# THE
# SAVAGE
# SHORE

**David Hewson** is a former journalist with *The Times*, *The Sunday Times* and the *Independent*. He is the author of more than twenty-five novels including his Rome-based Nic Costa series which has been published in fifteen languages. He has also written three acclaimed adaptations of the Danish TV series, *The Killing*.

@david_hewson davidhewson.com/blog/

*Also by David Hewson*

# THE
# SAVAGE
# SHORE

A NIC COSTA MYSTERY

# DAVID
# HEWSON

**BLACK**THORN

First published in Great Britain, the USA and Canada in 2019
by Black Thorn, an imprint of Canongate Books Ltd,
14 High Street, Edinburgh EH1 1TE

Distributed in the USA by Publishers Group West and in Canada by
Publishers Group Canada

First published in 2018 by Severn House Publishers Ltd,
Eardley House, 4 Uxbridge Street, London W8 7SY

blackthornbooks.com

1

*British Library Cataloguing in Publication Data*
A catalogue record for this book is available on request from the British
Library.

ISBN 978 1 78689 485 4

Typeset by Palimpsest Book Production Ltd., Falkirk,
Stirlingshire, Scotland.
Printed and bound in Great Britain by Clays Ltd, Elcograf S.p.A..

If justice is taken away then what are states but gangs of robbers? And what are gangs of robbers themselves but little states?

St Augustine, *The City of God*

# PART ONE

## Martinis for a Marmoset

Extract from *Calabrian Tales*, by Constantino Bergamotti
(1898-1955)
first published 1949

### Chapter IV: The Garduña

In the eighth century, when the Moors ruled much of the Iberian peninsula, there was a priest named Apollinario, a hermit who lived in a cave in the hills above Córdoba. One day the Virgin Mary came to him in a dream and declared that he was destined to be the saviour of his native Spain, forming an army to drive the Muslims from God's beloved Catholic nation.

Flattered as he felt by this divine revelation, Apollinario was reluctant to take on such a task. He was a priest not a soldier, let alone a general. The Moors were everywhere. They were for the most part benign rulers, willing to tolerate those of other faiths, builders of great mosques and libraries, creators of a rich and philanthropic civilisation. How could one unworldly priest fight such a power? And with what?

Seeing his doubts the Virgin reached out and gave him a silver bracelet from her wrist. When Apollinario touched this precious item he knew that her strength, which came directly from God, now lay within him. In this way began the Garduña, Apollinario's sacred army, warriors of the night, fighters determined to rid Europe of Muslim domination.

With the private blessing of the Church, this band of holy villains grew to thousands, all of them sworn to destroy the followers of Allah, not through bloody confrontation on the battlefield, but by stealth and treachery and theft, the stiletto in the dark, the artistry of tricksters, every criminal device available, since the Arabs, being heathen, merited neither mercy nor forgiveness. Over the centuries the Garduña quietly gathered like-minded men to their cause, honing their skills as assassins and vagabonds, murdering, raping, robbing, and pillaging, slaying Muslims, Jews, and any Christians who opposed them, before seeking, and gaining, forgiveness for their sins.

Around 1670 the Inquisition, which had used their talents to such effect, began to turn on its loyal servants, seeing them as a pernicious criminal element that threatened the Vatican's own temporal power. Throughout Spain thousands of loyal members were arrested, many executed, the rest stripped of homes and possessions, thrown into dank prisons, their families left to starve in destitution. Those of Apollinario's children who remained fled into the hills whence they came, hiding their identities, surviving as best they could by virtue of the only talents they knew.

Three of the boldest, Catalan brothers Osso, Mastrosso and Carcagnosso, found themselves trapped in the city of Barcelona, with the king's men standing between them and their mountain home, knowing they were the greatest prize of all since they had in their possession Apollinario's precious silver bracelet given to him by the Virgin. Outflanking the soldiers of the Inquisition in the dead of night, they stole a flimsy fisherman's dory from the harbour and cast themselves upon the mercy of the waves. This was in November of 1673, at the beginning of a vicious winter that straddled the length of the Mediterranean, one which would witness the sea freeze in Siracusa, beggars die of bitter cold in the grand avenues of Alexandria, and snow cover the Temple Mount in Jerusalem for weeks on end.

The brothers fought to control their little boat on the wild waters of the Balearic, hoping to reach Mallorca and safety in Palma, where some of their Garduña brothers had found sanctuary. They were God's thieves, not sailors, and knew nothing of navigation or seafaring. So fierce was the storm that their flimsy boat was tossed about like flotsam for eight long days and nights. These young men grew weak and confused, fearing their lives would be lost on the cold grey ocean, each in turn clutching Mary's holy bracelet to his chest, praying for deliverance.

Perhaps the Virgin was listening, even through the tempest. Starving and close to madness, finally they found themselves beached in Sardinia, near to the city of Cagliari, stranded in a nation which spoke their native Catalan and was, in law at least, still beholden to the kingdom of Castile.

Yet this was not true Spain. They were on the borders of the east, close to a mythical world of pirates and bandits, thieves and ruffians, the Hinder Sea of the Jews, the Mesogeios of Homer, the Mare Nostrum, following in the footsteps of so many others like them, the Vikings and the Normans, the Turks and the Saracens. And the greatest brigands of all, the Romans.

On this foreign soil these three brothers rediscovered themselves as a new Garduña, lying, cheating and stealing now from the wealthy and barbaric Sardinian lords. Their fortunes rose. Their stock improved. Soon they came to see that one island was too small to encompass three such ambitious and talented men. With many tears and embraces, each knowing that separation was the only alternative to division and death, they bade each other farewell and set off to establish their individual fortunes, Mastrosso to Naples, Osso to Sicily, and Carcagnosso to Reggio at the tip of Italy's toe in Calabria.

Here is the history of the south, Garibaldi's Mezzogiorno, written with the blood spilled by these three brothers from Spain and those who came after. In Naples, Mastrosso began the brotherhood that came to be known as the Camorra, the name coming from *capo morra*, meaning boss of the crooked street game by which the innocent are fleeced of their wages. Not that alley tricks for a pittance were the Camorra's principal interests for long.

In Palermo, Osso took a similar path, his creation coming to bear the name Cosa Nostra or Mafia, the origins of which are challenged by many, and perhaps impossible to pin down. The third brother, Carcagnosso, made the longest, hardest journey of all, to the bare, bleak land at the foot of Aspromonte, the last remaining fragment of ancient Greece in Italy. With his sons he came to form the 'Ndrangheta and here the etymology is clear: the Greek *andragathia*, meaning 'those who are full of a strong goodness'.

It is natural that they should choose the ancient tongue of the eastern Mediterranean to describe themselves. Calabria is but the modern face of Magna Graecia, 'Greater Greece'. The language of Aristotle and Demosthenes remains more audible in our local dialects than in the demotic Greek heard today on the other side of the Ionian.

'Ndrangheta.

Strange, impenetrable, unpronounceable, fearsome. The name of 'the honourable men' seemed made for the sons of Carcagnosso as they seized Calabria, populating its inhospitable mountain ranges, its primitive ports and fishing harbours, bringing a kind of society, of civilisation, to an impoverished and neglected hinterland about which Rome and Florence and Milan cared nothing.

While the Mafia grew greedy and sought fame and riches in America, while the Camorra quarrelled, turned corrupt and untrustworthy, the 'Ndrangheta alone remained true to the Garduña, the sum of their fathers, nothing more, nothing less, their blood running pure from generation to generation.

The crones in the mountains say that somewhere in the bare, cold hills of Aspromonte may be found a grotto containing the silver bracelet of the Virgin Mary, given to the timid monk Apollinario somewhere outside Córdoba in a distant era when Andalusia rang to the cry of the muezzin, not the plainchant of the Holy Church. And by the altar in this hidden lair lies the tomb of his loyal follower, Carcagnosso.

A fairy tale for children? This is possible, so perhaps it has no part in history. What remains undeniable is this: only in Calabria does the spirit of the Garduña live on among 'the honourable men'. They serve still, strong in their silence, asking nothing more than loyalty, obedience and their due, infected, like the Greeks before them, by the spirit of the land, which is wild and free, invincible even to time itself.

At three o'clock on a sweltering late summer afternoon Emmanuel Akindele sat behind the counter of the Zanzibar feeding Jackson the marmoset his first fierce cocktail of the day.

A thin, nervy thirty-year-old, Emmanuel had been rescued off Lampedusa the previous spring. Two thousand dollars that cost him to the Libyan people smugglers, pretty much all his family back home in a Lagos slum possessed. He'd thought himself dead already by the time the Red Cross boat came along and pulled him from a sea so cold it seemed to freeze his bones.

Now, in a kind of life, he spent hour upon hour with this sad and savage little animal, a miserable bundle of bone and fur, barely the size of a cat. Something trapped and helpless, and probably beyond hope. The creature kept thrusting a skinny arm through the bars of its rusty metal cage, holding out a grubby shot glass. A simian alcoholic and Emmanuel couldn't think of anything else but to dull its senses in place of his own.

He'd inherited Jackson when the gang boss put him into the Zanzibar nine months earlier, after he'd earned what the mob men called promotion from pushing cheap counterfeit bags to the tourists on the beach at Locri. The creature was part of the furniture in the cramped, windowless bar, like the broken Playboy pin table, the cheap paintings of Marilyn Monroe, the satellite TV system with an illegal card to pick up premium sports channels from around the world.

He'd thought about letting the monkey go. About driving out of the grey and sprawling city to one of the bare back roads that led to the desolate hills rising from the coast. There the sparse tracts of scrappy brown vegetation reminded him of the countryside back home. He could see himself taking the cage out of the boot and watching the scrawny broken animal limp off into the dry, barren lower reaches of Aspromonte, the sprawling mountain that rose behind Italy's extended toe like the humped back of a slumbering giant.

Jackson would be a corpse in a few hours, a day at most. Nothing foreign lived long in that bleak wasteland. Some things were dead before they even got there. The gang men who employed him, members of the Calabrian mafia, the 'Ndrangheta, saw the place, with its wildernesses full of snakes and spiders and, some said, wolves too, as their natural home. The worst thing that could happen to a man was to be told he was going for a 'walk in the hills'. You never came back. This was where the mobsters took their victims, where they hid the men and women they kidnapped for money, slicing off a finger or an ear when they needed to raise the temperature a little. Even life in a cage, begging for drinks, getting laughed at by the scum who made up the Zanzibar's clientele, was better than abandonment in that brutal, inhospitable expanse of desolate rock and thorns.

The bar was empty, as it usually was at this time of the afternoon. Customers didn't begin to turn up until five or so and they didn't stay long once their business was done. He had beer and wine and unbranded bottles of spirits that could, at a push, be turned into cheap cocktails. There were even a few panini and packets of cheese and cold meat from the supermarket should a rare soul feel hungry. Not that any of this was of great importance. The Zanzibar was a covert market place and he was its tame host, there to serve and nothing more, certainly not to listen because that could prove very dangerous indeed.

This lost little dive, an airless converted storeroom in the back streets of sprawling Reggio, served as an illicit stock exchange where millions of dollars might be exchanged over a couple of glasses of warm Negroni and a shake of the hand. Five minutes away on foot down a narrow industrial road lay the port, a place where boats large and small, legal and nefarious, came and went through the Strait of Messina, past Sicily, out of Europe altogether. Some sailed east, to Turkey, the Balkans and beyond, bringing back narcotics and human traffic, women and cheap labour for the black market. Some went south, to Africa, another continent, his own, which was, Emmanuel often reminded himself, nearer to Reggio than Rome. As far as he could see those vessels returned with much the same kind of goods too, just ones that sometimes bore a different colour and a price tag that was yet more cruel.

On occasion the merchandise found its way into the Zanzibar. He wasn't happy with that idea. The dope, hidden in the storeroom, could put him in prison for years, even though he didn't stand to take a cent of profit from its sale. The men and women he had to hide sometimes . . . He'd got used to the look in their faces, the mixture of fear and self-loathing. They, like him, had started on the journey to Europe out of naive hope and desperation, seeking only what any human being ought to regard as his or her right: some way to earn a decent living with a little dignity.

That fantasy ended in the back streets of Reggio when the scales surely fell from their eyes. Watching the bright, sharp spark of fear in the faces of the women was the worst. They never used females to sell fake bags to tourists or run bags of dope out to the chains of pedlars. There was only one reason for them to be here.

He hated the Zanzibar and the tiny, dingy room above it, one entirely without windows, where he was forced to live. When he got back home, not rich but no longer dirt poor, he'd shout the truth out loud. The men who tempted you out of your home, who dangled riches and luxury in front of your eyes as you stood there, stupid, transfixed, on the doorstep of your miserable little shack, these lying bastards were nothing more than the missionaries and hard-faced, white company men of old, waving trinkets with one hand, hiding the vicious tools of enslavement, a gun and a Bible, tight behind their backs with the other.

Europe was no place for men like him.

That message was one he would deliver soon. Emmanuel was both terrified and proud that, over the previous few months, he'd managed to skim some money from the meagre cash passing over the counter of the Zanzibar. Soon he would have enough stashed away to buy a one-way economy ticket back to Lagos. The route would be the long way round, from

Catania in Sicily to Bucharest then Addis Ababa, and finally home. He didn't dare countenance the direct flight, through Rome. The men from Aspromonte would be mad as hell because stealing from them was the worst thing a man could do, an automatic death sentence, carried out without a second thought. They had people everywhere in Italy, maybe beyond, not that he liked to think about that possibility. Emmanuel had worked hard to convince himself that once he was on his plane out of Sicily, headed briefly for Romania, he'd be free of them for good, and that was what he wanted most of all.

The marmoset broke the daydream by rattling his shot glass hard across the bars of its cage.

'Stupid little animal,' Emmanuel spat at it. He snatched away the glass and threw in some fresh peanuts instead. The animal screeched furiously and flew at the bars, yellow teeth bared, its tiny, insane eyes glowering at him. 'Eat something. Eat now or I shall take you out to Aspromonte myself. You go play with the wolves there. See who wins.'

It kept on screeching and screeching. The two of them had been here before. The creature would never give up. It had no reason.

He sighed, filled the glass with booze, a cheap gin copy decanted into the real bottle, not that any of his customers were fooled. Then he passed the drink back through the cage, getting his fingers out of the way as quickly as he could. The thing had sharp teeth and claws and liked to use them. He didn't know why he felt sorry for it. Or rather he did, but was reluctant to admit the truth. In the animal's lost and miserable eyes he saw himself. This was self-pity and Emmanuel, a proud and independent man who left Nigeria for no other reason than to win a better life for his family back home, loathed such a trait in anyone, most of all himself.

Yet the marmoset amused his customers. A little monkey in a cage, a trapped animal that liked to drink and would even puff at a cigarette or something stronger given the chance. This was Europe. Even in the grimmest Lagos dive they never stooped to such games.

The solid front door to the bar opened and two shapes

entered. The Nigerian squinted against the brief entry of sunlight trying to make out who it was.

One of them, a big man, very big, was shutting the door carefully and turning round the sign on the front so it read 'Closed'.

Jackson the marmoset was watching them too. He downed his little shot glass and held it out for a refill. The creature's feeble arm was shaking. Emmanuel wondered whether it was the hooch or something else.

'Can I help . . .?' he began to say again, then stopped.

They'd turned and this time he remembered what Rocco, the boss from Aspromonte, had said only two hours before.

These were the men he was supposed to look out for. Both middle-aged, both wearing winter jackets, heavy ones, even though it was boiling outside. The big one was hefty and muscular with an ugly, scarred face that might have met a razor some time. The other seemed very different. More a business type, tall, erect, a touch pompous. Cultured, bald, with a very tanned face and a silver goatee, he seemed the kind of man who possessed a natural and unquestionable authority.

Neither of the individuals who had just walked into the Zanzibar gave the impression they smiled much or were likely to any time soon.

The Nigerian's phone was on the shelf behind the counter. Casually, so that they wouldn't notice, he pressed the shortcut key on the handset so that it auto-dialled the number the boss gave him in case of trouble.

He'd only had to use that once before. The call was all it took. No need for an explanation or words at all. It was an alarm in itself, one that identified the source. The gang men had arrived in minutes. Clearing up the mess they left behind – blood and teeth and worse – took a lot longer.

'We need to talk,' said the cultured one with the goatee.

He was staring at Jackson in the cage.

'It's a monkey,' Emmanuel replied without thinking.

The other one grunted something obscene then muttered to his companion. They had unusual accents. Roman maybe. Emmanuel had been in Italy long enough to notice.

The tough-looking guy walked round the bar, picked up the cage quite gently, placed the silent, scared monkey in the back office and closed the door.

'Talk about what?' Emmanuel wondered.

The bearded man looked tired and a little strained. They were both sweating in their heavy jackets. 'My name's Falcone. This is my colleague, Peroni. We're here to discuss insurance.'

He laughed then. It was ridiculous. The most amateurish shakedown he'd ever seen. They even gave him names, real ones too, he thought, from the sound of them and the easy way they spoke.

'I don't need insurance. Listen. If you know what's good for you get the hell out of here right now. This place may look a dump . . .' He smiled brightly at the garish bleak interior of the Zanzibar. It was a dump, a dreadful one. 'All the same. The people who own it are class. Of a kind. You don't want to meet with them.'

The two looked at each other.

'Trust me,' the one called Falcone said. 'You need insurance. You need it badly.'

He nodded at the other guy who reached inside his thick winter jacket and pulled out a shiny black handgun.

'No, no, no . . .' Emmanuel murmured, thinking all the time about the little shack he called home, his wife, their three kids there, wondering as he did on a daily basis why he'd been fool enough to leave it. 'Please—'

Peroni stared at him, shook his big ugly head, pointed the gun and fired.

When the call came the three men from Aspromonte were sitting in a battered white VW van on the waterfront in the small town of Villa San Giovanni, twelve kilometres north of Reggio, the strong, sharp stink of fresh-killed swordfish still wafting round them. Ferries meandered across the Strait of Messina between Sicily and the mainland. In the middle distance the gentle shape of Etna rose to the perfect azure sky like a gigantic beached barnacle left behind by the Great Flood. A grey-brown wreath of smoke curled around the summit of the volcano. The mountain had been grumbling for nearly a week. Fontanarossa airport in Catania had closed for a few hours through poor visibility from the ash. At night, from the ghost village of Manodiavolo in the Aspromonte foothills where one of these men was living, a thin red line of livid fire was sometimes visible as lava trickled then died in the Valle del Bove.

To two of them this sight was nothing new, nothing strange. Rocco Bergamotti and Santo Vottari were Calabrians through and through. They had grown up in the shadow of the mountains, children of the badlands behind Reggio. Rocco was the son of the shadowy capo of the Reggio 'ndrina, the local unit of the 'Ndrangheta, a man known only to the locals as 'Lo Spettro', the Phantom, since few knew who he was, what he looked like, where he lived. Rocco was his visible lieutenant, holding the rank of *crimine*, the senior officer delegated to pass on the orders of the local lord to his troops. Santo Vottari was, like every member of the 'ndrina, a blood relative of the capo and his family, in his case a distant cousin, from a family well down the ranks. They shared the same southern Mediterranean looks: swarthy, with black wavy hair, dark, darting eyes, and lean, muscled bodies that always looked ready for a fight. Rocco was an inch or two shorter and skinnier, a handsome man with a quick and easy smile. Santo laughed a lot, though his face was coarse and exaggerated, that of a peasant straight from the land. Almost everywhere they went there was a pair of designer sunglasses tucked into their black hair, even at night. They were known too, quietly acknowledged in cafes and bars, stores and garages, the length of the coast around Reggio, from Melito in the east, on the Ionian Sea, to Bagnara Calabra in the north, on the Tyrrhenian, just beyond the Strait of Messina.

The third individual had found it difficult to take his attention away from the volcano across the water. The idea of a chasm in the earth, a living window into the fiery hell beneath the surface of the everyday world, continued to appal and fascinate him. He was a touch shorter and paler, just turned thirty, dark-haired and striking, with an accent quite unlike their sharp, coarse guttural Calabrian, littered with dialect and terms from Greek. Nor was he fully a member of the Bergamotti or any other 'ndrina, not yet at least. There was an act required of him, a sacrifice demanded before he would be allowed to become a 'man of honour'. A rank that would only be attained through the shedding of blood.

Santo listened to Rocco issue the order to move from the back seat then started the van and began to pull off the beach-side road.

'Hey, Maso,' he said to the man in the passenger seat. 'You got stupid people in Canada too?'

He'd learned to respond easily to the alias they'd given him. That was important. His life, and those of others, depended on it. Tomasso Leoni – Maso he was and would be until this game played out. He reached down into the footwell for the briefcase they'd given him. 'There are stupid people everywhere.'

'Take your word on that. I never got around to travelling much. Went to Germany once and then it all turned nasty. Jesus. Vendettas. Dead men in a pizzeria. Who needs it?'

Maso took out the handgun from the briefcase and checked the magazine. He recalled reading about the 'Ndrangheta war that had left eleven men dead in Frankfurt and Cologne. The two 'ndrine involved were from the north of the region. The feud had never spread this far.

'You worried?' Rocco asked from the back seat.

'Not much.'

Etna had disappeared. They were driving through suburbs of low white houses and uniform apartment blocks. Reggio was maybe fifteen minutes away.

'Tell me about the mooses,' Santo demanded, for the third time in an hour.

'Guelph is just a town,' he said patiently. 'One hour east of Toronto. You don't get moose in town any more than you get wolves in Reggio.'

Santo grinned. He had very white teeth, crooked and sharp. 'They got us in Reggio. We're wolves, aren't we?'

'We're wolves,' Rocco repeated from behind, his voice a tone lower, his accent a little less coarse. 'Just drive, will you?'

'A man's gotta be curious,' Santo objected. 'I never met a

guy from Canada before. I never even knew we had family over there.'

'It happened seventy years ago,' Rocco told him. 'Back in history. What's history to you?'

Santo turned onto the main highway south. 'Nothing. If it happened seven weeks ago wouldn't be none of my business. Not if you say so, boss.' He stabbed a finger across the dashboard at his passenger. 'You remember that.'

'I will.'

'You remember. You do this right. Shoot these stupid thieving bastards in the head. Good and proper. The way it's supposed to be. Bullets cost money. Shouldn't need more than one.'

'I don't give a shit where he shoots them,' Rocco barked. 'Or how many shells he uses. He can kick them to death for all I care. Or take them to the hills, put them in a cave with you, asking stupid questions about mooses and Canada all the time, boring the life out of them. What the hell?'

Santo nodded. 'What the hell? What the hell? That's right. What the hell?'

The man now determined to think of himself as the minor criminal Maso Leoni, not the state detective Nic Costa, had learned much about the 'Ndrangheta of late. How unlike its two great rivals, the Sicilian Cosa Nostra and the Neapolitan Camorra, it was. No one prospered inside the Bergamotti 'ndrina on talent alone. It was a true family, one bound together by direct blood ties. Without them one was always an outsider. With them absolute obedience was essential. His position still had to be earned.

He lifted the handgun above the dashboard and said, 'I shoot them.'

'Put that damned gun down!' Santo yelled at him. 'What are you? Soft in the head? They do that in Canada and no one minds, huh? Waving guns round on busy roads like this? Jesus, Maso. You got a lot to learn if you wanna be like us.'

'You do want to be like us?' the man in the back asked.

'Yeah. Never wanted anything more.'

The shot didn't go near Emmanuel but it shattered the grubby cracked mirror behind the bar. His fingers clung to the plastic

counter of the Zanzibar as he stood still as a rock, breath
frozen for a moment, aware there was nowhere to run, no
chance to hide.

This was too crazy, even in the upside-down world of the
'Ndrangheta.

He thought of the gun in the drawer by the cash register.
The Bergamotti made him keep a firearm. He didn't like the
thing, didn't ever want to use it, even now. These two looked
so much better with weapons than he could ever hope to be.

So he held hard to the sticky counter, trying not to shake
as he looked at the ugly hulk with the scar. There was something wrong there, something odd in his scarred and battered
features.

He didn't like doing this, Emmanuel thought. Maybe he
wasn't cut out for robbing either, any more than he felt born
to running an illicit shebeen for Italian mobsters and their
fellow-criminals.

'I apologize, friend,' the big man said in that curious accent.
'My finger must have slipped. I'm getting old and careless
these days. Please God it doesn't happen again.'

Jackson was screeching from the back room, terrified by
the noise of the shot. The little monkey's high-pitched bawling
went on and on. Then Peroni moved slightly to one side and
cracked a shell through the office door.

The shrieks got louder. Jackson wanted a drink, Emmanuel
thought. A big, strong one. So, for once, did he.

'Insurance,' the leaner, sharper looking man who'd called
himself Falcone repeated. 'We want five hundred now. Five
hundred weekly. You can afford that, can't you?'

'Five hundred?' Emmanuel asked, exasperated. 'You're
gonna get yourselves killed, both of you, for five hundred
euros?'

'You heard.'

'Might as well ask for five thousand, man. Dead's dead
whatever. Don't you understand who you're ripping off
here?'

Jackson's cries got louder. Peroni started firing again,
pumping lead into the mirror, the pinball table, the lines of
grubby cocktail tumblers that sat on a shelf behind him. Glass

and metal and wood started to jump up and down inside the airless little dive that was the Zanzibar. Emmanuel stopped counting the shots, grimaced and put his hands up to his ears. The racket was worse than the monkey's terrified screams.

When the gun clicked on empty the lean one pulled out a weapon and pointed that across the bar.

'Who exactly?' he asked.

'You don't know? This isn't Rome, friend. You're in Calabria. It belongs to the 'Ndrangheta. They're kings here. The government. The army. The church. You don't mess with them. You never, ever steal from them. If you do that makes you a walking dead man. And me too.' Emmanuel opened his long arms wide, aware of the sweat patches that had grown beneath them. 'For what? You tell me. Five hundred stinking euros? Please. I did not come here for this.'

'What did you come for?' Peroni wondered.

Emmanuel stamped his fists hard on the bar, feeling something sting at his eyes. 'I came 'cos I thought I had to. I came 'cos I thought . . .' He stared around the grubby interior of the Zanzibar, realising what a fool he'd been. He shook his head. 'Don't matter. Go ahead. Do what you want. Shoot me. Who cares?'

Falcone walked behind the counter, went to the cash register, opened it, then stared at the meagre collection of notes and coins there.

'There isn't even five hundred here,' he muttered. 'Where's the rest?'

Emmanuel reached inside his shirt for the key then, with both hands, lifted the chain that hung round his neck, got it over his head and held it out to them.

'There's a safe in the back room. With Jackson. I just keep the key for them.'

They stared at him and Falcone asked, 'Who's Jackson?'

'The monkey.'

'Show us.'

The marmoset was hunched on the bottom of its cage, silent, miserable. As he entered it rattled its little shot glass once across the bars then caught the mood and fell back into a quiet sulk.

Emmanuel had never looked inside the safe. He didn't want to know what it contained. Didn't want to think about what they used it for. The 'ndrina men came down from the hills and dipped in and out as they pleased. They only gave him a key in case a visitor needed to collect something, and when that happened he made certain he never watched.

The two men stood behind him as he crouched down and opened the metre-high iron box that sat on the floor next to the desk.

The light was bright in the little room. The big guy's weapon grazed the back of his neck the moment they saw what was inside.

'I had no idea,' Emmanuel said honestly, mostly to himself. 'Truly. I had no idea . . .'

The top shelf of the safe contained at least five brand new handguns still in clear plastic wrapping. The middle was full of packs of ammunition. The bottom contained more shell boxes and wad upon wad of neat new one-hundred euro notes bound together with the paper bands they came in from the bank.

He felt mad at them for doing this to him. It was worse than dope. There was enough here to put him inside for fifteen years or more. He was an African. Not even a true member of the 'ndrina, because for that you had to have the blood. If he'd gone to jail for owning the key to all this illicit weaponry and suspect money everything would have fallen apart. The monthly remittances home. The chance, one day, of a better life, back in his own land. The Calabrians looked after their own, sent round a moneyman each week with allowances for the sick, the wounded and the relatives of those who'd gone to jail. No one was going to do that in Lagos.

'Bastards. Bastards . . .' he whispered.

The hard metal of the weapon disappeared from his neck and the voice said, 'Get back.'

Peroni hunched down and picked out the wads of cash. Emmanuel gazed at the wads of notes. It was more money than he'd ever seen, so much he couldn't begin to imagine what it might buy.

'Ten thousand a bundle,' Peroni said, whistling as he counted them. 'Ten bundles. You must sell a lot of beer.'

'I swear to God I never saw any of this before.' He glowered at them. 'How the hell did you know it was here?'

'You should follow the news,' the other one said. 'Someone stopped a wages van for the hospital eight days ago. It doesn't take a genius . . .'

'And I'm just their stupid little bagman,' Emmanuel murmured.

'Looks like it.'

Falcone opened his thick coat and beckoned to the other. Peroni passed each bundle over, one by one, and watched it go inside some deep pockets there.

'A good day's work, sirs,' Emmanuel said, watching the money disappear. 'They're gonna take you for a walk in the hills and carve your heart out for that.'

'You think?'

Peroni was looking at him, clutching at the last bundle. The gun, reloaded now, was in his left hand.

Emmanuel stood there and sighed. 'No. I know. Just shoot me and get it over with. You. Them. What's the difference? I'm dead anyway, just as dead as you.'

'Take it,' the man insisted, holding out the money. 'Go on.'

Emmanuel took a deep breath. 'This your idea of fun?'

'You can go and run somewhere. How about that?'

He looked serious. They both did.

'Who in God's name are you?' the Nigerian asked.

'No one you need worry about,' Falcone said. 'Take the money. Get out of here. Don't talk to anyone. Don't stop running till it's safe to turn around and look behind you. Do we need to say this twice?'

He stared into their eyes and wondered what he saw there. Nothing was what it seemed in Calabria. He was just a kind of slave in a theatre of nightmares. Unworthy of being told the truth.

All the same his fingers fell around the smooth bundle of notes. Ten thousand euros. It felt as if he were touching something magical. His eyes strayed to their faces. 'They're coming already. You're the ones who'd better run.'

'I'm sure you're right,' the lean one said, stroking his silver goatee, seemingly unworried.

Without another word the man in the heavy winter jacket, now more thick and uncomfortable than ever, turned and walked back into the bar then out of the door into the bright afternoon sun. The big one followed and didn't look back. Emmanuel watched them go.

Jackson the marmoset let out a muted squeak and rattled the bars once with its glass.

The Nigerian waved the bundle of bills at him. 'Not any more, little monkey,' he said. Then, more quietly, 'Not from me.'

There was a way out at the back. A steel security door that led to the yard. He could be gone in minutes, hot-wire a car down by the docks, drive as carefully as possible to the ferry, cross to Sicily, the airport at Catania. Then the first flight to Bucharest, anywhere so long as it was outside Italy. With the kind of money he had he didn't have to wait any longer. He'd be rich once he got home. If he could stay out of the hands of the men from the hills.

Emmanuel Akindele raced upstairs, packed his small suitcase with what few belongings he had, picked up the pictures of his family from the cupboard by the bed, then let himself out into the narrow alley behind the Zanzibar. It stank of cats, bad drains and rotting rubbish.

He'd just reached the perimeter of the building, and the lane that led to the warehouses by the docks, when he heard the noise of a vehicle drawing up in front of the club.

'You know what I think?' Santo Vottari said as the van pulled into the cul-de-sac by the Zanzibar.

Two tall figures in heavy jackets were walking towards a Lancia parked in the shadows by the side of the industrial unit on the left. They didn't look back as the 'Ndrangheta men arrived. They didn't even seem to notice.

'What?' Maso asked.

'Picking yourself up off the floor. That's what counts. The way a man deals with that is what defines him. We all got it coming to us. Some day. You get knocked down. You climb back in the ring. Try again.' He touched Maso's arm. 'Guess you know that. What with you getting kicked out of Canada and everything.'

'I didn't get kicked out. I left.'

'Got a little push though, didn't you?'

Maso didn't look him in the eye. 'I don't want to talk about it.'

'Picking yourself up. That's good. If you get the opportunity.'

He was aware they were both staring at him.

'You understand what I'm saying?' Santo added. 'What we're saying?'

Maso glanced at Rocco Bergamotti in the back. His dark, intense eyes were on the two shapes heading into the darkness of the alley. 'That I only get one chance?'

'You only get one chance and that's more than you're worth,' Rocco agreed. The men outside had stopped a few paces from their vehicle and were talking, one of them on the phone. 'Your people in Canada done nothing for us for years. Nothing except send Christmas cards which does not merit us wet-nursing some punk who fouled up over there and now thinks he can come back home, not that it is home, and pick up where his old man left off thirty years ago.'

'My father—'

'—is dead,' Rocco cut in. 'What gratitude we had went in the coffin with him. We've fed you, told you what you've got to do. That's enough. We owe you nothing. This isn't college or some kind of charity. The 'ndrina looks after its own, that's a given. This is a society. Give and take. You got to earn your living because that's the only way we get to look after one another.'

'You sound like my old man,' Maso grumbled.

'Shame you didn't listen to him more. Who do you think we are? Some grubby little crime family living off the scraps they can steal from everyone else?' Rocco banged the window. 'This isn't Sicily. Or Naples. The people out there are our people. If they toe the line, pay their dues, we look after them. It costs but what they get back—' he took out a short cigar, tapped the end on the glass, then lit it – 'is security. Not a kick in the teeth like they get from the government. From Rome.'

Santo was laughing.

'What's so funny?' Rocco asked.

'That black guy we put in there. Emmanuel. I'm the one that gets to run him, remember?'

'Right,' Rocco muttered.

'He's the scaredest little slave we ever had. Christ this will freak him out.'

Maso let the handgun rest in his lap. He looked out of the window. The two men walked past their Lancia then disappeared into a shadowy corner. One of them was taking some cash out of his jacket as they vanished. It looked as if they were about to divide up the money.

'Go deal with them,' Rocco said. 'We won't help. We won't even watch.'

'We won't?' Santo asked, surprised. 'I'd like to.'

'No. He's on his own. Go on, Maso. If it all works out, tonight we give you your due. You get to make the grade. One step on the bottom of the ladder.'

'That's if those two don't kill you first,' Santo added. 'They look pretty serious to me.'

Rocco pointed at the alley ahead and clicked his fingers.

Maso got out of the car, stuck the gun in his waistband and walked towards the shadows.

When he turned the corner he saw them. They weren't on the phone any more. They stood there, as if waiting for him. The big one was smiling. The other had an expression that was harder to read. A gun hung loose by his side in his right hand.

'Ciao,' Peroni said, still grinning. He lifted up his right hand. It was full of clean, new hundred-euro notes. 'You come for some money?'

'You're alone?' the other asked.

'That's right.'

The two looked at each other then the lean one with the gun brought up the weapon and said, 'Well . . .'

Maso fired. Six shots, the whole magazine. Carefully, deliberately. He couldn't afford any mistakes.

When it was over, when the noise and the smell of powder was beginning to dissipate in the thin, polluted city air, they were on the ground stretched out in the crazed position he associated with corpses, arms and legs akimbo, their thick winter jackets ripped and torn, thick with blood.

He didn't want to look at their faces. Instead he pocketed the gun, bent down, opened up the coat of the one with the silver goatee, found some money and ripped it out from the pockets.

The notes were in his fingers when Santo Vottari and Rocco Bergamotti rounded the corner.

'See. I knew you could do it,' Santo said, scooping up some of the one-hundred euro bills flapping around the rubbish on the dry and grubby ground. 'Next time you might want to pop them in the head. Do things easy. Particularly when there's two of them. If these morons knew what they were up to you'd be the one who was dead.'

'If they knew what they were up to they wouldn't be stealing from us,' Maso told him, and waved the cash in his face.

'True,' Rocco agreed.

They watched him. He was the boss.

'Santo,' he said after a moment, 'go buy some food and drink. Something nice. Special. Take it back to Manodiavolo. You're done for today.'

'You got two bodies? And you want me to go shopping?'

Rocco hesitated for a moment then asked, 'Was I unclear in some way?'

Santo shook his head immediately and said, 'No, no.'

'Good. We'll deal with these two. We got the van. They can go in the hills. I don't want bodies around this place. Makes work for everyone.' He scanned the grim industrial area around them, sniffing the air. 'No one here's going to say a word. We'll deal with the African. Maybe move him along somewhere. The guy doesn't look right behind a bar anyway. Put him back on the beach pushing bags. He can hassle the tourists there. More his kind of thing.'

'Sure,' Santo said. He turned on his heels, ambling back towards the waterfront, walking with the punk-roll gait the 'ndrina men liked, whistling all the time.

Maso looked at Rocco Bergamotti.

'Is that enough?' he asked.

Rocco moved close, took his arm, clasped his hand. His

breath smelled sweet. His eyes were sharp and dark, intelligent, dangerous.

'We're honourable men. Don't you understand that yet? You should. I like you. We all do. You fit in here. You'll make a good soldier. Now . . .' He stared at the two still shapes on the ground and grimaced for a moment. 'Let's finish this.'

Emmanuel stayed in the shadows by the back wall of the Zanzibar, trembling, trying not to breathe, scared and silent as a mouse. In his left hand he was carrying a cheap fabric holdall with his few belongings.

The wad of money the two men had given him was safe for the moment, buttoned into the inner pocket of his shiny black jacket, pressing against his chest like some cancerous lump.

He wanted to scream at the motionless shapes on the ground a few short steps away, to say, 'Didn't I tell you? Weren't you warned?'

There was no way he could run to the waterfront. Santo Vottari might see him there, and if he did he'd know something was wrong. The whole of Reggio was his enemy. The Bergamotti 'ndrina ruled over this land like brigands, warlords. It was their territory and everyone within it answered to their power. There was no one he could trust, no place he could go.

The only answer was to hot-wire a car, find an airport – Catania, Reggio, even Lamezia or Crotone in the north – and flee Italy for good somehow.

Or walk back into the Zanzibar, pour two large drinks, one for Jackson the marmoset, a second for himself. Place the money he had back in the safe, crack his head against a door to make it seem like they'd hit him, then make out the Romans somehow overlooked a little of the money as they fled.

He didn't like lying but it was a talent he'd had to learn.

The window at the back of the bar was open. Rocco and his murderous hood were still talking. They didn't seem remotely interested in what might have happened to him or the Zanzibar. There was, perhaps, time to creep round, crawl back through the escape route he had taken only a minute or two before, and try to work on some story to convince them he was still theirs after all.

Selling fake Gucci to gullible foreigners wasn't so bad compared to this. He didn't, in truth, have much choice.

Emmanuel Akindele had convinced himself, was ready to turn and scramble back inside the little prison that was his home, when he found himself watching them again.

He froze, cold as ice on this hot afternoon. Struggling to believe what he was seeing.

In the black shadows of the industrial park on the edge of the city at the toe of Italy he tried to understand, and failed. There was only one thing he could hold onto with any conviction, and that was the certain knowledge he had to run.

# PART TWO
## The Wine-Dark Sea

### Calabrian Tales

### Chapter VIII: Scylla and Charybdis. Sleeping Monsters

On a warm summer's day at the coast it is difficult to believe that two of the most fearful sea monsters in mythical history once inhabited the waters of the Strait of Messina.

Scylla and Charybdis lived on opposing sides of the strip of sea separating Sicily from the Italian mainland, a channel so narrow, said Homer, that a soldier could fire an arrow from one bank to the other. Fable would have us believe Scylla possessed six necks, each topped by a vicious, snarling wolf's head with a triple row of sharp teeth. The beast had an insatiable hunger for passing flesh and was, accordingly, able to snatch six rowers at a time from any vessel within reach. She was characterized by the ancients as a hazardous promontory of jagged rock jutting into the sea, able to pierce the hull of a battleship as easily as that of a fisherman's rowed felucca.

Charybdis was the daughter of Poseidon and Gaia, a covetous sea-nymph punished for stealing the oxen of Heracles. Zeus threw her into the ocean, turning the unfortunate creature into a monstrous mouth that would swallow the waters thrice daily, devouring anything within reach, be it ship or sailor. A whirlpool in other words.

In modern Italian these two venerable deities translate as Scilla and Cariddi. The first is now the name of a tall, snag-toothed cliff rising from the Sicilian coast near Messina and stabbing into the sea channel at its narrowest point, a feature that can still easily be imagined as a threat to a careless captain. For local mariners today Cariddi represents an unpredictable confluence of powerful currents sweeping from the opposing Ionian and Tyrrhenian Seas as they meet in the funnel-like straits and battle one another like maritime wrestlers.

This is most noticeable, and most dangerous, in the narrow stretch of water opposite the rock that was once Scylla. The effect is deemed to be more benign than it was in ancient times but the whirling waters may still engulf a small sailing vessel if the master is unwary. Cariddi also lends its name to the charming fishing hamlet on the coast at the foot of Aspromonte.

One other legacy these mythical creatures have left us: the local saying which speaks of finding oneself 'tra Scilla e Cariddi', betwixt a rock and a whirlpool. In other words, to be faced with the choice of two unwelcome alternatives, both perilous, both unavoidable. Those of us who inhabit this reclusive little corner of Italy have endured poverty, repression, earthquakes, war and famine over the centuries. 'Tra Scilla e Cariddi' is a place we know all too well.

Ten days earlier … .

There was good food on the table and the limpid blue of the Tyrrhenian murmuring beneath their feet. Sicily swam in the distance, distorted by the visual phenomenon the waiter called the 'Fata Morgana'.

Teresa Lupo made a note of the term in her little black Moleskine book. Calabria felt like a new country, a new world almost. She'd heard there was an optical illusion of this nature, one that distorted the horizon of the island opposite until the rocky promontory there seemed extended, duplicated in places, like a fantastic tangle of fairy-tale castles. But she'd never expected to witness it in person.

Silvio Di Capua, her young deputy from the Rome state police forensic department, had squinted at the dreamy landscape through his thick round spectacles and muttered something about temperature inversions. There would be a scientific explanation, she knew, but that didn't take away the magic. They had been in the small coastal town of Cariddi for four days now. Rome, with its cares and chaos, seemed almost distant, unreal.

In different circumstances this would have been an interesting holiday. Gianni Peroni, colleague and lover, at fifty-seven some fifteen years her senior, sat silent, distracted, his chair turned to the water that lapped at the feet of their platform over the sea, his disfigured yet kindly face wreathed in thought and perhaps doubt. Leo Falcone, his inspector, a cultured, diffident man, lean and elegant, of the same age though a more introverted nature, was running his fingers over the menu wondering, as he so often did, whether he'd chosen as wisely as he should. In a pale pink polo shirt and perfectly-ironed white slacks he easily passed for a playboy on holiday.

Even Di Capua looked as if he didn't have a care in the world, leaning back in his wicker chair at their lone table on the pedana, a wooden platform for ten or twelve customers, no more, built above the gentle waves, chubby arms folded over a plain black T-shirt, alternately scanning the still blue sea then checking the web and his email on his phone.

They were all part of the act, here illicitly, pretending to be successful Roman business executives celebrating a lucrative deal and planning the next. It was important no one except a handful of civil servants and senior officers in the Rome Questura knew the truth. One day soon, they hoped, they would reel in the biggest prize the state police had seen in years. A mysterious figure in the hierarchy of the 'Ndrangheta, one who would turn *pentito*, state witness, and take down any number of crooks and fellow travellers. A man the authorities had heard much about over the years, appreciating the power he wielded, bloodily at times. But known to them only by his nickname: Lo Spettro, the ghost.

It was an odd mission to be pursuing on the outside deck of a fish restaurant. On this hot, clear afternoon they seemed to be the only visitors about. From behind the restaurant they heard the occasional buzz of a moped navigating the single lane, too narrow for cars, that was the main street of the fishing quarter. Gulls soared lazily in the clear air scouring the gentle blue waves for food. The town itself stood above them, clinging to the steep hillside rising from the sea to Aspromonte, growing progressively more modern as it approached the busy autostrada from the north to the ferries for Sicily at Villa San Giovanni. They had fetched up in the fisherman's quarter, a quiet, exquisitely pretty part of Calabria, a kind of paradise set behind a single line of tall, narrow waterfront homes, some still with boats in the footings, ready to brave the Strait of Messina, searching for a living the way men must have done here for a couple of millennia. One old and elegant house, the furthest north in the street, set apart from the rest on its own stump of rock, was theirs for the duration, a six-bedroom holiday let with a terrace over the water that was to be the local control centre, connected by encrypted data links with their colleagues in the Centro Storico Questura back in Rome.

An extraordinary vessel moved slowly across the shining sea no more than four hundred metres ahead of them. It was long and slender, with an extended metal prow running to twenty-five metres or more, like a long ladder, and a tower half the height towards the stern. There was a man at the top, scanning the calm waters that sat like slowly-moving glass beneath him. At the end of the long ladder on the prow stood another figure, erect, eyes fast on the gentle waves. In his hands was a long five-pronged spear, the kind she associated with images of ancient Greeks painted on the side of jars in a museum. Much like the emblem painted on the bows: a dark, wide-open eye surrounded by cerulean blue, something that would not have looked out of place in the Phoenician cabinet in a museum.

'I hope he doesn't catch anything,' Peroni said, watching the boat edge past at a speed that was little more than walking pace.

'Why?' Falcone asked.

'How many swordfish are left? You look at the way we take everything we can lay our hands on. The greed. The excess . . .'

Teresa reached over and squeezed his hand. This assignment hadn't pleased him. Peroni was ill at ease with everything at that moment. He was too honest a man to be happy pretending to be someone else. The state of the world, confused, dangerous and out of sorts, had begun to weigh on his mind, along with the plain truth that Falcone had, yet again, thrust Nic Costa into the front line with scarcely a second thought, the some-what fragile Rosa Prabakaran at his side. She'd no idea how to comfort him when he felt like this. He'd always been the rock, and not just for her. This task was difficult enough. If he faltered . . .

The waiter had returned bearing two platters, each full of tiny dishes of tempting looking antipasti. All of them fish. They seemed to eat little else here. The sea was their larder and they visited each and every day. This was their third meal in the place. Realising they were staying nearby, not visiting day trippers, the waiter had introduced himself as Toni and begun to offer extras – glasses of a dark, bitter spirit at the end of the meal, once a plate of delicately sliced prickly pear – as thanks for their custom. The locals, it seemed to her, were friendly in a distant fashion, always keen to keep a customer, inquisitive about one's motives.

'Not here, sir,' Toni announced. He had a charming smile and a dark and handsome face marked by a scar close to his left ear. A knife, she thought. Definitely a knife. 'In Cariddi we hunt the old way. A strong arm, a keen eye and a spear. If those men catch one fish today they're lucky. Two. Three . . .' He glanced at the sky. 'Someone up there is smiling on us.'

Silvio Di Capua waved his phone in the hot, sparse air. He had a knowing look on his face. Teresa should have guessed what he'd been looking at as he watched the sea. 'According to this the Mediterranean swordfish is an endangered species.'

Toni frowned then walked inside. One minute later he returned with the silver head of a swordfish, young and small, still with its long sharp spike intact and eyes that shone. Cleaved at the neck, the flesh there was pale but so fresh it might have been killed that morning.

'See this?' He pointed to a crossword of four crude slashes across the creature's right cheek. 'That's the *cardata da cruci*. My cousin's fingernails made those marks the moment they landed her in the boat and quelled her thrashes. We do not fish here. We hunt.'

'It's a beautiful creature,' Teresa said quietly, staring at the dark, glistening eyes.

'It is.' The head was almost too heavy and awkward for him to hold. 'We've been hunting here since people spoke nothing but Greek. Or earlier. In Spain, in Sardinia, they use long-lining or worse, nets. No one would dare try such a thing in Cariddi. They would not find themselves welcome. Why would we destroy one of the few precious things we have?' He nodded at the steep green mountain behind them. 'Calabria is a poor country. We possess so little. What we can grow. What we can catch. To lose the *pisci spata* through greed or vanity . . .' His expression lightened. 'I know you think we're all dumb. Trust me. We're not that stupid.'

'No one who lives in such a beautiful place and manages to keep it secret can possibly be stupid,' Teresa said.

It was true too, she thought. Just as it was true that the rest of Italy did look down on this strange, almost foreign part of the country. Few Romans knew it, except as a brief stopping place on the way to their holiday in Sicily. Few much cared. The wine wasn't good enough. The food, though cheap, was deemed unsophisticated. People spoke of the south, the Mezzogiorno, with a shrug and a sigh. It was a lost world beyond both comprehension and rescue, not that it seemed to seek salvation.

'For the benefit of those with a sensitive disposition,' the waiter announced, nodding at the rolls of exquisite-looking fish on the plates in front of them, 'these are swordfish. From my friend here, as fresh as you'll ever find.'

He left, the severed head in his arms. They leaned over the table and examined the selection of little dishes: squid and tuna, bright red shrimp and tiny octopus. Falcone got his fork in first. The rest weren't far behind. No one left a scrap. The food was astonishing, twice the quality and half the price of home.

Teresa looked round, making sure there was no one within earshot, not unless they had smuggled some very fancy listening equipment into one of the ancient, crooked houses next to the restaurant, which seemed unlikely.

'Four days and we're still in the dark. Is there a plan, Leo?' she asked. 'If so, are we to be allowed to know about it?'

Falcone removed a scarlet shrimp from its shell very delicately and examined its pink body, like a baby's finger, before popping it into his mouth. 'We don't even have a name for this man,' he said when he'd finished. 'We don't know why he suddenly wants to rat on his fellow criminals. We're not entirely sure he's serious.'

'That's comforting,' Peroni grumbled. 'We've just sent two bright young officers out into that wilderness up there—' he glanced at the bare mountain behind them – 'without a clue what's in store for them.'

Falcone nodded, seemingly accepting the point. 'What else could I do? That's what our new friend in the 'Ndrangheta demanded.' He gazed at Peroni. 'Seriously. Tell me. What else could I do? You understand this better than I. Please.'

'He does?' Teresa asked, watching Peroni. 'How come?'

'The Bonetti case.' Falcone said simply.

The Bonetti case.

She tried to recall the details. It must have been eight years before, and her memory was hazy. All that she remembered was that it was not a pleasant story. A crook turned pentito. Then there were consequences.

'You dealt with that, Gianni?' Silvio Di Capua asked. 'Before my time. I remember the name from the papers.'

Peroni took a deep breath and said, 'That was back when I held rank. It was my case. Bonetti was a well-connected pimp. We had him under surveillance when I was running vice. A weak guy. Scared of everyone.' He grimaced. 'Me in particular. One day I bullied him into thinking the only way he could keep himself out of jail was to start squealing. The idiot believed me. I can be a good bully when I feel like it. Or at least I could back then.' He shrugged and looked briefly ashamed. 'I beat him about a bit. Reckoned he wouldn't complain. He didn't dare.'

The details still eluded her.

'And?' Teresa asked.

'The guy went to court and coughed up everything he knew. We sent down two of the biggest hoods in Lazio and a handful of their lieutenants.' He grabbed a glass of water from the table and took a long draught. They weren't drinking wine. It wasn't right somehow. 'Couple of days later someone shot dead his wife, his brother and his seven-year-old son. The brother was driving the little boy and his mamma back from school. One day later we found Bonetti in his safe house hanging from a rope in the bathroom. I still don't think he killed himself. He didn't have the guts. Someone got there.' His eyes didn't leave Falcone. 'Someone who knew where he was. One of us. A cop. A lawyer. We never did find out.'

Di Capua was tapping away at his phone again.

'Please, Silvio,' Peroni said quietly, putting his hand on the young forensic officer's fingers as they dashed across the screen. 'You don't need to know any more. The point is—' he closed his eyes as in pain – 'once we step outside the system like this anything goes. We're as bad as them.

Sometimes they can be as good as us. It's not black and white any more. The consequences can be . . .'

Teresa did remember. It came back in a sudden, hurtful flash. The papers carried pictures of the Bonetti child. He was a lovely-looking boy, so it made the front pages, a photo of a gap-toothed kid with a head of bouncy black hair, and a big, broad smile. His death would have broken Peroni's heart.

'I don't get why he doesn't just come in,' Di Capua said. 'Call and tell us where to pick him up. Have done with it. Nice and simple and—'

'Nothing's nice and simple here,' Peroni said with some heat. 'Do you really not understand why he won't do that?'

Silence then she said, 'Tell us, genius.'

'First, the men around him would kill him if they knew. There's maybe a hundred people employed inside that 'ndrina. If any but his closest family have a clue this is going on I'd be very surprised.'

Makes sense, Teresa said. 'And the second?'

'Because there's a price to be paid. He won't just hand himself over. Not without getting something in return.'

'I know that!' Falcone's temper was shorter than usual. 'There'll have to be negotiations about immunity from prosecution. Where he'll stay. How we'll bring him to court. I understand that. I expect it. We'll check everything they tell us. Every location for a meeting. Everyone we encounter. I won't risk a single officer—'

'You're risking them already,' Peroni pointed out.

'We'll check out what they tell us—'

'You shouldn't have sent Rosa.'

Falcone looked baffled. 'Why not? She's a serving officer. She volunteered—'

'Because she's got feelings,' Teresa said. 'For Nic. Did you really not notice?'

He stared at her, his tanned face immobile, trapped, she thought, between shame and anger. Falcone was a cold man and to make matters worse he knew and hated that in himself. 'We all must distance ourselves from our emotions,' he said and seemed embarrassed by the words. Then, as if to change the subject, he picked at more food.

'They won't,' Peroni said eventually. 'Lo Spettro and his people. Their emotions tell them that nothing matters except themselves. Their family. Their clan. Their blood. Do you think they'll give us real names? Do you imagine for one moment they'll tell us the truth about anything? This guy hasn't been scared into standing up in court and talking. Not by us anyway. He hasn't had a sudden attack of conscience. It doesn't work that way. There's a reason we're here, a reason he'll never tell us, not unless it serves his purpose. This is their game. Not ours. And it's going to be dirty. That's just about the only thing you can take for granted. We're on their level now. Best not forget it.'

Falcone carried on as if he hadn't quite heard. 'We assemble the facts. We verify them. We've got all the equipment we need in the house. Links into Rome. When we need something the people there—'

'Intelligence . . .' Peroni's voice had a cold, mocking tone, one she'd never heard before. 'Listen . . .'

He got up, grimaced at the food on the table, looked around him. 'You keep staring at your computers hoping they'll tell you something if you like. I want to understand what kind of place this is. What kind of people we're dealing with. I'll see you back at the house when I'm ready.'

'I'm in charge here!' Falcone barked, suddenly cross. 'You will do what I say. *Agente*!'

He spoke Peroni's rank in haste. It was too loud. She looked around. There was no sign of the waiter, no other customers in earshot. All the same this argument was foolish.

'I think,' Teresa said, 'for all our sakes you two had better calm down.'

Peroni shook his head and walked into the dark interior of the restaurant. She saw him climbing the stairs up to street level, nodding at the waiter who was at the till, on the phone. Taking a reservation she hoped, not that the place seemed to attract many customers.

A few short years before Gianni Peroni and Falcone had been equals, both inspectors, Peroni perhaps more highly regarded than the dry and stoical Falcone. Then his world had collapsed, along with his marriage, through a simple mistake made in the heat of the moment, a brief and stupid affair that brought down everything.

This was before her time. She didn't regret any of it. She couldn't. She was selfish, and it was his downfall that had brought them together.

In all the years she'd known the man he'd never behaved like this. She wanted to tell herself it wasn't like him. Not the Peroni she'd come to love. But the Peroni who'd had an affair while married with kids was a stranger too and occasionally she'd wondered where he'd gone.

Falcone was staring at the menu again, embarrassed, lost for words. Silvio Di Capua caught her eyes and pretended to whistle.

'Do you want something else?' Falcone asked, not looking at her.

'Just coffee,' she said. 'Let Gianni go his own way, will you? He has a kind of . . .' The phrase 'emotional intelligence', a cliché she loathed, sprang into her head. 'He knows what he's doing, Leo.'

'I don't doubt it.' For once Falcone looked unsure of himself. Then he scowled and added, 'But do I?'

Two hours before his colleagues sat down for their meal on the Cariddi waterfront, Nic Costa had pulled in by the side of a narrow mountain road twenty-two tortuous and winding kilometres away and once more checked his directions. They were deep in the mountainside behind Reggio, with a breath-taking view back to the point at which the Tyrrhenian gave way to the Ionian, Homer's wine-dark sea, the waters once owned by ancient Athens. In places hereabouts the locals still spoke a kind of Greek. Another thing that set them apart and made the place feel foreign. He could see the coastline and the ragged shore of Sicily across the shimmering azure gulf. Cariddi, he guessed, was just out of sight, lost behind a massive spine of rock that hid the western shore.

A lone eagle hung in the air over a craggy bare peak to their right. They were in the upper ranges of Aspromonte, more like the Alps than the south. It was a wild, deserted region where some took to skis in the winter. Houses were few and mostly confined to a scattering of hamlets. Those they had long left behind and scarcely met another car on the road. It was ten thirty in the morning and there was still the smell of fresh dew in the pine-scented air.

'We should have brought the satnav,' Rosa Prabakaran said from the passenger seat of the rented Fiat saloon.

The young policewoman was dressed in jeans and a white cotton shirt. A small silver crucifix hung around her neck on a chain. She had sunglasses on her head and her dark, serious Indian face bore a little make-up. The two of them were playing the part of tourists, lovers on a brief holiday. The pretence appeared to work on the pair of young armed Carabinieri officers in bulletproof vests who'd stopped them in the lower reaches of the mountain, asking for ID and their intentions. The men had glanced at their fake identity cards then sent them on their way, shaking their heads as if to say, 'Why bother?'

The air was so thin and clean, the land so untouched by civilisation, the language of the locals so different, he found it hard to believe he was still in Italy.

'And what exactly would I have asked it?' he wondered, amused that they were beginning to play the part of a bickering couple with such ease.

She looked at him and laughed. He felt, for a moment, embarrassed.

They had been given no place name. No directions to or from a nearby village or town. Only an anonymous message by mobile phone, passed on from Lombardi, the Justice Ministry official who led the small support team in Rome from a private office away from the prying eyes of the Questura. He said they were to follow a particular route into the mountains and look for a marker: an old, abandoned farm tractor, rusting, with a red seat. Then drive three kilometres along the narrow track by its side and wait. Which was what they were now doing.

Searching for what? The prospect of taking in a local gang lord, one who had somehow communicated his willingness to turn pentito, though how exactly, or why, none of them had been told. All he knew was that they were chasing a ghost and they never came when you called.

He got out of the car and looked around. Rosa followed, putting on her sunglasses, looking every inch the pretty holidaymaker. He couldn't help but glance at her, the same way the Carabinieri had earlier. Without her drab work clothes, away from the everyday cares of the job in Rome, she seemed as unexpected as this foreign and unfamiliar landscape.

They were still on the western side of the mountain. The steep stretches of rock and vegetation around them were, for the most part, lush and green from the incoming wind and rain. Tracts of woodland meandered up the slope towards an unseen peak. Thickets of strange tall weeds dotted with straggly prickly pears ran along the meandering lines of what he assumed must have been winter torrents. On an irregular patch of high grass pasture in the distance a herd of sheep or goats – it was difficult to tell from this distance – grazed with the lazy, unconcerned nonchalance their ancestors might have possessed two millennia before.

There seemed to be some kind of a building in a clump of low woodland a few hundred metres up a rough stone path ahead. A thin curling line of smoke was rising from the crooked rusty chimney on the roof.

'I'm going to take a look,' he announced.

'Me too.' She was by his side in an instant, linking her arm through his. 'Not on your own. What if they're watching? We're a couple, aren't we?'

He scanned the nearest line of woodland, a tangle of weak, lanky trees that looked undernourished. In winter, the books said, it would be thick snow here. Men who lost their way were lucky to survive. Somewhere close by, on the bare, high plateau, lay complexes of caves where the 'Ndrangheta kept their prisoners and kidnap victims, and buried their dead too. He wondered what the local police and Carabinieri knew of the kind of people they were trying to reach, understood too that he would never dare find out. Everything about this venture was covert. An idle word to a stranger could cost them their lives.

A few moments after they began to walk up the path a figure emerged from the hut in the woods. Costa could make out that it was a very diminutive woman in a shapeless brown dress. As they got closer he could see she had shoulder-length grey hair that hung flat against her tanned head. She stood there, watching them, hands on bony hips, a short, compact woman, very sure of herself. A cigarette hung from her lower lip, almost extinct. There was a woodpile by the porch, an axe notched into the topmost log. Ragged washing hung on a line running from the front wall to a post by a patch of herbs. He could detect the distinctive and gamy smell of meat on the musty smoke that hung around the place with a permanence that suggested there was a fire burning here always.

The woman stared at them, leaning against the rotten wooden frame of the door. Her arms were bony and the colour of old mahogany, as if they'd been stained by smoke over the decades too. She had the drawn, judgemental face of a medieval saint. Her small, sharp eyes never left them. When they stopped in front of her he could see the pupils were milky from what looked like the onset of cataracts. She might have been forty or fifty or more. Costa couldn't begin to guess, though it did occur to him that she might seem entirely different in another context. There was something theatrical about her, as if she were an actress about to begin a performance.

'You make such a pretty, pretty couple. I don't see so many young people around here. Don't see much of anything at all.'

She had a hoarse voice, that of a hardened smoker, and a severe southern accent of the kind he was beginning to recognize.

Rosa smiled and unhooked her arm from his.

'Thank you,' she said.

'What do you want?'

Costa glanced around the place. She seemed to be on her own. 'We were looking for someone.'

The woman crooked her head to one side as if listening and asked, 'Who?'

'We don't know his name.'

There was brief, sarcastic laughter. 'What are you? Psychic?'

'Not exactly,' Rosa countered.

'There's no one here except a crazy old woman. What can I tell you?'

Rosa shot him a rueful glance. She hated making mistakes. She was too quick to pass judgement too.

Costa pulled out his wallet.

The woman raised an eyebrow. 'You think I have something for you, Roman?'

'Perhaps.'

She finished the cigarette and ground the stub under her foot. He couldn't help but notice she wore no shoes.

'I'm the *santina* of this hill. Do you understand what that means?' The little woman took two steps towards them and peered up into Rosa's face. 'You should know what I'm talking about, girl. Skin that colour. Face as pretty as a picture. We all came from the east, in the beginning. Even those fools—' she nodded at the road – 'in the city.'

Rosa caught his eye. It signified something to her anyway.

'A santina's a fortune-teller, isn't it?' she said, amused, like a child discovering something new at the fair.

The woman's narrow, expressionless face was marked by deep, dark wrinkles in her walnut skin. Too much sun. Perhaps working the fields. Though it could just as easily come from an excess of time spent on the beach. Costa could see the pearly glint in her eyes more clearly now. He wondered how good her sight truly was. There was another smell too. Something alcoholic with the fragrance of mountain herbs was on her breath.

'No,' she said, leaning forward, looking into their faces in turn with her damaged, half-opaque eyes. 'Your fortunes are your own to tell, not mine. All I do is see. While the rest of you are blind. Fifty euros. Then I'll tell you what you want to know.' She held out a bony hand. Costa pulled out the money and handed it over. 'What you don't as well if I feel like it. Which may be of more value.'

He handed her the money. The santina brought the cash right up to her face, peering closely at the notes. Then she stuffed the wad into the pocket of her shapeless dress, kicked open the door with her filthy bare foot and said, 'Come in.'

The shack was little more than a single dark room with a rickety table, a few chairs and a blackened stove leaking smoke. A huge bubbling pan sat on top alongside a collection of battered pots and a tin kettle. In the corner, on a set of drawers, there was a tiny portable TV, a radio and a small black and white photograph of an old man with long white hair and a dark felt hat, the kind mountain shepherds wore.

The woman closed the door, walked to the table and turned on the light, a single bulb dangling from a twisted cable. The curtains were closed on the front windows. The rear ones had no fabric at all but faced directly onto the woods. A thick line of silvery tree trunks fought each other a metre or so away from the glass. The place probably never saw much sun at all. It stank of mould and stale smoke, humanity and the rank odour of cooking meat.

The santina walked to the table, picked up a bottle, and poured three shot glasses of dark spirit.

'Drink this,' she said. 'It's good. You get your money's worth here.'

'It's a little early for me,' Costa said. 'And I'm driving.'

'The Carabinieri won't bother you. They don't come this way. They know if they do they won't go home.'

Rosa eyed him, amused, and took a gulp, then began to cough and choke. Costa tried the stuff and just about managed a sip. It tasted of the mountain: of earth, wild herbs, and raw potent alcohol.

'Sit down.'

They took two old rickety wooden stools on one side of the table. The woman perched on an ancient dining chair opposite, one that had a cushion to raise her to the same height. The light of the single bulb fell above her face. She had the things she needed there already and her hands fell readily to them. A pack of Tarot cards. Two scarlet candles, blackened wicks curling like seared tendrils, half burned and attached to the bare cracked wood by swirls of long-hardened wax. She lit them and Costa could see, next to the cards, what looked suspiciously like the dark scrawny paw of a small animal, severed at the elbow or knee.

This was an act, he thought, a performance that had been prearranged for the rare tourists who came to Aspromonte seeking something more than the usual local colour.

'No crystal ball?' Rosa asked.

The santina glared at her then leaned across the table and peered at the silver crucifix around the young agente's neck. 'Christ stopped at Eboli. Didn't you know? This is the south. Jesus won't help you here.'

Rosa cast Costa a querulous glance.

'Give me your hand,' the woman said, nodding at her. 'The right one.'

She obeyed and placed her dusky arm across the table. The santina took her fingers and turned them over to look at her paler palm. Then she traced her nails along the lines there, peering hard at the skin as if searching for something.

Rosa seemed perturbed. Costa wasn't surprised. He'd dealt with fake clairvoyants before and understood that they needed to instil a little fear into those they robbed. In Rome he'd hauled one or two into court when they picked on someone too poor, too gullible for the offence to pass. It was impossible to do more than rein in a few when time allowed. The national obsession with the occult was ubiquitous, fodder for an ever-increasing number of TV channels. Millions of good Catholics seemed to follow these supposedly dark arts without so much as a second thought.

He recalled an incident when his father was alive. A government minister from the south visiting a hospital for disabled children and being pictured secretly making the sign of the horn behind his back, a traditional gesture for warding off the devil. Marco Costa had known the man responsible, a fellow politician, though gullible and right-wing. He'd sworn in fury at the picture when it appeared in the newspapers. The story had produced a howl of outrage from liberal commentators offended that a senior politician should give credence to the popular prejudice that the disabled somehow attracted their impairment through an association with evil. What was it his father had said? It was seventeen hundred years since Constantine decreed Italy was a monotheistic state. Still the pagan gods refused to die.

'You know why we're here, signora,' he said, looking at the santina. 'Kindly earn your money.'

'I rarely disappoint,' she replied, and traced her dirty nails across the lines of Rosa's right hand. 'Wait your turn.'

The woman's fingers moved quickly across her dark skin. Rosa twitched automatically, affected by the swift, purposeful gestures she made, then rapidly withdrew her hand.

The santina was staring at her. 'I feel sorry for you,' the woman said. She scowled at Costa. 'He doesn't know. He doesn't care.'

'Know . . . what?' Rosa asked.

'You pretend you're his lover and hope one day this game will turn to truth. You fool him. You fool yourself, perhaps. You do not fool me.'

'I don't know what you mean . . .'

Rosa had her head down, eyes averted. Costa suddenly felt hot and uncomfortable. 'Signora—'

'If one day you should find your way to his bed . . . enjoy that moment. The pleasure will be fleeting and pain not far behind. Now you . . .'

She reached for him with both hands, her sharp, hawkish eyes fixed on his face. 'The right, not the left.'

Her strong, bony fingers snatched at his with a touch that was coarse and leathery but purposeful, like that of a surgeon. She moved with a subtle, practised touch, probing the crevices and lines of his skin.

The santina frowned, looked uncertain of herself for a moment, then stopped, still gripping him, but staring at the table, thinking.

'What is it?' Rosa asked.

'This is his story. Not yours.'

The woman dashed at her face with one hand, as if rubbing some invisible spot.

'My story . . .' Costa said with a sigh. 'What is that exactly?'

He caught his breath. Rosa uttered a low, frightened murmur. The woman's head went back, her cloudy eyes rolled upwards into her head then, as he watched, feeling his skin turn cold, a line of livid shiny red emerged flooding from behind the lids. A trickle of thick blood began to run down each cheek with the precise vertical symmetry of the tears on a statue of the Virgin in some distant chapel.

A trick, he said to himself. A cheap, fairground ruse.

Something smuggled in her fingers in that curious movement a few seconds before.

She took away one hand and wiped at her cheeks with her arm. The red sticky stain smeared across her face like cheap make-up.

'Very good—' he began to say.

'Be silent!'

Her milky eyes were on him again, filmed with gore. 'Tell me. Why do you expect others to bury your dead? Why? That is what infants do.'

He tried to take his hand away. She held onto him, tightly, with extraordinary strength.

'I don't pretend to understand these riddles,' he murmured. 'If you will excuse me . . .'

She looked at his palm and placed a long stained finger in the centre. 'I see your parents here. Your mother and father. I see another woman. Your dead wife. You loved them all. Still I feel their bodies inside you because, in your childish selfishness, you refuse to let them go.'

'Signora . . .'

'Is this your idea of devotion? To keep their rotting carcasses in your head as a reminder of your pain? What would their dead mouths say to you now if they could speak? Would they thank you . . .?'

'Enough!'

The woman let go of him then folded her grubby arms across her chest. 'I can only tell you what I see. Your future is yours to direct, not mine.'

For some reason he couldn't understand the light bulb above the table was beginning to swing slowly, to and fro. Then he heard something outside, a noise. A car perhaps. Another smell cut into the noisome rankness of the shack: the acrid stink of a cigar.

He couldn't get her words out of his head.

'This is not why I came,' Costa insisted.

'To seek the dead? It's exactly why. Who do you wish to deceive with these lies? Others?' Her dirty fingers indicated Rosa. 'This girl? She would be your *inamorata*. As big a fool as you.'

Costa got to his feet and said to the young agente, 'We're going.'

The santina grinned at him. She had very white teeth, too perfect for a country crone. 'Tanato we called him in the old tongue. The god of death. Twin to Hypnos, sleep, though fools may mistake the two. Unlike his twin he is a generous and curious spirit. If you keep calling his name he will hear. He will come. When summoned.'

'I'm not going to listen . . .' His hand cut the air, as if it could wave away her words.

'Bury those you loved, before they come back to consume you for good.'

'Nic . . .' Rosa begged.

He wanted to scream at the ugly little crone. Wanted to burn down this grubby, stinking shack around her ears.

'Nic?'

She was trying to draw attention to something. His rage blotted out her voice and her concern. Almost. The woman was right. They were losses that marked him, shadows from the past. They would not leave and a part of him was glad of that.

Rosa Prabakaran's deep brown eyes glistened in the darkness. There was fear in her face.

The door was open. Two shapes filled it. A man and a woman, almost as tall as each other, and of similar appearance. Siblings by the look of it. They wore modern, fashionable clothes, brightly coloured, expensive, as if they were dressed for a social engagement, not an appointment in a squalid shack with a dwarfish witch who claimed to be living like a wild thing on the distant, isolated western reaches of Aspromonte.

The man had a short-barrelled *lupara* shotgun across his arm, broken over his elbow, its leaden length incongruous against his bright pink shirt. The woman glanced at it for a moment in disapproval. Her hair was short and very black framing a pleasant round face that was disfigured by a faint but long scar on her right cheek. Her shirt was white and short-sleeved. Lurid tattoos of dragons and other mythical creatures crawled down her right arm to the wrist, so many they obliterated most of her olive skin.

'They came alone?' the santina asked, nodding at Costa and Rosa.

'They came alone,' the woman replied in a voice that bore the same southern burr. 'We watched them all the way.'

'Good.' The santina pointed at Costa. 'You will see the man you seek when our family knows it can trust you. How else may we proceed? Do you understand the risks of what we do? How few know of this?' She stood up quickly and thrust her filthy hand into his face. 'You can count them on these fingers. Before you may get close to him we must be sure you deserve our faith. Those who know nothing of what he's planning surround him like hawks and would kill us all if they knew what he intended, as is their right. You will make them treat you as a brother in the 'ndrina. One of their own. Then, and only then, you may see him. Then, and only then, will we be able to find some way to allow him to escape into your world and become a pentito as he wishes.'

They had thought this through, so much more than Falcone and the rest of the little police crew in Cariddi. This was their game, their plan.

'What do you want of us?' he asked.

'Your patience. Your obedience. Your trust. This will take time. You have no choice. Neither do we.'

He listened, trying to understand. 'What exactly are you asking of me?'

She laughed just for a moment and he saw again those white and perfect teeth. 'You must join the 'ndrina. We've a story that will explain your presence. You can be a newcomer, a fugitive from a distant relative in Canada. You will follow our orders. There is no alternative. Our men will only trust those in the blood who earn their confidence. Without that your presence around the *capo locale* would arouse suspicion. They would kill you first, then us. So forget who you were. Become what we tell you. Otherwise you go home empty-handed. Or in a box.'

'Rosa—' he began.

'This woman stays here,' the santina interrupted. 'I shall be her *manutengola*. Her keeper.' She glanced around the surroundings. 'I have a spare bed. She will not suffer. You have our word.'

'I'm a hostage?' Rosa asked, incredulous.

'You're a guest. If he—' she jerked her head at Costa – 'deceives us then you become a hostage.' The woman glowered at him. 'Don't let that happen, police man. We make stalwart friends but heartless enemies.'

'This was never part of the arrangement . . .'

'What arrangement is that?' asked the woman at the door, stepping into the room. She was about Costa's age and there was something troubled about her he thought. The tattoos, the scar, the darting, anxious eyes. She held out her hand and he took it for a moment. 'My name is Lucia Bergamotti. This is my brother Rocco. My aunt you have met already. The person you seek is my father, the head of our 'ndrina. Lo Spettro they call him. A man who risks his life, all our lives, everything, to help you. There is no arrangement. No bargain on our part. Not yet. Once he can trust you then he will do what you wish. But only if he's promised immunity from prosecution and an absolute guarantee of his safety and ours.'

'And in return?' Costa asked.

They glanced at one another and he found it interesting she was the one who spoke.

'In return he will lead you to a meeting of the heads of the organisation within Calabria. You may detain them—'

'We know their names, signora,' he cut in. 'We know where most of them live. If we could prosecute them we—'

'My father will tell you things you've never guessed at.' She looked at her brother again. 'In addition he will give you Andrea Mancuso. *Il Macellaio*. The Butcher of Palermo. You know who he is.'

Costa didn't know what to say. Mancuso was the *Capo dei Capi*. The head of the combined Sicilian mobs. Overlord of the Costa Nostra, on the run for almost two decades. Over the years both the police and the Carabinieri had been close to capturing him, only to be defeated by a whisper from a traitor in their own ranks.

'You will have the 'Ndrangheta capi, the lord of Sicily and the names of all their tame politicians,' the man said. 'If that's not enough we can take you both for a walk in the hills right now.'

'Names,' Rosa muttered.

'For some,' the woman replied. 'Others in person. There'll be a meeting soon. A summit if you like. We'll tell you where and when. You'll need many men to take them. Organisation. Discipline. All the same . . .' She looked uncertain of herself for a moment. 'There may be blood.'

The man joined them. He had a ready smile, a charming one, and his right hand gripped the barrel of his shotgun.

'There's always blood,' he said to Costa. 'Signore. Please. The women in this family . . . no sane man wishes to argue with them. Do as my sister and my aunt say. You ask a lot. Our father is willing to oblige with a generosity no man like him has ever shown you before. But we need a little in return.' He smiled at Rosa. 'Your phones. Your documents. Any weapons.'

'We have no weapons,' Rosa hissed, beginning to flail her arms. 'I didn't agree to this. Any of it. I won't . . .'

The man called Rocco Bergamotti hitched the shotgun off his shoulder, snapped it shut and pointed the barrel straight in her face. He wasn't smiling any more.

'Rocco . . .' his sister said quietly from behind.

The gun stayed straight and level. 'If you do not agree then I kill both of you here and now. You know us. No cop I do not own has ever been this close and understood what I am. Please. What alternative do you leave me?'

Costa walked in front of the weapon and pushed the barrel to one side. 'I will go with you. My name is—'

'I know your name already,' the man cut in. 'Tomasso Leoni. If ever I find I'm mistaken I will not be responsible for the consequences. You understand, Tomasso?'

Costa hesitated. Flies were buzzing round the grubby little shack. The santina lit another cigarette.

'*Si*,' he said finally. 'Tomasso Leoni.'

Gianni Peroni walked the length of the narrow alley that was the single street of old Cariddi, a cobbled lane separating the seafront houses from the terraces at the foot of the hill. He didn't know what he was looking for. He didn't know why he'd walked out on Falcone and Teresa. It wasn't the memory of the Bonetti case, not entirely. In comparison to their current task that was almost routine. Everyone had known the true identity of the man they were seeking to protect. They had understood the names of his enemies as well. It should have been much easier to keep the two apart.

Here, without the benefit of conventional backup, with only a secret link to a handful of officials working covertly in Rome, everything was different. They were clutching at shadows, unable to control the pace of events, waiting until the moment the elusive, nameless figure they sought would make himself known.

Two young fishermen in blue denim shirts and jeans wandered past on their way to the horseshoe-shaped port set beneath the wrecked castle on the cliff above. The modest walled harbour was home to a handful of flat, sharp-bowed skiffs and two sword-fishing vessels – feluccas – with their towers and long ladder prows. One of the men carried a huge glass-bottomed bucket. Peroni had watched them use this the evening before. They sailed out as dusk fell, arranged the bucket beneath a bright light, then dipped it into the sea from the square stern of the skiff, peering beneath the waves looking for fish. It was almost an hour before Peroni saw them cast a modest net into the water and another before they returned with a catch so small it barely filled a single box. Enough to feed a few mouths in the village, not sell. Toni, the waiter, spoke the truth. No one hereabouts was greedy, not when it came to the ocean anyway.

The pair entered the shadow cast between the buildings on either side of the street, deep in conversation, their arms interlocked, their heads close in conversation. They possessed an open familiarity one would never have seen between two men back home.

Peroni thought of the equipment in the rented house. The computers. The high-speed encrypted links to the team in Rome. He barely knew Lombardi, their linkman running the liaison office. Their lives depended on strangers. Still, he had to assume the men and women behind him were intelligent, committed professionals.

The problem was they didn't appreciate what Calabria was like. No one could without being there and this worried him. He'd read every file on the 'Ndrangheta he could lay his hands on and even, for once, a little history. It was still insufficient, like trying to comprehend a foreign country described in an unfamiliar language. He appreciated how easy it would be for Nic and Rosa to disappear forever into the vast, green emptiness of Aspromonte should they set a foot wrong. Men and women had been vanishing in that bleak wilderness for centuries. It seemed to have been the land of brigands since time began. The imperial Romans struggled to control the region. Spartacus had been cornered by Crassus as his slave revolt began to wane, only to escape and die elsewhere. The warring states of the Renaissance viewed the region as untameable. Even Garibaldi had to beg permission and support from the bandits in the mountains when he invaded from Sicily in 1862, promising to enter Rome victorious or perish beneath its walls, and managing neither. Peroni could find no reason to believe that computers and intelligence systems would be any more useful against a cunning and knowledgeable outlaw army than the regiments and generals of previous generations.

There was too much staring at blinking screens, too little staring into people's faces. He was a practical man. His career had hit its peak some years earlier and then he had fallen spectacularly through one stupid personal mistake. His own talents and weaknesses were as familiar to him as the damaged lines on his battered features. He had no great grasp for technical matters, no thirst for dry, impersonal knowledge. One recent history book on southern Italy apart, he'd barely read anything outside a case file in years. It was hard enough wading through the dreary, jargon-laden and often illiterate material that counted as evidence these days. Increasingly of late he'd contemplated taking retirement. He was fifty-seven. His cautious and frugal nature had left him with close to fifty thousand euros in the bank and enough service to generate a pension that would suffice, even with the support he still had to provide for his children and ex-wife in Tuscany.

What stopped him wandering into Personnel and filling in the forms? He knew exactly. There were still times when he loved the work, most of all being near Teresa, admiring her bright intelligence and the way it could close a desperate case just as everyone else was giving up. He adored those rare occasions when they finished at the Questura on the same shift and could walk home together, arm in arm, just like the Cariddi fishermen, through the busy, cobbled streets of Rome to her little apartment in the Via del Tritone, picking up a pizza or something simple along the way.

This was the most magical part of his life, the best he'd ever known, and he couldn't imagine being without it. Even if such a belief in the permanence of things was an illusion, like the curious mirage that distorted the coastline of Sicily across the Strait of Messina, turning it into a fantasy land of rocky castles and unreal mountains.

Something else kept him chained to the Questura. Over the last few years he'd watched Nic Costa turn from a quiet, introverted young man into a decent, close friend, a good man, one full of integrity and hope, even when fate dealt the cruellest blow and stole away the woman he'd loved. Nic had a burning inner fire of decency that was both infectious and necessary since it reminded those around him, awkwardly at times, of the reason they picked up the badge in the first place. He could even chase the weary cynicism out of Leo Falcone, mostly anyway. Watching him at work filled Peroni with the enthusiasm that came from seeing an investigation conclude with some measure of success, at a private cost perhaps, but always with an absolute sense of dedication to the wronged and the innocent. That was important, and their young, occasionally naïve colleague would never let them forget it.

'How the hell can we do that here?' Peroni muttered to himself.

At best they would take a bloodthirsty criminal into custody, keep him alive, provide him with a new identity for the rest of his days which he would spend as a free man elsewhere, doubtless in comfort. Perhaps a few crooks and bent politicians would go to jail. Others would soon take their place. It was justice of a sort. A very modern and Italian kind it seemed to him.

Peroni was surprised to discover this pessimism within himself. It was not typical, familiar or welcome.

He needed a coffee. He needed someone to talk to, someone new.

At the very end of the lane, a couple of hundred metres along from the house they had rented, on a rock and cement plateau overlooking the sea, stood a lone fisherman's cottage with tables and beach toys outside. At the front a woman and a young boy were carefully stacking a huge supply of gigantic green water melons next to a large sign indicating a price that seemed to Peroni, familiar with Roman shopping, ludicrously cheap. The restaurant where he'd walked out on Teresa and Falcone apart, this seemed to be the only place in the whole of old Cariddi where a stranger could buy a drink.

He ambled over and asked for a caffè. The tables and chairs had seen better days. The tall, slender woman behind the counter was extraordinarily handsome, with piercing eyes and the chiselled, tanned features of the wife of a fisherman or farmer. She wore a simple black dress, the kind the peasant women wore in the hills. Her long dark hair was tied back simply with nothing more than a blue elastic band. She waved at him to sit down. This was meant to be more than a simple drinks stop. There was everything in the shack: meat and cheese and bread for panini, postcards and maps, swimming gear, beach balls and toys. A little home business that provided all the seaside visitor needed. Not that there were any tourists about except him, and the way the young boy was carefully brushing dust from some buckets and spades it seemed they had been absent for some time. The lad was her son, surely, eight or nine, no more. He had the same engaging dark eyes and angular face. A fetching kid with a shy and nervous smile when he noticed he was being watched.

He doesn't have a father, Peroni thought immediately, and wondered why that seemed so obvious, whether it could really be true. These thoughts came to him sometimes, and he knew their source. They came from memories of his own children, now in their late teens, fast becoming adults, their younger, more carefree selves lost forever.

A good, strong, generous cup of coffee arrived, and with it a slice of watermelon for free, both brought by the boy, still sporting a diffident grin. Peroni sat back and watched the interplay between him and the woman who was fussing behind the counter of the little cabin, cleaning things, checking the very old yet shiny coffee machine. They shared something familiar and loving, though there was a distinct nervous awkwardness to them too, as if a storm was lurking beyond the brilliant blue sky, waiting on the other side of the vast mountain above them.

The child came back with the bill: one euro.

'This coffee is so good I think I'm back in Rome,' Peroni said, planting a two euro coin in the kid's fingers and closing them with a gentle grip to say: no change.

'Rome?' The child's eyes grew wide with wonder. 'Rome?'

'You've been?'

'Never,' his mother said, and then looked a little guilty, as if shocked by the cold tone in her own voice. 'One day maybe.'

'I went to L-L-Lamezie . . .' the child stuttered.

Peroni had passed through the place driving south. A provincial little town a hundred kilometres away. There was a regional airport there. It didn't look anywhere to remember.

'Was it good?'

The kid looked at his mother and said, hesitantly, 'Yes.'

The old cop stuck out his massive hand. 'My name's Gianni.'

'R-R-Roberto.'

His tiny hand felt soft and warm. It brought back memories of Peroni's kids when they were tiny.

'He has a problem with speaking,' his mother said.

Peroni nodded. 'Me too. At that age. I stuttered all the time. Much worse than you, Roberto. People couldn't understand me. The kids at school. They were horrible.' He made an exaggerated comic expression of disgust, like a clown. The boy laughed. 'You don't worry about it. One day you'll wake up and it's gone for good. You just have to be patient and do what your mamma and the doctors tell you.'

'Doctors . . .' the woman said quietly and shook her head, staring at him.

From the expression in her face, both dubious and a little

grateful, she knew Peroni had never stuttered and wanted him to see that.

A battered black Fiat drew to a halt in the adjoining road. The driver, a lean man in shades, hooted the horn and got out. The boy's eyes fell to the ground and stayed there. The woman looked nervous. Her hands went immediately to the till.

'Roberto,' Peroni said, turning his chair to the ocean. 'You stay and talk to me. I'm new here. I know nothing about Cariddi. You tell me.' He pointed at the gentle blue waves, and a large rock that rose from the water like a prehistoric arrowhead wreathed in seaweed. 'My friend and I have a bet. I say there must be a story behind a rock like that because little fishing villages always have stories about rocks. Always. My friend's a good guy but he's a smart-ass from the city. He says no. It's just a stupid lump of rock. If I win, he pays me ten euros.'

He took a five-euro note from his pocket and placed it on the table. 'Maybe he's right. Maybe not. But if you know a story about the rock I win, see? We share. Five euros for you. Five for me. A deal?'

The child's face lit up again and he said, 'The r-r-rock of Odysseus.'

'Who?'

The boy gripped his arms around an imaginary object. 'Odysseus. He sailed by there. When the monsters wanted him, Scylla and Charybdis.'

'Best thing to do around monsters,' Peroni agreed. 'Keep going. See. You spoke well.'

Roberto giggled and placed a skinny finger to his lips.

Peroni picked up the money, bent down, stuffed the note in the pocket of Roberto's short trousers then whispered in his ear, 'The secret is never think before you speak. Just say what's in your head. If you've a good heart, and I can see you have, what harm can come of it? That's what I did anyway. Worked for me.'

He took out his phone and switched it off, patted the child on his young head and said, 'Sit in front of me, there, and tell me some more stories. But quietly. Let's not disturb your mamma.'

\* \* \*

He did listen, but not so much to the boy's slow and stumbling recounting of the landmarks of the horizon: the cliffs and bays, the further rocks, and the unseen volcano of Stromboli, a bright beacon of fire only visible in the sky on a clear night across the dark and gleaming sea.

It was a strange place to eavesdrop on a cold, hard hood shaking down a woman for money. Peroni was determined not to look but for one moment his resolve failed him and he glimpsed the two of them at the counter, the woman distressed, the sour-faced man in black leaning forward, touching her breast suggestively, laughing as she brushed away his hand, looking at her as if to say, 'Maybe not today. But one day, huh? You'll have no choice.'

Peroni found it so hard to stop himself getting up and inter-vening directly, physically if necessary, to stop what was going on in the humble little cabin.

Instead he made sure little Roberto kept looking at the sea, telling stories about mythical people and monsters and a time when the world didn't hurt quite so much. He couldn't get involved. He had no power, no authority. No identity he could reveal either. Besides . . . this was Calabria. What would happen to her and the boy once he was gone? He'd read the files on the 'Ndrangheta. He knew the consequences, and so would she.

So he took in the boy's tales, told in a voice that faltered very little after a while. When the business at the cabin was done Peroni waited a few minutes, pretending to sip at his coffee, engaging Roberto in another conversation, and one more imaginary bet that won the kid ten euros this time.

Then he got up, went to the counter and paid. There were tears in the woman's eyes, and fear too.

'I need some things for my vacation, signora.'

'What sort of things?' she asked wearily, wiping at her face with her sleeve.

He ambled into the cabin and looked at the dusty items on the shelves. Walking methodically around the cramped space he picked up a pair of fake designer brand sunglasses and some swimming trunks that were far too small, ten postcards, a couple of bottles of wine, some water and two bottles of suntan oil that were years past their use by date, so old the print was fading on the labels.

'I want to get to know this place,' he said, scratching his grizzled grey head. 'What I'd like more than anything is a history. A proper one . . .'

She went to the back and pulled out a leaflet for a book with a fading watercolour cover and the title, *Calabrian Tales*, by Constantino Bergamotti.

'It's old,' she said. 'And expensive. And I have to order it in. Not many people write history here. Even fewer read it.'

'Same in Rome and we've lots.' The cover was blue with a black pencil line drawing of Cariddi.

'Bergamotti,' he said. 'Funny name.'

The way she smiled at that, the first smile he'd seen, made her look very pretty.

'It's not real,' she said. 'A little joke here. Whenever anyone wishes to hide who did something they say, "It was the Bergamotti". Bergamotto is the fruit we grow. One of the few things we have that is ours alone, unique. Look.'

She picked up a couple of jars and some bottles and packets. There was jam made from the fruit, liqueur, soap, bath oils. Most of them had a picture on the label of something a little like a misshapen lemon.

Peroni took the soap from her and sniffed it. The curious citrus fragrance was exotic and alluring. 'I'll take those.'

'The book could take a week to turn up. Sorry. Perhaps longer.'

'We'll be gone by then.' He flourished a hundred. 'We just sold a business in Rome. We've got a little money to spend. Maybe we could invest it here. Who knows? Back home they rip you off, every single day.' He watched her and said, 'The city's full of thieves.'

'That's the world, isn't it?'

He extended his right hand. She took it gingerly. 'Gianni. Gianni Romano.'

'Elena Sposato.'

He nodded at the cottage and then the sea. 'Your husband's a fisherman?'

'My husband's dead,' she said straight away as she packed his goods into two old and wrinkled plastic bags.

He tried to see into her eyes but it was impossible. 'I'm sorry. A watermelon, please. And some oranges.' There was no change in the till. The hood had taken everything. 'No worry, signora. I'll be back another time. The coffee here. The view . . .' He patted Roberto on the head. 'It's beautiful.'

'What sort of business?' she asked.

'Public relations,' Peroni said, then threw a few coins on the bar as a tip, wished them both farewell and walked back to the road.

The black Fiat had gone. But Falcone was there and he looked furious.

'You might at least keep your phone turned on,' he grumbled as they left the village.

'Apologies,' Peroni said with a shrug. 'I wanted to listen in on someone's conversation. It was work, Leo. I assure you.'

He was driving, Falcone in the passenger seat, Teresa was in the back. Silvio Di Capua had stayed in Cariddi to work the machines in the house, liaising with Rome if needed. It seemed a futile exercise. Until they could understand more of the task ahead none of them had a clue how to act, though Peroni's gut instinct told them this was not necessarily bad news, or perhaps even unexpected. If the mob had wanted to kill a couple of cops they would have left the corpses on the doorstep. Not what was posted through the door of their rented house while they were dining: an envelope with a map marked with latitude and longitude co-ordinates for a satnav unit and a simple message written in a cultured hand: 'We have your man. We do not want your woman. Pick her up. Both are safe and will remain so if you do as we say. The car we will take care of ourselves. It will find a good home.'

He navigated the first of the series of sharp hairpin bends that crossed beneath the main A3 autostrada running from Salerno to Reggio then pointed the hire car up into the hills.

'Listen to what?' Teresa asked.

He glanced at her in the mirror. Only briefly. He was trying to follow the constant spoken instructions of the satnav. It was taking them onto a single track road as steep and circuitous as any mountain lane he'd ever encountered.

'A young widow getting hassled for money by some creep.' He looked at Falcone. 'Maybe he was the one who dropped off that message. The moron had thug written all over him. They don't even bother to hide it here.'

He couldn't forget the look of fear and loathing on the woman's face when the jerk reached out and stroked her breast. Or his lascivious, expectant smile.

'I don't think she had enough to keep him happy. Not money anyway. I'd like to know why her husband's dead. There must be a library in the village somewhere. Newspapers. Up the hill where the modern houses are. I'd like to go there. I'd like to talk to this woman some more. She's got a lovely kid—'

'What?' Falcone snapped. 'What? Two of your colleagues are out there somewhere and all you can think about is going to a library?'

Teresa, puzzled, asked, 'Since when did you start reading?'

'What else is there to do? The message said they're safe.'

'The message? You trust a bunch of crooks?'

Peroni turned and looked at the irate man in the passenger seat. 'We trusted them enough to send them Nic and Rosa in the first place, didn't we?'

Falcone was going red and the language, for him, was getting unusually rich.

There was a narrow passing space on the corner of the next bend. Peroni watched the view open up as he approached it. The panorama was astonishing. It ran back to the ragged coastline and across the strait to Sicily. Etna stood majestic in the distance, a puff of smoke near the summit. A little to the north he could see what he presumed to be the Aeolian Islands and, nearby, Stromboli rising like a sea limpet just as Roberto, the widow's kid, had promised.

Peroni pulled in, turned off the engine and waited for the man next to him to calm down a little. When Falcone finally shut up he said, very calmly, 'Let's get this straight once and for all, Leo. We're not police officers here. You're not my superior. I'm not yours to order around as you see fit. As far as Calabria's concerned we have no legal status, none of us. No authority. Nothing. I value your opinion. I admire you. We're friends. A mark of true friendship is that we get to speak frankly with one another. So listen. I don't have to take your pompous crap and bite my tongue as if we're in Rome. OK?'

He leaned forward. Falcone's angular, tanned face had lost a little of its colour. There was still anger in the man's eyes but something a little like self-recognition too.

'I've got more of a feel for what's going on here than you'll ever have and you're smart enough to know that,' Peroni added. 'You got that note for two reasons. First, to let us know our people are safe and that we should come and collect one while the other gets to talk with someone important. Second, it's their way of telling us we're here at their discretion, their pleasure. They know where we live . . .'

'How's that possible?' Falcone demanded. 'We arranged that house through Rome—'

'Doesn't matter,' Peroni cut in, waving him into silence. 'There's no point in worrying about it. This is another country. It belongs to them. I'd be amazed if they didn't know who we are, what we're doing, from the moment we turned up. I know you hate that idea. I appreciate you want to be in control. But listen to me please. We're not.'

He took Falcone by the arm and repeated, 'We're not, Leo. If we ever begin to think we are, or worse, behave that way, then Nic or Rosa or maybe all of us could be in danger. We're at their mercy. That doesn't make me happy either but we'd better learn to live with it. Don't forget. If what they're offering is real, and we have to assume it is, they're risking a lot more than any of us. Remember what happened to Bonetti and his family? He was a minion. Imagine what they'd do to one of their bosses.'

Teresa was silent, watching him in a guarded way he didn't see often.

'As long as they feel they're running this show we've nothing to fear. They want something from us. Something that's in our gift. That's why they asked us here.'

'What could we have for them?' she asked. 'Aside from the obvious—'

'The obvious being solitary exile for a man who's currently king of his castle here,' Peroni cut in. 'Why would he exchange that for a life in which everyone in his family could get killed at any moment?'

They were silent.

'You see the problem,' he added. 'Maybe they'll tell Nic once they trust him. Maybe they'll keep him too until they get the answer they want.'

He thought twice about saying what was in his mind then realized he had to. It was foolish to pretend they could approach this case as if it were some routine inquiry handed down from on high in the Questura.

'Put yourselves in their shoes. What would you do? Would it be any different? We've got to learn to see things from their point of view. To work with them. Like I told you earlier. We don't bring in people like this by thinking we're sweet-talking nuns. You may have to hold your nose from time to time because some of this is going to stink.'

Falcone watched him then shook his head.

'Why don't you run this operation?' he asked straight out.

'Oh that's right. Turn clever.'

'I mean it.' Falcone breathed a deep sigh then repeated, more softly, 'Really. You're right. I'm out of my depth here. I should have passed the whole business on to someone else.'

There was a reason they were out on a limb, a good one.

'We're here because we're the only ones smart enough, or dumb enough, to meet the job description. Oh. And the answer's no. I won't run the operation for you. The things that you're good at are important. Discovery. Intelligence. Planning. You can be doing all that stuff while these people in the hills think we're sunning ourselves by the beach. Me . . .' He thought of the pretty woman and her shy, scared little kid and found himself taking his eyes away from the mirror. 'I'd just like to hang around Cariddi. Talk to people. Get a feel for what's going on. We may need that.'

He gazed down at the coast. It was beautiful, utterly unspoilt. Perhaps, from the point of view of those who'd owned this remote green jewel for a few centuries, worth fighting for.

'You know what separates us?'

Falcone stared at him. 'What?'

'You just want to bring in the bad guys. Throw them in

court. See them go to jail and then move on to whatever happens next. I want more than that. I want to talk to them. They're interesting. You can learn things. You realize we're not so far apart. They just come from a different place and the way they see things is as strange to us as we are to them.'

'I don't even want to think about that,' Teresa complained from the back.

'Then leave it to me,' Peroni said and started the car.

Rosa Prabakaran was waiting for them outside a little hovel of a shack set against a dark clump of trees at the end of a stony path. Peroni took a good look around. There were tyre tracks in the brown dirt and, close to the door, a half-smoked cigar. Nothing else. He scanned the rocky outcrop above them. Someone was probably watching from there right now. Not that it mattered.

'Are you all right?' Teresa asked.

'How did you find me?'

They told her about the note and what it said.

'They took Nic . . .' The young agente seemed upset. 'They made him think they were keeping me as hostage. It was . . . a lie. An act. A performance. Everything. The things they said . . .'

Peroni thought there was a little extra colour in her cheeks at that moment.

'There was a woman. A santina . . .'

She led them into the little shack. Something was cooking on the stove. He thought it smelled good. Meaty, like the best country food. There were two bottles of mineral water on the table, one sparkling, one still, and a basket of bright red apples.

'That's what the witch leaves you, isn't it?' Rosa muttered looking at the fruit. 'The woman said to stay here and wait. You'd come. Then she took our car. I wasn't going to walk anywhere, was I? I don't know where we are. I don't know how far it is to the nearest village.'

A long way, Peroni thought.

Falcone asked her about Costa and what had been discussed. Peroni listened, not wanting to intervene. He meant what he'd said earlier. Falcone was good at detail, at chasing down hints and rumours, turning them into fact. These were rare skills, ones Teresa shared, and quite unlike his own.

But people . . . people were more difficult. Unpredictable. Hard to pin down. Peroni liked that. Not many of his colleagues felt the same way.

Rosa left the most significant part to the last.

'They said they would give us Andrea Mancuso. From Sicily. In person.'

'Jesus,' Peroni whispered. 'What have we got ourselves into? Do you believe that, Leo?'

Falcone didn't seem to be listening. He was wandering round the shack, lost in thought.

'The woman . . . the santina . . . she lived here,' Rosa added.

Peroni went to the sideboard by the front window where the curtains were closed. There was a portable TV and, in an ancient wooden frame, a photo of an old man with very white hair. He looked kindly and intelligent, with a knowing smile. Like everyone's favourite grandfather. He wore a black hat and behind him there were mountains, the bare rocky outcrops of Aspromonte.

'What's a santina?' Teresa asked and looked unimpressed by Rosa's answer: a kind of Calabrian fortune-teller.

Peroni pressed the button to turn on the little TV. Nothing happened. He followed the cable. There wasn't even a plug on the end.

'Nobody lives here,' he said. 'It's just a . . . prop.' Like the envelope with the directions that came through the door while they ate. 'Somewhere they use when they need to. They've probably got scores of places like this around Aspromonte.'

But would they all have a photo of what looked like some-one's grandfather? He wondered. Behind the back of the sideboard with the TV he saw something else and bent down to retrieve it. Teresa looked at the object in his hands. It was a rag cloth with a stain on it.

'Blood,' she said, with the authority of the professional. 'I guess. Old. I'd rather not think what they got up to here.'

'Did they say how they'd get in touch?' Peroni asked.

'No. When Nic offered to go with them that was it. I thought the old woman would stay with me. That I'd be here for weeks. She said she'd be a manu . . . manu . . .'

'Manutengola?' Peroni suggested. He'd read about them in the files.

'That's it.'

'It's what they call someone paid to keep a prisoner. For kidnapping or something.'

Rosa picked up an apple. 'An hour after the others had left she offered me one of these and said goodbye.'

He stifled the amusement inside him. 'Not what you expect the first time you meet the 'Ndrangheta, is it?'

Falcone placed a finger over his silver goatee beard and held it to his thin-lipped mouth, thinking. Tall, urbane, he looked quite out of place here in the wilds.

'They're uncertain of themselves too,' Peroni suggested. 'We're just going to have to wait for them to make a move. If they have to pretend Nic's one of their own . . . if that's what it takes to get him close to whoever this man is . . . it could take a while.'

'It's not as simple as that,' Rosa said.

The others waited. 'There's a summit. A council or something. All the mob bosses are coming somewhere here. He's offering a time and a place. So we can take them.'

Peroni groaned. 'We'd need the army for something like that.'

'It's what they said, Gianni. There was a man and woman too. They looked like brother and sister. They said . . . they said there could be violence.' She looked close to tears. 'We can't let this happen. We can't leave him in there. I wouldn't trust any of them. They'd kill him just like that.'

'We have no choice . . .' Falcone looked at Peroni. 'Do we?'

'None at all.'

'But . . .' Rosa's voice was close to breaking. 'We can try to find them. There has to be something here we can use.'

Teresa picked up the stained cloth and the glasses on the table then pulled out a plastic evidence bag and placed them inside. After that she got an old cardboard box in the corner and started packing away the plates and cooking utensils. There would be prints. They would not, Peroni thought, be easy to check.

'You should leave them,' he said.

She looked aghast. 'Leave them?'

'Yes. What can you do? What forensics lab would you trust? We can't talk to anyone outside. They'd know, however well you disguise it. Can't you see? They're more scared of their own people than they are of us. When they want us to know who they are they'll tell us. Besides, how does it look? We're trying to build trust. And all the while you want to walk round one of their little lairs picking up everything you can find and stuffing it in an evidence bag.'

'For Christ's sake, Gianni,' Rosa cried. 'He's your friend. He's . . . one of us.'

'That's precisely why we do nothing,' he said, watching Teresa carry on putting things in bags.

'Leave it,' Falcone ordered. 'Leave it all. He's right.'

She stopped and asked, 'Is there nothing we can do?'

'I keep saying it,' Peroni grumbled.

'I've got a name,' Rosa chipped in hopefully. 'They're called Bergamotti. We can start with that.'

'True,' Peroni agreed with a quick grin none of them understood. 'We can.'

# PART THREE
## The Fist of Rock

### Calabrian Tales

### Chapter XI: A Place Called Manodiavolo

The belief that the world is not entirely as man sees it lies deep in the heart of every true inhabitant of Aspromonte. Perhaps it stems from our Greek blood. A pagan relic in our character that centuries of Catholic teaching have failed to erase. I believe this to be true but only in part for the land itself is as much to blame as the breeding of its inhabitants.

This is the territory of enchantresses and demons, of magicians and those who fall under the spell. Walk through the bare hills of Aspromonte in mid-summer, smell the fragrance of the mountain herbs crushed beneath your feet, and you find yourself in a kind of Arcadia where the modern world is far distant. What lurks behind that brittle patch of brushwood? Dionysus with his ithyphallic satyrs? A mischievous covey of Pan's thuggish fauns, half-man, half-goat? Or simply the snake of Eden, waiting, fangs bared, for the next innocent Eve to wander past, wide-eyed and waiting for the fall?

In our solitary corner of the Mezzogiorno no one knows. And so we tread these winding mountain paths with trepidation, constantly aware that mysteries lurk unseen, not least within ourselves.

Manodiavolo – Hand of the Devil – is now a ghost village, an unkempt collection of ruins set beneath the squat peak which gives the place its name: four low round outcrops that serve as clenched fingers, and a slender plateau that, with a squint, may be deemed to resemble a thumb. From the position of the latter it's clear to see this is a left hand.

The hand of the devil. Hence the name it has lived with since the Middle Ages.

The first community was founded here in the sixth century BC by colonists from the distant Greek city of Chalcis. The surrounding orchards and pasture brought the place wealth. The Romans later extended the village, building a small castle and defensive walls to protect the nearby seasonal river used as a traffic route into the mountain. In the twelfth century those wandering barbarians the Normans – Vikings in all but name – invaded southern Italy and placed the area under the control of a baronial family named the Abenavoli. In the way of the Calabrian nobility, much interbreeding and internecine strife followed. In 1686 the entire Abenavoli clan was massacred in an argument over the hand of a beautiful woman. Some say you can still see the bloody fingerprints of the slaughtered appear on the walls of the ruined palace at night and in the church of Saint Dionysius (who was named after a Greek cleric, pope for a while and born in Magna Graecia) where they sought sanctuary in vain.

The hamlet in the hills was never to recover. From that murderous point on the place seemed cursed, damned. In 1738 the village was badly damaged by earthquake. Half the inhabitants decamped to nearby Melito Porto Salvo. Those who remained formed a bickering, divided community rent with vendettas and violence. By the 1930s the population had fallen to a few hundred or so. I was living in Reggio at the time. No one visited Manodiavolo willingly. The place lived in the shadows. Few of the inhabitants made their way to the coast except to sell goat meat, fruit and vegetables and honey in the markets. Nor did we speak to these strange and surly people, whose dialect seemed impenetrable even to those used to the Griko of the mountain folk.

And one day they were gone. The story is this. On an August morning in 1938 the priest of Saint Dionysius was found dead in the church. A terrible sight. The man lay on his back in front of the altar, mouth agape, eyes wide open as if frozen by a sudden terror. The father was found by the baker, a man more superstitious than most. He swore that as he stood over the dead man's body the entire building shook and groaned as if about to collapse. The eyes of the statue of the Virgin above the altar ran with blood. A ghostly wail struck up crying one word in Greek: leave.

The baker was notorious for being a drunkard I should add, usually out of his senses from an hour after his loaves left the oven.

Terrified, he ran out into what passed as Manodiavolo's main street shrieking about what he'd heard. It was, as the village schoolteacher soon pointed out, two hundred years precisely since the last earthquake had struck the area and the day of the present alarm, July the thirteenth, was the anniversary of the slaughter of the Abenavoli, a Friday too. Only the week before the unfortunate priest, an eccentric man from Florence, had preached from his pulpit like a latter-day Savonarola, threatening all manner of retributions from heaven because of the ungodly behaviour of the locals.

Being a young man at the time, and one who was not averse to searching out ungodly behaviour wherever it might be found, I was unaware that Manodiavolo, a place where the average age seemed to be around fifty-eight, was such a veritable nest of sin. Nevertheless the locals, confronted with the frightful corpse of the man who had warned them of their coming fate, were in no doubt. The Hour of Judgement was upon them. A terrible destiny awaited any who ignored the ghastly cry howled through the church of Saint Dionysius by the shade of the dead god Pan, fellow to his namesake, for it could be no other.

So they fled. Every man, woman and the handful of children who made up the population of Manodiavolo. In a matter of hours they packed everything they owned into whatever manner of transport they could lay their hands on, from donkeys and carts to an old tractor that plied up and down the hill ferrying those tremulous folk down to the coast.

By the time they reached the shore the tale had multiplied tenfold. Now the little village beneath the devil's fist ran wild with shrieking demons bringing pestilence and death to any who stayed. In the space of a day a spot that had been home to mankind for almost two and a half millennia was deserted, a crumbling ghost given over to rats and stray dogs to wander its alleys and hovels, its palaces and halls. Nor would any who departed that day dare to return.

This was Manodiavolo's fate that August day in 1938. Now it stands as a sad collection of ruined houses, the church spire toppled by age and neglect, the buildings marked by the black eyes of shattered windows. Home to vagabonds alone, though that is another story.

They were bickering, in an amicable, combative fashion, from the moment they told him to get in the car.

Rocco wanted him blindfolded.

Lucia said not to be ridiculous. He'd no idea where they were, least of all where they were going. There was no reason for his colleagues to try to follow. If they were that stupid then the whole idea was doomed in any case. Besides, she added with a glance behind and a quick smile, they would take their guest for a long ride first. A random tour of Italy's toe, his new home, Calabria, just to make sure.

He didn't argue with his sister. So Nic Costa kept quiet and in his head repeated his new name, over and over. Tomasso Leoni. Maso for short. From Guelph, somewhere in Canada, a country he couldn't imagine.

Maso. Maso.

Then he sat back in the soft leather seats and watched and listened. Brother and sister, he thought. Not twins as he first wondered. Rocco, the older one, looked the part of the Calabrian hood, moneyed, powerful, confident. Stubble on a tanned and knowing face, easy to smile, easy to fall into a scowl too. His clothes seemed fashionable. A polo shirt with a logo. Light blue trousers. A fat, expensive-looking digital watch that he looked at, tapped periodically and once spoke to, briefly, in a rapid dialect that was impossible to understand. There was a strong and pungent smell of cigars about him, smoked and raw. He kept them in a shiny brown leather case attached to his belt with a fastener that looked as if it could as easily bear the weight of a holster. A criminal of rank. He'd seen men like this in Rome, southerners usually, from Naples or Sicily. Never the 'Ndrangheta of Calabria. They seemed to shun the city. Or if they were around, remained invisible.

Lucia told her brother he couldn't smoke when he tried to reach for a cigar. Then she pulled her hair back and clamped

it in a tortoiseshell grip. That way he could see better the
similarity in their features. Rocco looked like a man who'd
lived his life outdoors, in the mountains, by the beach, even
on the sea. She had a more urbane, worldly appearance. There
was the scar, faint, something another woman might hide with
make-up. The darting green eyes. A round face, olive skin,
dark eyes always alert as if something unexpected might lurk
behind the corner. An interesting woman. Damaged somehow
along the way.

The difference was there in their voices: his sharp, quick,
unthinking; hers slow, calm, quiet, reflective. There were the
personal tics too. His constant fidgeting, the way he patted
the cigar case from time to time even though he would not
be allowed to smoke. While she would toy constantly with a
plain silver bracelet on her left wrist, old it seemed, perhaps
a family heirloom. A beautiful item which clashed awkwardly
with the lurid tattoos, wild patterns of dragons and unidentifi-
able monsters that ran down her arm. The santina, her aunt,
had glanced at them with distaste as well, as if they were
relics of a past they all wished to forget. Brother and sister.
They made an interesting pair, with the faintest hint of irrita-
tion and perhaps rivalry between them.

The moment the car found the road proper Rocco turned
up the air conditioning so that icy air seemed to blow at them
from every vent. She muttered something, pulled a plum-
coloured pashmina out of a bag on the floor and dragged it
round her bare, tanned shoulders. Another tattoo, a small,
delicate one, was etched upon her left shoulder blade: an image
of the Virgin Mary in blue.

'Are you warm enough in those cheap clothes of yours,
Maso?' she asked with a quick glance in the back. 'My brother
believes he's a polar bear.'

'Yes. Thank you.'

The car was an Alfa Stelvio SUV, the Quadrifoglio, Rocco
said, which meant nothing to him but supposedly it could
outrun anything the police or the Carabinieri owned except
for the couple of motorway Ferraris they gave to their favourite
officers. All wheel drive, all weather machine. Perfect for the
mountains.

Maso. Tomasso Leoni.

An hour away from the santina's shack Rocco stopped the car on a solitary lane. There was a parking spot where someone had fly-tipped trash: blue plastic bags, household rubbish, sawn-off conifers. Beyond that a spectacular view to the coast, the outlines of hamlets running along the edge, between them wild bays set by the calm blue sea. He took out a handgun from the glove compartment, waved it idly behind him and said, 'Just so we are clear . . . if you try to run I shoot you. If you annoy me I shoot you. If I ask you to do something and you don't—'

'You shoot me.'

'He learns quick,' Lucia said with a smile.

'It's important he understands.'

'Brother. He's given himself into our hands. I think he understands. Don't you, Nic?'

The first test.

'Nic? Who's Nic?'

Her smile grew wider. 'An old friend of yours. Maybe you'll meet him again one day.'

'Maso. Tomasso Leoni. I'm from Guelph, Canada. You know it?'

'No.' It was Rocco. 'No one in the 'ndrina knows it. Why do you think we chose that place?'

She placed her arm over the car seat and said, 'We had relatives go there a hundred years or so ago. After the earthquake in Reggio when people here were starving in the streets and no one outside Calabria gave a damn. They took a boat. Some of them stayed in touch. Not now. They became . . .'

Both men waited.

'They became . . . ordinary. Normal. In their terms. Not ours. May we go now?'

He didn't argue.

The Alfa had the biggest engine money could buy, Rocco said, and did his best to prove it on the many stomach-churning chicanes, up and down hill, around the coast. Lucia rolled her eyes when she was able.

After three hours on circuitous roads they stopped at a

half-deserted palace beyond a sign for a hill town, Gerace. From what he saw it was a place that, had it been in the north, would have been on the tourist map, gentrified and turned into a bustling complex of hotels, apartment rentals and restaurants. The mansions and squares were elegant, mostly baroque, a few older, and spoke of former riches and grandeur. But many were shabby and a good few boarded-up as if abandoned. Christ stopped at Eboli the santina had said. In other words, civilized Italy never came this far south. Never thought about these places.

Greek, Lucia told him as they sat down for dinner on the terrace, this whole area was once Greek. The name Gerace came from *hierax* which meant sparrow hawk. Then she spoke a little of the local dialect he'd heard her use earlier, a kind of Greek too, impenetrable, closer to the language of the ancients than the version heard in Athens or so she said. He listened and couldn't make out a single word. The sound was strange, exotic, enticing. Like her and he guessed she knew it.

Rocco grimaced at his sister, pointed at a place by a ribbon of pale beach along the Ionian and made a caustic comment about the futility of history. It was a town called Locri, he said. A well-liked politician was murdered there some years before, an event the man trying to think of himself as Maso Leoni vaguely remembered. Though there were so many violent deaths in the south over the years it was hard to pick any out in particular.

'We didn't shoot him,' Rocco added. 'Never would. That was a mistake. Some of the families are run by fools. They piss off people for no good reason. They think the world never changes.' He stared at the one untouched plate on the table. Mountain lamb, *caponata*, potatoes and greens. 'You got no appetite?'

'Not meat. I don't eat meat.'

'Fish?' Lucia asked.

He shook his head.

Rocco groaned then took hold of his plate, scooped off the succulent lamb and handed the rest back. 'Oh God. Who chose you?'

'He's Canadian,' Lucia told him. 'He's allowed to be a little strange.'

Just after ten the next morning they told him to get back in the car. This time she drove, not as fast or as rashly as her brother. As far as he could work out they took a series of narrow mountain passes that led from the Ionian west to the Tyrrhenian, through dense, uninhabited forests, across bare high plains. Finally they emerged close to Tropea on the coast, stopping for lunch at a tavern somewhere outside town. Rocco vanished to make calls he said and meet someone. The two of them ate mostly in silence: spicy '*Nduja* sausage for her with the local red onion salad, and for him a local dish *lagane e cicciari*, pasta with chick peas and garlic at her suggestion.

'It's not so bad eating just vegetables,' she said, sipping at a small glass of white. 'Years ago that's all people could afford. *Cucina povera* isn't a fashion here. It's a necessity. People won't think you're weird, Nic.'

The pasta, broad and soft, was delicious. 'Who's Nic? I'm Maso. Tomasso Leoni.'

She frowned, a sign of approval. 'I apologize. This game can get tedious. You must try to appreciate our concern.'

'I came here to meet your father. How long—'

'That's not a question I can answer. Or Rocco. It's not our decision. We do as we're told. There are reasons the Bergamotti 'ndrina has survived and ruled here for nearly a century. That's one of them.'

She raised her glass and tapped it against his. The wine was strong and coarse. 'Another is we don't answer questions unless we need to. And we're invisible. Here's to a successful conclusion for all of us. Though our lives will change forever, while yours just for this little time.'

She pulled at her hair. It was raven black, very straight, very sleek, cared for in a practical way. Everything about her seemed like that. He could imagine her as an athlete or something strong, determined, forceful. Someone in charge.

'The santina . . . Who is she really? Your mother?'

Lucia laughed. 'No. My aunt. My mother's dead.'

'Sorry.'

'It was . . . some time ago.'

'Your aunt. Her eyes . . . the cataracts.' She waited until he said, 'They were lenses, weren't they? It was an act.'

She raised her glass in a toast. 'Very good, Maso.'

'How much of this is like that? A piece of theatre?'

A shrug, then: 'A good actor isn't acting, is he? A good actor's the part. So who knows? You keep on asking questions . . .'

He raised his glass then downed a draft. 'Just . . . trying to be friendly.'

'So I see. Clothes. Do you like Paul and Shark?'

'Not the kind of thing you buy on a police salary,' he said without thinking.

She stared at him, hard, unamused.

He groaned. 'Oh dear. Got that wrong.'

'One more night on the road, I think. Blurt out something like that around the people you're going to face and we're all dead. I'll call Rocco and he can meet us later.'

She threw a hundred on the table and didn't wait for change. Then she cast a glance at him, after the sea, thinking.

'What is it?' he asked.

'You keep looking at me.' She tapped her arm. 'At these.' Then her cheek with the scar. 'At this.' He said nothing. 'Like they shouldn't be there.'

'I didn't mean to.'

She folded her arms and stared straight at him. 'OK. Let's get this out of the way now. I went a little crazy when I was younger—'

'I don't need to hear this.'

'But you do.'

'Lucia—'

'Shut up and listen. Maybe it'll help you understand a little about us. When Mamma died I was nineteen. There was a local war. Just a little one. All the same some bastards from the north shot her. They thought my father was in the car. So . . .' She closed her eyes and he thought: the memory was still raw. 'I kind of lost it. Didn't see the point in anything. Hung around bars. Got stupid. Got . . . careless. They were bad times all round. None of us knew what might happen. I kind of . . . had a lot of men. You can drown yourself in people sometimes. Make them blank out everything. You know what I mean?'

'I think so,' he replied.

'No you don't. So there I am hanging out in some beach bar at three in the morning, waiting for Rocco to come and pick me up. Out of my head. Stupid. Some kid comes up and waves a knife in my face. Wanting me. If he'd asked nicely back then . . .' She stopped and brushed away a stray strand of hair. 'I'd probably have said yes. But he didn't. So he cut me and got what he was after anyway. Then Rocco turned up with some of the guys and took him away to the hills.'

She finished the last of the wine. 'They never told me but I heard. They cut his cock off, stuffed it in his mouth, let him choke on it. Dumped him in a ravine somewhere. Never told his parents how to find him and they didn't ask too hard. You don't disrespect the *capo*'s daughter. You don't make her mad. Even when she was a little slut like me.'

'You don't do that to any woman.'

'Not hard to tell you're from somewhere else.'

There was an awkward moment between them. An intimacy broached.

'You didn't need to tell me that.'

'Wrong, Maso. I did. That kid with his knife, dead in the hills. That liberated me. That made me look at myself and realize what a mess I'd become. There's a bunch of bones up there I'd thank if that were possible.' She leaned forward. 'That's how things are here. Raw. Real. Dangerous. Remember that.' She jabbed a finger on the back of his hand. 'Now we go.'

In Gioia Tauro they stopped at an out of town clothes store where she said he needed enough clothes for a week or more. She chose the shirts, the trousers, the canvas shoes of summer. The rest she left to him. Almost a thousand euros, paid again in cash.

As dusk fell they arrived at a deserted *agriturismo*, a farm

with lodgings somewhere in the hills not far, he felt, from
Cariddi. A man and, he assumed, his wife busied around
carrying cases and fetching food and drink. They never once
looked anyone in the face. Rocco was there already. She told
him about the clothes.

'All this trouble and expense,' he said. 'I trust it's worth it.
Anyone who wants to be one of our soldiers must shoot. Can
you?'

Lucia groaned and left them, shaking her head.

'If necessary.'

'Let's see.'

Rocco lugged a small suitcase out of the back of the car.

At the back of the farm, next to a pen where black and pink
pigs ran around snorting and shovelling at the earth, he opened
it. Night was coming on and they must have been at altitude.
There was a chill breeze rolling down the mountain. The place
smelled of wild herbs and livestock. A small arsenal sat in
Rocco's suitcase. Two handguns. Two machine pistols, stacks
of shells. They emptied ammunition into targets among the
trees until the light began to fade, the pigs running round,
squealing in terror all the time.

'So you know how to handle a weapon,' Rocco said after
he emptied the last magazine. 'You need to learn to keep your
mouth shut. I don't have time to wet nurse you. Nor does my
sister, whatever impression she may give.'

He didn't know what to say.

'One other thing, Maso. Don't confuse geniality for
friendship. With anyone you meet.'

Back in the house, after a change of clothes and a shower,
a simple supper was waiting, roast pork for them, grilled
vegetables and cheese for him. Rocco vanished again to make
some calls. Lucia had changed into a white silk shirt and blue
denims. He'd chosen something from the clothes she'd bought
him: a purple polo and green chinos.

'Paul and Shark suits you,' she said.

'Thanks.'

'Do you ever think of colours? Purple and green?'

He looked at himself and said, 'Not much.'

'What's wrong, Maso? You look troubled. We've been your

guides. Taken you places most people don't see. Bought you food and clothes. And still . . .'

He wondered whether to say it but there seemed nothing to lose. 'The woman who was with me—'

'She looked foreign.'

'Her father came from India. She's Roman born and bred.'

'Which is foreign to me.'

He raised his glass and accepted the reproach.

'Is she your lover?'

'No. A colleague.'

'My aunt believed otherwise.'

'Your aunt was wrong. Rosa's sensitive. I'm worried about her being a prisoner. If you'd wanted a hostage you'd only to ask. We could have found someone stronger.'

She reached over and stole a slice of chargrilled aubergine from his plate. 'I should eat more vegetables. I do when I'm home.'

'Where's home?'

'I can't imagine the state police would simply offer up a hostage if a bunch of criminals asked for one. Can you?'

A reasonable point, he said.

'Quite. You've nothing to worry about. We didn't keep your friend. She's back with your people in Cariddi.'

He nodded, thinking. 'Then why—'

'Because my brother wanted it. He likes a little drama. But we have much on our minds and my aunt would make a terrible manutengola. She goes nuts around other people. As others go nuts around her. We spared your friend. Your . . . colleague.'

There was a commotion by the stables where they were staying in converted blocks. Rocco on the phone, animated, angry.

'Don't let him know I told you that. You won't run. You have a . . . determined look about you. Like someone who wants to see things through.'

'Thank you for the clothes, signora. The food, the wine, the company.'

'My name is Lucia. Kindly use it.'

'Lucia.'

She poured him more wine, then a glass for her.

'At least you drink. Tomorrow you go to your final destination. Be wise. Be careful. If in doubt about anything . . . come to me. No one but me.'

In Cariddi the days after Costa's disappearance seemed to drift into nothingness. It was as if the team there were trapped in an extended, dreamlike Fata Morgana of their own. Falcone spent hours on an encrypted line to Rome telling no one else much about what he was discussing. Peroni, bored and a little anxious, had hung around the seafront bar of Elena Sposato, talking to her and her son Roberto, drinking lots of coffee and occasionally the odd beer. The place was called the Kiosco Paradiso though there seemed little heavenly about it. The thug in the dark suit came back every day at the same time, drank a beer or a brandy he never paid for, leered at the woman behind the counter, ignored both the boy and Peroni, then left.

Teresa had taken to long walks along the beach beyond the rocky headland and solitary swims while Silvio Di Capua had played with his techno toys. And Rosa . . . she worried Peroni most of all, not least because Falcone seemed oblivious to her emotional state.

In their own, interior silences, they felt crippled and helpless, waiting on news of what might have happened in the hills, knowing that there was only one source from which that might arrive. The Bergamotti. Who did not exist, as Peroni knew full well, not that he had told the rest of them. There seemed no point and something in Falcone's manner told him that it was best not to add another layer of complexity to the situation. And so they waited, on others. Nothing he could say or do would change that one bit.

He'd taken to visiting the little café twice a day, talking to the charming young son and the woman too, though that was never easy. He'd asked again about the book and its author, Bergamotti, and she'd repeated what she'd told him before. The name was an alias, a mask people used to hide behind. When she said that there'd been a look in her eye, cautious, close to fear. It made him realize people hereabouts were forever heedful, keen not to step on the wrong toes, offend someone with higher connections, utter an unfortunate private thought. There was no way one could ask a direct question. To say to the young Roberto, 'How did your father die?'

Only other sources could provide those answers which was why, as the morning zephyr from the hills began to conquer the cool breeze off the Tyrrhenian, he found himself once more alone on the rough concrete terrace of the Paradiso, scouring the news services on his phone. One question only he'd asked the boy that morning: what was your father's name?

Paolo Gentile.

A fisherman. That was all he had. Nor did the search engines know much more.

The second macchiato of the day sat in front of him as Peroni's fat and clumsy fingers stabbed at his personal phone looking for information on Paolo Gentile, late of the town of Cariddi in the province of Reggio Calabria. After a couple of minutes he knew little more. Gentile had died the previous November. A death notice in the paper described him as a loving husband to Elena Sposato and father to little Roberto, a much-admired crew man on the boats, both the swordfish feluccas and local inshore craft, that operated out of the town harbour. One story had a photo of him: an unsmiling man with receding hair, a careworn, lined face, hard and dark. Nothing about how he died, aged thirty-four. Not a hint of illness or accident.

There were footsteps close by. It was the woman, so he quickly put his phone in his pocket, looked up and smiled. Elena Sposato had brought him a plate of watermelon, the scarlet flesh so fresh the juice was running off the plate.

'On the house,' she said. 'You spend so much time on my terrace. Not with your friends.'

'Another macchiato, signora. Please.'

'That would be three in little more than an hour. Too much coffee is bad for you. Eat the watermelon. You're a big man. You need to watch your heart.'

'I do.'

She pushed the fruit at him and went back to the bar. The thug was there, tapping his keys on the counter.

Peroni had his police phone with him but they weren't supposed to use those here. There was always the chance someone on the inside, someone corrupt, might see he was in Calabria working, not on holiday as the office supposed. It was a slim chance it seemed to him and if something untoward had happened to Paolo Gentile then it would surely be on the database somewhere.

He looked around him, aware that Falcone would fly off the handle if he knew about this, then started the phone, logged into the internal intelligence network and typed the name. It was a cursory report from the Reggio Questura network. A Cariddi fisherman found shot dead on the beach one winter morning. Cut about as if tortured. A criss-cross of four parallel marks had been scraped on his chest, seemingly by his murderer's fingernails. The report called it a '*cardata da cruci*'. It seemed to mean 'carded from crosses', as if the man's skin was wool to be teased. Peroni realized he'd heard it once before. Seen it too. Those marks scratched into the right cheek of the decapitated swordfish they'd been shown in the restaurant by Toni, the talkative waiter.

The case was marked unsolved. There had been no activity on the investigation, such as it was, in ten months. Whoever murdered Paolo Gentile was still walking free.

'And you had his skin underneath your nails, you bastard,' Peroni whispered to himself. 'They must have pulled in someone . . .'

But if they had it wasn't on the system. He quickly closed down the work phone and stuffed it back in his jacket. It was the only way he was going to find out what happened to Gentile. Still, perhaps using the thing was unwise.

The unwanted visitor was on his second coffee and grappa. Free no doubt. Or rather Elena, who had vanished into the kitchen, had paid. The man in black swigged down his coffee and drink and looked ready to follow her in a moment.

Peroni got up. He was fast for his size and age. Six strides from the terrace to the counter and his hand was on the man's arm before he could take a step towards the little terraced house behind the bar where Elena and her son lived.

'A word, sir.'

Two sly eyes stared back at him. He had a narrow, cruel face and a smile that was halfway to a sneer. Close up it wasn't hard to see the suit was old and worn and there was something shabby about him, about the black Fiat he came in too which had more than its share of dents and scratches. A lowly foot soldier out to get what he could, perhaps without the knowledge of his betters.

'Friend,' Peroni began, still holding him, though it was obvious this was not welcome.

'I'm not your friend. Take your hand off me.'

'Of course.' Peroni did so and held up his two arms by way of apology. 'I'm sorry. I didn't mean to offend you. Not in the least.'

Honour, Peroni thought again. The intelligence he'd read in Rome used that word a lot.

'All I want is a favour. A good deed. The kind of thing a benevolent man like you would willingly and graciously give.'

'I don't even know you.'

Peroni smiled, leaned over the bar, took the grappa bottle and poured him another shot. 'My old priest in Tuscany always said the gifts we give to strangers, with no expectation of reward, are the ones that get us into heaven.'

All he got back was an uncomprehending glare, then: 'What are you after?'

'Your understanding. Your compassion. Your forbearance.' Nothing at that. 'The lady here is troubled for a variety of reasons. I think . . . business is bad. She's on her own. A widow.'

The man reminded him of low-level hoods back home, the kind who collected 'insurance' from small traders too scared to refuse.

'I know who Elena Sposato is. Don't need you to tell me.'

Roberto was kicking a football along the pebbled beach alone, while in the distance a gaggle of kids of a similar age played together. Either they ignored him or he felt too shy or scared to join them.

'Her son's a solitary child. They have their problems. A little sympathy is due.'

The man laughed and it wasn't a pleasant sound. 'Sympathy?'

'Quite.'

'You mean thinking a widow's an easy screw, huh? Desperate

for this?' He made an obscene gesture with one arm and gyrated his hips like a lousy dancer in a bad rock video. 'I know what you want. You want to get your cock there first and leave the local guys behind—'

Staying calm was hard. 'No. Not at all—'

'You bastards from the north are all the same. Looking down on us.'

It was hopeless. Peroni knew that. Perhaps he had from the start. He'd been foolish and maybe now he was making the situation worse. Of more concern he could feel his temper start to rise, a rare event these days, and one that never boded well.

'All I ask is that you leave her alone. You would earn my gratitude.'

'And if I don't.'

The words came unbidden. He found himself leaning forward, close enough so his breath touched the man's face, the way he used to scare lowlife like this in Rome, leaning on pimps and dealers and other such scum.

'You will earn my lasting ingratitude. Which any man with half a brain will find unwelcome.' He stroked the guy's greasy, unwashed hair. 'There is a brain here somewhere, friend. Tell me. Isn't there?'

A silence followed, one he knew so well. It represented the moment a dispute slipped subtly from mere argument to an outright clash of wills. One man wins, the other backs down. This gang minion was lean, cheeks hollow and pockmarked, eyes dead. Peroni could take him down with two quick blows to the gut and a swipe across the face. Nothing to it. He looked a coward at heart, a minion who got his kicks from picking on frightened people. Women. Kids. The old. The lowest they had around here and something had happened that meant no one kept him in line.

But if he did give way to his instincts and beat the punk to a pulp . . .

It was years since Peroni had even had that thought let alone the urge. His temper had gone or so he thought until this wild, raw land reminded him it only slumbered. And what would that short and satisfying explosion mean for Elena Sposato?

For the team in the house down the street? For Nic Costa, lost in the wilds of Aspromonte?

'Think about it,' Peroni said and patted his shoulder, which was stained with dirt and the grey-white speckles of old dandruff.

Then before anything else could happen his phone rang. The personal one.

'Are you hanging around that damned bar again?' Falcone asked.

'Coffee. That's all.'

'Get back here. We have a visitor.'

They were waiting for him in the first-floor dining room at the front of the rented house. The furniture was modern and pale blue and arranged in a way that seemed to say: this place is for temporary visitors, not a home. But around the walls ran tiles depicting the swordfish hunt back in the day when it was down to teams of strong men in rowing feluccas, a harpooner on a modest prow, a spotter up a short mast. Beneath the blue drawings were the names of famous fishermen, poems and, on a few, tales of their deaths, lost to cruel sea or the thrashing blade of an angry fish. Stories, it seemed to Peroni, were never far away in Cariddi and carried a weight they never possessed in Rome.

From the window he could see the thug had left the bar, doubtless in a foul mood, consumed by a mix of fear and anger. Threatening him was not a wise move any more than the sly, perhaps irresponsible, check on Paolo Gentile. Not that he'd regretted either. Close up to the weasel-faced creature he'd felt that spark of fury that had, on occasion, caused him difficulties as an inspector policing the brothels, pimps and hookers of Rome. Something in Peroni always responded to the sight of a woman being bullied and abused. The only reason that hadn't happened of late was that he'd been bounced back down to agente, the lowest rank, when he fell from a kind of uneasy grace, and moved to duties that took him away from the grim world of exploitation and trafficking. And he'd met Teresa Lupo who had tamed him. Or so they both believed.

Three or four hundred metres along the shore Elena Sposato

was wiping down the counter though he doubted it was necessary. Roberto hadn't moved from the beach where he continued to kick his old red ball against the rocks quite alone.

Teresa was on the terrace smoking. Something she hadn't done in years. Then she threw the cigarette over the wall into the sluggish turquoise waves and marched back, barely looking at him. Rosa was silent standing in the corner. Silvio Di Capua kept tapping nervously at his iPad. Falcone was in quiet conversation with Lombardi, the thin, unsmiling man from Rome who had set up this strange mission in the first place after the tipoff from the south.

He must have driven all the way, Peroni thought. It was just after one in the afternoon. An early start from Rome would get him here in six or seven hours and Lombardi, an officious pen-pusher who seemed to flit between the Ministry of Justice and its various outposts as he wished, was just the kind to start off at the crack of dawn. As usual he wore a suit, blue, largely uncreased in spite of the journey, and carried a leather portfolio case under his arm, one he always seemed reluctant to open, at least in Peroni's presence.

'We need to talk,' Falcone said and summoned them to the table. A vase full of artificial flowers sat incongruously at its centre. 'Have we swept the room?'

'Every morning,' Di Capua said a touch testily. 'As you asked.'

'Why bother?' Peroni wondered, taking the chair next to him. Teresa seemed to want to be with Rosa for some reason. 'They know we're here. They know who we are. Why would they want to bug us?'

'Precautions,' was all Falcone said.

Lombardi took the seat by his side and opened his portfolio. There was a lined pad there. Completely blank. He said nothing so Peroni asked, 'Since our lives are on the line here . . . may I ask where this intelligence first came from? About our mysterious pentito's sudden burst of conscience?'

Lombardi looked no more than thirty-five. Doubtless he had a fine degree, possibly from an international school, and could speak any number of languages. He'd never worked in the field. That much was crystal clear from the way he spoke and acted. The messy, asymmetrical task of law enforcement was for him a matter of intellectual rigour. A game, a kind of chess, played on a board composed primarily of unwitting and unknowledgeable pawns.

'We're not in the habit of making information widely available—'

'It's hardly wide,' Teresa cut in. 'Is it? There are five of us here. In the front line.'

Lombardi hesitated for a moment. 'We were approached through channels.'

'Channels?' Peroni asked.

'Channels. We have all manner of channels open. With criminals. With foreign organisations—'

'Terrorists, you mean.'

'As a general rule we achieve more through talk than force. For that to continue it must remain discreet—'

'Nic's in there with these bastards,' Rosa cried. She'd been quiet, sullen, weeping sometimes, ever since he vanished in the hills. Guilty too that she'd been allowed to escape. 'He's in there—'

'Let the man finish,' Falcone ordered.

'Thank you. We had a message that the capo of the Bergamotti 'ndrina was willing to give himself up and turn pentito under certain conditions,' Lombardi went on. 'Those conditions are to be communicated to you here. Once met he will surrender to you. That's as much as I can say.'

Peroni waited. To his astonishment that was it. 'Mancuso? The other mob capi he's promising us?'

Lombardi wriggled on the blue chair. The table shook as he did so. Nothing in this place was built to last.

'We need to know where we stand,' Peroni added.

'What are you accusing me of?' the man snapped back.

'Nothing. I'm merely trying to understand a complex situation. Did you have any idea he was going to offer you the most wanted man in Italy? Someone who, if he talked in court, could bring down a government maybe if he wanted. Simple question.'

'No . . .'

'Thank you. Mancuso and the 'Ndrangheta are, it seems to

me, at best friendly enemies. Do you have any idea why he
might come to Calabria in the first place—'

'None.'

'So it might be a pack of lies,' Teresa suggested. 'Our whole
reason for being in Calabria . . . Nic lost in the hills . . . all
based on nothing?'

Lombardi closed his portfolio case without writing a line
on the pad. 'He summoned us here for a reason. It would
appear that's more complex than we appreciated. It doesn't
mean there's no opportunity. Or that he doesn't want to turn
pentito—'

'Do you even have a name for him?' Peroni demanded.

It was the first time he'd seen the man from the ministry
blush and that didn't last long. 'As I said . . . they call themselves the Bergamotti—'

'It's an alias.' Peroni realized his voice was too loud. There
was nothing he could do about it. This didn't seem a place
for self-control. 'Bergamotti's a name they use to hide behind.'
Lombardi stayed silent. 'But then you know that and never
saw fit to tell us. A name—'

'South of Lamezia our sources of intelligence are slender
and rarely reliable.'

All of them waited for more. It didn't come.

'If you don't have even a real name,' Teresa said to break
the silence, 'how do you know any of this is what it seems?'

Again nothing, then Lombardi shrugged. 'You think we
should just ignore an opportunity to take the capo of the biggest
'ndrina in Calabria? The boss across the water as well? We
have to determine what the offer is. How to respond. What
the gains might be, what the cost.'

Falcone was watching him intently. If Mancuso and some
of the other capi gathered for a summit they wouldn't come
alone, he pointed out. There'd be guards, a small army of men
with weapons. The couple who took Nic Costa spoke of the
potential for violence.

'We can't deal with that. Just the few of us.'

'You won't have to,' Lombardi replied. 'We'll bring in
the necessary forces once we know a time and place. Best we
keep the locals out of it if possible—'

'Jesus Christ,' Peroni cried. 'You're talking about a pitched battle. God knows where. With one of our men inside it. Supposedly pretending to be one of them . . .'

'We always understood there was a risk,' Lombardi replied, almost in a whisper. 'We are prepared.'

He saw it then. The briefest of glances exchanged between Falcone and the man from the Justice Ministry, and at that moment Peroni understood.

'Prepared?' He shook his head. He wanted to scream in Leo Falcone's face. 'Prepared? You knew they were going to take one of ours. You sent Nic and Rosa out there knowing one of them wouldn't come back. You bastard!'

He was halfway across the table, trying to grab him by the jacket, when Teresa leapt in, yelling, batting at him with her flapping hands and arms.

That, and that alone, stopped him picking Falcone up by the scruff of the neck.

'You knew?' Rosa gasped.

'Men like these require reassurance,' Lombardi answered. 'There's only one way they know to receive it. A . . . guest. Given to a manutengolo—'

'You seem to know a hell of a lot about them,' Peroni barked.

'It's my job. It's what I do. Intelligence. Organized crime.' He pointed at his chest with a pale and clerical finger. 'That's me.'

'He isn't a guest.' It was Teresa. 'They want him to make out he's one of theirs.'

Lombardi laughed and that made Peroni even madder. 'If they knew he was a police officer how long do you think he'd last?'

There was a packet of cigarettes on the table. Something else that Peroni had bought from Elena Sposato that he didn't need. He grabbed them, got up and headed for the terrace, lit one, looked along the coastline. It was rough and rocky, savagely beautiful. A place they should only visit since they could never belong. A place that could tear them apart. Perhaps was doing that already.

Someone came to his side. Falcone and it was all Peroni

could do to hold back his fiery temper at that moment and
distil his anger into a simple statement. 'You knew, Leo. You
knew all along.'

The silver goatee looked thinner than it used to. There were
age spots on his shiny bald scalp. We're all getting old, Peroni
thought. Past it. Beyond this crap.

Falcone grabbed a cigarette from the packet then the matches
Peroni had snatched from the table. With Teresa that made
three of them smoking again, out in the clear, fresh sea of
Cariddi, a place that deserved something better.

'I'm sorry,' he said. 'I felt sure they'd pick her. They
wouldn't harm a woman easily.'

Peroni took a deep breath. 'I've never punched you, have
I? Not once. Much as I've been tempted.'

A frown and then: 'I think I'd remember that. If it would
help . . . feel free.'

'So this is why you've been so cold and distant? Even for
you.'

'It's not easy, Gianni.'

'It isn't for any of us. We're not going to be the same after
this. You know that, don't you?'

Falcone took his arm. He had grey, emotionless eyes but
there was something in them at that moment. Fear perhaps,
or even concern. 'We keep our heads. We look after one
another. We do what they say.' A pause and then: 'We get him
out of there in one piece. What happens to the rest . . . I don't
give a damn. Lombardi can bring in the army for all I care.
We're just here to deliver an invitation and wait for them to
come back with a time and place.'

Peroni wanted to laugh. 'You really think it's that simple?'

'If we make it.'

'And Rosa?'

The scowl again, a judgmental frown of disappointment.
'She can go back to Rome with Lombardi and book a vacation
somewhere. A real one. I don't want her round the Questura
in this state. She might say something. We don't need her here
anymore. Not now.'

'All heart,' Peroni said and removed Falcone's fingers from
his arm. 'You really are.'

Thirty years they'd known each other and he wondered what that was worth.

'Heart won't get us through this,' Falcone retorted.

'Gentlemen . . .' Lombardi had stuck his head outside the door and was blinking against the harsh afternoon sunlight. The temperature had picked up. Even with a sea breeze the heat felt searing. 'I must return to Rome.'

'She'll be packed and ready in a minute,' Falcone told him, nodding at Rosa.

He stayed on the terrace and saw them as they left. She was weeping as she walked down the narrow lane to the small car park at the end, tugging her little case. Lombardi saw fit not to help her. Peroni and Teresa watched. Falcone couldn't bring himself to do that so he bustled through some messages on his phone. Aspromonte loomed over them all, a rocky giant casting its long shadow over the coast.

'Where the hell did you go, Nic?' Gianni Peroni whispered to no one at all.

Manodiavolo was a desolate place, quite unlike anywhere he'd ever seen, a two-hour drive away through the back lanes of Aspromonte. The ghost village deserved its name Hand of the Devil, sitting beneath four rugged finger outcrops and a flat, plateau thumb. It was as if a dead god of old lay buried beneath a fractured landscape, one desperate hand emerging from the grave. Ten or fifteen kilometres away – it was difficult to tell on the journey – lay the coast, a thin line of ribbon development running along the strand beyond Reggio. Even Rocco slowed for the single winding, rough track that took them there, all four wheels of the Alfa struggling to keep a grip.

At some invisible point in the grey-blue waves the Tyrrhenian Sea of the west met the Ionian of the east and succumbed to its strength and exotic power. Turning the corner between the two was marked in curious ways. The vegetation turned harder, sparser, perhaps because the rain was less frequent. The air felt and tasted entirely different to the sea breeze of Cariddi. This mountain atmosphere was perfumed with wild herbs and scorched grass from flash fires, rent by the cries of crows and eagles circling in the whirling eddies.

Their eventual destination lay in a secluded plateau beneath the bare outcrop of the mountain, perhaps sixty or seventy houses in all, most now reduced to rubble, homes for peasants and labourers long vanished to the city or exile in other lands. A few were larger, some attached to shops. An old grocery store with a rusting sign collapsed over the door. A bakery, the oven visible through the walls, a long-handled peel still resting by its side and what looked like a burnt batch of loaves black as charcoal by the charred logs behind.

The one inhabited building was on the tiny village square next to a dead fountain of toothy dolphins and crumbling putti in front of the half-collapsed church, its broken, crooked spire snag-toothed against the rocky thumb. A shield on the front wall bore a heraldic device of three dragons, rampant, beneath, in ornate stone lettering, 'Palazzo Abenavoli'. It was a four-square building, grand and once, surely, the home of the rulers of this little community hidden away on Aspromonte. Two storeys high, built from pink tufa that must have been imported, so different was it from the grey stone all around. The style was late baroque and reminded him of Noto, a place in Sicily he'd once visited on holiday: all ornate curves and cornices, balconies and crumbling masks and gargoyles. Anywhere else the architectural authorities would be busy with their reconstruction plans and notices banning all unauthorized work. But Manodiavolo, like so much of Aspromonte, was either forgotten by Rome or judged not worthy of attention. So here there were no such restrictions, not that the place seemed greatly neglected.

They got out and Rocco and Lucia introduced him to the lone resident of the Palazzo Abenavoli, his manutengolo of a kind. A more genial sort it was hard to imagine. Uncle Vanni they called him, a portly, smiling man of sixty or so, completely bald with the round and pleasant face of a country monk and a belly that spread over the waist of his canvas country trousers. He was, he said, the guardian of Manodiavolo, a kind of caretaker-cum-peasant farmer who kept the ghost village in some kind of order. A look in Lucia's face said as they first met: indulge this old man, we love him. And there was a country simplicity about him, obvious in the way he bustled round, excited, embarrassed almost, by the arrival of a visitor from afar, a rare event and one, it seemed, that needed to be greeted with an old-fashioned warmth and generosity.

'He's from Canada,' Rocco said.

'Canada?' Vanni asked in a deep, slow voice that seemed to say: where's that?

'His name is Maso Leoni,' Lucia added. 'Our guest. He'll be here for a while. Let's make him welcome.'

Vanni nodded to say he understood.

'A guest is always welcome in the palace of the Abenavoli. Come Maso. Come.'

And with that the Bergamotti climbed into their scarlet Alfa and began the slow and snaking journey down the rocky track back to the coast.

'We will make a mountain man of you,' Vanni declared that first day after they'd gone.

'Which means what?'

'Which means you learn our ways. Our history. How . . . how we do things on Aspromonte. Come. Let me introduce you to your new home. Can you read?'

'I can read,' he said as they walked through the open palazzo doors.

'Don't be offended. Not everyone can. I do my best but . . .' Vanni grimaced. 'I'm just the dumb peasant uncle. My eyes are a little slow. But I don't need to read. So who cares?'

The place was vast and dusty in all those parts Vanni didn't use. But upstairs there was a tidy room waiting for him with a four-poster bed covered in a scarlet velvet spread. A desk stood by the double windows from which there were breathtaking views to the coast.

'This was for the lady of the house if she didn't wish to be with the lord. Which happened often with the Abenavoli, one reason they died.' He patted Maso's arm. 'Don't worry. None got killed in here. They decapitated them outside by the fountain. Sometimes I hear their screams.'

He waited for a reaction then winked. 'Just kidding. There's nothing to fear from ghosts round here. The only ones that remain are harmless. Here.'

From a drawer in the desk he retrieved an old hardback book with a grey linen cover.

'*Calabrian Tales*. Constantino Bergamotti,' Maso said. 'A relative?'

'My late father. A good book. A true book. Or as true as any of us can manage. I lend that copy to every guest I have. Perhaps you'll understand us. If you do please let us know for we understand ourselves very little these days.'

There was a photo on the desk too. The same good-natured old man in a shepherd's hat he'd seen in the santina's cottage.

'This is him?'

'No.'

'He looks like you.'

Vanni laughed and stroked his head. 'That's my brother. He has that wonderful head of hair. I take after my mother's side. He's different. Lucky man. Older but he's not as bald as a rock like me.' He tapped the grey cover. 'It's an entertaining book. You'll have time to read it between your work.'

'How much time?'

Vanni shrugged. 'If my nephew and niece knew they didn't tell their idiot uncle. But then they tell me little. I'm a fool who keeps this place alive for when they have guests.'

An answer he'd expected.

'Then . . . how much work?'

The old man slapped his shoulder, hard. 'I like you, Maso Leoni. You ask good questions. Lots of work because work makes a man round here. Idleness is a sin. You agree?'

'I—'

'Good,' Vanni declared. 'We have a little electricity from some panels on the roof. Enough to light a couple of bulbs. The water must come from the well. When you wish to bathe you fetch it yourself. I'm your host. Not your servant. Now make yourself comfortable. In an hour we dine.'

He seemed to know about the meat and fish already. Wild mushrooms from the mountains, fresh tomatoes and rocket, grilled aubergine, a pungent cheese, all local, were on the table when Maso Leoni came down to the dining room. They ate beneath dusty paintings of old nobles, then Vanni showed him around the village, told him the names of most of the people who'd lived in the ruined houses, the habits of the innkeeper who drank more than his customers, the love life of the baker's wife whose adventures beyond the oven would have served as another tale in the *Decameron*.

There were two donkeys tethered behind the palace, Silvio, dark, almost black, and Benito, silvery grey, named after the two politicians Vanni said he loathed the most.

'Though unlike those vile creatures these are benign fellows and sometimes a great necessity.'

He showed him how to feed and water them, how to avoid their hard hooves should they decide to kick, then watched as Maso mucked out the stable and took the manure to a heap composting for the vegetable garden at the back.

In the evening they ate much the same food again, this time from a brazier set up by the fountain in the piazza. Vanni brought out a pitcher of rough country wine that was so golden in colour it seemed wrong to label it white.

'You must be tired,' he said as they finished. 'I will clear the table and wash up. Your turn tomorrow.'

'I've many questions.'

'I'm sure you have. But I told you. I am their simple country uncle. I keep house. I keep my peace. They tell me nothing except someone is coming and will be here a little while.'

He poured his guest another glass of the wine. It tasted good once the first shock was over.

'Perhaps a week I think. There's an event coming, or so I gather. A meeting of some kind. I am instructed that we'll need food and wood to cook it. Charcoal. Have you ever made charcoal?'

'No. If—'

'I'll make a good man of Aspromonte out of you. Lots of work to be done in that respect but it will happen. Now. Go read that book I gave you. Please.'

The night was warm and he was glad of the mosquito net around the bed since the hot, dark air seemed alive with insects. An owl or some predator seemed to live in the roof space above his room. He heard it moving, squawking and at some point in the early hours arrive back with living prey, a mouse or a young rabbit, which it tore to pieces as the thing shrieked and howled above him.

After which, exhausted, Maso Leoni slept.

On the second day they walked downhill to the orchards where line upon line of bergamot trees stretched for a kilometre or more down the craggy slopes. The fruit looked like green oranges and would not be harvested until November, Vanni said.

'Then we bring up workers from the coast. Africans. *Clandestini* in the main,' he said, using the slang word for immigrants. 'They're good men mostly and grateful for the pay. Here . . .' He pulled a fruit off the tree and ran a thick nail through the pith. 'Smell.'

The fragrance was nothing like he expected. Musky, smoky, with only the faintest hint of citrus.

'Where do they go?'

'All over the world they tell me. I'm a farmer. What happens when these green jewels leave our land concerns me not one whit. Some go to perfume. Some go into a tea the English like and name after some lord . . . I don't know. Food and syrup and drinks . . . Ask Rocco. If you're lucky you may even get an answer. Now. We work.'

Four hours they spent pruning the trees, picking off insects – Vanni would use no products – and once dealing with a wasp's nest lodged between two branches. Then lunch, bread and cheese eaten in the field with water and that same rough wine. Then more work.

He went to bed gratefully at nine that night and if the owl came back he didn't hear.

At breakfast the third day Vanni announced it was time to learn to burn charcoal like the *carbonari* of old. On the eastern side of the hill the site was almost ready and looked much like an ancient burial ground unearthed. An inner circle of logs, each cut precisely, the same diameter, a metre and a half high, stood upright. Then there was an empty circle for the flames. Finally an outer ring of logs to be completed. Vanni

had strong arms, the rolling gait of a farmer, and set about
the task in a familiar and determined fashion.

'Come on, Maso,' he cried, pointing to a pile of logs stacked
beneath the trees. 'There's a feast a-coming and they'll need
this for sure.'

All day long they worked until they'd completed a log
mound, ten metres across, pretty much airtight or so it seemed,
though when, close to six in the afternoon, Vanni lit it, holes
appeared and needed to be sealed quickly with sand and dirt.

Another hour they spent at that. He felt exhausted.

'Are we done?'

'Done?' Vanni cried with a laugh. 'We haven't yet started.
Go back to the palace. There are two sleeping bags in the
room next to the kitchen. Some insect nets and poles. Bring
them. Fetch us some food and drink. Some water. Whatever
you want.'

'I can't carry all that myself.'

In the dying daylight, his face outlined by the flames of the
fire, Vanni stared at him, baffled.

'Of course you can't. That's why you and Silvio will make
three journeys. Maybe four. Off you go. No time to waste.'

It was a good kilometre up the hill to the palazzo, the donkey
grumbling by his side. Four trips they made and then, laughing
for no good reason, the two of them ate and drank and talked
of nothing much at all around the fire.

There were insects everywhere, all of them seemingly with
stings and teeth, but most stayed clear when the smoke from
the mound turned dense and enveloped the clearing in the
woods. At some point – Vanni had said to leave his watch
behind because of the heavy labour they faced – he fell asleep
on top of the bag. Then Vanni shook him awake and said a
*carbonaro* could rarely sleep on the job. There was work to
do, tending the charcoal mound, filling in gaps, damping down
areas that Vanni deemed too hot, opening up those he thought
too slow to take.

The moon was bright and the hillside so lacking in artificial
light the stars seemed alive above them. For the first time
since they came south he found himself thinking of his
surroundings alone, not Rome, not the team in Cariddi even.

They said he was to become a mountain man and perhaps that transformation had begun.

He slept for a while until Vanni woke him and said he needed help stoking or damping or just looking round the glowing mound, poking at places, seeing all was well.

'You don't make charcoal in Rome, do you?' he asked idly as they watched the inner timber starting to turn from livid red to a dullish shade inside.

'I've never been to Rome,' he said and was surprised how easy he found it to lie. 'I'm from Canada.'

The old man nodded, a smile on his face, dark red on one side from the warm flames of the fire, cold silver on the other from the light of the moon. 'What was I thinking? I must have mistaken you for someone else. In Canada . . . you make charcoal there?'

He poked at the nearest timber with a spare branch. 'I live in a town. I guess someone must. In the country. Maybe if I go home one day I'll find out.'

'Perhaps,' Vanni agreed.

What time it was he didn't know. Or much care. Between sleeping and working they spent the night by the charcoal mound. Then Vanni shook him awake one last time and he asked, 'What do you want me to do?'

The old man laughed. 'Just look, Maso. This is your first time in Manodiavolo. We have miracles here. You must see. The dawn. You see? The beautiful dawn. There's none better anywhere in the world. Or so I'm told. I'm a foolish old man who's guardian to this magical place. What do I know? You tell me.'

Vanni half-dragged him to his feet and guided him to the edge of the clearing, by a stand of trees, their leaves rippling in the soft morning zephyr. Dawn was breaking over the tip of Italy, a sliver of light rising in the east from where the Greeks once came to rule this land. The rays ran like liquid gold across the Ionian, a stream turning first into a river and then becoming the sea itself. The two of them stayed by the ridge and watched as day broke over the Strait of Messina, over Reggio and the coast, over Sicily and the giant cone of Etna across the water, extinguishing the dim circlet of fire he'd seen at the summit the night before.

'This is our land and there's not a man among us who wouldn't die for it,' Vanni said. Then he reached up to the tree and pulled down some fruit. It was still dark. He didn't know what was in his hand when the old man offered it to him.

'Just an apple, Maso. That's all. Not poisoned. Nor does it come with consequences as far as I know.'

The fruit was hard, a little sour and like everything else around here seemed to carry a perfume of its own.

'Now back to the fire.'

Three or four more hours they laboured until, in what must have been the middle of the morning, Vanni declared the charcoal mound well prepared, and ready to sit cooling for twenty-four hours after which it might be used.

They trudged back up to the palazzo, filthy, sweaty, stinking of wood smoke. Maso's expensive Paul and Shark clothes would probably never survive this. Just as well he had some more.

As they approached the village square from the side he heard the insect whine of a two-stroke engine toiling against the steep slope of the track as it led into Manodiavolo. It had stopped by the time it emerged. Someone was by the dead fountain, a figure in blue jeans, blue jacket, blue helmet with a smoky visor.

'Lucia,' Vanni cried and waddled towards her, arms out ready for an embrace.

She removed the helmet, climbed off the scooter and retreated from him in horror.

'Don't you dare touch me with those filthy hands. Don't. Don't.'

He agreed, though visibly disappointed. 'We've been working. Don't be harsh.'

'The same goes for you, Maso. Keep your distance. You look like two mountain goats straight out of the midden. What have—?'

'We needed charcoal. So the two of us obliged.' He gestured at Maso. 'Meet my new carbonaro. A sharp apprentice, learns quick. I'll keep him if I can.'

'Oh.'

It was hard to tell if she was impressed or not. He tugged

at his shirt, stained with smoke, torn in places from the branches.

'Sorry. It's ruined.'

'Then I'll bring another. I know your size. The colour wasn't right anyway.'

'Thanks . . .'

She sniffed at him. 'You need a bath. Some food. Some drink. Be quick. I've something to show you and it's best we're moving before my brother gets here.'

Vanni walked over to the well head at the edge of the square, took off the wooden cover and grabbed the bucket that sat there at the end of the rope.

'You know how to do it,' he said. 'You first.'

As a man who called himself Maso Leoni struggled with a tin bath and an iron bucket, thirty kilometres away on the upper slopes of Aspromonte, a chubby officer of the state police, half-spilling out of his misshapen blue uniform, rang the bell of the rented house in Cariddi where Falcone's team had fallen into a routine of idle, restless days, staring at computer screens, waiting on messages from Rome that never came.

Teresa Lupo pulled back the curtain, saw the officer there and muttered a low and powerful curse. They all came and looked, then shrank back not wishing to be seen.

'I'll deal with it,' she said before anyone else could move.

They stayed upstairs in the dining room with the pale blue furniture that was starting to get on Peroni's nerves. It clashed somehow with the perfect sea and sky beyond the bay windows. Across the terrace he could see the bar. No customers. Roberto sitting on a cheap plastic chair at the front peeling potatoes or something. His mother inside presumably. Making no money. Wondering when the idiot with the battered black Fiat might come back.

'You know the story,' Falcone said. 'If he comes in stick to it.'

Business people from Rome celebrating a deal. Thinking about what to do next with the money. There hadn't been time to fix fake IDs. Lombardi was supposed to come up with them later but it never happened. If the local police waded in demanding to see their cards it wouldn't take long before what cover they had was blown. As far as the local Bergamotti clan was concerned that was long gone, perhaps had been from the start. But they didn't want the police or the Carabinieri in the loop, not unless it was necessary at the last moment. The news that the biggest pentito in years, a man whose true identity was known only to an inner circle of confidantes, was about to give himself up, could break safely in one way only: after the event.

Peroni thought he had an idea why the uniform man was at the door, probably knocking up people all over this part of Cariddi. He hoped he was wrong.

Ten minutes later Teresa came back, sat down, said nothing, just kicked the basket full of washing waiting to be ironed if anyone could be bothered. They hadn't brought so many clothes with them. No one had expected to be in Calabria so long. The day before she'd declared they needed to start using the washing machine. Silvio was first in line, then Peroni. Then she did Falcone's for him since he seemed to have no idea how to manage it himself.

'What did he want?' Peroni asked.

'He wanted to know who we were. What we were doing here.' She stared straight at him. 'If any of us were police officers. Seems someone accessed their network from outside and something pointed to Cariddi.'

'What?'

'It's alright, Leo. I looked baffled and told him the story. He didn't seem particularly bright. All they know is someone went into their network through a mobile connection. Could be from anywhere in town. I think he was the station idiot sent out on a hopeless job—'

'You,' Falcone yelled at Silvio Di Capua, 'are supposed to route everything through Rome. Christ. Communications. That's the only reason you're here—'

'Thank you,' Silvio cut in. 'I'm flattered. I am routing everything through Rome. There's no way anyone in Reggio can see our traffic.'

'Then how—?'

It was another hot and stifling day even with the breeze off
the sea but it seemed to Peroni perfectly capable of turning
hotter.

'It was me,' he said. 'Sorry.'

They fell quiet and stared at him. He guessed he ought to
take that as a compliment. Gianni Peroni, once an inspector,
a man who made a big mistake and paid for it, was supposed
to have turned into an old, wise hand, always cautious, never
rash, the kind of officer you needed in a difficult corner.

'Gianni,' Teresa said and something in her voice hurt him
most of all. 'What the hell were you thinking?'

'I was trying to find out something. Something local. There
seemed no other way—'

'It was her, wasn't it?' she interrupted. 'That woman from
the bar. You can't leave that place.'

That threw him. 'She's in trouble—'

'That's all it is?'

Her tone of voice had silenced Falcone too.

'Yes,' he replied, trying with some difficulty to stifle his
temper. 'Of course that's all it is. I made one brief inquiry
into their records system. Can't have been in there for more
than a couple of minutes.'

'If it had been longer they might have got a fix.' They all
relied on Silvio for technical issues. He was trying to get
Peroni out of a hole. 'They can't have done that, Gianni. We're
fine.'

'We're not fine,' Teresa muttered.

'I said I'm sorry. It was a mistake. Won't happen again. It's
just . . . sitting around here . . .'

'We don't have much choice,' Falcone pointed out.

'Maybe not. But you think about it. The mob, these
Bergamotti . . . we don't know who the hell they are. We don't
even know the real name of the man who's supposed to be
about to surrender to us. How or when we take him in.'

'We don't have much choice,' Teresa repeated.

'They know who we are. Where we live. What we do. The
people we're hiding from are our own. The police. The
Carabinieri. It's like someone flipped a switch and everything's
the opposite of the way it should be.'

Falcone struggled to his feet. He shook his head, glanced at Peroni just the once and said, 'Don't step out of line again. I need some fresh air.'

'Me too,' Teresa grumbled and the two of them walked out.

When he came out of the bathroom clutching nothing but a towel Lucia was waiting by the bed, a pile of fresh clothes in her hands. She smiled at his embarrassment and patted the shirt and trousers on the thin cotton sheets.

'Wear thick socks and tuck the bottom of your jeans into them. We have bugs and spiders and snakes where we're going.'

'Where's that?'

A wink. 'Somewhere a man like you has never been before.'

'If you don't mind . . .'

He nodded at the door. She sighed theatrically and walked out.

Ten minutes later he was downstairs, dressed as she'd ordered. Lucia had changed too. Rough khaki trousers and a chequered shirt, her black hair tied back in a practical bunch behind her head. She looked older like that. Looked as if she belonged in these sparse and inhospitable peaks and valleys high above the coast. The tattoos apart. He didn't mind them. But somehow they didn't fit.

Vanni had brought two of his donkeys but she declared they weren't needed. Beasts of burden were for old men like him. They were young. They could walk the hills.

If her uncle was offended he didn't show it, just passed over a couple of water bottles which she stuffed in a rucksack and handed over for Maso Leoni to carry. The day was hot even with the breeze that came from altitude. They'd need it.

'There's one path up where we're going. One way only. Stick to it,' she ordered. 'Stay with me. Do as you're told. Be grateful.'

And then, his arms aching from lugging and turning logs all night, his legs weary, they set off.

The path was made for beasts of burden, strewn with their droppings in places, rocky and hard. It snaked upwards from behind the ruined church of Saint Dionysius, through a cleft in the rock that formed the index finger of Manodiavolo, into a long and shadowy passage that stank of mould and damp and something else. Creatures were chittering above them, flying swiftly through the dark, some close.

'Bats,' she said. 'They don't scare you, do they?'

'No,' he replied as they emerged on the other side.

Here the way ahead became narrower, steeper, and the fist of Manodiavolo hid the coast completely. They were in a sloping rocky bowl on the high slopes of Aspromonte, a bleak, bare peak which seemed to be earning its name, the harsh, the rugged mountain.

A thin plume of smoke was rising above the low pines, from the charcoal mound out of sight somewhere below. He could tell that from the smell and in his imagination see the thing they'd created: like a blackened prehistoric funeral chamber where a long-dead king of fable rested on a smouldering pyre.

'Do you live in Manodiavolo?' he asked as she forged ahead, not pausing once for breath.

'Are you serious?'

'Yes.'

'No one lives there all the time. Except Vanni. He loves it. He looks after the orchards and the vegetables. He keeps the place in order as much as he can. And when we have . . . guests to be housed . . . he sees to them as well.'

'Is he really your uncle?'

'Of course. Why would we lie?'

He joined her by the rock. Lizards scurried at their feet and he saw a slender green snake slide into a patch of thorns close by. 'You're about to tell me I'm asking too many questions.'

'No. Ask what you like,' she said and passed him the water. 'Just don't expect answers to everything.'

Something cast a shadow over them briefly. The vast spreading wings of a mountain bird, an eagle or a buzzard, gliding over the tree tops.

'Where do you live?'

'Why do you want to know?'

'Because . . . people are shaped by places. For good. For bad.'

Lucia scowled, at the view, not him.

'I want to smoke but it feels wrong up here.' She pulled out a pack of cigarettes, glared at them, then put them away. 'My father's big on education. He had none. His own father had none though he still managed to read a lot and write the book Vanni left you. Kind of. He always pulls it out when we have . . . guests.'

She waited.

'It doesn't seem the work of an uneducated man.'

'I said he didn't have an education. That's not the same. There's a lot you can do for yourself. Not me. After that little incident on the coast – my tattoo phase – Father sent me to Lausanne in Switzerland. Business Studies.'

She stifled a very dramatic yawn.

'Oh.'

'When I walked out of that he bought me a tiny villa in Capri. Out of the centre. Away from everything. To keep me out of trouble.'

'It worked.'

'Is that a question?'

'No.'

'OK. It worked. But now I'm back. For a while anyway. He needs me. You know Capri?'

A distant memory, a weekend away with Emily. 'I remember us paying a fortune for two warm beers in the Piazzetta.'

She laughed but not for long. 'Your wife died. She was murdered.'

'I'm Tomasso Leoni from Guelph. Never married.'

'I'm sorry. It sounded like a test. I didn't mean it that way. Your real name's Nic Costa. I know all about you. It's OK. I can say that. It's just you that can't.'

'No . . . offence taken. Capri—'

'I never go to the Piazzetta. It's for tourists and movie stars. My little house is near the Villa Jovis where a nasty emperor called Tiberius used to live. Across the road there's a place called Salto di Tiberio. His leap. They say he used to have servants who pissed him off pushed over the cliff. Once a fisherman climbed all the way up with a lobster he'd caught. A gift for his beloved emperor. Tiberius was so frightened he had the shell and claws rubbed in the poor man's face. Then a soldier pushed him over the edge.' Her hand briefly touched his arm. 'It's not just the criminal peasants of Aspromonte who display a heartless streak at times.'

'What do you do?'

Again that self-deprecating shrug. 'I try to paint. I try to write. I'm no good at either but I try and then I read. History mostly. I walk as well. Capri's a little place but there's a lot of it if you know where to look. Then when my family calls I come.'

Something melancholy seemed to flit around her shoulders. At that moment, for the first time since he left Rosa in the hills, he did not feel alone.

Eyes on the stark and desolate landscape she said very quietly, 'When Tiberius was dying they say his adopted son was announced emperor prematurely. And when the old man recovered he went into his room and smothered him in his bed. Dynasties don't always pass from one generation to the next in peace. I like history. The one thing it teaches us is we learn nothing at all. And yet we're defined by everything that went before. Here especially. It's like there's ghosts all round you.'

'Caligula,' he said. 'The adopted son.'

'Gaius Julius Caesar Augustus Germanicus to give him his proper name. They must have fine and well-stocked libraries in Canada.'

She stood up, removed the clasp behind her head, shook her hair free and touched the old silver bracelet on her wrist, unconsciously he thought. A habit. A tic.

'That book. You read the chapter about the Garduña? Spain. Apollinario. Where we, the Sicilians, the Neapolitans, all came from.'

'A fairy story, surely.'

She turned and stared at him and he felt he'd said the wrong thing once more. 'If enough people believe a myth is it a myth at all? There's a pope in Rome who might feel otherwise. He's the master of a million places built on nothing more than stories and parables written by men long dead. Men who perhaps never existed. Yet walk into the places where they worship and you can feel the faith so many have left behind. Is that . . . real? Or not?'

He was an atheist, he replied. Born and bred into him by his late father.

'You must still believe something.'

'Right now I believe I'm a man from a town called Guelph, somewhat bemused, with an interesting and charming stranger, waiting to know what happens next.'

'Interesting,' she repeated and squinted into the bright afternoon sun at the narrow rocky path ahead of them. It meandered through a bower of low bushes struggling to find purchase on the steep mountainside then vanished into shadow. 'What happens next is you meet a fairy tale.'

At that she set off up the track, walking briskly, not looking to see if he followed. Where else was there to go?

Peroni went onto the terrace and lit a cigarette. He was back in that vile habit even though he hated it. Silvio came out and made soothing noises. They wouldn't trace the call to his phone he said again. They surely couldn't, not without going back to Rome and asking for details on the login. And that would take them straight back to Lombardi who'd doubtless log the transgression and throw it in Peroni's direction should there be blame to apportion at some stage.

'Thanks,' Peroni told him. 'They're mad with me, aren't they?'

'Leo's mad with everyone at the moment. Himself most of all. We need to start doing something.'

'Except we can't.'

Silvio was the office innocent in some ways. A geeky guy of thirty more interested in science and technology than people. Everyone liked him.

'No. Guess not.'

'And Teresa . . .'

Silvio had worked with her ever since he joined the force after university. They were close. In a way he idolized her because she was something he'd never be, a loose cannon in the Questura at times, always bright, always asking awkward questions others didn't dare.

'You've been spending a lot of time in that bar,' was all he said. 'She notices everything.'

'Jesus . . . the woman there's a widow twenty odd years younger than me or more. Come on. You know me. Teresa knows me.'

'This isn't Rome, is it? We're different people somehow. Pretending to be. Like actors I guess.'

It seemed an uncharacteristically perceptive comment for the man from Forensic.

'Tell her—'

'For God's sake, Gianni, you tell her. You live with her. She needs to hear it from you.'

He patted Silvio on the arm. A nice guy, always struggling with his own private life. Keeping a girlfriend was never that easy. He worked too much, didn't care about his appearance, sometimes seemed the most pasty-faced geek in Rome.

'Just so you know . . . I need to warn Lombardi,' Silvio said, heading for the room where he kept his laptop. 'If he doesn't know already.'

Peroni went to the edge of the terrace. The smell of the sea, all salt and freshness, rose to swamp him, make him feel giddy for a moment so strong and powerful was its presence. To his left the boats bobbed in Cariddi's little harbour. A couple of feluccas, a dozen or more smaller craft. No one seemed to be fishing. As he watched, Teresa and Falcone ambled along the short stone pier, deep in conversation. He wondered what he could say to make things better. Words weren't the problem. This place was.

The two of them sat on a bench and watched a couple of men start to scramble across the boats. Soon they'd be putting to sea, perhaps chasing swordfish. He'd spotted the larger felucca out first thing that morning, a man atop the tower, another with a harpoon at the end of the long ladder extension to the front.

He didn't want to see this any more so walked to the other side of the terrace and looked back towards the Kiosco Paradiso.

The black Fiat was there. The creep was out, leaning on the bonnet, shades on his greasy scalp, a cigarette in his narrow, thin-lipped mouth. He was talking to the fat cop who'd been at the door. These two knew one another, that much was clear.

The punk laughed. The cop laughed. Then the punk briefly wound his arm through the man's blue jacket and whispered something in his ear.

A nod then and there was something in the way they two of them stood, looked, talked, laughed that made a little red fire light up at the back of Gianni Peroni's head.

Then the cop slapped the thug in the black suit on the shoulder and walked off towards his cheap little Fiat saloon parked up on the pavement at the end of Cariddi's narrow waterfront lane.

Sometimes things happen and you didn't need to be clairvoyant to see them coming.

The punk threw his cigarette in the water then strode over to the bar with obvious purpose. He barked something at Roberto who jumped, shrank back and started to head off for the beach.

'Get out of here, kid,' Peroni whispered, thinking of his words. 'I got business with your mother. And the fat jerk of a local cop just decided to look the other way.'

The black suit watched Roberto slink off then went to the kiosco and vanished into the shadow of the door at the side.

To hell with it, Peroni thought. To hell with Teresa if need be. Right was right and wrong was wrong. Forget that and you might as well never get out of bed.

'And I got business with you,' he murmured staring at the little shack of a bar along the way.

The boy had vanished by the time Peroni reached the Paradiso. So had the shabby local cop. There was no one outside on the battered plastic chairs, no one on the beach, no one in the little lane that ran behind the terraced fishermen's cottages. It was the middle of a scorching afternoon. The people of Cariddi were elsewhere, maybe at work, on the sea or just inside hiding from the heat.

He knew this was a mistake. He'd fouled up already, making the illicit call into the local network, and got away with that. Not that it made much difference. Elena Sposato was still

getting pestered by the creep in the black Fiat and probably
would long after he and the rest of the team made their way
back to Rome. Over the years hard experience had made him
connect actions with their consequences. But sometimes you
overthought things. Sometimes you needed to act in order to
flush out what would happen next. They did that all the time
in Rome, in real police work, a world they tried to make black
and white as much as possible, not the messy shade of grey
they'd fallen into in Cariddi, as wide as the sea in front of
him and just as likely to drown them.

A bare concrete platform, badly laid, covered in ridges and
cracks, formed the Paradiso's front terrace over the rocks. He
walked to the front and scanned the pebble beach. Roberto
was nowhere to be seen and that bothered him.

Then there was a gentle, frightened noise from the side of
the ramshackle building, where they kept the bins and the
empty crates for beer and soft drinks. Peroni walked over,
trying to trace the source. He could just make out a timid
shape buried behind the mound of giant watermelons lined up
by the counter. A sign, two for three euros, almost hid the
boy.

'Roberto,' Peroni said in a quiet, authoritative voice, and
held out his hand. 'Come on. Come out. You're safe with me.'

He didn't move.

'Where's your mother?'

The kid's eyes flicked to the left and behind him.

'You're safe, son.' He heard his own voice and thought:
there was a strain of anger in that already so it was hardly
surprising the boy stayed where he was. 'Stay there then if
you like.'

There was no way of stopping this. Nor should there have
been. He knew what was happening behind the rusting garage
door. Knew too he couldn't ignore it. Whatever anyone –
Teresa, Falcone – felt. Whatever the consequences.

He had to edge past a couple of empty barrels of used
vegetable oil waiting for the pickup truck. As he did so he
heard her. Heard them. She was crying, hurt, furious, somewhere inside the grubby garage. Her sobs mingled with his
rhythmic moans.

'Bastard,' Peroni grunted and lifted up the garage door. Light flooded in as the thing squeaked on rusty hinges. Two shapes in the corner, against a pile of sheets and rags, that spasmodic movement he was expecting. Elena Sposato shrieked louder as the bright summer sun fell on her spread-eagle legs and flailing arms. The man was on her and so engaged he didn't seem to notice.

'Bastard,' Peroni said again and told himself, as he went to pull them apart, there would be a point at which he'd stop. A moment where he could go no further. Though in truth the best thing for them all would be if he followed his instincts, beat the moron till he breathed no more, then dumped his sorry corpse in the bright blue waters of the Tyrrhenian Sea.

His left hand went out to grab the mop of black and greasy hair beneath him. His right balled into a terrible fist, one drawn so the hard white bone of his knuckles showed through pale and fleshy fingers.

He didn't say another word. It seemed unnecessary.

A narrow rocky corridor snaked between two high and craggy ridges ahead. All around the plants and shrubs and trees were sparse, scrubby, almost alpine, clinging on for life among the few brown-grey patches of earth around. The path through the rugged hillside blocked all views back to Manodiavolo and the coast so he couldn't guess how high they were or how far from the nearest road. The air was fresh and cool. The heat of the lowlands seemed far distant.

The only sign of visitors along the way was the odd mule dropping and, once, a spent sweet wrapper by the stub of a cigar. Then they rounded a towering spike of weather-beaten rock and he saw ahead the opening to a cavern, so small it seemed impossible to believe the place could be of any importance. As they got closer there were signs of activity: scrawls on rock, paintings of eyes and crosses and, on a flat, stone face a good metre tall, what was clearly a dagger drawn, blood dripping from the blade in scarlet paint, poised over a torn and ragged heart.

The entrance was little more than an inverted vertical slash in the massive slab of granite that rose to a stark point above them, the summit of this particular peak on Aspromonte.

'You need to duck,' she said, taking a small LED torch from her belt. 'Stay close.'

A chilly darkness swallowed them up the moment they crouched and stepped inside, a fresh draft of mountain air seeming to rise from ahead of them, like breath from a sleeping giant's throat.

'Here,' she said, and in the shade passed him a torch. 'Our secret place. The Chapel of the Holy Clasp.'

It had a dank and mouldy smell, tinged with incense, like the interior breath of the mountain itself. Ahead the stony track widened, the roof grew taller. Within the space of twenty or thirty metres he was able to stand freely. Then she stopped, found some larger form of lighting installation by the wall, turned it on and his breath briefly stilled inside him.

It was a refuge for secret worship and devotion hidden deep inside this solitary peak of Aspromonte. Rows of low wooden chairs ran from side to curving side with a narrow gap between. The walls were lined with paintings, mostly representing martyrdoms: Saint Lorenzo on his gridiron fire, stabbed by soldiers as he was burned alive; Catherine with her wheel of torture; Sebastiano bound to a tree and pierced by arrows.

'Sacrifice,' Lucia said in a hushed and cautious tone. 'We're fond of that idea.'

But the light drew them to the altar and as he approached he saw why. A cleft ran through the rock above the raised rostrum, out to the open air. Glass covered the vent as it reached the chapel but the light, bright now from the clear summer day, fell through, caught the silver and gilt crucifix on the plain stone table and flooded onto something that lay on a wooden stand in front. A bracelet, he saw, remembering the chapter he'd read in Vanni's book.

'Apollinario's?' he asked.

'Mary's or so they claim,' she replied with a dubious nod. Lucia raised her wrist and showed him the bracelet there. 'Look. I have a copy. My father had it made.'

He came and stood in front of the crucifix. The silver clasp was without ornament and the metal had lost a little of its

sheen over the centuries. He wanted to touch it and she saw
that and her look said, Why not?

'It seems wrong. Anyone could come in here and steal this
thing . . .'

She laughed. 'And how far do you think they'd get? Touch
it. They say it brings . . . knowledge.'

'Not luck?'

'No. We don't believe much in luck. Only the fortune we
make ourselves. Touch it.'

The metal was soft and warm somehow and he didn't want
it in his fingers long. 'I don't feel right here.'

'No. You're a foreigner. But I doubt the Holy Mother will
mind. That fairy story you read? The Garduña? The three
brothers from Catalonia?'

'Yes?'

'Meet one of them.' She pointed to a pale block of stone
half-hidden in the darkness. 'Carcagnosso. The brother who
brought us here.'

It was a grave, he realized. A rock sarcophagus, so old it
looked as if it belonged in a museum. There was no inscrip-
tion, only a neat line of three black holes, each big enough to
take a couple of fingers, drilled into the upper third.

'They loved him so much from the start, the Greeks here,
they buried him in the old way,' she explained. 'With those
holes through his tombstone and copper pipes into his mouth.
To feed him until he rises again in the afterlife.'

She leaned against the altar so the light from the cleft above
caught her face. 'The church banned that centuries ago. It
came from the old religion, the pagans, you see. Still, this is
Aspromonte. Once in a while the men who followed gather
here, pay homage. They feed Carcagnosso wine and milk and
honey through those holes, like our ancestors did when he
was first buried. And afterwards they get down to business.
No one outside the 'ndrina and the clans has witnessed this
and lived. You must be the first—'

'When?'

She seemed disappointed by the question. 'That's for my
father to say. A group of the masters of the three clans who
started life as the Garduña . . . they will gather to say thanks

in front of Mary's bracelet and feed their long-dead saint. Then a summit. Alliances to be forged. Vendettas to be ended one way or another. Business opportunities. Threats from outside. Some of these men – they will all be men – your people will know. Finding them here will be of no use. They've escaped prosecution in the past and will in the future. But some . . . will be those you've been searching for year after year. And some you will know only by reputation. Andrea Mancuso for one. The Butcher of Palermo. And my father . . . They will all be here. It will be quite unlike any summons to the Chapel of the Holy Clasp they've ever witnessed.'

She faltered for a moment then took his arm and led him back the way they came, until they emerged blinking in the bright sun by the entrance.

'There are two paths to this place only,' she said, pointing to the route they'd come, then a side track leading off to the east where the Ionian was just visible between two distant crags. 'Our people will go back to Manodiavolo this way, my father among them. There he will go into your custody provided you meet conditions he will soon outline to you himself. The rest, the Sicilians, the men from Naples . . .' She indicated the eastern path. 'There's a space near a mountain road about a kilometre down. They'll park there. They won't want to linger. Everyone knows it's dangerous to gather like this, especially for no other reason than sentiment and tradition.'

'You said it was for business.'

She shook her head and he found he couldn't take his eyes off her. High in the mountain she looked so at home. As if the peaks and wild land around them were a part of her. 'Only in part. Mostly it's a ritual. An offering of thanks. A prayer for the future. We bring in a priest brought in for the occasion. A man who may one day wear the red hat of a cardinal. We've friends in many places. It's best you never forget that.'

This was all deliberate. The 'ndrina using Lucia to set out the first part of the plan. Though how he was meant to communicate it to Falcone and the team he'd still no idea.

'So you want us to take them where they leave their cars? Down the hill?'

'Not in the chapel. That would be wrong. Not in Manodiavolo. Nowhere near us. My father will be there. You'll need plenty of men. Armed. If some of them are local I wouldn't mention where they're going until it's too late for them to refuse. You might find a sudden outbreak of sickness has gripped their ranks. And at least one of them will talk.'

He went a little way down the second track. The space she must have been talking about became visible after a while, surrounded by mountain pines. A rugged 4×4 was parked there already, no one visible near it.

'There are . . . hurdles to clear before this can happen,' she told him. 'Come now. It's time to go home.'

'Hurdles for me?'

'You're very quick,' she replied with a bright smile. 'It would be best if you hid that. But yes. Hurdles that are very much for you. Now . . .' She tucked the torch back into her belt. 'We must go.'

They were halfway down the track, emerging from the shadowy corridor between the crags, when the man with the shotgun pounced. He was about the same height, swarthy, muscular, with shiny, wavy black hair, a pair of sunglasses pushed back on top. The weapon he held in his strong, tanned arms was a short-barrelled lupara shotgun with a wide khaki strap running round his back. He held it diagonally across his body and grinned at them, like a hunter who'd found fresh prey.

'Pretty lady,' he said in a heavy Calabrian accent, looking Lucia up and down. 'Out wandering the hills. Just the two of you. Did no one tell you there are wolves up here?'

She folded her arms and leaned against a rock, sending a couple of lizards scurrying into the cracks.

'Do you know who I am?' Lucia asked.

'I said. A pretty lady. Wandering places she shouldn't. Some foreign creep with her.' He cocked his head. 'I heard you talking on the way. What the hell kind of accent's that?'

'What do you want?' Maso Leoni asked.

He shrugged. 'Oh just the usual.' A grin. A wink. 'Money. And from this pretty lady . . . a kiss.' He gripped his groin briefly with a free hand and made a coarse gesture. 'To begin with. Run away, foreigner. Leave us now. We've business and—'

It wasn't hard. They were just a couple of steps apart. He jabbed his elbow out, quick and sharp, took the guy in the chest, got both hands on the barrel of the shotgun, held it firm, brought up the stock and slammed it hard into the side of his head. The newcomer shrieked with shock and pain. At that moment he wrestled the strap from round his shoulders, got the shotgun free, kicked him once in the shin, watched as he went down to the hard ground.

The barrel was in the crouching man's face in three or four seconds, no more. For some reason the newcomer was laughing in between holding his head, still glancing at Lucia with that same avaricious expression he'd had from the start.

'What do you want me to do with him?' he asked.

'Say hello,' she said with a scowl. 'Santo Vottari. Meet Tomasso Leoni. His friends call him Maso, I believe.'

'Maso it is then.' The man struggled to his feet, brushed himself down, stuck out his hand and winked at him. 'They said you came all the way from Canada. Your old man kicked you out for being a pain in the butt. That right?'

There were two tests here. Being able to deal with a threat. Being capable of keeping a secret too. Santo Vottari had to be a foot soldier, probably with no idea what was going on. It was important to keep it that way.

'I guess I was a pain,' he replied. 'I always wanted to come here anyway. It's where we're from.'

Santo frowned and moved his head from side to side, in doubt. 'Doesn't make you one of us.'

'He's working on it,' Lucia said. 'Pretty well.'

'Good. Sorry about the little game.' Santo nodded in her direction. 'It was her idea and what Lucia wants Lucia gets. Can I have my shotgun back now?'

He handed it over. Santo slung the thing over his shoulder as if it was a part of him.

'Well done,' she said. 'Both of you.'

Then she walked ahead, out into the bright afternoon, taking the path back to Manodiavolo.

Santo waited, let her get ahead. When Lucia was out of earshot his sharp elbows nudged Maso Leoni in the side.

'She is a pretty thing, the capo's daughter,' Santo whispered. 'One day I'm working my way into those tight pants. You watch. Well . . .' He corrected himself. 'I don't mean . . . watch.'

A bird cried somewhere. A hawk or an owl.

'Welcome, friend,' Santo said and patted his shoulder. 'You can handle yourself. That's a start.'

Peroni was in the kitchen washing his hands when they got back. He'd no idea where Teresa and Falcone had been but from Leo's grumbling it sounded as if they'd tried a different restaurant and found it wanting. Silvio must have been in his room glued to the laptop as usual. They'd bumped into one another as Peroni returned and the eager young man from Forensic had taken one look at him, muttered a rare curse then vanished.

His knuckles were raw and bleeding. His chest hurt. The thug had fought back when Peroni dragged him off Elena Sposato. More than expected, which was a big mistake on his part. Everything was different in Calabria. Punks who'd whine and run away back in Rome the moment you whispered boo stood their ground here.

But not for long.

'Good evening,' Peroni said as Teresa came into the kitchen, placed her bag on the table. 'Could you possibly find me some plasters?'

Falcone must have heard. He zoomed into the room straight away and asked, 'Why?'

He grimaced and showed them his battered and bloody hands. 'Sorry, Leo. Truly I am.'

Teresa was shading her eyes and saying, 'Oh Christ.' A few other things besides.

'I can't just stand to one side and watch. I won't. Best send me back to Rome right now—'

'We can't, you fool!' Teresa yelled at him. 'What have you done?'

He shrugged, dried his hands. They stung. If he hadn't held

back somewhat he might have broken something. Then he
walked out to the terrace and they followed him. The Kiosco
Paradiso was closed, the front boarded up. No watermelons
for sale. No sad little kid playing on the rough front terrace.

'Probably something stupid,' he murmured. 'But necessary.'

Lucia went down the hill as fast and nimble as a mountain
goat. The two men followed at a distance, Santo Vottari chat-
ting all the way. About her. About how she'd gone a little
crazy with men and drink and drugs on the coast. Then got
herself sorted, wouldn't marry and preferred to live somewhere
else, north, he thought, though he wasn't sure. The Bergamotti
– he called them that – were the most secretive of the
'Ndrangheta families. They kept their real name hidden and
worked through a strict hierarchy of ranks. The foot soldiers
at the bottom only dealt with the men above them. He was
one of the lucky ones who'd met Lucia and her brother. Only
a handful ever encountered the capo, Lo Spettro, the head of
the clan. Santo had heard stories over the years. He was a man
in his mid-sixties or so, a widower who moved around Calabria
and further afield as he wished, issuing orders through his
family, Rocco, Lucia and their aunt Alessia.

'You're lucky to get in with the boss guys so soon. You
something special, Maso?'

'I don't think so.'

'They must.'

He tried to keep his eyes on the fast-vanishing figure ahead
of them. They were nearly back in Manodiavolo. He could
see the church, the little cemetery full of shattered headstones
behind the hill, the sign of the old shop, half-off on rusty
hinges, the bakers with the wrecked stone oven inside. In the
courtyard by the fountain was something new: a shiny little
Fiat Cinquecento, white with a red stripe on the side. The
ghost village had another visitor.

As they rounded a bluff covered in thorns and rampant ivy
Santo reached out and put a hand on his shoulder to stop him.
'Jesus. See that.'

There was a man seated at a table brought out into the
middle of the little square. He wore a navy blue felt hat, what

looked like a pale linen jacket and matching trousers. As they watched he removed the fedora, let loose a head of long white hair. Then Rocco appeared carrying a tray of beer and some kind of food. The man in the photo in the santina's hut. And in the palazzo.

'That's him,' Santo said in a needless whisper. 'Has to be. Lo Spettro. The capo.'

'How do you know?'

'Snow-white hair. Rocco told me about that the other day. Christ. Who are you, man? You got Lucia coming to see you. Rocco. Now the big guy . . .'

She was walking into the courtyard, smiling, kissing her brother first, then the man in the linen suit, embracing him with a familiar, loving hug.

'He never comes and sees the troops,' Santo murmured. 'Jesus. I wish I'd known.'

'You think the capo of the Bergamotti sends out invitations?'

Santo eyed him, not suspicious, just surprised. 'You're a fast one. They teach that in Canada?'

'Doesn't need teaching.'

'That accent of yours sounds more like Rome to me.'

'My uncle came from there not long ago. Mostly I talk Italian with him.'

The man with the shotgun over his shoulder wasn't really listening. He was watching what was going on in the square.

'Come on, Maso,' he said. 'Let's get this over with. Our betters are waiting on us.' Then a frown. 'Something's going on here. And something going on . . .' He rubbed his hands and winked. 'That's opportunity.'

After they descended the last hundred metres or so he let Santo Vottari go first since he seemed to want it. Rocco introduced them and for the first time gave the capo of the 'ndrina a name: Gabriele Bergamotti. While Maso stood back and listened, Santo bowed, got on one knee, placed the shotgun on the worn cobbles of Manodiavolo, and started a rambling speech about how grateful he was to be a humble member of the finest, most honourable 'ndrina in the world. How dedicated, how loyal, how willing to do anything to prove his worth in the hope – his eyes stole towards Lucia at that moment, which seemed to amuse her – the sincere wish that one day his fidelity might be rewarded if the capo saw fit.

The man with the white hair sat on a wicker chair, sipping at a beer, splitting pistachios with his nails, listening. He didn't smile. He didn't scowl. He didn't look bored. Just nodded as Santo got on with his meandering speech.

It ended as Vanni returned breathless from the lane that led to the fields, Silvio and Benito, the donkeys, tugging a pair of carts laden with charcoal fresh from the mound the two of them had built the day before. The old man seemed able to direct the animals through a few gentle words and gestures alone. No need of a bridle let alone a whip.

'That was very good,' Gabriele Bergamotti said when there was a gap in the kneeling man's devotions. 'I'm fortunate to have such a loyal and decent soldier among our ranks—'

'None more loyal, boss. None more eager—'

'Good.'

Gabriele smiled then and showed a set of fine, too-white teeth, doubtless false, the entire set. His face was pleasant, round, genial, not careworn in the least, that of a friendly grandfather. Though his blue eyes seemed very sharp, almost northern in appearance, the colour of the Tyrrhenian off Cariddi the day they arrived. There was Norman blood – Viking in origin – throughout the south, in Sicily and the toe, and some-times, in the hair, the skin, the eyes. Or so the book they'd given him, written by this man's father, claimed.

'My poor brother's struggling with the burden he's bringing up from the fire,' Gabriele announced in a deep and friendly, almost theatrical tone, with only the slightest accent of the south. 'Be a good man and help him, will you? I would be most grateful. And so I'm sure will he.'

'For you, boss, anything,' Santo replied and after a salute went off to take instructions from Vanni who was waiting by the cart.

He came forward. It seemed expected. Gabriele looked him up and down. As Nic Costa he'd been close to many powerful individuals. Even the president of Italy for a while. This man had the same presence about him, as if he was able to treat every occasion as a performance, the world a stage on which to stroll.

'There was a real Tomasso Leoni,' he said. 'We chose that name because of him.'

'Who was he?'

'My teacher. Here. We had to stay at home. It wasn't safe to go to any ordinary school much as he would have liked it. Me too. Still, my father insisted I receive an education.'

'You never told me about a teacher,' Lucia said and Rocco nodded at that.

'So much of the past is misery,' he murmured. 'Leoni was a good man. A very knowledgeable fellow too. One time the Sicilians came for us when there was a dispute.' He gestured round the crumbling, deserted village. 'Here. I'll show you something.'

He picked up a handful of nuts and got up, easily. A fit, strong man, tall, still imposing.

'Follow me.'

They walked up the steps of the church, past the broken spire, into the cemetery behind. Many of the headstones were in pieces, the names worn away by age and the harsh mountain weather. In the harsh afternoon sun crooked cypresses cast spiky shadows across the broken monuments and the jigsaws of cracked paving. There couldn't be more than a hundred graves here, most of them centuries old.

'We prevailed in the end but that day Tomasso gave his life for mine. So in a way for yours too.' He stopped and pointed at a bare patch of ground covered in weeds. 'We buried him hereabouts. I wanted to put up some kind of monument but my father forbade it. Manodiavolo was supposed to be a place for ghosts, he said. It would be wrong to try to bring it back to life. Who knew what that might summon?'

His foot scraped at the earth with the toe of a polished brown brogue. 'A very well-read gentleman. Learned. He helped my father with that book that bears his name. To be truthful I suspect Tomasso wrote most of it. But without the Bergamotti it would never have been published. So we earned our name on the cover.'

He came up close and stared in Maso's eyes. There was the fragrance of beer and something sweet on his breath and his icy blue eyes shone as if lit from inside. 'The new Tomasso Leoni. I hope you prove as intelligent and dutiful as the good man who bore that name for real.'

'I'm here for a reason. You asked for it. I need details. Dates. Agreements. When can we—?'

'It's too early to start asking when.'

He could see there was no point in arguing. One other question then. It had to be asked.

'Why are you doing this? I think we're due an answer there.'

The old man scowled. 'Does the giver need to explain the gift?'

'On this occasion . . . it would help.'

Gabriele Bergamotti looked around him. 'This world is changing. It's not the one I grew up in. A place of honour and duty. Somewhere the 'ndrina cared for its flock. We had to. No one in Rome would lift a finger for the people of Aspromonte. Now . . . everything's about money and power and influence. Who you are, what you believe no longer matters. I don't want my children swept up in that nonsense. You can take me. You let me live my days free in the place of my own choosing, a small villa I own on Burano where I will watch the fishermen and the hunters on the Venetian lagoon and never trouble you again. Lucia and Rocco you never touch. You don't go looking for them or asking what they do, where they get their money. All of which will be legitimate so you'll have no cause. The rest of the 'ndrina . . .' He glanced at Santo Vottari across the little piazza, grumbling as he picked up filthy charcoal from the cart. 'Do with as you see fit. Is that reason enough for you, Roman? Are you able to agree?'

He nodded and said the truth: all of this could be arranged. It was nothing less than they'd expected.

'Good. We need you to be able to move freely between us and your colleagues, Maso. Until you're seen to be one of us, accepted, that is not possible. These men suspect everyone and everything. So it will be a perilous journey. First of all, appreciate this. No one here understands who you really are except me, my two children. And my sister Alessia. Not that I wish her involved any more than she has been. Fools like that crude swaggering footman my son brought here—'

'Santo's OK,' Rocco objected.

'How many times must I tell you?' His voice rose, became hard and domineering. 'You must look into a man's eyes. I did when he was fawning on the ground. There's nothing there but darkness.'

The vehemence seemed to take Rocco aback and he didn't like it. 'If you say so . . .'

'I do. That man's the creature of whoever pays him. He must never know. Nor Vanni. My brother's a poor and hopeless fool, too simple for our schemes. You understand this? I'm asking my children, Maso. Not just you.'

The two of them looked at one another.

'We understand,' Lucia said before her brother could speak. 'Don't worry.'

'Don't worry.' He laughed. 'We'd all be dead in the morning if any of them knew what's in my head. All it takes is a single traitor and every one of us here will be in the ground like my poor teacher back there.'

'How long will that take?'

Gabriele smiled and took his arm. 'A few days. Perhaps a little more. We're the 'ndrina. A meritocracy my father always said. See? He learned a lot from your namesake. A man earns his place in our ranks through what he does. We require that you become one of us. For that . . .'

The smile vanished in an instant. Another man seemed to take his place, a harder, colder individual.

'For that you need to act like one of us. You must do what we all do to earn our place.' A smile, a hard pat on the shoulder. 'My boy . . . you must kill and be seen to kill. Really . . . it's as simple as that.'

# PART FOUR
## A Time to Kill

Calabrian Tales

### Chapter VI: The Gladiator of the Sea

I n May giants of the deep begin to move from the far Atlantic through the straits of Gibraltar into the warmer depths of the Tyrrhenian. Tuna, fin and sperm whale join native sharks and dolphin traversing the three-kilometre stretch of swirling water between Scylla and Charybdis. The fisher folk of Cariddi have sought these creatures for as long as men have sailed this southern tip of Italy. But here the most prized of all is never caught by net or barb. The Gladiator of the Strait, so-called for the weapon that forms its bill, is hunted, one by one, in a slow and theatrical ritual upon the gleaming waves, a ceremony so old none knows whence it came.

The swordfish is a valuable catch, prized up and down the coast in season. Elsewhere greed rules and men trawl the ocean ceaselessly with lines and hooks, grasping at everything they can kill. In Cariddi we hunt in a singular, respectful fashion, one that may reap thin rewards but leaves sufficient of these magnificent creatures to return another year.

This annual preoccupation is never without risk. The pisci spata, as we call it in our native dialect, is as powerful a fish as swims the sea, faster than the sleekest motor vessel made, weighing as much as a hundred kilos, all muscle and ready to slash at enemies with a long, sharp bill that can rip the hull of any small wooden craft foolish enough to come too close. My uncle Beppe lost half a leg to a thrashing male on the deck of a rowed felucca when he was fifteen, one damp June day off Messina. A year later he was back on board, climbing the tower in an ungainly fashion to spot for prey and

steer the vessel towards its quarry. He never held the harpoon
again and went with that regret to his grave.

We live, as I have said, in a land where myth is real and
this annual quest for the pisci spata is one more ritual that
defines us. These vessels are no ordinary fishing boats, being
designed for the swordfish season alone. During the summer
they can be seen slowly cruising this part of the Tyrrhenian,
men scouring the waves from their high spotting towers, a
harpooner perched on his *passarella*, a long iron bridge at
the front protruding from the bows, eyes on the surface, spear
in his upright arm, much like a figure from a mosaic of old.
Ancient symbols of respect and good luck, eyes and holy
emblems, decorate the hulls.

The colours of the craft, often black, green and red, are said
to date from Phoenician days and ward off evil spirits. Once
a fish is finally landed on the deck the captain of the vessel
will utter a prayer of thanks to his patron saint, '*San Marco
è binidittu*'. Blessings for Saint Mark. A piece of bread or a
peach may be placed in the dying fish's jaws. After which, by
way of gratitude, the skipper will carve a lump of raw flesh
from the wound the spear made and offer it to the harpooner
who may well devour it on the spot.

Nor do we treat these magnificent monsters of the deep
with anything but deference. Famous battles with legendary
specimens are recorded in paintings, on wall tiles, in the many
songs that praise the prey we seek. Men weep as they kill the
bravest; for swordfish are admirable and amatory creatures.
They come to mate somewhere between Messina and the
waters around the Aeolian Islands. Monogamous, they swim
in pairs, like man and wife. And like a loyal husband the male
is both covetous and caring for his bride, a failing that the
wise hunter will use to his advantage.

The process is much as it was back in my uncle's days
when swordfish were taken by wooden boats rowed by sturdy
teams of oarsmen. The spotter scans the sea from his turret,
looking for signs of rising fish, a flash of tail, the moment a
fin breaks surface. Once a pair is seen, the felucca steers nearby
and the harpooner stays poised upon his passarella, a five-spear
weapon in his hand. If luck is with him he will find the

skittish, cautious female first and aim for her. The creature's distress brings her mate to her side immediately, offering a second chance of prey.

After the sharp barbs of the harpoon have found purchase, the victim is given a long line to escape to the depths, tiring itself, spilling scarlet blood into the ocean for an hour or longer. Then, when its weakness is apparent, the exhausted fish is hauled aboard, one man taking the deadly sword in a rag to still the weapon while another dispatches the creature with a long, sharp knife.

If the catch is the female then her mate will be close by, sometimes attacking the boat wildly in an attempt to free her. With luck, he will soon follow her onto the deck. But if the male is killed the lady will never linger. Shy or simply faithless, she'll flee to find another. Which is why there are many songs admiring the courage and faithfulness of the male and none that praise the lady. Fidelity is much valued in this corner of Calabria, and disloyalty viewed as a sin.

Ashore the prize is sold to middlemen who will ship it to the markets of Naples, Rome and Venice at a fantastical margin. Or, more likely in Cariddi, someone will fetch a wooden trestle from their house, stretch out the silver corpse upon it and butcher delicate pale slices streaked with fresh blood for anyone who'll pay.

The season is short. Come the darker, colder days of autumn the Gladiator of the Strait moves back to the grey Atlantic. Different, conventional vessels ply the Strait of Messina seeking more mundane, smaller catches.

Should you come across a swordfish on your travels there is a simple way to discover if it was one of ours, dragged from the ocean the old way, not with cruel and indiscriminate hooks and nets. When the creature sighs its last upon the deck, before the morsel of fresh flesh is offered to the harpooner, the skipper will reach down with his hand and scrape four fingers down the fish's right cheek with his nails to scratch a lattice cross. This is the *cardata da cruci*, as necessary a benison for its passing as that murmured, 'San Marco è binidittu'.

Those four gouged, criss-crossed streaks say, 'This death is our doing, this creature's agony the price it pays to keep us fed.'

I cannot count the times I've seen the cardata scratched upon that shining, silvery skin and on every occasion I have wept. Then ate. Happily. Greedily. Content, wiping the tears from my eyes. In Cariddi, the Bergamotti and our like do not shrink from death any more than we recoil from tomorrow.

Each year the swordfish swims to its fate in the treacherous waters between Scylla and Charybdis. Each year we work our way to our own end too.

We are at one with Ecclesiastes. All things have their seasons. A time to be born, and a time to die; a time to plant, and a time to pluck up that which is planted; a time to kill, and a time to heal; a time to weep, and a time to laugh; a time to mourn, and a time to dance; a time to love, and a time to hate; a time of peace, and a time of war.

T he next morning a shiny 4×4 with a Sicilian number plate was parked in the square. Leaning on the bonnet was a tall, muscular individual with a bull-like head, more obvious since he kept twisting round to observe the abandoned village around him. He wore a brown corduroy waistcoat over an open-necked white shirt, a gold chain visible beneath, matching trousers, heavy country boots. A red and fawn checked coppola cap sat tight to his scalp, pulled down to the ears. He could have been an extra from a gangland movie of old were it not for the modern smart phone in his right hand which he was using to take photographs. He stopped and squinted at Maso as he emerged from the palace after a solitary breakfast of a single pastry and strong coffee. Santo was by the man's side, saying something behind his hand. Then Lucia came out from the kitchen, gave Maso another pastry and touched his arm.

'The Sicilians are here,' she said and waved to the car. Santo, misreading the gesture, waved back. 'God. That idiot never gives up.'

'The Sicilians?'

'His name is Gaetano Sciarra. Think of him as Mancuso's lieutenant. Il Macellaio's nephew, here to check the lie of the land. To see if it's safe for him to cross the water and pay homage in the chapel of our lady.' She blinked and he thought that wasn't just the fault of the blazing morning sun. 'It's nothing you need worry about. Do as you're asked. There needs to be a death today.' She took his arm again and smiled at him. 'Don't worry. It's not what you think. Now eat your cornetto. I chose one with ricotta. You need a full stomach for what lies ahead.' She laughed. 'I hope you can keep it down.'

'Which means . . .?'

She didn't answer. Didn't seem to notice the question. Her brother had stormed out of the old church, phone in hand, a look of fury on his face. He was listening, not talking. Then with a quick, barked curse he cut the call and stood alone by the crumbling porch, beneath the remains of the fallen campanile, thunder in his dark eyes.

'Tonight the sun will set around eight thirty,' she whispered, still staring at Rocco across the square. 'There's a special place to see it. A magical spot. If all goes well I'll take you there.' Santo Vottari was watching them. Her hand came away from his arm. 'Somewhere we can talk.' Then, more loudly, 'Go to your work, Tomasso Leoni. Strike hard. Strike well. Come back and we can greet you as a man of honour.'

A quick aside, murmured in his ear, 'Not that I think you need it.'

'Lucia!' Rocco barked from the church.

She left. He walked over to Santo and the newcomer, was introduced, got an attentive, scrutinising look in return.

'Canada?' the Sicilian asked and he could hear the difference in their voices, the subtle shift between the Calabrian and the accent across the water. That was something he'd come to learn.

'Guelph.'

'Where's that?'

'Ontario. A hundred kilometres west of Toronto. You've been?'

'Why would I go somewhere that cold?' Sciarra grunted and pushed his cap up his forehead, watching Rocco Bergamotti and his sister all the time.

'It's as hot as here,' he said, remembering what he'd read about the place. 'This time of year.'

'So why are you in this dump?'

'He's a relative,' Santo cut in. 'Did something bad back home. Here to learn the ropes.' Santo punched his arm, hard. 'We'll see if he can.'

'Not with me,' Sciarra replied. 'You go play your little games. I got talking to do.'

They watched him walk over to the Bergamotti.

'Something's happening,' Santo said. 'Told you.' His smile was fixed and artificial. 'But maybe you know that already. Got something to show you.'

They walked out of the square to a patch of spare ground where an old Land Rover was parked diagonally across the shattered cobbles, a battered trailer at the back. The vehicle he'd seen the night before, parked in the spot in the hills. Santo's. He pulled up a blue tarpaulin in the back and retrieved a long handled spear that might have been a prop in a movie.

'Here,' he said. 'This is yours. The big man's son is going to skipper us. He's damned good. That guy can spot a fin where the rest of us see nothing but a wave. Do what he says. That way you might come back alive. After that . . .'

He went quiet. Rocco was marching towards them. He didn't look any happier.

'We're ready to go, boss,' Santo said. 'I called the crew. Got the felucca ready. There's plenty out there. You could be scraping your nails on a dozen if you want.'

'No time for that. One's enough. You take him, Santo. I got work to do.'

'You want me to skipper?'

'Don't be stupid. You don't know a damned thing about it. Let the men down there do it. It's their job.'

Santo nodded, said nothing.

'Get me a fish on the truck by two at the latest. They can bring it back here. After that . . .' Rocco stared at Maso who wondered what he'd done wrong. 'We got other blood to spill. Here . . .' He threw Santo a set of car keys. 'I'll call.'

Then he went back to talking to the Sicilian.

'Something's really up,' Santo said again. 'He's pissed off as hell and that's not good. Things happen round you, don't they?'

One hour later Gianni Peroni was sitting alone on the terrace of the house in Cariddi, scanning the seafront, north to south. He couldn't go back to the bar which was now, he saw, open again, though quite without customers. Falcone had swiftly lost his foul mood from the incident there, the way he usually did. The man was incapable of harbouring grudges and could only focus on the moment in hand. Teresa was different and remained mad as hell. Silvio had slunk back to his computers and the odd message from Lombardi.

He threw the stub of his cigarette over the balcony into the blue waves, felt briefly guilty about so many things, not just that, then saw a decrepit grey Land Rover draw up next to a white van at the low curved parking place half a kilometre away by the harbour. A familiar figure stepped out.

'Christ,' he muttered. 'Nic.'

Except it didn't look much like the man he knew. He might have been one more local, getting ready for the boat.

He thought about the possibilities then rushed back inside and found them in the kitchen where Silvio was making coffee.

'Nic's out there. He's—'

'Where?' Falcone demanded.

'The harbour. It looks like they're getting ready to go out on one of those boats. The swordfishing ones.'

'What the hell for?' Teresa asked.

'To make him look local,' Peroni answered straight away, and wondered why he could see that and they didn't. It seemed so obvious. 'They're trying to convince the people with them. I guess . . . We can't set foot out of this place until he's gone. It's too damned risky.'

At other times Falcone might have objected to him giving the orders. Not then.

'Well,' Teresa said, 'at least we can watch. We've got binoculars, haven't we, Silvio?'

'Good ones,' he agreed, pouring the coffee. 'The best. I can film him if you like.'

'Don't,' Peroni cut in. 'Don't do anything that makes it look like we're interested.' He scowled. 'I've been a fool enough there.'

They didn't argue. All the same, after a while, the four of them assembled on the terrace, taking the chairs there, putting bread and cheese and salad on the table. All this was normal. No one could object. He wondered what Rosa Prabakaran was doing at that moment. Forgetting about Calabria he hoped. She was better out of the place.

Then a modern, low-slung felucca edged slowly out of the port, a man atop the tower steering from a wheel set in front of him as he scanned the still and gleaming water. Nic was there on the deck with three or four men showing him gear and gesticulating at the ocean. Rome had never seemed so far away at that moment.

'It's a test,' Peroni said, mostly to himself. 'It's what they do. Like it's the army or something. And you're just a foot soldier headed for the line.'

The felucca cleared the little harbour and settled into a snail's pace cruise barely a kilometre from the coast. Another, almost identical vessel, was running parallel in the stretch of sea towards Messina. From the taut line and cries at the front of the passarella it seemed they were already into a fish.

'Poor guy,' Peroni murmured. 'You hate hurting anything. Killing it . . .'

But he also knew his duty. There was no choice.

Settling back on the hard plastic chair of the terrace, Peroni watched his friend and colleague walk warily along the horizontal ladder, step by careful step, a weapon in his hand. A harpoon. Like an ancient spear. The figure atop the tower was shouting, pointing. Something soon would die. And with its blood the men of the Bergamotti 'ndrina would decide to trust this strange newcomer more. Perhaps.

'We should never have come here,' Peroni said to himself. 'There's something . . . wrong.'

He thought about another cigarette but that seemed wrong too. Before he could make up his mind there was a hammering on the door, loud, insistent, violent.

'I'll get it,' Peroni announced, rushing to be first. He'd been expecting a visit of a kind.

Two men were on the doorstep. A local with wavy dark hair, a pair of sunglasses above his tanned forehead, expensive clothes, a striking face, full of fury.

'We should not be meeting like this,' he said in a gruff Calabrian snarl.

The man in black didn't look as bad as Peroni expected. He didn't think he'd broken any of the bastard's bones. The nose maybe which was now bloody, purple bruised and swollen, and both his eyes were black and bleary as if someone had poured a bottle of ink over his face.

'You're lucky,' Peroni said to him, surprised. 'I thought

I'd hurt you more. But . . .' He opened the door wider.
'Come in.'

He had what felt like a long and heavy gladiator's spear in
his sweating hands, a rope round his waist that snaked back
to the mast where three locals watched him, both amused and
appalled. He was a Roman. Boats meant nothing. Even on the
gentle swell of the Tyrrhenian, a salty breeze blowing in his
face from Sicily across the strait, he found it difficult to focus,
to balance, to think of anything but the swirling sea beneath
him and the creatures there, the swordfish scything through
the waves.

Santo Vottari puffed out his chest and told him how to do
it: use both hands, strike hard and deep. Then one of the
locals, a burly man with a scarred, tanned face covered in
greying stubble, spat in the water and told Santo to shut up
and listen. The harpooner was the most important actor on
the felucca after the skipper, steering and spying from the
high tower above them. They couldn't understand why such
an important task had been given to a foreigner. They didn't
like it. But this bizarre instruction came on the orders of the
Bergamotti. However much they objected they were never
going to say no.

Use one arm only for the strike, the fisherman said, your
strongest. A single, certain aim, at the silver flank close behind
the gills. Avoid the head with its giant circular eye. That was
too bony for the five spears of the harpoon to do much damage.
All that would happen was that the fish would be startled and
wounded, but the barbs wouldn't bite and so the line couldn't
hold. All they would have was a wounded creature, fleeing to
the deeps.

'Like this,' the man said imitating the sudden, short jab of
a swordsman certain of his target. 'Then release.' His fingers
flew open. 'Imagine you're throwing a spear or a javelin straight
in the neck of the man you hate most. Find the spot and he's
ours. Miss it and you hurt the poor creature for no purpose at
all.'

Santo didn't argue. These men looked as if they wouldn't
brook that.

Twenty minutes out the captain on the tower shouted something in a vernacular so crude and local he could barely understand. A long, outstretched arm pointed to a stretch of turbid water a good thirty metres to the right, towards the shore. Something must have been visible from the skipper's lofty lookout but all he could see was the waves, all he could smell was the sharp and briny sea. Behind lay the waterfront of Cariddi with its tall terraced fishermen's homes, most with boathouses in the basement. Then Aspromonte rose in a series of harsh, spiking peaks, rock and forest, barely a house or building visible. Somewhere there he and Rosa had met the santina and nothing had been the same from that moment on. Somewhere nearby on the coast Falcone and the team were gathered waiting on him to bring news of the fateful meeting in the hills.

'Maso! Hey, foreigner!' cried a brisk voice from the mast. 'You awake down there or dreaming you're in bed with your boyfriend?'

He grinned at that, tapped his forehead and held the harpoon high in his right hand by way of answer.

'Good. We got a lady on the bows. You do her justice, nice and quick.'

Two more steps and he was at the very end of the passarella, balancing like a ballerina against the steady rhythm of the waves. There was something ahead of him dashing through the blue which, now he was close to it, was nothing like the wine-dark sea the book spoke of.

A flash of silver swept alongside the iron bridge, something skittish about it though the fish was massive and powerful, at least a good three metres long.

'The flank behind the gills,' someone yelled again. 'Not the head.'

The fish was both scared and curious he thought. Then, so quickly he caught his breath, the beast broke surface and he found himself staring at a wide, circular, glistening eye. It looked almost human and was gazing straight at him.

He jerked back his right arm the way they said, did his best to aim and threw the harpoon, hard and straight, filled his lungs with the briny air again as he watched the rope snaking after it, heading for the fish.

'Christ almighty,' the skipper yelled from the turret. 'Did you hear a single damned word I said?'

Most of the spear points missed. Two caught the swordfish close to the eye, briefly held, then fell free the moment someone behind tightened on the line. The thing made a sound like a baby's squeal and vanished beneath the surface.

'Sorry,' he said, though whether to the fish or the men behind him he didn't know.

'Pull it in!' someone yelled. 'Pull it in, Maso. That was the lady. You got her husband mad now and he's coming for you. Pull it in.'

A second silver shape was scything through the water. It was slimmer, sleeker, a little smaller too. But filled with purpose, swimming towards him faster than seemed possible, like a weapon charged.

The long sword broke surface, cut a savage shape against the bright blue sea then tore the waves.

'Get the harpoon in your hands, foreigner,' the skipper bellowed. 'Do that now. It's you he wants. Get—'

He reeled in the rope until he could get his wet and slippery hands clamped round the weapon's shaft. Thought of what they'd said to him, the fisherman's instructions, not Santo Vottari's braggadocio. Like a speeding bullet the male was closing hard. He waited for the moment, then jabbed forward with all his strength, released the stock and watched the five-forked spear tear through the air.

'It was him?' the man in the Paul and Shark polo asked the shame-faced figure in black by his side. They were in the living room, curtains closed. The air was close and stifling, the day the hottest yet.

'Him. The big bastard.'

'Good. Now go wait in the car. I'll drive you home shortly.'

A moment the bruised and battered thug hesitated then he was gone.

Falcone started talking, not that Peroni heard much. He couldn't avoid Teresa Lupo's miserable stare, the one he always got when he'd done something wrong. Even Silvio Di Capua looked out of sorts. The mission was delicate, dependent upon their invisibility. And he'd broken cover so brutally, for them with so little reason.

'Besides,' Falcone finished, 'it's time we spoke direct to your side. Face to face.' He hesitated. The visitor hadn't even given a name. 'You are?'

'Rocco Bergamotti. I'm the son of the man who's seen fit to offer himself to you. If anyone else in the 'ndrina knew you were here.' He raised his shoulders in an expression of dismay. 'We risk everything and you fools play games like this.'

Teresa's judgmental stare turned on the newcomer at that point. 'You took Nic. You and your sister. You played those games with Rosa. Terrified her.'

Another shrug. 'And now the Indian woman's gone.'

'You're watching us.'

'Of course they're watching us,' Peroni snapped. 'In our shoes . . . wouldn't you?'

Rocco sighed and took a half-smoked cigar out of his jacket pocket, then lit it and waited.

'I'm sorry,' Peroni said. 'I shouldn't have hit him. I tried to warn him off. If he had half a brain he'd have listened.'

'If I had half a brain I'd cut you all loose. Get rid of that man you sent us. He still sticks out like a sore thumb.'

Peroni nodded at the windows to the terrace. 'He's out there now. Trying to catch a swordfish for you.'

Rocco grimaced.

'As if that's enough.' He leaned forward, frowned again. He'd already decided what he was going to do. Peroni understood that. All the same he had to pretend this was some kind of negotiation. 'So how am I supposed to handle this? We tell you to keep your heads down. Stay anonymous. Instead one of you beats up a foot soldier of mine. It's not something we can ignore. Ordinarily . . .' He smiled at Peroni. 'You're a big guy. I'd have set three on you. Just to be sure.'

'Three?' Peroni asked. 'They'd need to be good.'

'They would be—'

'Enough of this.' Falcone was getting mad. 'We've been sitting here for days waiting on you to come up with a date. You've got an officer of ours—'

'You don't have the faintest idea how hard this is. We're offering you Mancuso. Do you think he hops in a cab the moment we send him an invitation? He plays games. Checks us out. Then, when – if – he decides he's coming gives us twenty-four-hours' notice if we're lucky. They're Sicilians. They don't own that island any more, not the way we own this place. They're nervous.' He shook his head and cast another dark glance at Peroni. 'I should throw this big bastard to the wolves, the rest of you along with him. And the guy you gave us.'

Falcone couldn't think of anything at that moment. Or Teresa. Silvio kept his head down. He was a backroom guy. This was probably as close as he'd ever got to a real-life hood and the sight seemed to petrify him.

Honour, Peroni thought. It meant something here, still.

'You haven't asked why I did it?'

Rocco laughed. 'He said you got pushy. It matters?'

'Pushy. Pushy? You think I look that sort?'

The Calabrian seemed interested.

'The woman over there in the bar,' Peroni went on. 'She had a husband. A fisherman. Paolo. Someone murdered him. Scratched his face with nails. Like a mark. Maybe he pissed off you guys. Wouldn't pay—'

'Paolo was one of ours,' Rocco cut in angrily. 'Don't talk about him like that.'

'What happened?'

'He got into an argument with some idiot from the 'ndrina in Locri. Over a bet. The moron killed him.' That shrug again. 'He paid. He won't be back. We're even.'

Peroni nodded. 'Paolo Gentile was one of yours.'

'Like I said.'

'So I guess that bar is too.'

'You people will never understand,' Bergamotti replied. 'You can't. We all own a little of everything here. This is our land. We share.'

Peroni thought about that and said, 'So that's why your friend in black kept pestering Elena Sposato for money she didn't have? For favours? That's why I caught him trying to rape her in that poky little storehouse they've got while her damaged little son sat crying on the beach.'

'What—?'

'All this crap about honour and how you guys are like some caring, responsible alternative regime or something . . . that's just bullshit. Because one of your small-time hoods can pick on a helpless widow and try to rape her. Would have too if I hadn't come along and dragged him off.'

'Gianni.' It was Teresa. 'I think that's enough.'

'No.' He got up. 'It's not even a start. Tell me, Signor Bergamotti. Or whoever you are. Is that what honour means round Cariddi? Some foot soldier of yours gets himself killed and it's just fine that one of your hoods goes round and makes his widow's life a misery? Taking what little money's she got? Drinking his caffè corretto for free? I guess she's just a woman. And they don't count much round here except for bed.'

The Calabrian puffed on his cigar and glared at him.

'If I'm wrong,' Peroni added, 'just say.'

'I need one of you,' he said as he finished the cigar and threw it out of the open window onto the terrace. 'A guest.'

'A hostage you mean?' Peroni said.

'A sign of goodwill. A guarantee you'll behave better in future.'

Peroni couldn't take his eyes off the man. That brief lecture about honour had affected him.

'And Elena Sposato?' he asked.

'Signora Sposato is the widow of one of our men. She'll be treated with all due respect. We do not let our people starve. Nor do we tolerate their abuse. By anyone.'

'Good—'

'You didn't hear me. I need one of you.'

Peroni rubbed his big hands and said he'd pack a case.

Rocco laughed. 'Not you. I got other plans for you.' He nodded at Falcone. 'And him. Your friend in our midst needs to kill more than a fish to win his honour. We'll organize a little theatre. No.' He smiled at Teresa. 'She'll do.'

'Not a chance,' Peroni told him. 'Not in a million years.'

'Gianni.' She got to her feet. 'If it's just a question of a few days with strangers I'm fine with it. Besides the atmosphere round here . . .'

'No.' It was Silvio who spoke up. 'You're needed here—'

'We're all needed! We're one down as it is.'

'I'm just handling email and phone calls. Anyone can do that.' The little technician looked terrified but determined all the same. 'If you're going to take anyone take me. It . . . it will be comfortable? Won't it?'

Rocco Bergamotti laughed. 'Good Aspromonte food. Coarse company. When this is over you'll have such tales to tell.' The smile vanished. 'Not that you'll tell them, of course. It will be as if it never happened.'

Teresa still didn't look happy but for all her squawking her deputy remained dead set on going. While she was in the middle of her rant about why he couldn't, Silvio walked out and came back two minutes later with a small bag.

'I don't suppose I can take my phone?' he added.

'No,' Bergamotti told him. 'No phones. Clean mountain air and a hard bed. A week I think at most. You'll lose some of that fat and see a different world.'

'Sounds like a holiday,' Silvio answered. 'More than this place.'

Teresa went and hugged him. 'You don't have to do this. We don't have to give this man what he wants.'

The Calabrian sighed and looked at his watch. 'Today we set these wheels in motion. Or not. He comes with me or it's best all of you leave this place directly. Nor will you see the friend we have again. That will be impossible. We've extended a great degree of generosity in your direction. A little gratitude is now in order.'

He waved his hands: you choose, the gesture said.

'I've never been without a phone,' Silvio moaned. 'Not as long as I can remember.'

'Maybe it's time to start. Go wait outside in the car. It's the red Alfa.'

One more embrace from Teresa, a long one and she was close to tears, then Silvio Di Capua was gone. Peroni didn't know what to say any more. This was his fault. All of it.

Bergamotti waited until the front door closed then pointed at Peroni then Falcone. 'This afternoon you'll take a drive. To Reggio. Give me a phone number. I'll send you a map.'

Immediately Peroni scribbled his on a piece of paper and handed it over. This was his game now.

'I'll call in a little while and give you your orders,' Rocco Bergamotti added. 'If you know what's good for you, for that little guy outside, that man of yours on my boat . . . you follow them. Every last detail. This is my world you're in. My rules. My say-so. Do this right and the guy we've christened Maso Leoni will be bringing you good news very soon. Get it wrong and I got nothing to offer. Nothing you'll like. You understand me, policemen?'

'They do,' Teresa said and didn't wait to see him go.

Falcone sat in a chair, brooding. Peroni went back to the terrace. The bar across the beach was open. Elena Sposato was out front on the phone. She saw him then she turned away and he wondered what he'd truly done.

Upstairs he heard noises and he knew straight off what they were. Teresa clearing his things out of their bedroom, throwing them into the tiny space with a single bed next door.

Five sharp barbs bit into the fish's side, deep into the silver flank behind the gills. Someone cheered. The creature seemed to let out a sharp high scream, twisted once in agony trying to free itself, failed, then arced like an acrobat, diving deep beneath the boat.

Rope began spinning out all around his ankles, feeding into the thrashing waves.

'Jump, you fool,' Santo yelled as the crew began to flock around the loops left on the deck.

Just in time he managed to hop into the air as the line was about to snag his legs. The remaining loops vanished over the side, dragged into the sea by the fleeing swordfish. Breathless, looking at the bright shower of bubbles rising from below, he leaned over the passarella and tried to understand what was happening beneath the vessel.

'Cut the sightseeing,' the skipper yelled. 'Get over here. We're not done yet.'

He took the horizontal iron ladder step by unsteady step back to the deck. The rope was still spinning out, the speed diminishing though none of the men came near. It was still

fast enough and rough enough to tear the skin from your hands
or tug the unfortunate over the side.

The man atop the tower clambered down, patted his arm,
then offered him a draft from a hip flask. He took it: a bitter,
medicinal shot of booze caught fire in his throat and mingled
with the salt spray there.

'Took me five goes before I struck good,' the man said,
beaming at him. He had crooked, tobacco-stained teeth, a good
few missing. 'You got him second time. Shame about the lady.
She'll be looking for a new mate now. If only . . .' He glanced
at the rope still spinning slowly over the side. 'If only those
barbs of yours will hold.'

The rope was thick, the colour of the tobacco on his teeth, and
tethered to a winch by the foot of the tower. All the men were
waiting for the moment the length ran out and he understood
immediately why: at that point the harpoon might break free from
the fish's flank and the catch escape, wounded but at large.

'If you know a prayer,' the captain muttered, 'that fish is
yours . . .'

No prayers, he thought. None at all. But then the rope
tautened, shuddered and groaned like the string of a gigantic
instrument played by an invisible bow. No one breathed for a
second or spoke a word.

It held.

'Silent prayers are the best,' the skipper declared with a
grin. 'Now . . . take a break. You look done in. The rest of
the work is ours.'

The best part of fifty minutes it took. The injured swordfish
fought to begin with, so hard it rocked the boat from side to
side at times. As the minutes passed its strength waned. A
good half hour after he first stabbed the harpoon into its side
they saw it again, a gleaming shape, moving sluggishly beneath
the limpid surface, a red stain of blood leaking in its wake
like ink behind a paintbrush.

Not long after they pulled the creature to the boat side. A
good fish, the skipper said, big for a male, powerful and still
angry. Two men took to the sharp sword with oily clothes
while another stabbed claw hooks into the side and landed the
still-thrashing creature on the deck.

The skipper seemed to be reciting some kind of prayer. He thought he heard the words 'San Marco è binidittu' in coarse Calabrian. After that the coup de grâce was delivered with a swift, sharp blade, straight behind the neck into the brain. The fish had beautiful eyes, clear as glass, a dark and lustrous blue. They dulled at that. Then, covered in blood and slimy scales, the captain bent down and with his four outstretched fingernails carved a lattice cross on the bright silvery blue of its right cheek.

After which he stood up and sniffed the air. 'I'm told we must return you to the shore, foreigner. You've other duties to fulfil. What the Bergamotti want they get. We've hours left in this day and other gladiators to pursue. Come . . .'

He put a boot on the fish's flank and yanked the harpoon barbs out of the flesh. Dark blood spilled from the wounds as the man bent down, went to work with his knife once more, and carved out a hunk of pale, fresh flesh from the nearest laceration in the shining skin.

'Here,' he said, holding out the lump. 'If you want to be a man of Cariddi you eat this now. Not the skin. Just the flesh. Up to you.'

He bent down and washed the blood off in a bucket of seawater someone had scooped from the side.

'Come on, Maso,' Santo Vottari said, nudging his arm. 'This is no trick. Not some stunt we play on outsiders. Eat. Fresh fish. The best pisci spata you'll ever get.'

It was the size of a chicken's egg. He was in his teens when he'd infuriated his father by telling him he was a vegetarian. Barely a piece of meat had passed his lips in all that time.

But Costa wasn't here, not now. The swordfish at his feet, its blood dripping back into the ocean whence the creature came, the man who was beginning to think of himself as Tomasso Leoni brought the morsel of its pale and slippery flesh to his lips and took it between his teeth.

'Taste good?' the captain asked.

'Tastes wonderful,' he said and took another bite.

They all watched him, approving or so it seemed.

'You could make one of us maybe,' the skipper said with

another slap of the arm. 'In a year or ten. Now.' Someone
started the engine. 'The shore.'

Silvio sat in the back of the scarlet Alfa determined not to say
a word. Just listen. The man in the passenger seat in front of
him was called Fredo. He gathered that from the driver, Rocco,
the one who was in charge. Fredo sounded worried, scared
maybe, from the moment they set off.

Then the car worked its way along the winding local road
that led beneath the main north-south *autovia* and found a
narrow track up into the hills. There were homes for a while,
little more than shacks, most with tidy gardens full of summer
vegetables: tomatoes, peppers, aubergine and the long gourd
they liked in the south, the snake courgette some called it, the
*cucuzza*.

It all seemed so mundane. Like somewhere in Campania,
the area he came from. Where his mother still lived; not that
he visited as much as he ought. But this seeming normality
was, he understood, an illusion. Soon the shabby bungalows
vanished and in their place came wild and rocky hillside, the
track forever winding its way upwards, past hairpin bends that
leaned over dizzying chasms and left him clutching at his
stomach. Rocco drove so fast the car lurched towards the edge
from time to time. This was, he felt, deliberate. He was angry,
with Peroni but with the man in black too. And Fredo felt that
anger.

Thirty minutes in they stopped on a bend that had been
widened as a passing point. There was nothing around but
bare mountain, a few trees and, on the left, a dizzying way
down, a dry torrent, a line of rock and shingle that would
surely be overflowing in winter when the snows came.

Rocco switched off the engine then turned to the man in
the passenger seat beside him and said he wanted a
conversation.

'Sure, boss,' Fredo said but nodded at the back of the car.
'With him around?'

'He's a guest. I'll be driving him to his manutengolo soon.
We'll feed him. Keep him. Give him a little holiday in the
hills for free.'

'Thanks,' Silvio said and the man behind the wheel barely noticed. 'Do you want me to step out?'

'No. Don't. Fredo. Elena Sposato's the widow of one of our men.'

Nothing.

'You know that, don't you?'

'Yeah.'

'Paolo was a good guy. Should still be here.'

'Yeah.'

'And you've been picking on her. Getting money out of her. Messing with her. She's got nothing anyway, her and the kid.'

Silvio watched as the man in black shrank in front of him, crouched down in the front of the big Alfa, put his hands together as if to pray.

'I'm sorry, boss. I'm really sorry. I'll make it right. I'll pay her back. You tell me what you want.'

Rocco wound down the window and lit his cigar again then sniffed the mountain air. 'You get no wages for the next two months. Every cent goes to her.'

A pause then: 'Sure.'

'You don't go near Cariddi. You can go back to running crap to the immigrants down the beach. Hell. I ought to put you shifting that shit yourself.'

Fredo didn't say anything at that. Not a word.

'Also,' Rocco added, 'you can get the hell out of my car and walk all the way home from here. I'm sick of the sight of you. The smell of you. Damn. I don't believe I'm not doing more than this.'

'Gonna take me hours, boss,' Fredo whined. 'From here.'

'I know where we are. I know what I'm saying. Get out and start walking. You might get home before dark. If not who cares?'

A pause then Fredo said, 'She's a widow. Looked lonely. Pretty woman when she could be bothered to smile. I was just offering company—'

'Get the hell out of here!' Rocco bellowed and for a moment he looked ready to stamp out the cigar in Fredo's eye. He leapt across and grabbed for the passenger door. 'Get your stinking hide gone . . .'

Silvio had rarely seen anyone move so fast. The man in black tore off his seat belt and slid outside the Alfa, then stood on the dirt road by the hairpin bend shaking, looking ready to piss himself. After that he kind of saluted, turned and began to shamble slowly down the road, back the way they came.

Rocco was looking at him in the mirror. 'That big friend of yours.'

'Peroni. Gianni Peroni.'

'He's got a temper.'

'I never saw that before,' Silvio replied. 'It's like we're different people here.'

Rocco nodded. 'But he's a smart guy. He knows what's best. He'll do the right thing.'

'I don't know anyone I'd say that about more,' Silvio told him honestly. 'He's the straightest man I know. That's why he . . .' Rocco's eyes were burning in the glass. 'That's why he couldn't do nothing,' Silvio went on. 'It wouldn't be right.' He was glad he said it, glad he didn't back down.

'Maybe not. All the same you do as you're told.'

With that he brought the Alfa back to life, jabbed the pedal, made the powerful engine start to growl and hum. Then looked behind, through the rear window, beyond Silvio, at the man in black ambling down the road, hands in pockets. Fredo was by the corner, beyond him nothing but the blue horizon of sea and sky over the ravine below.

'The little shit,' Rocco murmured, then stabbed his foot on the pedal and hit reverse. The scarlet machine screamed back on the rocky, pebbled road, angling towards the edge above the chasm. Silvio closed his eyes and tried to remember what it was like to pray.

The man in black screamed as the rear end took him, screamed more when he realized where he was headed. Then he was gone and Rocco was fighting to get the car back into gear as the wheels fought for purchase on the crumbling edge of the hairpin.

Silvio looked. He had to. There was nothing but space beyond the shrieking wheels, a ragged gap in the mountainside, trees and maybe a stream far, far below. And a black shape wheeling downwards, arms flailing, body bouncing

against the craggy sides. Until finally the man called Fredo
vanished into the trees that ran in a crooked line down the
little valley towards the coast.

The tyres took. The Alfa pulled away. Rocco seemed to
settle into a steady pace after that, as if it had all calmed him
somehow. Ten minutes later they stopped in the middle of a
high plain. Prickly pears struggled by the side of the road
alongside patches of flowers he didn't recognize. There was
what looked like a shepherd's hut made of coarse stone at the
end of the track. A man in rough clothing was standing there
leaning on a stick, a huge dog by his side, an alpine hat on
his greying head.

'It's not exactly five stars,' Rocco said. 'But then this isn't
a holiday. For any of us. His name's Mirco. I hope you like
eating meat. He does.'

Silvio Di Capua didn't need to hear more. 'Thanks,' he said
and got out.

'Hey, Maso. You got stupid people in Canada too?'

Calabria as well.

Rocco had made sure Santo Vottari saw very little of what
had happened outside the back street bar in Reggio. Two
men viewed almost entirely from behind. Then a brief performance. Finally their bodies, seemingly bloody on the grubby
ground. A scene from the kind of tragedy that might have
played out on the Greek stage hereabouts a couple of
millennia before. The Calabrians seemed good at play-acting.
They knew their lines, their props, could manage all the acts
and stages.

He'd done exactly as he was asked. Fired blanks, not at
Falcone and Peroni directly because a part of him wondered
if they were blanks. But they didn't even generate a tiny cloud
of dust. Rocco, thus far, was to be trusted it seemed. When
Santo scuttled off as ordered, a little puzzled but disinclined
to argue, Peroni and Falcone got off the ground, discarded the
heavy coats now stained with fake blood rubbed as Rocco had
ordered. Then looked round, brushed the dust off themselves
and wondered what came next.

'Next you go home and wait,' Rocco said. 'That was good.

Now they can see Maso here is one of ours. If I let him come and go no one will take much notice. He does my bidding.'

'Maso?' said Peroni.

'Tomasso Leoni.' He held out his hand. 'Pleased to meet you.'

'When does your man hand himself over?' Falcone demanded. 'Mancuso and the others? This is going on too long.'

'When we say,' Rocco replied and glanced at his watch. 'If all goes well in our discussions with the Sicilians, perhaps a day or two. We have their go-between here. He'll go home this evening. If he's convinced . . . Maso here will let you know.'

'Why the delay?' Falcone wondered.

'How long will it take for you to understand this? Because I want my family to come out of this alive. So you wait until I say. The locals would come tomorrow if my father summoned them. Mancuso isn't one of us. He's as cautious as a cat. Got reason to be, hasn't he?'

'True,' Peroni said. 'How are they treating you, Maso?'

'Well.'

'I trust Silvio will get the same.'

'Silvio?'

'He's enough to think about already,' Rocco cut in. 'Your men are our guests. Safe with us as long you two keep your heads down and your temper. You have my word. Now. Go home . . .'

One more glance around to make sure no one was looking.

'We got some money from the safe,' Peroni said, holding out the cash. 'Lots of interesting things in there.'

'We're busy people.'

'So I gathered. The African. Your slave. I gave him a wad and told him to get the hell out of here. An act of charity. It always bodes well, don't you think? I mean . . . we don't want witnesses. Your usual way of ensuring that doesn't work for us.'

Rocco took the cash. 'Plenty more where he came from. So long he's out of the way and silent that's fine with me. When there's news Maso will bring it. The day we move he can be the runner between us. Don't tell anyone until the last moment. Don't go near Elena Sposato. Don't make me think of you till I want to. Otherwise my patience may run out.'

'Sure,' Peroni replied. 'Leo?'

Falcone looked a little lost.

'I don't want tricks, Bergamotti,' he said. 'If you screw around . . .'

A sudden anger flared in Rocco's swarthy face. 'You Romans talk too much.'

'If—'

'Leo . . .' Peroni had his hand on Falcone's arm. 'It's time we left.'

Falcone was about to say something but thought better of it. The two of them walked back to their rented Lancia.

'That big man I like,' Rocco said as it drove steadily out of the estate. 'The other I don't know.'

Maso watched them leave. 'Why?'

'He seems . . . out of his depth. A dangerous habit round here.'

There was a charcoal grill set up in the piazza of Manodiavolo when they got back, a table with a white lace cloth by the side, Lucia fussing over the plates and cutlery, Gabriele Bergamotti drinking wine in a silence. Vanni was roasting long red peppers and aubergine on the embers, turning them until the skin was black, then putting them on foil, peeling them, pouring dark olive oil on the pulp. Slices of raw swordfish from the catch and fresh bread accompanied it.

Santo Vottari broke off from lugging wood to pat Maso on the arm and say congratulations.

'One last thing and you're a man of honour,' he said with a wink. 'Almost one of us. In twenty years maybe . . .'

'One last thing?'

Lucia seemed to hear. She glared at Santo and he went back to the wood pile. The Sicilian, Sciarra, was there. From the sound of it he was advising Vanni on the imperfections of his charcoal, something that didn't go down well.

Gabriele came over, added a few languid words of congratulations and said it was time to eat.

'Are you done with him?' Lucia asked, nodding at Sciarra. He was in conversation with Santo now. She didn't seem to like that idea.

'The Sicilian you mean? Or Rocco's idiot friend?'

'Sciarra.'

'I've told him we have a mass to be held in the chapel at a time that suits his uncle. His safety's guaranteed. After which we will talk business. That's as much as I can do. It's their decision now.'

Not long after Gaetano Sciarra left and they had a kind of improvised banquet. Raw swordfish, sharp and fresh with lemon juice, roast vegetables from the fire, bread and wine. He tried them all. He was the man they wanted now. Santo was allowed food from the spread but had to eat it with Vanni at a separate table by the old wellhead. Not that there was much talk between the old man, his children and their guest.

When Lucia was clearing plates from the table Rocco got up and told Santo to take a couple of days off. He wouldn't be needed for a while.

Santo didn't move. 'For nothing? I thought maybe we'd got some business coming. That Sicilian guy seemed to think so . . .'

'Leave the Sicilians to us.'

Santo nodded and said, fine. Then went off to look for the scooter that they kept at the stables down the hill.

Lucia didn't talk much at all. Except when all the fish was out of the way and they were eating prickly pear scavenged from the hills. Then she turned to him and whispered, 'You smell. Fish. And the sea. Which is not unpleasant but I think it's time you lose it.' She nodded at the palazzo. 'There's water inside. Cold as ice. Off you go.'

The light was fading as he came out of the bathroom, shivering from the cold water. A loud roar of the Alfa signalled Rocco driving out of the piazza, his father in the passenger seat. It seemed that Manodiavolo was left to Lucia, Vanni and him alone.

He felt tired, odd, different. A key had been turned, a lock freed. He was, if not accepted, at least no longer quite such a target of suspicion. Finally they seemed to be moving towards their goal, the defection of Gabriele Bergamotti and the capture of the mob kings he was luring to the chapel in the hills.

'Get dressed,' said a soft voice from the shadows. 'We're not done yet.'

He blinked and tried to peer into the dark.

'I'm naked.'

'Most people are straight out of the bath.'

'This habit of yours of wandering in and out of my room—'

'Whose room? This is our palazzo. You're our guest. I come and go as I please.'

There was a set of clean clothes on the bed. New, a designer brand he'd never have picked for himself. She'd been shopping for him again. He grabbed them, retreated to the bathroom and put them on.

Lucia was standing by the door when he came out. She was in a casual cream shirt and jeans looking very pleased with herself. A small purple leather bag hung over her shoulder.

'Is it the cocktail party now?' he asked.

That made her laugh. 'I don't do that kind of thing. Any more than you.'

'Back in Canada,' he said carefully, 'cocktail hour's a ritual.'

She came right up and looked him square in the eye. 'It's alright. There's just you and me here. Vanni's downstairs but you can forget about him. Rocco's off to see some woman of his in Reggio. My father . . . well, he's gone as well. I don't know where and I don't want to. That creep Vottari too, thank God. You can . . . you can drop the act for a little while. If you like.'

But that, he thought, was dangerous. It was allowing that it was an act at all.

'Where are we going?'

She didn't look at him when she said, 'For a little walk.'

'One last thing . . .'

'Santo Vottari's a loud-mouthed idiot. Come on.' She took his arm. 'Let's get it done.'

There were a couple of solar panels on the palazzo roof but they powered nothing more than a few bulbs downstairs. The rest of the building was given over to candles and oil lamps that now lit the stairway and hall, sending a warm, soft aura swimming over the crumbling plaster, the stone floors, the lighter spaces on the walls where paintings must once have hung. Portraits of a lost family of aristocrats ruling Manodiavolo he guessed, the Abenavoli. Long dead from one more Aspromonte feud.

Hands running through dust on the ancient balustrade, they descended and walked out into the empty piazza by the church. The last of the summer sun dappled the snaking, shimmering channel that stood between Calabria and Sicily, a distant neck-lace of street lights defining the shore. Across the strait stood the mound of Etna, the only clouds around clinging to its side like needy children, the red haze of its volatile summit a dim rim of fire against the darkening sky.

She took his hand for a moment and he felt her fingers close on his.

'There are better sights than this,' she said then led him out by the church, past the cypresses in the cemetery. The night was alive to the sound of insects, perfumed by herbs and trees and mountain flowers. They wandered through a tangle of trees, onto a track just wide enough for a mule with evidence that Silvio or Benito or both had been here recently. Five minutes later the path ended at a flat stone platform that served as a solitary panoramic gallery over the coast. As day turned to velvet night, the sky a painterly chiaroscuro somewhere between dark blue and black, they sat together on the hard rock, staring at the sea. They were, Lucia said, above the point where the Ionian ran into the Tyrrhenian, where east met west in front of them.

'That way,' she said, aiming a long finger back to the coming darkness, 'five hundred kilometres for the birds, lies Patras. Greece. Where most of us came from in the beginning. South—' the straight and certain finger moved – 'six hundred kilometres and you're in Tripoli. Africa.' Another turn and he couldn't stop watching the way her raven hair shifted in the scented breeze. 'West. Beyond Etna. Then . . . I don't know . . . a thousand kilometres or more and you're in Spain. When I was a kid I used to sit here on my own, listening to Rocco shooting birds and anything that moved, imagining all those places. Imagining I'd visit them one day. And never come back. Then Mamma died. Everything changed.'

He didn't know what to say.

'I'm sorry. I shouldn't harp on about that.'

'Say what you want,' he told her. 'I'm happy listening.'

She shuffled closer to him. 'You are, aren't you?'

'You're a good talker. Who wouldn't be? Why Capri?'

'Because it's little. Because it's an island. They can keep an eye on me there. Not that I need it any more. My wild days are over. I am old. I am tamed.'

He didn't speak.

'You're supposed to tell me I'm not old at all.'

'I didn't want to argue.'

'You're very different. I don't meet different men. Funny.'

'But why Capri?'

Lucia wrinkled her nose. The scar on her cheek had a new texture, a different aspect in the moonlight. It didn't bother him in the least. The mark was like the tattoos, a sign of age, of experience and pain borne in earnest.

'To try to find who I am. That's what hermits do, isn't it?'

'I don't know.'

A laugh then: 'You're the worst liar I've ever seen. That's different too. Don't try it round my brother.'

She opened her bag and looked inside. There was something in her face he couldn't read. Doubt. Regret perhaps.

'You killed a fish.'

'I did.'

'You pretended you'd killed your friends.'

There seemed to be nothing she didn't know and he wondered again: who was the second-in-command here? Rocco or her sister? 'Your brother said I should. I didn't have much choice. Neither I suspect did they.'

'No. We don't offer people choices. Only certainties. Do this. Do that. Obey. Or else. This man you know . . .'

'What man?'

'Nic Costa.'

Still the tricks . . . 'Never heard—'

'Sshh . . .'

She shuffled right up to him, placed her fingers over his mouth.

'I told you already. We're alone. No need for lies. Not . . . here.'

He'd been remembering Rome at that moment, the time his wife died. Scarcely a day passed without that intruding into his thoughts. The santina had seen that so easily. Perhaps Lucia had the same gift. He knew why she had brought back that memory too. It was a recollection of how it felt to be near someone. The joy, the possible pain of closeness.

'I don't think anyone's ever safe,' he said.

'This little place is mine. Here, the two of us. We are. There's no need to play that game. You understand? Nic? Nic?'

He picked up a pebble and threw it over the edge of the rocky platform. Like a kid he guessed.

'You're not very good with women, are you?'

'Ah. You noticed.'

'Maybe you just picked wrong.'

'No.' He shook his head. 'Not that. Never that. Well . . . rarely.'

Lucia hunched up her knees, wound her hands round them. The tattoos weren't so garish in the gentle twilight. 'Go on.'

'Things didn't work. I tried to make them. I couldn't. I dreamt I could. But it didn't happen.'

Her eyes were closed then, a smile on her face, and he thought he could look at that for a long time. Just look.

'Dreams,' she whispered. 'When I was little I used to sleep out here sometimes. To see the sun rise. My father always said the wolves would come for me. They never did. I heard them though. I heard their lonely cries. They didn't scare me. Then I'd come again in the evening and watch it vanish into the sea. Like the sky was on fire and that big blazing ball was dousing itself at the end of another day the way it had to. I used to read the old stories in Grandfather's book. There was one about Helios, the sun god, who drove his chariot across the earth to bring us light, day in day out. I'd dream that one morning he'd come down from the heavens and take me. Let me ride with him back up into the stars, beyond the moon, beyond everything. Live forever in a place where there was no pain. No hate, no fear, no death. The things kids dream.'

'Soon this will be over. You can be back in Capri.'

'Where I will return to being a hermit. What about Nic Costa? Tell me about him.'

What to say? He never thought much about himself. There was always the job, the cares and worries of others to occupy his days.

'He gets up. He goes to work. He comes home.'

'On his own.'

'Maybe.'

'No.' She shook her head very firmly. 'Not maybe. The lonely recognize each other. It's one of the few gifts we have.'

She was taking something out of her bag. He couldn't see what. 'What's he thinking now? This absent Roman?'

There was a pen and a notepad in her bag. He took them and scribbled out his private number on the page then put them back.

'That one day he'll go back to Capri. Maybe see a little villa near where a cruel emperor once killed men for no good reason. Perhaps find someone there he'd like to meet again. In different circumstances.'

'That's a nice dream,' she whispered, pulling back. 'Do you like chocolate?'

'Not much.'

'Romans are so strange.' A bar of something came out of her bag. 'This is from Modica in Sicily. It's like the Aztecs used to make. No one else sells chocolate like this. With cinnamon.' She broke off a piece and placed it in his mouth. 'If you hate that we have nothing more to say to one another—'

'It's delicious,' he mumbled. And it was: grainy, hard, dry and full of spice.

'Something nice before something not so good.'

Now she was holding a short knife, its sharp point sparkling gold in the dying sun. And a piece of card.

'There's one last thing that has to happen. If you're to be a man of honour they all can trust. I'm sorry. You must bear a mark. It's going to hurt a little. I wish . . . My father should be doing this but he had to go away. He said it was for me.'

She lifted up the card. 'Read this. You don't need to understand the words. They're . . .'

He took a quick breath, unable to take his eyes off the glinting blade.

'The words, Nic. The words . . .'

'"In this holy night, beneath the sky, the starlight and the shining moon I bless the holy chain—"'

'Hold out your right hand. Keep talking . . .'

'"I deny all previous affiliations . . . up to the seventh generation" . . . Ow . . . Ow!'

She'd cut him, a small crescent in the fleshy part beneath the thumb.

'I apologize. It was necessary. Be grateful. If it was my father he'd have gone much deeper. Keep talking. Say the words . . .'

He did. Not that they made any sense. The wound was short and not too deep, no worse than he'd had when working clumsily on his father's old Vespa back home. But it would be visible.

She peered at it and said, 'If this were real I doubt that'd do. A man's supposed to be marked for life but that'll be around for a week or two, no more. Still, enough.'

He sucked at the wound as she watched.

'Stop that,' she ordered. 'It's childish and highly unsanitary.' Then she pulled out a bandage and plaster too, took hold of his hand, staunched the blood with some muslin and began to treat the cut.

'There. And now your torturer kisses it better.' Her lips closed briefly on his hand. 'I'm sorry. We're primitives. We live by rituals. They're broken ones now. You've been initiated by a woman. That'll never do. If the likes of Santo Vottari knew they'd never believe it. You tell everyone it was my father. When they see the wound. You'll be one of us.'

Over the ocean to the west the golden ball of fire was almost gone. He'd never known a sunset like it.

'Trust no one but me,' she begged. 'Not Rocco. Not my father even. No one but me.' She took his hands. 'Promise.'

'I promise, Lucia Bergamotti. Which probably isn't your real name, is it?'

'Not true!' She pretended to be hurt. 'Entirely. Lucia is.'

'And Bergamotti?'

'A mask we hide behind when there are dangerous strangers about. We're still Greeks at heart. We like our disguises.'

'Am I a dangerous stranger?'

'Oh, very.' Her fingernails stroked his hand around the wound and he thought of the skipper of the felucca making his mark on the flank of the swordfish that morning. 'You Romans are such sweet talkers.' Abruptly she folded her arms. 'My real name is Lucia Ursi. So we're bears, in truth. Sometimes cuddly. Sometimes not. It's best . . .' She seemed to be wondering as if this was a mistake. As if she'd uttered some secret that might be damaging. 'Best you don't let anyone know I told you.'

Night had fallen so quickly it felt as if the world had turned upon its axis in a matter of minutes. The moon was out and made her smile so bright.

'Come,' she said, standing up, holding out her hand. 'My man of honour.'

By the light of her torch they wound their way back to Manodiavolo. There were fewer candles inside and no sound except Vanni listening to old music on his radio, something he did most nights.

'My uncle loves no one's company but his own,' she said and led him upstairs.

In the room she threw open the windows and stayed there in the moonlight.

The evening was full of the sounds of the wild. The screeching of hunting owls. Distant dogs or perhaps even wolves. Vanni's mules braying as if they were uneasy and someone was stalking their stables. The whirring of unseen insects and once, he thought, the rattle of something like quiet footsteps on the cobbles outside.

Suddenly she turned, came close and said, 'So do I say goodnight?'

'I . . .' He thought perhaps he was blushing. 'Lucia . . .'

'Lucia, Lucia, Lucia . . . I know my name. Even if you're not sure about yours.'

'Your uncle . . .'

'The only keeper I have is myself.' She laughed. 'God you are quite terrible at this.' Her fingers closed on his shirt and popped the topmost button. 'Does this awkwardness extend to . . . everything?'

'I . . . don't . . .'

'How would Maso Leoni behave? A wannabe Canadian hood. How—'

He kissed her then. She giggled as his fingers wound their way through her soft hair.

'He's not here. I am. And . . .'

Entranced he watched her throw off her shirt, arms over the head the way women did. Something he always marvelled at and he didn't know why.

'You talk too much,' Lucia told him. 'Kindly undress me. Then I'll do the same for you. After which . . .'

He didn't need asking twice. The fire was on them, a state of being without words, without real thought, occupied by nothing but physical pleasure and the sweaty heat of closeness in the thin and fragrant air of Aspromonte, beneath the filmy skein of the mosquito nets that tangled with their bodies as they moved.

Soon the only sounds left were their own: the rhythmic squeal of ancient bed springs, the damp, insistent joining of two bodies wound tight to one another upon the soft and sagging mattress. Finally two cries close to one another, wordless, desperate, full of an agonized joy like animals in the night.

Outside the window, hidden in the crumbling portico of the church, Santo Vottari listened to the sighs and moans from the window, wanting to light a cigarette, never daring. He wasn't supposed to be there. Rocco had told him to take his scooter down the hill to the little apartment the 'ndrina paid for on the edge of the city. But then Rocco had vanished himself, like the Bergamotti woman whose interest in the newcomer was obvious.

So he'd wandered off into the hills, lupara over his shoulder, wondering if he might come across a rabbit, a hare, a wild boar even, and maybe manage to bring it down with a clean enough shot that he could sell it on. But there was no game around, not until he saw the two of them winding their way to the stone platform at the edge of the eastern slope.

Spying on people was one of his pastimes. He liked to see what they got up to when they thought they were on their own. So he positioned himself in a stand of white fir and watched, getting hard, getting bitter just thinking about her. The way she touched him. Looked at him. This strange foreigner seemed to get such special treatment, and nothing Santo Vottari saw in the man could possibly merit it. Even with a fish to his credit and the murder of two men in the back alleys of Reggio. Not that Santo Vottari had witnessed him do it, or seen the guys himself. Yet here he was, a foreigner, right at the heart of the 'ndrina. So close to them that even the capo Gabriele had come out of the shadows and now appeared more interested in the newcomer than one of his own, a man who'd spilled blood over the years and risked his life for the clan.

The moment he saw Lucia cut Maso Leoni the way the capo was supposed to, he understood something here was very wrong. Though he'd keep that to himself for a while. It was hard to know with whom he might share that particular secret. Except, perhaps, the Sicilian Gaetano Sciarra who'd seemed more friendly than most of the Mancuso bunch and had left him a phone number to call if he should ever be around. Though that would have to wait. If Rocco heard he'd been talking to them directly there'd be hell to pay.

So, feeling coldly impotent, he'd tailed the couple back to Manodiavolo and hid in the shadows when they went upstairs. Then listened as they made love slowly, eagerly, taking their time.

Anywhere else and he'd have walked in when they were finished and laughed as he blasted them both with his lupara. He'd done his best to impress the Bergamotti bitch over the years. All to no purpose. They all knew she'd gone off the rails when her mother died in the local war. Got into drink and dope and banged any man who took her fancy on the coast until the family stepped in. In truth she was just one more Calabrian slut, the capo's daughter or not. A loyal soldier

ought to be good enough, ought to merit a step up after all
the years of service that began when he was thirteen acting
lookout, selling dope at school.

All the same there was nothing he could do. Harm her and
they'd chase him to the ends of the earth and cut him apart
piece by bloody piece.

Somewhere above in the bedroom of the old palace that
was supposed to be used for guests, hostages left to the
company of the old fool Vanni, nothing else, Lucia laughed.
Happy with the stranger who seemed to be leading the kind
of privileged life a man like him, a peasant from the hills,
good with a knife and a gun, not much else, could never
expect.

One day, Santo Vottari thought, should the opportunity arise,
I will make them look at me. I will lock that bedroom door
and make her scream and yell the way a woman should.

They'd finished. Then it sounded like they were about to start
again. This was more than he could bear. Quietly as he could
he wheeled his black Aprilia out of the piazza, sat on it and
freewheeled down the bumpy track. A hundred metres down
the road he turned the key so the little scooter coughed into
life, its headlight cutting through the darkness as he trundled
slowly, bitter and indignant, down to the coast.

# PART FIVE
## The Sicilians

### Calabrian Tales

### Chapter XVI: The Land Across the Water

The Strait of Messina is a narrow stretch of water, treacherous on occasion as we've discussed. Yet the world on the other side is so different to ours it may as well be an ocean. Sicily and Calabria are neighbours thanks to geography, nothing more. In temperament and in breeding we are races apart.

Calabrians cherish their Greek heritage; Sicilians are proud of their polyglot origins. True you will still find traces of Ancient Greece in places, but so many foreign invaders have crossed that soil since: Carthaginians, German Vandals, Ostrogoths, Byzantines, Arabs, Normans, yet more Germans the Swabians, the Spanish . . . And not long before I write the invasion of a very large number of Americans. All have left their mark in Sicilian faces, pale and swarthy, in blue eyes and green, in hair that may be black as the Africans or a Scandinavian blonde.

Relatives some may be from the arrival of those Catalan brothers three centuries ago, but even in the dark arts of criminality they differ too. We have the 'Ndrangheta, a quiet, self-effacing and purposeful fraternity that, in many ways, acts as a quasi-government in the shadows. The Sicilians are louder, more interested in money and power and women than the tedious task of keeping people fed. Their organisation is best called the Cosa Nostra – 'our thing' – though it is commonly referred to as the Mafia as well. Where Cosa Nostra comes from no one knows for sure. Mafia probably stems from the Sicilian adjective *mafiusu* which may mean 'swaggering' or 'fearless'. Or perhaps both.

Modesty has never been a Sicilian virtue. As evidence I must quote the historian Giuseppe Pitrè who wrote: 'Mafia is the consciousness of one's own worth, the exaggerated concept of individual force as the sole arbiter of every conflict, of every clash of interests or ideas.'

Also I must cite this bold statement, 'if by the word "mafia" we understand a sense of honour pitched in the highest key; a refusal to tolerate anyone's prominence or overbearing behaviour . . . a generosity of spirit which, while it meets strength head on, is indulgent to the weak; loyalty to friends . . . If such feelings and such behaviour are what people mean by "the mafia" . . . then we are actually speaking of the special characteristics of the Sicilian soul: and I declare that I am a *mafioso*, and proud to be one.'

These last are the words of the 'liberal' professor of law and son of Palermo Vittorio Orlando who was, albeit briefly, prime minister of Italy, a onetime Minister of Justice, and now, as I write these words in a nation recovering from one more terrible war, a Roman senator for life.

I trust you understand, dear reader. The food is good, the island beautiful in parts, the history, the monuments, the ruins more visible than our own. For all that the Sicilians will always have ideas above their station. One forgets that at one's peril.

Two days after he fled Reggio, terrified by the sight of men rising from the dead, Emmanuel Akindele found himself in the attic of a derelict warehouse on the southeast coast of Sicily, the steady blue of the Ionian just visible through the single filthy window at the end of the room.

The place smelled of damp and drains and dust. Across the water, over the bridge, was the island of Ortigia, a beautiful-seeming haven for tourists and locals who could afford the rent. But he was in the grim industrial area at the edge of the city, running south. Next door was a burnt-out petrol station and on the other side a wrecker's yard. Just along, on a patch of waste ground leading to the water, a circus had set up shop. Big tents, not much in the way of an audience that he could see, but there were beasts there. Maybe a miserable lion or elephant. Their cries rang out, night and day. He'd read somewhere that the Italians were, out of kindness, on the verge of banning animals in circuses. While all around them desperate men and a few women from distant, impoverished nations tried to eke out a living any way they could.

In Reggio he'd discovered he couldn't hot-wire a car as easily as he thought. The ones in Italy were newer, harder than the rusting lumps of metal back home. Terrified he'd be found and someone would ask why he'd run with so much money stuffed inside his jacket, he'd stumbled into the heart of the city, caught a bus to San Giovanni, taken the ferry to Messina, plucked up the courage to buy a ticket for the train.

All the way he'd looked at the faces around him. Especially the men. The way they stared back made him yet more scared. Six hours later, close to midnight, he found himself outside Fontanarossa airport which was pretty much closed. He knew he didn't dare brave it anyway, trying to pick up a ticket to Africa with nothing but cash. Might as well have put a sign over his head: something bad going on here. So he slept in a bus shelter overnight, trying to swat off the persistent, hungry mosquitoes, and in the morning made a call to the one man he knew living somewhere nearby.

He was desolate but he had money, more than he'd ever known in his life. That was worth something after all.

The man he'd called was his cousin Chuk, two years younger, smarter, always itching to come to Europe even when they were young. They'd made the journey to Libya together, Chuk dealing with the people smugglers, haggling, laughing with them, charming everyone he could with a smile that seemed to fill the whole of his big round face. He was a hefty guy, handy with his fists when they were needed. But usually they weren't. While Emmanuel held back, shy, scared, reluctant to engage with all these strangers along the way, Chuk walked in, put on that big grin, opened his arms wide, made loud, theatrical gestures, roared with laughter, killed all the fears and doubts before they could grow large and swamp them all.

Chuk was always going to make a go of things, wherever he fetched up. When finally they got on that last boat and had to be rescued off Lampedusa he was the one who somehow talked his way out of the camp, got in touch with men who knew the people smugglers, begged them into taking the two of them off that hot, cramped island, and give them a break. Anywhere. Doing anything. That was part of the deal.

A deal that, for Chuk, turned out to be Sicily where they got separated. Chuk to Siracusa and a tourist-fleecing operation managed by the local mob. While Emmanuel got sold off to the 'ndrina in Reggio. For three hundred euros. He'd learned enough Italian by then to understand just what he was worth.

Chuk had called a couple of times in Reggio, over the moon with the luck he'd had. Emmanuel hadn't wanted to disappoint him by saying he was stuck behind a grim bar for criminals feeding martinis to a marmoset. So they talked of all the opportunity there was in Italy and, on Emmanuel's part, how much money they could send back home. Not that Chuk mentioned Lagos much at all. This was his home now. There was no going back.

It took till the afternoon for him to get through so he spent a scary, solitary day hanging round the airport, making himself scarce. Then when Chuk finally answered he caught the bus south to Siracusa, a place he couldn't imagine. Tourists came here in their droves. He saw them walking out of the airport in their expensive clothes, getting into fancy cars, heading off for the fleets of coaches. But the bus to Siracusa wasn't so fancy. The one big sight along the way was familiar from home: a vast oil refinery clogging up the coast, kicking smoke and fumes into the air. Then he turned up at a poky little bus station, read Chuk's instructions from his phone, and walked his way to the edge of town.

It was late by then and the only spectacular thing around was the sunset, a burning ball of fire falling across the mountains and the bay. It took him the best part of an hour to find the derelict warehouse and then a good ten minutes banging on the door before Chuk answered.

'This a social visit, is it?' Chuk asked, a little wary.

'Couldn't take Calabria any more,' Emmanuel said. 'Just need a bed for a couple of days. That's all.'

Chuk looked him up and down then asked if they'd been feeding him. 'You look skinny and starved.'

Whereas he seemed happy and well-fed. 'I just . . .'

He couldn't say a thing at that moment. He knew he'd burst into tears. Seeing his cousin, hearing his voice, was a reminder of home, of the family he'd left behind.

They walked a couple of hundred metres down the road to a roadside stand where Chuk bought him a burger and a beer. After that Emmanuel returned with him, took the sleeping bag he'd indicated in the attic and, for the first time in ages, fell fast and soundly asleep.

When he woke the next morning Chuk was up already. Bright sunlight was streaming through the window, cutting a shaft through the dust and flies in the attic. Now it was day he could see the place was filled with cardboard boxes, half of them open, the contents neatly arranged on the hard timber floor. Emmanuel couldn't work out what was going on. The stuff was African of a kind: masks and gaudy baubles of necklaces and bracelets, carved wooden antelopes, lurid shawls and bandanas.

Chuk was sorting through them, putting them round his hefty arms, singing a little song.

'Hey, cousin,' he said when he realized his visitor was awake. 'Get dressed. You can use my other robe. It's a bit big for a sparrow like you but the girls will like it.' Then he walked over to the side of the attic and pulled out a long Arab-style gown in a garish leopard print. 'We gotta sell a hundred euros of crap before midday or the Sicilians gonna get pissed off.'

Emmanuel shook himself awake and asked where the bathroom was. It turned out to be a tap downstairs. 'Why are you dressed like that? No one dresses that way. Never seen a guy back home put on that crap unless he was on the stage.'

'We're on the stage,' Chuk said, not pleasantly. 'We been on it ever since we left Lagos. Don't you get it? You play your part, man. Or they're gonna come along and kick you off into the gutter. Put that thing on. Time to go.'

The two of them looked like clowns from the circus across the way. All the same they walked into Ortigia, across a pretty bridge, and began pestering tourists sitting outside the cafes there. Chuk was so good at this. Even if the people, couples mostly, never wanted to buy a thing – and most of them didn't – he had a way of making them feel entertained, almost grateful for his smiling attention. So he picked up something out of sympathy and those little numbers soon began to mount. By eleven they'd got a couple of free coffees and two cheap pastries from a cafe guy, another Nigerian Chuk knew down by the port. He'd made his hundred euros twice over. Emmanuel hadn't sold a thing.

They stopped in the main square by a spectacular cathedral and sat on the steps, Chuk always eyeing the passers-by, noticing the ones who glanced at the gaudy junk on his arm.

'What do you want, man?' he asked. 'I can't keep you. No one keeps someone else here. It's Italy. You earn or you starve or you beg.' He slapped Emmanuel's arm. 'And I don't see you being a good beggar either.'

He could feel the wad of notes slapping against him

underneath the stupid leopard print gown. 'I got enough money to pay my way back home.'

Chuk put his big head back and roared like a lion that just heard the best joke anyone had ever told. 'You been drinking on the quiet?'

'No. I mean it. I hate it here. I'd rather starve in my own back yard. With people I know. Not be a slave to these criminals.'

'You think I'm a slave?' He sounded angry.

'No. I didn't mean—'

'I got money. I get girls from time to time. This life is good if you just work at it. One day soon they'll get me a shop. All you got to do is earn it. Nothing else.'

But we're not the same, Emmanuel thought and didn't want to say.

'I miss Linda. I miss Jonny.'

Chuk scowled and shook his head. 'If you go home all the money you send back stops. You think they'll welcome you?'

'Yes. I do.' He hesitated. 'I said. I got some money. Enough.'

Chuk was staring at him. 'How much enough?'

'A couple of thousand. If you can find someone who'll get me there. A boat might be best. Back to the other side. I don't think . . . I don't like the idea of flying.'

His cousin leaned on his elbows and shook the rings and bracelets and leather belts he was carrying. 'None of this is mine, you know. It's theirs. If I steal a single thing they'd cut my fingers off . . .'

'It was a gift.'

'A gift? How much?'

He was never good at lying and besides Chuk had a way of staring at you till you told in any case. 'Five thousand. You take a thousand for yourself. Just get me out of here. I don't care how.'

He didn't much like Chuk but he always trusted him. They were family and family counted. Besides . . . how many options were there?

'You're a good man, Emmanuel,' his cousin said, patting his knee, staring at him with those genial brown eyes that seemed to charm everyone. 'You should never have made this journey. It wasn't for you.' He laughed. 'Any more than selling shit to tourists.'

'No.'

'Go back to the warehouse. Wait for me there. I'll see what I can do. Tonight we'll go and eat somewhere good. Celebrate you going back. I'd do it myself, you know. If I could earn a living there like I do here. Can't. Just can't.'

They got up outside the duomo of Ortigia, two tall black men in exotic costumes, and embraced in a way that made a few passing tourists stare. Then, grateful a corner had been turned, Emmanuel walked to the derelict warehouse on the edge of town and waited.

Chuk returned at eight that night, all smiles and good news. It was arranged, he said. First thing in the morning someone would come to pick him up, take him down the coast to a port called Pozzallo. From there he'd catch a fast catamaran to Malta where a man would meet him, arrange a passage to Alexandria and then a flight to Lagos. The journey would cost the best part of three thousand euros, not counting his own cut.

'So,' he added, 'you pay me now and from that I'll take you for a meal. A good one, cousin. Who knows when we'll meet again?'

The food was the best part of two hundred euros, more than he'd earned in Reggio in a month. Chuk ate and drank heartily: lobster, squid, exotic fish Emmanuel had never seen before, lots of Sicilian wine, then strange bitter drinks and sweet cannoli filled with ricotta. He didn't have much of an appetite but Chuk kept forcing drinks on him. So a little woozy and confused, his stomach churning from the strange rich food, he'd gone to bed on the sleeping bag and woken with a stinking hangover.

The bright sun was cutting a shaft through the dusty windows. Two men stood there, arms folded, outlined by its beams, looking down at him.

'Is it time to go?' he asked, still drowsy.

His eyes focused.

'Not quite,' said Santo Vottari. 'The Zanzibar misses you,

Emmanuel. I miss you. That stupid little monkey too. Screeched so much when I went there yesterday I took it out back and drowned the thing. The black guy we got in your place just doesn't have your touch. So . . .' He crouched down on the floor and smiled. Chuk was in the corner, putting on his robe, riding his rings and bangles and tourist crap up his arms as if nothing had happened at all. 'What's up?'

Two more days passed, two more hot and sleepless nights. That first time they slept together they woke to an empty Manodiavolo. Vanni was working somewhere out in the perfumed bergamot orchard down the hill. Rocco had stayed with his friend on the coast. Gabriele was Lo Spettro once more, gone from the place, where she wouldn't say and Vanni, when he finally returned, seemed not to know.

The hours were empty but delightful. He wanted to know who she was and how this place made her. So the two of them walked the hills where she showed him the places she'd discovered as a child. Empty caverns filled with bats, salamanders and spiders as large as any he'd ever seen. Ravines where waves of pink oleander were in full bloom and spindly tamarisks ran down the river bed. Dense woods of holm oak and pine, beech martens and black squirrels scurrying in front of them across the forest floor. Once, stopping by a low tree at the edge of a mountain torrent, she shrieked with laughter and pointed out a snake, more than a metre long, lounging in the branches.

'A *cervone*, city boy. Remember the name. The calmest, most kindly creature you'll find hereabouts. Look.' She extended a long finger towards its black-striped head. The serpent's eyes glistened back at her, a forked tongue flickered, and he waited for it to strike. Then the creature simply yawned, wound its tail more tightly round the branch, and climbed a little higher.

Lucia watched entranced and said, in a reverent low voice so as not to frighten it, 'The peasants call her *sacra* and believe she lives for decades, and when she's very old grows a horn and feathers on her head. *Ciao*, cervone!'

The snake slithered off into the upper branches at that.

A few words of the local Greek dialect she taught him. *Ilio* for the sun. *Silene* for the moon. *Agapi* for love. *Miso* for hate. *Zoi* for life. *Tanato* for death. Aspromonte didn't mean 'rugged' or 'acrid' mountain as the Italian suggested but came from the Greek *aspros*, white, and referred to the glistening mica sheets found in rock formations on the high crags. Or so she said.

'The only bitter things here are men,' she whispered in his ear when they stopped to eat prickly pear and cheese for lunch beneath a glade of fir trees over a panoramic view of the coast. 'And they're just travelling through.'

Weary, sated, full of the wild summer days they'd return to Manodiavolo as the sun began to wane. He'd no idea of the exact hour but always Vanni was there, grilling his peppers and aubergines on the charcoal they'd made, fetching coarse country bread from the oven. Never asking questions. Always pleased to see them.

After a while he'd leave them with a carafe of rough red wine, go to his room and listen to loud music: dance bands and jazz. And not long after they'd be in bed where different noises came to life.

On the third day after he killed the swordfish and pretended to murder Peroni and Falcone he woke alone, wrapped in crumpled sheets like a swaddled infant. The sun was high in the sky already. He checked his watch. Eight thirty. He hadn't slept this late in years. There were voices in the piazza. Gabriele was at the table in the centre again, Vanni by his side. Lucia came out from the palazzo with coffee, fruit and pastries. Then she looked up at his window and waved.

He did his best to bathe in icy water from the bucket and came downstairs. She met him in the hall, kissed him quickly, and said, 'Let's just pretend for now. My father . . .' She frowned. Her face seemed paler, careworn in the morning light, the scar more pronounced. 'Something's happened. He's got a lot on his mind.'

'What do you want me to do?'

'Be Tomasso Leoni. Be him every second of the day till this is over and I'm gone from here. Back in Capri where I belong.'

Another quick kiss then she ushered him out into the daylight where he blinked against the brightness.

'Maso,' the old man said and waved a welcoming arm. Rocco was there now, his scarlet Alfa parked in a lazy diagonal by the wellhead. 'We have coffee. We have cannoli. Fruit if you want it. Mountain ham.'

'He doesn't eat meat,' Rocco said straight off.

Vanni listened and nodded his head. 'Perhaps that's because he's Canadian. People are different in different parts of the world. Or so I'm told. I've never set foot outside Calabria as my brother here knows. It seems I'm not . . . wise enough for that.'

Gabriele reached over and took his arm in a strong grip. 'And what would you do if you travelled? Who'd look after this place? Who'd deal with those mules of yours? They love you so much.'

Vanni gazed at him. 'They're donkeys. Call them asses. Not mules. You've spent too long away from Aspromonte.'

Rocco grunted and said, 'Give them to the Sicilians and they'll turn them into mortadella.'

'I'm fine with fruit.' Maso sat down. Lucia came over and poured him coffee. 'What do you want me to do today? Go fishing?' He hesitated. 'Go hunting.'

Gabriele turned to his brother and suggested he take a look at the animals. Vanni hesitated for an instant then wolfed down one final cannolo, got the message, and wandered off to the abandoned warehouse by the church, a place he used for storing all manner of things, from grain and wood to an ancient, rusty motorbike.

'He knows when he's not wanted,' the old man said, watching him go. 'If only all my family were as obedient and biddable.'

Rocco stared at the table. Lucia patted her father's head and said, 'We're an awkward bunch. I wonder where we get it from.' And left.

There was a long silence over the cannoli and the coffee. Then Gabriele turned to his son and told him to try calling the Sicilians again, then the neighbouring 'ndrine. A string of names followed, easily, glibly, some he recognized, some he didn't: Canale, Ficara, Saraceno, Corigliano.

'Reassure them the summit will happen any day. Tell them they are in my thoughts as always. We'll keep our brothers safe.'

Rocco didn't move. 'If we have to say all that they'll get suspicious.'

Instantly, Gabriele snapped. 'They're suspicious already! They loathe the Bergamotti for who we are. Do as I say. Go to the office in Reggio. Make yourself visible to the men. We'll need them soon enough.'

With a grunt the younger man left and headed for his car. He revved the engine needlessly, and left in a cloud of smoke and dust.

'My son understands nothing,' Gabriele grumbled as the Alfa vanished noisily down the hill. 'All his life the Bergamotti have been the principals in the 'Ndrangheta in these parts. The cradle of the clan. Everyone pays us respect. More than that. A cut of all they earn. Or steal . . . so you'd put it. He thinks we'll live that way forever.'

This wasn't the moment.

'I think you should leave all this till later. When we get out of here. There'll be time to talk then. We can get everything down for the record.'

'The record . . .' Gabriele grabbed at a bottle of grappa on the table, swilled a few drops in his coffee cup and drank them down. 'What does the record say of men like me? We robbed. We killed. We looked after our own when no one else could be troubled to care. And then we died. I . . .' He blinked, looked ill for a moment. 'I do not wish to end my life in jail, young man. I will not. Gasping on a hospital bed in some hellhole prison in Naples or somewhere.' He jabbed a long finger at his broad, full chest. 'I've mediated in wars you people never knew about. I've saved good men who would otherwise have slaughtered one another over slights barely worth a mention. Why do you think they follow me? Someone who's sick? Tired. Worried for his children. Because of what I was. Not what I am. When they know . . . a wolf scents weakness. It has the smell of meat.'

He finished the grappa. A heady cloud of alcohol wafted

across the table, harsh against the herb-filled mountain air. 'You asked why I'm doing this. Do you not understand? I have no choice. None whatsoever. Lo Spettro they call me. Like I'm a ghost. A spectre no one gets to see. But this ghost's going to die one day and when that happens this all changes. My son's a headstrong fool who wouldn't last six months before one of his underlings, like that Vottari bastard, came along and shot him in the face. My daughter . . .' His expression became more mild. 'Were she a man could take my place. As could my sister Alessia. They have the strength, the courage and the intelligence. But the Bergamotti will never be led by a woman. It's unthinkable. And Lucia has an . . . unfortunate history.' His eyes narrowed. 'Though I imagine you know that already.'

He said nothing.

'Don't worry, lad. She's an adult. A formidable, intelligent woman when she chooses. What she does with her time is her business alone. Insofar as it does not affect the family.'

'I can guarantee your safety and theirs,' he said. 'So long as you testify, you can live anonymously where you choose. Lucia and Rocco. Alessia too.'

He laughed. 'My sister will be in New York shopping on Fifth Avenue before I find a boat in Burano and begin to shoot some winter ducks. There's only one place Lucia will go. That villa of hers in Capri. I could have bought the whole of Cariddi for what I paid for that. Still, it's worth it. She's happy, finally.'

'And Rocco?'

The old man's mouth fixed in something close to a sneer. 'My son is fond of the foreign and the exotic. Cities where we have influence and money but no tradition or culture to embarrass him. Bangkok. Australia. Melbourne. We have interests going back there more than a century. Poverty chased us out of Aspromonte. There's nothing better to instil a little ambition in a man. Though in time another generation comes along and forgets the sacrifices of their elders.'

He leaned forward and hammered his fist on the table. 'When this happens you must get us out of here immediately. The locals will know this castle of ours has fallen. There'll be a bloody war to see who seizes it next. As for the Sicilians

. . .' He looked, for one short moment, frightened. 'They must never find us. I know you think we're savages. But we're mountain wolves who kill for good reason only. They're wild beasts who murder for amusement.'

One last swig of spirit then he gripped Maso by the shirt. 'These hills will run with blood. Can you make sure none of it is mine?'

'I can try.'

The man's eyes were grey, intelligent, fixed, hurt by something that was hard to imagine. 'I'm glad you didn't say yes. That way I would have known you lied. Still—'

'Gabriele! Brother!' It was Vanni leading one of his animals across the yard.

'What does the old fool want now?' The old man sounded tetchy.

Vanni marched up, breathless, excited. The donkey looked at the two men, seemingly astonished.

'Well?' Gabriele asked.

'The day? The day!' Vanni's eyes were shining with delight.

'What about the day?'

'It's so beautiful. I've bergamot to care for. My animals. This place.' He touched Maso's arms. 'We have a charming guest. And Lucia here too. I feel a sudden happiness. Don't you?'

He left it there. Gabriele glanced at Maso Leoni as if to say: a fool, you see?

'What of Lucia?' he wondered.

'Haven't you noticed? She's so . . . happy. I don't know when I've seen her this way. Not in years. Not since she was a child and her mother was alive.'

A shadow seemed to fall over them at that moment. The brief tension was broken by the sound of the front door of the palace slamming shut. She was marching out, a leather jacket on, a crash helmet in her hand, a smile on her face.

'Maso here can clear the table,' she said as she turned up. 'Your domestic slave has other duties.'

'What duties?' It was Vanni who asked.

'Rocco called. Something in the office. He wants me there.' The three men looked at her. 'It seems I'm needed for chores

other than washing up and waiting on the table. And you.'
She winked at Maso. 'And him.'

Without waiting for an answer she headed for the stables.

'Help her push that Vespa out,' Vanni said. 'I left the wagons
in front of it. Didn't think the thing would be moving for a
while.'

He caught up with her as she slid open the thick oak door.
The place looked like a vast barn inside. Big and airy, the roof
half torn away. Straw stood stacked up to the left, Vanni's
carts blocked the rest of the way. They still stank of smoke
and burned wood. Lucia ran a finger of her leather glove along
the side of the nearest, looked at him and said, 'You've learned
so many tricks here, haven't you?'

In the shadows he came up and held her. He would have
kissed her but she retreated.

'Why do you have to go?'

'We've an office in the city. An estate agency. We do sell
property from time to time. I'm the name on the lease. It's all
genuine. If Rocco—'

'I'm here to protect you. All of you. That's not easy if you're
somewhere else.'

She shrank from him. 'Rocco's my brother. He asked. That's
how this family works. Don't worry.' Her hand came up to
his face. The silver bracelet copied from the ancient original
he'd seen in the chapel in the hills, glittered in the sunlight
streaking through the ragged roof. 'Nic—'

'Don't call me that.'

'It's your name. There's just the two of us. Not play-acting
for a moment. Oh, poor Nic. Poor, poor Nic. He's scared . . .'

She laughed, in a way he hadn't heard before, and in that
instant he saw a glimpse of what she must have been like
when her father intervened and found a quiet life for her in
Capri.

'I lost someone once,' he said. 'It scars you.'

'So did I. So does everyone in the end.' She traced a finger
on her cheek. 'And I've got a scar already.'

In the dark he held her tight. Her hand went to his neck.
She relented and they kissed this time, slowly.

'I'll be back soon enough. Now be a good boy. Fetch my scooter. It's against that wall.'

Five minutes later he watched her ride steadily down the hill.

So did Gabriele.

So did Vanni.

Then the white-haired man at the table poured himself another grappa. And Vanni came over, tried to smile, and said, 'My brother told me to show you the lie of the land. The tracks. The ways in and out. The places men can park.' He hesitated then added, 'Where they can hide.'

He didn't respond.

'I don't know why, Maso. I'm the village fool. It's none of my business. But we'll do it.' He scowled. 'I am at his bidding here. And yours.'

Gabriele seemed lost in a world of his own.

'My stick's in the stables. Let's go find it. An old man can't walk these hills without a little help.'

The stick was there, in the junk not far from where they kept the scooter. But that wasn't why he brought him there.

'Here,' Vanni said, and opened a long wooden chest, recent, the timber still fresh and pale. 'Look.'

Inside were weapons. Rifles and handguns still in their wrapping, boxes of shells.

'I may be the family fool,' Vanni said, picking up the nearest weapon, looking at it briefly then putting it back in place. 'But I'm not blind. They never tell me what they have in mind. But should there be another war . . .' He aimed the pistol at the wall and made a sound like a child's 'kapow'. 'You should know that here is where it begins.'

For the second time that long, strange week Emmanuel Akindele told himself he was dead. Santo Vottari, the cruellest of the Bergamotti foot soldiers he'd had to deal with in the Zanzibar, stood over him in the attic of the derelict warehouse in Siracusa waiting on an answer.

Chuk wanted to get the hell out of there. To put his stupid costume on and try to sell useless trinkets to the tourists in Ortigia. Maybe pick up a girl with his quick smile and superficial charm. But the Sicilian who came with Vottari wouldn't allow that. There was something they needed to know here, and it occurred to Emmanuel that it was, perhaps, more than the motives of a Nigerian slave who'd absconded with the Bergamotti's money packed in a wad against his sweating skin. Which was where half of it was now, no more. He didn't know why he told Chuk he had five thousand, not the ten the big foreigner had given him. Chuk was family, his cousin. But he looked so at home here. Places changed people. He'd wondered if it had changed him. Now he knew.

'Sit,' Vottari ordered then grabbed him and forced Emmanuel onto a chair at a rickety table by the window. Chuk stayed in a corner, silent, the Sicilian eyeing him in a way that said: don't move, you are mine.

'I'm sorry, boss,' Emmanuel said as calmly as he could. 'I had to go. I couldn't take that place any more. It wasn't me. It—'

Vottari's hand came out and swiped hard across his face. He'd had only one beating from the 'ndrina and that was at this man's hands. Unauthorized perhaps. For the most part they didn't resort to violence with their tame underlings. It wasn't usually necessary.

'You ran all the way here—' Vottari began.

'To see my relative.' Emmanuel laughed. 'See. I am the stupid one.' Then to the shadow in the corner, 'Thank you, cousin. If you—'

'You can't turn up here like this,' Chuk yelled at him. 'I got responsibilities. Men to answer to.'

Men like these, Emmanuel thought. Vottari. The Sicilian who was watching everything and didn't seem to want to say a word.

'He says he got five thousand euros,' Chuk added.

'Here . . .' Emmanuel took out the wad inside his shirt and placed it in Vottari's rough hands. 'Take it. Five thousand. I saved that. Every day I spent working for you it took. Every little tip. I just . . .' He wasn't going to cry. He wouldn't let them see that. 'I just want to go home. I don't belong here.'

Vottari waved the wad and slapped it against his free hand. 'That's a lot of tips. I never realized we were so generous.'

'Chuk—'

'Your cousin called us.' They were the first words the Sicilian uttered. His voice sounded different. Cold and hard and strange. 'He didn't understand why you were here—'

'I had to,' Chuk muttered from the shadows. 'I had to . . .'

'You're the property of the Bergamotti,' the Sicilian added. 'In the wrong place. For what reason—'

'I'm no one's property. I want to go home!'

Vottari pulled up a chair, set it back to front, sat in front of him, grinning over his folded arms. 'But why now?'

He had to weigh his options. Did telling them place him more in danger? Was there anything that could make his situation worse?

'That safe of yours . . . those two guys opened it. The thing was full of money. Of guns and all kinds of shit that could have sent me to jail for years. No one sends money back home to my people. Not if that happens.'

To his surprise Vottari didn't strike out at that. 'You were paid to serve drinks. Keep a monkey happy and the rest of us. Not trouble yourself with business—'

'I didn't have a choice!'

Santo Vottari laughed, put out a hand and patted him on the head. An unfeeling, condescending gesture. 'Poor little black man. Comes all this way thinking he's headed for freedom. Don't realize he's going to be a slave. Can't take it when his masters kill some thieving bastards who come round to rob them—'

'Wasn't that,' Emmanuel snapped.

What to say. What to hide.

'We shot those jerks,' Vottari said. 'This new guy did it. Canadian. Made him a man of honour. Thinks he's something special. Messing with Lo Spettro's daughter. Just cos he killed two bastards in cold blood. While I've done worse, ten times worse, and what do I get? A call from my Sicilian friend here wondering why you're hiding out in Siracusa not waiting on your masters.'

'Wasn't that,' he hissed again. 'Wasn't that at all.'

'Then—'

'Dead men don't rise,' Emmanuel cut in. 'Whatever the

bible tells you. That's just another lie as well. Dead men don't rise!'

That took them aback. The Sicilian pulled up a chair as well and said: carry on.

He didn't so the stranger pulled out a handgun and put it to his temple. In the corner Chuk began to whimper. Still Emmanuel said nothing.

'He wants to bargain,' Vottari said eventually. 'Who'd have thought it? Our little black slave thinks he's got something so precious he really thinks he's good for that.'

'Yeah,' Emmanuel told him. 'I do.'

'Then . . .'

He was sick of being treated like a cowering idiot. 'Time you shut up and listen, man. I got things to say. Got things I want in return. I want to live. I want my money back. I want you to let me out of here. Go down that port Chuk talked of. Take a boat to Malta. Never see you bastards ever again. Not in this lifetime.'

The funny thing was they seemed to like the fact he was almost yelling at them, biting back. It won him a little respect maybe, even if it was the kind of regard a man got on the way to the grave.

'Better be good,' the Sicilian said.

'Dead men rising,' Emmanuel said. 'How much better you want than that?'

So he told them. About the way the two strange Romans in coats smeared fake blood on themselves when the new guy came and fired pointless shots into the trash and rubble by the Zanzibar wall. Fell to the ground, pretended to be dead as Vottari and the crimine, the big man of the 'ndrina, Rocco, came round to see.

And didn't move an inch until Vottari shuffled off when Rocco told him to get out of there.

He watched as their eyes opened in amazement and for the first time since he set foot in Italy felt a little proud of himself.

'What did Rocco do?' Vottari asked.

'He watched those dead men rise and laughed. Then they talked. Then I took myself out of there and ran. All the way to my lying, cheating cousin when I thought blood meant something. Stupid, huh?'

'Any of them say something about Cariddi?' Vottari demanded.

'No—'

'Something happened there,' he snapped. 'I know it. Not seen that grubby little bastard Rizzo recently. The restaurant guys say people been hanging round.' He was thinking. 'Two big guys. A woman. Romans. They were Romans, huh?'

'I think . . . I don't know.'

The Sicilian put an arm round his shoulder and hugged him, tight. 'My name is Gaetano Sciarra. I work for big people here. Grateful people. You're a good guy, you know that? You don't have to go back to Reggio. Sicily's sweeter. We treat smart people the way they deserve. You'll like it here.'

'I don't want to be here,' Emmanuel said, too loud, he thought, until he saw the stranger's face and then thought again: maybe not. He'd been craven ever since he set foot on Italian soil. Even grateful for a while. But he'd always worked and he'd never begged. Whatever happened now at least, he thought, glancing at Chuk in his stupid African clown costume, he'd kept some dignity.

'I take your point,' the man said.

They went to the corner to talk, quietly but not bothering to make sure he couldn't hear. He and Chuk weren't important. Something else, it seemed, was.

Mostly the discussion seemed to be about someone they called Il Macellaio, the Butcher, a nickname spoken in hushed fear, almost awe. Then the stranger walked to the window and made a call in a dialect-strewn voice so difficult Emmanuel could barely understand a word.

Santo Vottari sat at the table, arms folded, waiting. He was the subordinate here. Just like when he was with the crimine Rocco Bergamotti.

The call ended. Gaetano Sciarra came back and the two of them talked. It sounded like Sciarra was giving out orders. All the time Chuk cowered in the corner, that quick smile of his long gone, his big white eyes on the grubby timber floorboards of the dump that was his home.

'Well,' Sciarra said suddenly with a clap of his hands. 'This was a profitable, a fortuitous day.' He came back and his arm wound round Emmanuel's shoulder. 'We owe you for that, my friend. Owe you dearly. Santo. Give him his due.'

'What?' Vottari didn't like that. Money only went one way for him.

'I said give him his money back. You Calabrians gone deaf or something?'

The wad came out. Emmanuel grabbed it the moment he could with a quick low grunt of thanks.

'Santo's driving back to Reggio now. I guess you don't want to go with him.'

'Never setting foot in that place again. Never working in some bar. With some screaming monkey.'

'You're African, man,' Vottari snapped.

'Yeah,' Emmanuel retorted. 'We got monkeys everywhere. We grow up with them. They live in our houses. We eat the things. Sleep with them. What do you know about us? What do you care?'

He'd never spoken to any of them like that before. It felt good. Stupid maybe. But righteous.

'The man wants to go home,' the Sicilian said with a last squeeze of his arm. 'He's earned that. Get your things. Go downstairs. You can pick up that ferry to Malta from Pozzallo. Your cousin can drive you.'

Chuk didn't move.

'Downstairs,' Sciarra said again.

He did as they asked. There wasn't much choice. Five minutes later Chuk came down with the keys for a rusty white van parked by the side.

'Get in,' his cousin ordered and didn't look his way.

Lombardi had turned up without warning from Rome. Marched into the rented house and said he wanted to eat. So there they were, Falcone, Peroni and Teresa Lupo dining with him outside on the Cariddi boardwalk at the restaurant they'd come to think of as their own. The same fish as they'd picked that first day: swordfish, shrimp and calamari. The same wine. The same attentive waiter, Toni, who kept asking questions. Was the young Indian woman coming back? And the quiet man with glasses who never spoke much? Where had they gone? And how long was everyone on holiday? It was unusual to have visitors in town for more than a few days, not that they weren't welcome.

Their answers were evasive and, Peroni felt, unconvincing. Everyone in this little place had some connection to the Bergamotti. From Elena Sposato in her kiosk cafe to the people running this restaurant. They might not have belonged to the 'ndrina but they knew someone who did. And if there was a little thing to be reported – a doubt, an overheard whisper, a suspicion – then that would be passed on. Because the Bergamotti were their people, their lords and masters, caring ones too who, for the most part, kept their wards safe. So long as everyone knew their place and did what they were told.

Lombardi watched Toni pour the wine then when he'd gone said, 'We can't keep this up. I'm going to have to put a deadline on this project. The longer it goes on the less I trust them. We still don't really understand what's in it for the Bergamotti anyway. Maybe . . .' He let out a long, pained sigh as if some perceived offence was personal, aimed solely at him. 'Maybe I've been misled.'

Peroni watched Teresa, knowing she'd be unable to stop herself speaking, knowing too what she'd say.

'If you're talking about pulling out,' she said jabbing at the man from Rome with a prawn head, 'forget it. I won't be coming. You seem to forget—'

'The longer we stay the more we risk detection by the Sicilians. The other 'ndrine—'

'Risk detection?' Peroni repeated. 'You mean they got us sussed? They've done that already. And stop talking like you're sending an email to your boss. Risk detection . . .'

'They've got Nic,' Teresa said. More softly she added, 'They've got Silvio.' She nodded at the hills that rose so quickly and steeply behind the village. 'If we walk away like craven cowards we leave them behind in some shallow grave up there among the rocks.'

Lombardi wriggled on his seat. 'We've lines of communication. Maybe I can persuade them to return to the status quo.'

Christ, Peroni thought. It was like listening to an office memo brought to life.

'Don't be ridiculous,' he said. 'The Bergamotti have put themselves on the line. They can't retreat from here. Someone would talk. Mancuso would tear them to shreds if he knew they'd been offering up his head. The other 'ndrine could sit back, tut tut, then march in and fight a war over the pieces. We're staying till this is done.'

'Falcone . . .'

Always turn to the senior officer, if you want to bring people in line. A civil servant through and through.

'We need a word,' Falcone said and led Lombardi to the edge of the deck. A couple of feluccas were drifting slowly across the horizon, men spying the blue water from their towers, harpooners at the end of the passarella, weapons in their arms. This place kept turning whatever happened. The pair's voices became heated until they realized the waiter was watching, maybe trying to listen from the door to the dining room inside. Then they came back. Falcone looked even more shifty than usual.

'Two more days,' he announced. 'Then we assess where we are and make a decision.'

Lombardi picked at a piece of swordfish, stuffed it in his mouth and mumbled through the shreds, 'I have to go.'

In silence they watched him leave.

'Two days. Two weeks. Two months. Two years,' said Teresa. 'Doesn't matter. I'm not leaving without them.'

Peroni raised a finger and said, 'Same here.'

'And what would you do, exactly?' Falcone demanded.

'If the rest of you vanish? If Lombardi scurries back to his office and starts to write a few memos to cover his back for when the inquests start?' Peroni pulled up his chair and frowned. 'I'd take the car up into those hills and go looking for them. Probably find myself a gun from somewhere if I could.'

'Me with him,' Teresa added.

'Lombardi will stretch to three days,' Falcone said. 'That's as much as I could get out of him.'

'Leo—'

'But you'll have room in the car for me,' he added and it wasn't a question.

Just a few words and they broke the atmosphere. Peroni smiled and raised his wine. So did Teresa. The three of them tapped their glasses together on the table above the gently churning water.

'Here's to Nic,' Peroni said. 'And Silvio. And us. I don't . . .' He was never good with words. 'I don't know—'

'You shouldn't have thrown him out.' Falcone was staring straight at her. 'He wanders round like a stray all the time. I kicked him over that nonsense at the bar. He's kicked himself. Plenty. You can see that. He doesn't need more from you.'

'These are private matters, Leo.' She looked shocked. Falcone was such a careful man when it came to anything personal. 'Stay out of them.'

'It isn't a private matter if it gets in the way of business. What happened with the Sposato woman's done with. She's fine. I checked. I went over there.'

He tapped his glass with Peroni's again.

'You went over there?' she asked. 'I was going to do that.'

'Well you don't need to now. I had a good cup of coffee. She knew straight away I was from here. Guessed pretty much why too. Seems a very smart woman.' He waited for her quiet curses to finish then added, 'She said some kind of . . . gentleman from Rome helped her out with a problem. It was awkward for a while. But she's grateful. It's in the past for her. That's how it should be with us.'

Peroni nodded, thinking this through. 'That little creep wasn't meant to be picking on her. I said these guys have got this thing about honour—'

'Doesn't matter what the cause is,' Falcone interrupted. 'She's fine. The boy of hers too. It's done with. You need to let him back into your room.' He looked at the feluccas on the sea for a moment. 'For one thing he's in the single right next to me now and his snoring keeps me awake. Also—'

'Enough! Enough!' she cried. Her hand came over and took Peroni's giant fist. 'He's back. I made my point. It wasn't . . . forever, Leo. He knew that. Didn't you?'

'Yes,' Peroni said because it was expected. 'Thanks and—'

Falcone wasn't listening. Lombardi had returned and stood at the restaurant door, beckoning with a wagging finger.

Ten minutes they waited. Ten awkward minutes. Relationships were best felt, he thought, not discussed. Emotions had no need of words. Of explanations. The two of them had fallen into each other's arms years before in the oddest of circumstances. Reluctantly almost. Cooped up in her little flat near the Spanish Steps, walking to work together in the Questura, they'd become a happy, settled couple and never even talked of marriage because there was nothing else they needed. Just one another.

Then came Cariddi. A test, he thought. Something that tore them out of the comfortable world of Rome and challenged them with a place so foreign it might have been a different country, a game of play-acting that made them live behind masks, disguise their feelings, their fears, their longings. Maybe it was good to be challenged. Maybe, with luck, you came out of it stronger. Once the masks were off.

She took her eyes off Falcone and Lombardi engaged in deep conversation by the water's edge. It wasn't hard to see she'd thought of something important, and he knew he was going to hear it.

'When we get back to Rome. Whenever that is,' Teresa told him in her loud and certain voice, 'I'm getting the workmen in to change that bathroom. It's an antique. I want one of those new rain shower gadgets. The sort where you don't need a door any more. You can't just let things ride.'

'Good idea,' he said and squeezed her hand. 'I can do some decorating if you like.'

Her eyes narrowed. 'Decorating? You've never offered to decorate before. Are you any good at it?'

'Slow but reliable. Very good value too.'

'You all over,' she said with a smile.

'Usually. Maybe not here. That woman in the bar . . . I was just trying to help. That's all it was. Never . . . anything . . .'

'I know. I know. I never thought . . . not for a moment. We're stuck with one another, aren't we?'

'For better or worse.' He raised his glass again.

'That's not a marriage proposal, is it?'

He hesitated, wondering what he'd said and how best to proceed. 'Not unless you want it to be. I mean—'

'Later,' she cut in. 'Leo . . .'

Falcone was coming back, a distracted look on his face that meant his thoughts were somewhere else entirely. The man from the Ministry of Justice had scooted off to the door and was vanishing past the waiter hovering there, looking ready to come and see what they wanted for dessert.

'Well?' Teresa asked when Falcone sat down, gulped at his wine, said not a word.

Falcone's phone rang. He answered straight away. The conversation seemed to be one-sided. It ended with one word: good. Then he was pouring more wine, still thinking.

'News by any chance?' Teresa asked.

'It looks like tomorrow. Lombardi was about to get in his car when he got a call from Intelligence saying something was up in Sicily. The Mancuso people were making plans to move. That was Rocco Bergamotti. He's heard the same. We should be ready by tomorrow afternoon.'

'All very quick,' Peroni noted. 'Lombardi one minute. The local hood the next. This feels stage-managed or something—'

'For God's sake! We've been waiting for this for weeks and now you're moaning.'

'Not moaning. I guess I hate the fact someone else is in the driving seat. They have been all along.'

Falcone downed more wine, watched in silence by the two of them. 'Lombardi's going to make arrangements about troops. He's shipping them in . . .'

'Troops?' Teresa asked, wide-eyed.

'He doesn't want to bring in the locals unless he has to. In case something leaks. Nic's going to come here in the morning. We'll find out more then.'

'And Silvio?' she asked.

'When it's done. When they're all safe. Till then he's their . . . guest.'

'Hostage. Let's use our words. Not theirs.'

Falcone's cold grey eyes turned on her for a moment.

'Hostage then. If you like. If you think it makes a difference.'

'And till then?' Peroni asked.

'We do nothing. We talk to no one. We . . . wait.'

The waiter came over.

'There are special *dolci* today,' he announced, all smiles. '*Crostata*, *crema* and *ciambellone*. Sweet *panzerotti* with *ricotta* too. All made with a *calabresi* speciality we grow along our rugged coast. A fruit. *Bergamotto*. Like a big lemon. You know it?'

'Coffee and grappa,' Falcone told him. 'We'll skip dessert.'

'Bergamotto's the aroma, the flavour of this part of the world, sir. You should try it. I'll bring you a selection. On the house. From me.'

Close to four in the afternoon Maso was back working with Vanni beneath the shadow of the fractured campanile. Manodiavolo was baking in the dry, still, summer heat. Insects everywhere, birds of prey soaring in the sky. They'd fetched a large beach umbrella out into the piazza for Gabriele who now sat in his customary chair at the table beneath its shade, sipping a glass of iced water with bergamot juice and sugar, reading a book. He'd caught sight of the title when he fetched more iced water from the palazzo: *Agamemnon* by Aeschylus. A play from what he recalled, not a book at all. Ancient Greek which was fitting for the surroundings but a curious choice for a capo known as Lo Spettro. The Bergamotti were odd and elusive creatures, difficult to pin down in the bright light of day.

The old man had returned in his little cinquecento just after two. He would, he said, be staying at the house that night, with Rocco and Lucia when they returned from the office on the coast. Something was afoot. It had to be. The atmosphere had changed. Even Vanni, who always appeared more focused on the day-to-day running of Manodiavolo and the happiness of his donkeys, seemed to have noticed.

Then there was the sound of a fast car racing up the hill. The scarlet Alfa 4×4 roared up the last few metres of cobbles, its front wheels flying briefly in the air, swerved, screeched to a halt by the old wellhead.

'No need to drive like an idiot,' Vanni yelled at Rocco as he clambered out of the front. 'We know you're one already.'

The younger man just glared at him and checked his watch.

'Where's your sister?' Vanni added.

Gabriele had seemed absorbed by the book but then he raised his head. 'Yes. Where is she?'

Back in Reggio he said. 'She's got her scooter, hasn't she? I'm not a damned chauffeur.' He'd got on a sky blue shirt and matching trousers, white shoes, the usual sunglasses back on his black hair. Casual looking; not that it worked. 'There's news. We need to talk.'

They sat around the table, Rocco with a beer, then a second, Gabriele sipping at his drink, Maso and Vanni with icy water from the well. The Sicilians had called that lunchtime, Rocco said. Mancuso was willing to attend the service in the chapel in the hills. Then sit down with Gabriele and the other 'ndrine capi and talk business.

'Am I meant to be party to this discussion?' Vanni asked. 'You usually talk business when I'm absent.'

'Yes,' Gabriele replied immediately. 'You know more about this place than anyone. You can find your way around like a mountain goat. We need the cavern ready.' He peered across the table. 'We need you to support us. Family . . .'

Vanni frowned. 'You know I'm no good at things like this. I'm not . . . a man of honour as you call it. I can kill a hen. An old donkey when he's crying out for deliverance. But a man . . .' He shook his head then growled, 'Leave me out of your plans—'

'We can't,' Rocco told him. 'This is our moment. Once it's passed nothing will be the same.' He hesitated and looked at Gabriele. 'You need to tell him.'

Silence, then Vanni asked, 'Tell me what?'

The old man took a deep breath. 'If everything goes to plan we leave here tomorrow.' He grabbed at the glass. 'By here I mean . . . everywhere. Reggio. Calabria. For good.'

Vanni glanced at Maso then turned on his brother. 'What in God's name are you talking about?'

'The end of the Bergamotti,' Gabriele said with a shrug.

'I'm going into retirement. And for your sakes, with a little help from our new friend here, I'm taking you along with me.'

'What if I don't want to go?'

'You don't have a choice,' Rocco told him. 'My father's turning pentito. He's going to give the cops Mancuso, Il Macellaio, the Butcher from Palermo. And a good few others.'

'What?' No one spoke. Vanni turned to Maso. 'So who, in that case, is this charming young man I believed to be one of your guests?'

Gabriele closed the pages of his book and slapped it on the table. 'He's a policeman. From Rome.'

'Rome?' ·

'You don't think I'd trust one of the locals, do you? Please. Listen. I'm old. I'm tired. There's no simple way out of this life unless it's in a coffin. It's either this or wait for the next war to come. This time it's one we lose.'

Vanni looked around him. 'I've lived here most of my life. This is my home. The place . . . the animals. The orchards. The fields. And now you're inviting policemen into our midst. I can't believe—'

Gabriele reached over and patted his hand. 'I know. I know. Always in your older brother's shadow. Always watching what I do . . . what I must do . . . a little fearfully. I asked you once if you wished to join us. And what did you say?'

'There's enough death in this world without us adding to it,' Vanni replied, and for the first time there was something hard and bitter in his voice.

'Violence is our business.' Gabriele emptied the jug of juice. 'Our trademark. Without it we are nothing. We are dead. All of us. You. Me. Our sister. Rocco and Lucia. Don't blame me for doing what's necessary. Only you grew up with choices. Never me.'

There were tears in Vanni's eyes then. Of pain. Anger too. 'And where shall I go then, brother? What future have you mapped out for me beyond here? The only place I know. The only place I love.'

'That you'll find out when we get there,' Gabriele said, not looking at him. In the stables one of the donkeys began to honk and bray. 'Your beasts are hungry. Go feed them. Whoever comes to Manodiavolo next will never harm your animals. They're needed here. We're not. Our time on Aspromonte is done.'

Vanni got up from the table, grumbling all the while.

'You'll live with it, brother,' Gabriele added. 'We all will. We must.'

'Am I such a simpleton I don't even get to know where?'

Gabriele considered the question for a moment then nodded. 'Of course.' He glanced at Maso. 'Tomorrow you can communicate this to your people down in Cariddi. They will agree. Like us they have no alternative. After which you must return here. I want you around for this . . . finale.' Watched closely by his brother, he ran a finger across the table as if drawing out a map. 'Lucia can return to Capri. Even if they know of the house there they've no business with her. Nor my sister. The Sicilians won't take it out on women who've no position in the 'ndrina. My son . . .' He glanced across at him. 'Well?'

Rocco's eyes were darting everywhere. 'I'll take a vacation. A place of my own choosing. A long way from here. The police don't need the details. You're the pentito. Not me.'

'Australia, I imagine,' Vanni muttered. 'It's always Australia when you want to hide. Who's going to feed my creatures? Who's going to look after them?'

'They're dumb animals,' Gabriele replied. 'Someone will come along.'

There was a kind of division between these men, he realized, not that he could discern the cause. He said, 'If you're out of Italy you're none of our business, Rocco. We'll need to keep your father safe for a few weeks. Vanni's no concern to me. When there are trials—'

'*If* there are trials,' Gabriele interrupted. 'Mancuso and his men have ways of avoiding that fate. Sometimes through their lawyers. Sometimes through other means. I'll take my brother with me to Burano. Perhaps I can persuade him to join me out wild fowling. He may baulk at the shooting but he'll eat the ducks sure enough.'

'I'm still here, brother,' Vanni retorted. 'You may address the village idiot directly.'

'We'll be safe,' Gabriele added as if he hadn't heard. 'It's a long way to the next house, with a bridge and a gatehouse to protect us. There'll be men. My men. Always.'

Maso nodded his assent. 'What time tomorrow? What can I tell my team?'

'I don't know,' Rocco answered. 'I'm waiting on the details. There's something . . . something they seem to need to clear at their end first.'

'But tomorrow it is?' Gabriele demanded.

'Definitely. The Butcher and his lieutenants are coming to the chapel. Most of the capi from the southern 'ndrine. All except Corigliano who's sick or something.'

'That bastard's dying in hospital,' Gabriele snarled. 'With an animal for a son who can't wait to steal his crown from the coffin. Corigliano.' He groaned. 'God . . . if a devil like him can live to die of nothing more than a rotten liver the world truly has turned on its head. I damn near murdered him two, three times myself. Corigliano we don't need to worry about. By the time the son ascends to his throne we'll have left this place to the wolves and the rats.'

Silence, then Gabriele lifted the water jar and said it was time to fill it with wine. Rocco took the hint and wandered off into the palazzo. The donkeys were still kicking up a noise. Vanni grumbled something about going off to care for them. Someone had to.

'Well, Maso,' the old man said when they were alone. 'I must call you that. For us it's your name. Our brief friendship is coming to an end.'

'You have a man of ours. A guest. Silvio. With a manutengolo out in the hills somewhere.'

Gabriele smiled. 'You've taken to our ways and our . . . vocabulary very quickly. I'm impressed.'

'Silvio—'

He shook his head as if this was a matter of no importance. 'That was my idiot son doing his best to improvise. Rather poorly. I wish he hadn't. But now . . .' His hand came over the table and gripped Maso's arm. 'Once we're safe so is he. I've no wish to harm your people. Why would I? I'd only suffer in return.'

It made a kind of sense. 'There's some way to go after this. A lot of questions.'

He laughed. 'But they won't leave that to you. They'll get the lawyers in. You're a man for action. For sticking your neck out. If you weren't you wouldn't be here.' He raised the empty glass as if in a toast. 'If you weren't my daughter wouldn't be so taken with a phantom who calls himself Tomasso Leoni. The only ghost in her life up to now was supposed to be her father.'

There was nothing he could think of to say.

'One more night. That's all you have. Make the most of my Lucia's company. You've made her happy. Because you're a stranger. Because she knows you won't be around for long. She's not one for permanency, I'm afraid. I trust you never fooled yourself on that.' He held out his hand. Maso took it. 'You'll always have my gratitude for making her smile. Not an easy task . . .'

Rocco was returning with the carafe in his left hand, wine spilling onto the old cobbles as he walked. His right held an expensive jumbo iPhone jammed hard to his ear.

The call ended when he got to the table. Wine was poured. Glasses raised. Gabriele told his son to keep quiet until Vanni could return and join them. When he came back the smell of the animals was on his old country clothes and he looked a little less crabby than before.

'You have news,' Gabriele declared. 'Share it with all of us equally.'

'They arrive in the afternoon.' Rocco gulped at his wine. 'The Sicilians won't say how they're travelling. I didn't want to pursue it. They'll meet us in the Chapel of the Holy Clasp at three o'clock. The service should last no more than twenty minutes or so. I've told the priest we have business.'

'Here?' Vanni asked. 'If we have guests we offer them food. I made all that charcoal—'

'It's not a social event,' Rocco broke in. 'I told them we've booked the restaurant in Cariddi. Toni has cleared all the reservations. We'll have the place to ourselves.'

'With the Sicilians it's never a social event,' Gabriele muttered. 'They'll leave their cars at the top of the old mule track. There you take them. Not in the chapel. The people would never forgive us for that.'

'Nor should they,' Vanni muttered. 'They'll never forgive us for any of this.'

'But we'll all be elsewhere, so what does it matter?' Gabriele raised his glass. 'To tomorrow. To a new life free of all these worldly cares.'

Four glasses met across the table.

'One more thing,' Gabriele added. 'I don't want Lucia around when this happens. There's no need. Tonight she can stay in Reggio with a friend. Tomorrow, first thing, she catches the train back to Naples.' He caught Maso's eye. 'Sorry.'

Vanni was shaking his head in astonishment.

'Is this thing you're planning so bad we can't face it as a family?' he cried. 'She doesn't walk out on people. Not even when she was sick she didn't—'

Gabriele wouldn't look at him. 'She's a woman. No place for her here. No place for Alessia either. If this turns bloody—'

'The best thing in the circumstances,' Maso cut in.

'Quite,' the old man agreed. 'Call your people on the coast. Tell them what you know. Tomorrow you should rejoin them. Your time as our guest will soon be over.' He smiled. 'I trust you found it . . . educational.'

He was barely listening. Manodiavolo without her seemed strange. Barren and wrong somehow. He went and made the call to Falcone as they asked. The men spoke quietly among themselves all the while. There was something here they didn't share.

When he got back Vanni said, 'Let me show you the lie of the land again. You only saw it before with Lucia. Perhaps you were distracted.'

So he went and got the old boots she'd found and they headed for the hills.

A shiny Lancia and a dusty Ford blocked their way out of the car park. Chuk said they belonged to the visitors and there was no way he was going to ask them to move. Emmanuel sat in the passenger seat waiting, barely a word spoken between

them, until Santo Vottari came down, Gaetano Sciarra at his
heels.

The Sicilian walked over and motioned for Chuk to get out
of the car. They spoke in whispers. Sciarra gave him a big
holdall. Then said something else. Chuk nodded. Vottari
climbed into the Lancia, Sciarra looked at the white van,
saluted with a wink, got in the driver's seat and tore out onto
the main road.

The holdall went behind the driver's seat as Chuk climbed
back in. Full of all the usual crap, Emmanuel thought. Cheap
bangles and wooden carvings of antelopes and elephants. His
cousin was the man's slave. He'd do whatever the Sicilian
wanted.

'Sciarra lives in Noto,' Chuk said. 'The other way. He's not
going home. The two of them could be in Reggio in a couple
of hours the way that bastard drives.' For a moment, as they
came slowly out of the car park, he glanced across and looked
at Emmanuel. He seemed scared for once. 'What the hell have
you done?'

Stood up for myself for once, he thought. Told the truth.
Held my head up high. Should have been brave enough for
that from the start. The moment the people smugglers came
round the shanty town all smiles, empty promises and
outstretched hands.

'Are you driving me to the ferry or not?'

Chuk was still in his stupid clothes, the long Arab gown
with the leopard print. He looked the way Europeans wanted
to think of men from Africa. Curiosities there to provide
amusement. Black clowns dancing to their tune.

'We could make a pair,' Chuk said. 'You stay here. We work
the tourists. Some of the girls—'

'I got a wife!' Emmanuel roared, slamming his fist on the
plastic dashboard. 'I got a family. What the hell do I want
with girls here?'

The van pulled out onto the narrow coast road. This couldn't
be the main highway to a port. It was narrow, rocky, little used.

'All you got back home is being poor. Don't matter where
you are the likes of us get to live in a prison. Question is
whether it's a comfortable one or not.'

Up ahead there was a line of green vegetation rising from what had to be a river running into the bay. The place seemed strange, exotic. Chuk caught him looking and said, 'That's papyrus. Like they get in Egypt. I'm picking up the vibes here, cousin. I could be a tour guide before the year's out. Throw these stupid clothes in the bin. Get myself a real apartment. A Sicilian wife and then I got a passport. Sciarra knows that. He doesn't care. There's always some other idiot to take my place. They're giving us a chance. Don't you see?'

No. He didn't. And there was no point in explaining why, even if he had the words.

'The chance to be a different kind of slave,' he murmured. Then more loudly, 'Don't you get it? I don't belong here. I want to go home.'

'Sound like a kid. Sound like a baby.'

'Kids and babies got more sense than us,' Emmanuel said and it was close to a whisper. 'They don't go selling themselves to crooks and smugglers getting fooled by stupid dreams.'

They were getting nearer the green line of waving plants. Maybe it was papyrus. They looked like giant bulrushes with bobbly heads, rising out of the banks of a slow, grey swirling river. He thought of bible classes back home and the story of Moses found in a basket in a place that must have been much like this. All his life people had been telling him fairy tales.

'When's the boat?' Emmanuel asked.

'Do I look like a travel agent?'

'You look like a fool. No offence.'

Chuk snorted at that, shook his head, and slowed down a little. The road was getting worse. Soon it turned into a track, ever more bumpy, headed for the line of water at the edge of the papyrus banks. Across the bay the island of Ortigia looked back at them, its soft stone shading from gold to pink in the summer sun. His cousin should have been there, selling junk to the foreigners, trying to pick up some loose woman for the night. Instead they were in a rusty old van headed nowhere.

He thought of Jackson the marmoset back in the Zanzibar. Dead now, or so Vottari said, drowned as if its sad little life

meant nothing at all. Which was probably right. It didn't belong
in Reggio any more than he. Something told him things were
going to get even worse there now somehow. Dead men rising
from the dusty ground. Vottari, a henchman of the Bergamotti,
driving off with the Sicilian. He knew how much those sides
loathed one another. Once, in the Zanzibar, he'd seen a knife
fight break out between a couple of men, one from Palermo
on the other side of the water, the other a Reggio thug for
whom violence seemed second nature. The Palermo guy had
won, then run for the door, never to be seen again. Clearing
up after that had been his job, accompanied by Jackson's
screams and the banging of that little glass against the bars
of his prison cage. Blood was never far away from that place.
Never far away from him.

'Where the hell are we going?' he asked as the track got
narrower and was surely heading for a dead end by the water.
There was nothing here but the tall green papyrus stems waving
in the hot summer breeze. After a shallow bend in the road
they were even out of sight of Ortigia across the water.

'Where you asked for,' Chuk said.

'Must be a tiny little boat to come here. Or you putting
me in a basket like Moses. Floating me up the river.
Cousin . . .'

He closed his eyes, knowing what was coming. In that dark
place behind his eyes there was a kind of comfort. He could
see his wife, his kids. Could smell the bad air of Lagos, hear
the neighbours arguing and playing music much too loud. And
knew he missed it all.

The van came to a stop. He opened his eyes. Chuk had
taken a gun out of the bag the Sicilian had given him. A
black automatic shaking in his hands. Emmanuel guessed
he'd seen a lot more guns than his cousin. They didn't scare
him anymore.

'I gave you a thousand euros,' he said very calmly. 'This
is what I get back?'

'Christ, Emmanuel!' His eyes were wild and there was the
glassy start of tears in them. 'Why don't you ever listen to
me? We could've made a pair. All you had to do was wear
these stupid clothes for a while.'

'This isn't my place. It never will be. If it's yours . . . good luck.'

The gun stopped shaking.

'I lied,' Emmanuel confessed. 'I took ten thousand from those bastards. Not five like I said. Even after the thousand I gave you that's nine left. You worked that out? You were always good with money. More than me.'

'Ten?' Chuk asked. 'Ten?'

'I can show you if you like . . .'

'Why do you always say things so late?' Chuk was starting to cry now, thick tears running down his shiny black cheeks. 'Why? I wouldn't have called Sciarra. We could have done so much.'

'Ten . . .'

'They said I got to kill you. Dump you here. If I don't do that they kill me. They mean it. These guys always mean the things they say.'

All the same Emmanuel reached inside his jacket and took out the first wad. Four grand left after Chuk's earlier cut. Then stuck his fingers inside his shirt and found the second he'd secreted there.

'Ten . . .' he said again and his cousin couldn't take his eyes off all that money.

It was so easy. One quick, hard punch to Chuk's eye, his left hand out to grab the gun. A shot went off and for a moment Emmanuel found himself full of fear and shame. He didn't want to hurt his cousin. Though maybe the Sicilians would do that for him.

But the bullet must have vanished somewhere beneath their feet.

Chuk was sobbing behind the wheel, wiping his eyes with the long sleeves of his stupid leopard print gown.

'You'd have done it too,' Emmanuel said, a little amazed, the weapon heavy in his hand. 'You'd have shot me just because some foreign bastard told you to.'

He kept on sobbing and didn't say a thing.

'Here.' Emmanuel counted out another thousand and held it out for him. 'That's more than I got. A chance. Give me the van keys. Take the money. Get out of here. Let's hope we never see each other again. Here!' He stuffed the money into the vest pocket of the lurid gown. 'And this.' He placed the gun in Chuk's lap. 'I don't need it.'

Maybe that last part was idiotic. But he didn't like the feel of the thing in his hand. And he didn't think Chuk did either.

He leaned over, grabbed the keys from the dashboard, popped open the driver's door and said, 'God go with you.'

Chuk left the gun on the seat, climbed out, went and sat on a boulder among the tall green papyrus rushes, head in hands, shoulders going up and down. Emmanuel pushed the weapon out of the door, shuffled over behind the wheel, turned the keys, started the engine. Took one last look at his cousin then reversed into a stand of brambles, eased the van forward over the rough ground and set off down the road.

He didn't know quite where he was headed. Just where he wasn't going back. That was enough in the circumstances. With money . . . more than enough.

Vanni took the two donkeys with them, for the exercise, theirs, for sentiment, nothing else. They wandered the same path he'd walked along with Lucia days before. A heat haze had gathered over the coast as the afternoon wore on. The complex shoreline of bays and ridges and promontories seemed to move like a mirage far below.

'Are you alright?' Maso asked as they stopped by a mountain stream to let the animals drink.

He and Gabriele didn't look much like brothers. There had to be five, maybe ten years between them. Vanni had the appearance of a farmer, weather-beaten, tanned, strong-armed with leathery hands marked by years of work. Gabriele had a patrician manner about him, that dignified silver head of hair, a natural authority. He wasn't sure the two men liked each other much. Or perhaps even were aware of their separate existences in the world outside.

'We always get pushed out of paradise, don't we?' Vanni said and sat on a rock, gazing back towards the strait below. 'That's what happens.'

'I'm sorry. It must hurt.'

He frowned. 'It doesn't yet. I'm still here. So are my animals.

A farmer can have them. That won't be hard to arrange.' He walked over to the donkeys, smiled as he stroked their rough, thick fur. 'All things come to an end. I knew it would happen one day.'

'Why?' he asked.

Vanni left the beasts and came up to look at him. 'Why do you think?'

'Because your brother feels he's no alternative. No natural successor in the family. The Bergamotti . . .'

Vanni laughed and shook his head. 'The Bergamotti. What nonsense is that? Lucia told you. We're really called the Ursi. The bears. The mountain bears. Who've roamed these hills and played these games for much too long.'

'She said?'

'Of course. She told me everything. Well.' He looked embarrassed for a moment. 'Not everything. I do have eyes and ears though.' His gaze became more fixed. 'Will you try to see her . . . afterwards?'

'I'd hope to,' he answered honestly.

Vanni shook his head and went back to the animals, shooing them away from the stream with a few gentle words of admonition before he returned. 'But you won't be Tomasso Leoni then. The world will be different. So will you.' He reached over and placed a hand on Maso's shoulder. 'At least I hope so. They've tried hard to make you someone else. It's only natural. Life on Aspromonte is much like a performance, like the Greeks used to put on round here all those centuries ago. Tragedy or comedy, or a bit of both, I've no idea. But this I do know.' He glanced back at the coast for a moment. 'Once my brother plays our final act tomorrow you must remember to take that mask off your face. Leave it on too long and the thing becomes a part of you. I wouldn't want that. Nor would she.'

They resumed their journey down the track, behind Silvio and Benito who seemed to know their way. Vanni appeared lost in himself for a while. Then he asked about Burano and the Venetian lagoon, the place where Gabriele seemed determined to take him. Did he know it? Was it anything like Aspromonte?

No, he said. It was wild and desolate in parts though across the water planes came and went from the city airport. And not far away lay the Dolomites, the peaks capped by snow in winter.

'Winter?' Vanni asked. 'That comes soon in the north I think. Tell me what it looks like.'

Fog across the ghostly waters of the lagoon. Wildfowl scooting through the mist. Small fishing boats throwing nets and cages into the grey water, hunting for mantis shrimp and crab, eels and lagoon goby hidden in the mud.

'You sound like you know that place?'

'A little,' he replied. 'Never enough. No one does. Like here.'

'No . . . swordfish?' Vanni asked with a grin.

'Nothing so big or grand or dangerous. I think you'll like it there. People have little gardens. Orchards. Vineyards.'

'They don't have fragrant bergamotti though.' His face was stern as they reached the stone platform where Maso had sat with Lucia that first day they became close. 'And I go from eating pisci spata straight from the sweet clean waters of the Strait of Messina to little fishies they have to dig out of the mud. Huh. I will never see this place again. I will never smell the perfume of those trees. My beasts. My fields. My mountain, Aspromonte . . .'

He sat down suddenly on a rock and wiped his eyes. After a while he asked, 'Did you learn anything from that book our father wrote?'

A lot, he said. About the people and the land. About history and myth.

'History is myth,' Vanni declared. 'That book's a pack of lies. Poor Leoni, our teacher, wrote it and my father had the nerve to put his name upon the cover after the man died saving us from one more war. He could read. He just couldn't write. After it came out he'd make us sit with him, going through the pages of those stories like every one of them was true. As if he wrote them. We are—' his hand swept the horizon – 'ghosts, Maso. My father was called Lo Spettro too. Born liars. Gabriele inherited that while I inherited Manodiavolo. I think I got the best of the bargain, don't you?'

'You can be happy in Burano. I'll come and see you. We can go fishing in a little skiff.'

He laughed at that. 'No. You think you'll find Lucia first. Make her happy. See that track?' Beneath them was the same rough way up the hillside she'd pointed out, the rocky ridges around it silhouetted against the bright sky. 'I was asked to tell you that's the way they'll come. That's the place you'll find them. Six hundred metres to the left there's another, rougher track, up along a dried-up torrent. Your men can hide in the trees. No one will see if they take care. Can you make it out?'

He walked to the edge of the platform and peered over the edge. A small wood of stubby firs ran downhill from the gravelly clearing where she'd said they'd park their vehicles. He could smell them from where he stood, a sharp resinous scent in the clean mountain air.

'It would be preferable if there was no blood,' Vanni added. 'I've always felt there's something holy to this hill. Something much older than our ancestor Carcagnosso. The Greeks worshipped here long before the Christians came. Call me superstitious but I doubt any spirits lurking would appreciate that stain.'

'No one wants blood,' he said.

'That's the other you talking,' Vanni told him. 'Not the man they think they made you.' He patted the nearest animal, Silvio. 'We should go back now. One last family supper for the Bergamotti in Manodiavolo. Tomorrow we will all be ghosts for real.'

He was barely listening. The fir wood was small, the trees spindly and bare. It wouldn't be easy to hide there unseen. The clearing was cramped, bounded on all sides by walls of bare pale stone. If violence broke out there'd be nowhere for anyone to run. A show of overwhelming force might be needed to persuade the Sicilians and the Calabrian capi to lay down their weapons. But a show of force required more cover than that little wood afforded. And if anything went wrong . . .

'You look worried, Maso.'

'We can do this. We've waited long enough.'

Vanni took Silvio by the neck and guided the two animals onto the path back home.

'I'm glad you feel confident. There was a story our father used to tell. From that old book. It used to scare me and as a child one always likes to feel scared from time to time. The old man always enjoyed that too. Putting the fear up people.' He screwed up his face as if trying to remember. 'Great God Pan is Dead. That's what it's called. Have you found it yet?'

'No,' he said.

'Well tonight, then. You should. Since Lucia has decided not to join us.' He smiled. 'Till tomorrow . . . reading may be all you've left to do. As for me—' he looked around them – 'I will miss this place. This life. It's all I've ever known.'

There was genuine work in the office. Real properties to manage, rents to collect, impoverished tenants to deal with, kindly usually. The Bergamotti were known for looking after their own and to Lucia that came easily. Whenever she came down from Capri for a few days she always spent time working there. She liked the people, especially Francesca the office manager, a distant relative who never mentioned the 'ndrina or their family unless it was necessary. For her there was only the job, a salary, a business to run, people to deal with. The two of them had become friends after Lucia's lost time. It was Francesca who found the villa in Capri, bargained for it with the local who'd been unwilling at first to sell until the money and the power of the Bergamotti proved persuasive.

The company's property empire stretched from the cramped slums of Reggio to holiday developments along the coast. There were tower block studios that would be condemned if the officials whose job it was to do so weren't on the 'ndrina payroll. There were family houses on the edge of the city, estates built with Bergamotti money, modern boxes with modern conveniences, often rented to those the clan knew at reasonable rents.

But Cariddi was a place for foreigners and tourists, the most beautiful town along the coast. There everything was about business and money. Those terraced waterfront houses now available for rent were either owned by a Bergamotti shell company or paid loyalty money to the clan in return for protection from any neighbouring gangs seeking influence. The restaurant the Romans had come to use so much was part of the property portfolio under the control of Alessia, Lucia's aunt, who stopped by from time to time to check the food and talk to the staff about takings. Falcone had found his way there through the recommendation of the titular owner of their house, a woman arts lecturer at the university in Reggio. Though in truth the deeds belonged to Alessia who picked up most of the rent, four or five thousand a week in the height of the season, and used her as a genial front.

A day in the office in Reggio's commercial quarter was a pleasant way to pass the time. Especially after Rocco vanished in a hurry after telling her to stay clear of Manodiavolo for the night. She'd been about to argue but he wasn't going to stay for that. The order came from on high, he said. So she could hang on in Reggio, finish the office work, then spend the night with Francesca and wait for news.

It seemed a little odd but in truth she didn't mind. There was something soothing, something normal, in dealing with emails, pretending to be ordinary for a while.

Francesca had showed her how to put new rental details on the various websites they used, tedious, repetitive work but she liked it all the same. Cariddi was getting ever more popular. Thanks to the international letting sites they were attracting customers from all over Europe and beyond to that little stretch of coastline north of Reggio. Growing up she'd felt she lived at the very edge of the world, a wild and savage place that only the brave or the foolish traveller would wish to visit. But times were changing. Not that she'd mentioned a word of that to Francesca. Soon the Bergamotti regime would be gone. Another would take its place, perhaps one that wasn't so benevolent to those who stayed behind.

The business was, to all intents and purposes, above board and quite free of criminal connections. It would continue, as would Alessia. Her mother had died in that gang war of long ago but that was judged an accident, an aberration. Men fought, men died, men won and lost. Wives and mothers had, for the most part, a kind of sanctity, and not just in the Chapel of the Holy Clasp. The Calabrians were sentimental. Men she knew to be heartless killers would weep at the loss of a favourite dog or a stupid movie.

'I am . . . done,' Francesca announced, banging her hands theatrically on the keyboard in front of her. Then she closed her laptop and said, 'How about a drink first? Then pizza? Maybe . . .' Francesca winked. 'Maybe we can hook up with some interesting guys. Who knows?'

It was close to six. There were cocktail bars on the waterfront, flashy places, all of them mob-owned or mob-controlled, though that was never obvious. All the same they'd be busy and there might be men there she'd know. Men who'd know her too. In the circumstances . . .

'Had my fill of interesting guys.'

'I meant interesting nice guys.'

'That type too.'

Francesca put a hand on her arm and gasped. 'Oh my God. You've got a boyfriend. Jesus. What's he like? Someone I know?'

'He's not a boyfriend. And no. You don't.' You never will, she thought.

'I am your best friend and putting you up for the night. You still won't say—'

'No . . .'

'Just one little drink,' Francesca begged. 'A Hugo Spritz. Barely any booze in it. Come on. We're done here. Let's go.'

Lucia grabbed her bag and keys and said, 'You're so damned insistent. Don't you have a man back at home to go to?'

'Nah. He's out working or something. Seems there's lots going on.' She was close to forty, never married, never had any long-term boyfriend as far as Lucia knew. Didn't want one either. 'He's walking round in that kind of funk they get when something's up. I'm not asking. Last time I did that he said he was going to rob a bank. Did I want to come?'

They headed for the door. She watched Francesca lock up.

'It was a joke. I'm sure.'

'Yeah. A joke. He's got some other woman. Round Locri way I think. It's fine by me. I don't want him hanging round the place all the time. I mean . . .' That smile again. 'Just say we meet two guys tonight. Just for tonight. What do you think?'

'I think you're a terrible person. One drink. Pizza. Your place.'

'You used to be fun. No. I correct myself. You didn't. That was someone else.'

There was a small private car park round the back. Just her Ford estate with the company logo on the side and Lucia's scooter in there now.

'You should come up to Capri some time. Meet a rich guy in the piazza. They'd like you there.'

'You mean I'm brassy and flashy.'

She was. All jewellery and gaudy clothes and a smile so big it looked as if it could reach across the strait to Sicily if it wanted.

'No. I just meant it might be fun.'

'A good kind of fun. Not the bad kind.'

'Don't do the bad kind anymore.'

She nudged Lucia's elbow. 'You can tell me all about him over a Hugo. Is he from round here?'

They walked to her car.

'Not exactly. I don't know . . . I don't know if it's going to go anywhere. Nothing lasts really, does it?'

'Best that way—'

She didn't finish. An old white van had turned up, tyres screeching, parked diagonally across the bays at the end.

'This is private,' Francesca yelled before anyone got out. 'You can't just drive in here and . . .'

The door was opening, Santo Vottari climbing out. Someone with him neither of them recognized. Same kind of build, same shades in the hair. But different somehow.

Santo marched up, took one look at Francesca and said, 'Beat it.'

'Don't talk to me like that you punk—'

'I said beat it. Me and Lucia got business.' He grinned. 'Her old man sent me. You want to mess with him?'

'Show some manners,' Lucia told him.

'Lady. It's best you go,' the other one said and he sounded different. Sicilian maybe. 'Please.'

'I'm not—'

'It's OK,' Lucia cut in. 'Leave me to talk to them. Teach Santo here some respect . . .'

'Plenty of things I could teach you in return,' he snapped back with a leer.

Francesca wasn't moving. 'Lucia. If you want . . .'

'I'm fine.'

''Course she's fine. She's Lo Spettro's daughter. Didn't you know that? Really? Didn't you know?' He nodded at the estate car. 'Get out of here. Her old man sent us on business. Don't want the likes of you gossiping about it either.'

She went after that. Lucia watched the car turn out into the street, Francesca looking back, worried. A Hugo Spritz would have been nice. She liked them. They weren't so strong as the Campari ones she used to down like beer back in the bad times on the coast.

'You never did know how to behave,' she said when the car turned round the corner. 'That'll come back to bite you.'

He laughed. Then reached out and touched the dragon tattoo on her arm, amused at the way she shrank from him. The stranger was getting something out of his pocket. A strip of fabric. It took her a moment to work out what it was.

'I like that,' Vottari said. 'Never noticed it before. I'm going to do the biting from now on. Did he do that to you?'

'Who?'

'The fake. The one who said he was from Canada. Did he bite you, honey?'

The piece of fabric was a gag. She saw that now, too late. They were on her and it didn't matter how much she struggled and fought and scratched and screamed. They were always going to win.

'What is this?' she yelled at them as they bundled her into the van, still trying to get the thing round her mouth.

'We need a guest,' the stranger said. 'You're not the only ones who've got that habit. Get in.'

The gag went round. They pushed her inside, tied her wrists, her legs as she writhed and tried to screech. The van must have had an animal in it sometime. She could smell the thing and there was a wire grate dividing the back from the seats up front.

No point in struggling. She knew that. They drove a little way and then she watched Vottari get out, saw what lay beyond him. The ferry terminal at Villa San Giovanni. Soon they were on the brief boat ride across the Strait of Messina and she saw the bulk of Etna rising through the window.

'Welcome to Sicily,' the man up front said when he hit the E90 autostrada. 'Be good. Then everything will be fine. *Tutto bene. Tutto.*'

# PART SIX

# The Grave of Carcagnosso

Calabrian Tales

### Chapter XX: Our Spartan Cousins

As we have discussed, the Sicilians trace their blood to many different sources. The small but significant contribution of the Spanish apart, in Aspromonte we mostly look to one place alone: east across the water to the Mani Peninsula in Greece, our mirror image since it also is mountainous, wild, remote and juts out into the sea, in its case from the Peloponnese.

The Griko tongue we speak has its roots here and echoes the vernacular of our modern-day brothers and sisters who now live in the region, the Maniots. They are a proud and individual race and trace their history back to the ancient city-state of Sparta. If the Maniots are modern-day Spartans then we are their kin, content with the hardship of mountain life, of self-sacrifice and a sense of duty. Indeed many of the sayings and customs of that legendary land, from the music of pan pipes to relics of the pagan religion, remain with us on both sides of the Ionian today.

Like the Maniots, the men and women of Aspromonte are famously terse when it comes to speech, never praising easily, uttering criticism frankly, whether it causes offence or not. A true native is also happy to sit through an entire formal dinner in silence if he or she finds the conversation so dull they can think of nothing of interest to say. You may, with good reason, call us laconic, meaning succinct and to the point, since the term comes from 'Lacedaemonia', the name – though little-used – of Sparta's territory. Plain speech without affectation and ornament suits our mountain ways.

One curious phrase from our ancient ancestors you will still hear today when a man of Aspromonte must face up to a difficult challenge, a heated dispute perhaps, or a battle with one of those interfering civil servants Rome sends us from time to time: *E tan e epi tas.*

Greek speakers among you will recognize this as 'with it or on it'. An innocuous and baffling injunction you may think. But this saying is as old as our hills, the very words Spartan women spoke to their husbands before battle, among them the most famous of all, Gorgo the queen of King Leonidas as he set out to meet the might of the Persian army at Thermopylae. Gorgo and her fellow Spartan wives were telling their men, 'Return with your shield . . . or on your shield.' In other words there were but two consequences ahead only: victory or death.

With it or on it.

Should you find yourself in a local tavern and hear these words my advice, dear traveller, is to finish your drink with alacrity and leave.

A line of summer mist ghosted across the Strait of Messina, bringing a Fata Morgana to the horizon off Cariddi. Hazy cliffs and towering make-believe castles seemed to hover there. Feluccas cruised lazily among them, men high in their turrets searching for elusive pairs of swordfish crossing the channel, the long ladder noses of their passarelle jutting out of the haze. It was ten in the morning and already the temperature was close to thirty, the air alive with insects, the sea so still it seemed to spread out before them like a vast blue pond.

Lombardi, newly arrived from Rome and sweating in his dark suit, had called a meeting, on the terrace Teresa decided, away from the house that had come to seem like a prison. Coffee and pastries sat on the table, along with some perfumed bergamot jelly Peroni had bought from the Kiosco Paradiso. The jar possessed a citrus fragrance he'd associate with this place forever, elusive, exotic, strange. The day before he'd plucked up the courage to wander over to see if they had any more to take back to Rome. But halfway across he'd noticed Roberto catch his approach and dash inside the cottage, afraid it seemed, desperate to warn his mother. Hardly surprising, Peroni thought with a shrug, and then turned back. At least they seemed to be back in business, and the jerk in the black Fiat had never returned to trouble them.

'When's Costa going to turn up?' the civil servant demanded.

The time had come. All they needed now was to use the inside knowledge he'd gained through pretending to be a foot soldier of the 'Ndrangheta then reel in their prize.

They'd had a phone call from him late the night before, a long briefing on what had been agreed for the family. There was no negotiation. It was exactly what Lombardi and the rest of the team had been expecting. Some time that morning Costa

would return to Cariddi to organize the handover. Falcone had
talked to him and sounded concerned afterwards, not that he'd
elaborate when Teresa Lupo tried to tackle him. She'd gone
to bed afterwards, tossed and turned so much in the heavy
heat she'd decided to try to sleep in the spare room after a
while. That hadn't happened he guessed from the way she
looked now. Her pale, full face seemed more lined than he
recalled in Rome. In all the years they'd been together he'd
never noticed her growing older, never given it a second
thought. She was Teresa Lupo, head of the Questura forensic
team, indomitable, awkward, fearless. Now in her early forties,
a fit, sturdy, determined woman who never let the world get
her down. That had changed as well.

'We don't know exactly,' Falcone told Lombardi.

Peroni couldn't stop himself adding, 'It's not like he can
make appointments.'

'Well I'm not waiting on him. Here's what happens.'

A civil servant first and foremost. He'd come with a plan
and that was what mattered, regardless of anything that might
affect it on the ground.

As they spoke a mobile control truck laden with all the
latest techno-toys was being parked off the highway behind
the city beneath Aspromonte, a few kilometres down from
Manodiavolo. A group of sixteen officers from a specialist
SWAT team based in Milan had flown into Reggio the night
before. Throughout the day a surveillance helicopter would
swoop around the area filming everything.

'Bad idea,' Peroni said straight off. 'What are they going
to think if they see that thing in the sky?'

'It's got military markings,' Lombardi retorted. 'We've got
them in the air all the time looking for smugglers. They won't
give it a second thought. The crew will be in direct touch with
us in the control van. We'll be able to talk to the team in the
hills. Liaise between the two.'

Peroni grumbled, 'The team in the hills from Milan? Who
don't have a clue where they are? Do they know what they're
here to do?'

He was evasive on that last point. Confront and capture.
That was all. They were hand-picked officers, expert in firearms

and dealing with violent encounters, assigned to anti-terrorism duties mostly of late. Peroni listened, heart sinking, and thought of trying to argue. They came here to spirit an old man out of the mountain clan that believed he was loyal to them, still their king. Not to battle their way out of a firefight in unknown territory against men who probably knew every last rock and ravine. But then he followed the way Lombardi was talking so quickly, so enthusiastically, about the scheme he and his colleagues had cooked up in a comfy office in Rome. Doubtless with whatever computers and software and game theory they used to calculate odds and opportunities. The time for argument was, he realized, long past.

The SWAT crew would approach Mancuso and the heads of the local 'ndrine after they left the solitary cavern and approached their vehicles in the parking space below – with force if necessary. Once detained, the men would be held in vans and driven north to a secure location close to Salerno in Campania. Out of caution local forces would know nothing of the trap, only that some important prisoners were to be transported along the autostrada late that afternoon and were not to be impeded.

'I don't want these men in 'Ndrangheta territory any longer than is necessary,' Lombardi added and Peroni couldn't help but laugh. 'What's so funny?'

'The world's their territory. They'll have lawyers on your back by the time you get there. The moment one of them can escape they'll be gone.'

'I'm lost as to the point you're trying to make.'

'The point,' Peroni said, close to losing his temper, 'is we're struggling to clinch one little local battle here. You think you can win a war. You can't. It's been going on for centuries. We should snatch this Bergamotti capo, whoever he is. Get him safe, make him talk, then take it from there.'

'Gianni,' Teresa broke in, 'he's offering us Il Macellaio. Mancuso. And all these others. We have to try.'

He couldn't get the dead Bonetti, wife, son and brother, out of his head. The only pentito he'd ever handled and that whole nightmare ended in blood. They all thought everything there would work out so easily too.

'It's not that simple. It never is—'

'We capture Mancuso,' Falcone cut in. 'We take as many as we can. This isn't an intellectual argument. It's the best chance we've had to jail some of these bastards in years.'

'They're like snakes, Leo. And this place is the head of Medusa. You cut off one . . . another comes along. We're not winning here because people, ordinary people, don't think we care. If—'

'I don't want to hear this,' Lombardi snapped. 'Are you in or out?'

It was getting harder to stay calm. 'You think I'm going to run away? Now? With two of our men, good friends of mine, out there? Hostages to these people? They could be buried in those hills any minute and we'd never see a trace of them again.'

'Good,' was all Lombardi said. And that was it. 'This is the way it's going to happen. Every detail's worked out. Your job is to see it goes through smoothly.' He looked at each of them in turn, then back to Peroni. 'I want you with the SWAT team when they approach Mancuso's people. We've a bunch of mugshots of local capi we think may be there. Identify them and get them in the van.'

Fine, Peroni thought, and picked up another pastry doing his best to ignore Teresa's bleats.

'Nic wants me with him,' Falcone said. 'The two of us will handle Bergamotti.'

Lombardi shook his head. 'I take him in. It was our intelligence that got you here. It's our money that's paying for this holiday of yours.'

The look on their faces stopped him saying more.

'It's me and Costa,' Falcone insisted. 'They know him. They know me by sight. If they see anyone they don't recognize the deal's off. That's what they said. That's what he passed on. Take it or leave it.'

There was a long silence then Peroni patted Lombardi's arm and said, 'Don't worry. We'll still say it's all down to you. There'll probably be a medal and a pay rise in the end.'

'Gianni . . .' Teresa murmured.

Lombardi lit a cigarette and blew the smoke into the hot

sea breeze. 'We need to handle the pentito carefully. I don't want to do anything that might spook him. Make him change his mind.'

'He's the spook,' she noted. 'Lo Spettro. Remember?'

'Lo Spettro. Who the hell do these people think they are? We got new intelligence a couple of days ago. His real name's Gabriele Bergamotti.'

'Intelligence from where?' Peroni wondered. 'Who keeps throwing you these breadcrumbs?'

'You don't expect me to answer that.'

'Actually I do . . .'

'It's . . . chatter.'

'You mean gossip? Third-, fourth-hand?' Peroni asked. 'Maybe they're the ones who are feeding us this bullshit. They've been pulling our strings from the start. You thought of that?'

'Enough,' Falcone cut in. 'We have to do it the way they asked. We've no option.'

A moment. He was outnumbered. 'Very well. You pick him up. Then bring him straight to me.'

He jabbed a finger at the giant iPad on the table. A map of Aspromonte was there, all the places Costa had told them about marked in detail: the cavern, the tracks, the wood where the team could hide, the clearing where the Sicilians and the visiting capi were due to gather after the service, before a meal in Cariddi that would never happen.

There was only one way in for the police team, only a single route out for the men they sought as well. It all looked very simple. Lombardi had placed the control van three kilometres down the hill on the main road leading east from Reggio. He was placing detention vans there too and would then route the prisoners directly north in a protected convoy all the way to the secure detention facility four hours or so away on the A2 coastal motorway.

'Bergamotti,' he went on. 'We've a plane waiting at Reggio. The general aviation terminal. You take him there straight away. Then you're done. You can go back to Rome. Take a break.' He glanced around at the terrace, the sea, the villa. 'Though I guess you've been enjoying one on us all this time.'

'Yes,' Peroni snapped. 'One long and lovely vacation. Where's the plane going?'

Lombardi squinted at the boats on the strange horizon. 'That you don't need to know.'

'You are going to stick to the deal? Nic told them it was agreed. The family. A daughter. A son. We can't touch any of them. That's the arrangement.'

'Any deal only covers the father,' Lombardi pointed out.

'No.' It was Falcone. 'It covers the family. A daughter. Lucia. A sister, Alessia. The son, Rocco. The women seem determined to look after themselves. There's a younger brother, Vanni. Who's of no interest to us whatsoever. Just a farmer from the hills. The capo wants to live out the rest of his days undisturbed with his brother in a villa he owns in Venice. We told him that was fine. The son . . . he's going to travel somewhere. We don't know.'

Lombardi didn't say a thing.

'If you go back on any of this,' Peroni added, 'the man will clam up. Everything we've done here will be wasted. All you'll get in court is an old man who's past his prime, close to giving up the game anyway, sitting there silent.'

The cigarette went over the balcony, into the pristine sea below. The man from the Ministry of Justice looked at his watch then checked his phone for messages. Only when he was ready did he say, 'You all know what you're supposed to do.' His long finger pointed at Teresa. 'You can come with me now. Get briefed on the control truck. The systems—'

'I know the systems! I'm not a bloody apprentice,' she pointed out.

'Good.' He got to his feet. 'I'll be with you in the van. If—'

The door to the terrace opened. It took a moment for Peroni to recognize him.

'Greetings, stranger,' Teresa said with a smile. 'You look different.'

He was in the neat, crisp shirt and trousers of a well-heeled Calabrian local, with a deep and weather-beaten tan and the ubiquitous dark shades in his dark hair.

'We need to go, Leo. Now.'

'It's not yet eleven,' Lombardi said. 'We're just getting people in place. There's time—'

'There isn't. The Sicilians just called. They're playing games. They're here already. They're meeting in the cavern at midday now, not three. Bergamotti had no choice.'

'Shit!' Lombardi roared. 'You told us three!'

The man in the linen shirt and pale fawn trousers stared at him in a way that made the civil servant fall silent. 'I told you what I knew. Arrangements have changed. Leo comes with me. The rest of you . . .' Falcone was grabbing his jacket already. 'If you don't move quick either there's a bloodbath up there. Or you lose these people forever.'

'Good luck,' Peroni shouted as they hurried off to the door.

Teresa was picking up her phone, her things, checking her watch. Lombardi looked flustered, out of sorts. A methodical man, Peroni thought. Used to having things run like clockwork to carefully-laid plans he'd mapped out well in advance. Which might have worked in Rome.

Something was happening in Manodiavolo. Santo Vottari just couldn't quite work out what. After they'd snatched Lucia the night before he'd wanted to stay with the Sicilians. There was a place they'd talked about keeping her, a remote country shack on the bleak coast between Augusta and Siracusa where petrol refineries dominated most of the shoreline. A day with her there could be pretty interesting. There'd be ways they could keep each other company.

Gaetano Sciarra had been kind of effusive in his thanks but still said no. The capo's daughter was theirs until they decided what to do with her. Which was the way of Sicilians. They only ever looked after themselves. They'd see him right, Sciarra insisted. He just had to go back to the Bergamotti and act as if nothing had happened. The family would know Lucia was in their hands soon enough. No one would understand she came courtesy of Santo Vottari.

There was a problem here though, several if he were honest. Every one of them making him feel uncomfortable as the lone foot soldier left lurking on the worn cobbles of Manodiavolo that morning. Until they gagged her, Lucia had been yelling all kinds of names at him in the white van as it drove to Villa San Giovanni and the ferry. If she came out of this alive, if the war, and there surely was a war to come, went the wrong way, he'd be the one in the Bergamotti's sights. They'd already seen to one guy lately, or so the whisper went. Rizzo, a grubby little seaside crook who'd been skimming and messing around in Cariddi. Rocco had taken him for a walk in the hills himself. It would only require a wrong word on his part for him to step down that same bloody, one-way path.

So he did as he was told and tried his best to keep quiet, which was never easy. Fear burned inside him, and a resentment too. He'd been a loyal servant of the 'ndrina for years and still couldn't afford anything but a simple rented flat in a Reggio tenement. All the same he turned up at Manodiavolo on his little scooter that morning as Rocco asked. Helped the simpleton uncle with some menial chores. The old man was there, Rocco, Maso Leoni. No one else. It seemed odd given he'd heard there was a service in the chapel coming up soon. They happened rarely, and always there was a reason. A deal to be brokered, a war to be started or brought to a close. They were occasions for the highest ranks alone, not infantry like him. Secretive gatherings, a kind of ritual almost, that most men in the 'ndrina could only gossip about. They were never going to see who stepped inside that cavern in the hills.

It was Sciarra who told him the meeting was on the cards, though he hinted that it might not happen in the way the Bergamotti planned. Whatever game Mancuso and his crew were playing they weren't going to let on, not to him.

In the square, mid-morning, around the table, Gabriele had told Maso he could take the Fiat on an errand to the coast. That was it. 'An errand'.

Watching the stranger manoeuvre the white cinquecento with the red stripe out of the square Santo couldn't help but feel a flicker of anger burning inside him.

'Who is that Leoni guy?' he wondered. 'Where the hell's he going now?'

Rocco had followed the car bumping down the track too. 'You heard what my father said. An errand.'

'I heard. I didn't understand. I thought I was the errand boy here.'

The capo's son was always so well-dressed. Today a pink polo shirt and immaculate white trousers, shades on his head, more expensive ones than Santo could ever afford. All the same he didn't seem himself. None of them did. The Sicilians must have been on the line to say they had the daughter. That was enough for a war in itself.

'Since when did you need to understand anything?' Rocco asked, squinting at him in the harsh morning sun.

It was hard to keep quiet. 'So this new guy killed a couple of punks and somehow got a cut on his thumb. I've been here years. Took me a long time to get that far. Didn't get a cut from your old man in person either. That dumb clumsy idiot Nino did it. How come a Canadian gets what I don't?'

'Somehow?' Rocco asked picking up on that stupid little slip.

'Don't matter,' Santo said and told himself: shut up while you can. The uncle apart, the Bergamotti seemed as sharp as a butcher's knife. Even the daughter. They didn't miss a thing.

An hour passed. Rocco kept making and taking calls, relaying them to the old man who sat in the square at a table by the dry, crumbling fountain, straw hat on, dozing in the sun, a jug of iced bergamot water in front of him. The brother, the bumpkin, had come back from the stables. He was pushing a cart full of vegetables from the fields: artichokes, peppers, tomatoes, aubergine. He didn't seem right. Not happy like usual.

Gabriele had a phone in front of him. It rang just the once. Afterwards he nodded, lifted his hat and beckoned with his hands. 'Boys. A word. Both of you.'

Pale hands, Santo noticed when they joined him. Didn't look as if they'd ever done a day of labour. Nor was there any sign of a cut beneath the thumb. Maybe those scars healed when you got that old. Maybe a capo was above getting cut.

Vanni was on an old stool peeling artichokes, throwing the hearts into a bucket of water laced with vinegar to stop them going brown. He didn't even seem to hear a word they said. That was funny too, Santo thought. The older brother was

smart enough and bold enough to run the biggest 'ndrina in
the south of Calabria and never let a soul know who he really
was for years. While his sibling looked like any other peasant
farmer, meant for nothing but the fields.

'As you may know, we've guests today.' Rocco refilled his
father's glass when he held it out. 'Friends from the north.'
The old man smiled, a genial beam. 'Friends from across the
water, here on a rare visit. It's been a long time since they
came and gave thanks to our lady and her silver clasp.'

'Sicilians?' Santo asked and hoped they didn't hear the
waver in his voice.

'You do keep asking questions,' Rocco grumbled.

'I'm . . . I'm just here to do what you want, boss. You tell me.'

The old man looked distant, a little past it at that moment.
'Sea urchins,' he said idly. 'Why have I not tasted sea urchins
of late? Maybe they're out of season—'

'Nothing's out of season for us,' Santo cut in. 'I can get
you *ricci* any time you like.'

'Ricci for Rocco.' Gabriele laughed. 'Except he doesn't like
them. Just for me.'

Vanni looked up from his artichokes, the sharp knife in
his hands. 'May and June those bastards in Brussels won't
let us fish for them. You can buy them straight just now.'
He waved the blade. 'Don't bother taking them out of their
spiny homes. I can do that.' He thought of something. 'Lucia
knows how to do that too. I taught her one day. When she
was little.'

Santo Vottari held his breath, praying he'd get out of this
place real soon. Quick as he could he said, 'You want me to
go find you some *ricci di mare*? I know a guy who dives, all
the best places, all clean and fresh. I can get them back here
in an hour.'

'Do that,' Gabriele ordered. 'Sea urchins. A bucket full. I'm
hungry.'

His brother finished the artichokes he was paring then threw
the last and the knife in the bucket. 'Take the van. Alessia's
restaurant wants these vegetables for their guests. They get to
eat home-grown. Not that usual shit full of chemicals.'

He wiped his face with the back of his hand. The dirt from

the soil went all round his cheeks. He looked like a sorry clown.

'We may be with our guests by the time you get back, Santo,' the old man added. 'If we're not around just leave them.'

'This thing in the cave,' Santo said.

'This thing,' Vanni echoed.

They were always picky about who was allowed to take part. Not minions like him.

'You want me there as well?'

Gabriele laughed and that hurt. 'It's not for the likes of you. Fetch what I asked. Leave it here. After that . . .' He waved a dismissive hand. 'Go play at whatever you want.'

They'd be gone to the Chapel of the Holy Clasp when he got back with the urchins. He just knew it. After which Santo Vottari would get the hell out of there. Hide out somewhere. Maybe even the Zanzibar with its new black guy behind the counter, a slave who now answered to him.

'Sure,' he said and went for the van.

'There's something wrong with that one,' Vanni said as the van vanished down the hill. 'He never looks you straight in the eye.'

Rocco was busy chewing on a cigar. Gabriele had resumed half-slumbering in his chair, hat over his eyes.

Vanni got up and went over to him. 'Did you hear what I said?'

A noise drowned out his words, one they rarely heard in that remote slope of Aspromonte. The sky darkened for a moment as a huge helicopter, khaki with army markings, soaring over the hillside like a gigantic insect blotting out the sun. They kept their peace, all three of them, until it vanished over the bergamot orchards, down towards the coast. As the racket diminished something else took its place. A black saloon driving into the piazza very slowly, as if each cobble needed to be approached with care.

'So many guests,' Gabriele said in a languid voice, almost bored. 'Such a busy day. Well . . .' He struggled to his feet, stretched his long arms, tipped back the fedora and squinted at the sky. 'I imagine it's only to be expected. The last act has begun.'

The car came to a halt by the fountain. Another of Rocco's foot soldiers was at the wheel. From the back a priest emerged, a tall, dignified man with the craggy face of a minor movie actor. He wore the white mantle known as a cope over his shoulders, with scarlet borders and a large gold cross visible on the back. The legs of his black suit trousers poked out incongruously at the hem, a pair of heavy boots beneath.

Gabriele tottered over, bent forward and kissed his hand. 'Welcome to our mountain home, Father. My son Rocco. My brother Vanni.'

'Rocco I have met,' the priest said. 'A few times of late. You, sir, are something of a hermit. Six services I've taken in Our Lady's chapel and never once has the capo . . . have you graced us with your presence.'

'Needs must.' He took the priest's arm. 'A man is required to play the role God gives him. I prayed for you, for our Holy Mother, for everyone all the same.' He felt the fabric of the cope. It was old and fraying in parts. 'This robe looks a little sorry if you don't mind my saying.'

'We're a poor parish. I'd rather spend money on my flock than clothes.'

'Very decent of you. We're both shepherds in our different ways.'

There was the sound of another car, a weaker engine struggling against the hill. Then the white cinquecento lurched into the piazza and stopped behind the priest's saloon.

'I will help a little with both—'

'That would be very welcome,' the priest said, suddenly cheery.

'Of course,' Gabriele replied. 'We all have a price.'

Two men got out of the Fiat. One familiar, the other a tall, aristocratic-looking stranger.

'We have guests from afar this time,' Gabriele said as they approached. 'Maso is from . . . Canada. Yes that's correct. Maso, meet our parish priest.' They shook. 'And you . . .' A smile. 'You must be his Roman friend. Welcome to Manodiavolo. Welcome to our holy place in the hills.'

The priest kept smiling. The newcomers said nothing.

'Rocco? I think it's time you went to greet our other visitors. The lady and her clasp have waited long enough.'

They watched him walk to the scarlet Alfa and drive slowly out of the square.

'My son will make sure they know the way,' Gabriele added. He looked directly at Falcone. 'We have everything in hand. Everything organized, as we promised. And you?'

'As agreed,' Falcone told him.

'I've been to Canada,' the priest cut in. 'Whereabouts—'

'Talk later,' Vanni told him brusquely. 'It's time to go.'

Gabriele wound his arm through the priest's white cope and led him to the overgrown cemetery behind the ruined church. A lively breeze was beginning to blow dead leaves over the cracked and crumbling headstones. As they walked ravens began cackling in the cypress trees.

'A short and pleasant walk,' he said, 'and then a short and pleasant service.'

The control van had a team of four specialists, three men, one woman, watching the monitors and following the communications channels. Teresa Lupo was familiar with the procedures, some of the equipment, none of the people.

It was almost eleven. Live links into security cameras at the ferry, at Reggio airport, on the main routes in and out of Aspromonte had been feeding into the bank of monitors in front of them since dawn.

'What do you want of me?' she asked.

'They say you've got a good eye and a good head,' Lombardi replied. 'Use them.'

She went through the logs. The van had been following all the traffic through Villa San Giovanni since six. It had access to the names of drivers buying tickets for the ferries. None of them came up on watch lists.

'They can't be coming today, Lombardi. If Nic's right about the timing they've left it too late.'

'I am,' he said, 'aware of this.'

'So they're here already.'

'Probably.'

He asked the female officer monitoring the video feed from the helicopter to tell the crew to make another sweep of the mountain over Manodiavolo.

'No.' Teresa put her hand on his arm. 'Don't do that.'

The woman held off, waiting for instructions. She didn't seem to have much confidence in him either.

'Why not?' he asked.

'They may be used to having helicopters buzzing round there. Doesn't mean they won't get scared off if you do it all the time. You have to be patient.'

He hesitated for a moment then told the operator to stand by. 'All we need do is locate their vehicles. Once we have that we can move. There's no need to wait for some damned pagan service in a cave. We find them. We move. And—' he nudged the man handling the radio links – 'get me Casale.'

That was the name of the captain in the team Peroni had joined. One of the few things Lombardi had confided.

She reached over and grabbed the mike before he could say a word.

'You're not helping, signora,' Lombardi said. 'I invited you here to watch and advise when necessary. Your assistance is welcome when I ask for it—'

'We agreed a process with these people. They go to that service. The Bergamotti leave one way with Nic and Leo. Mancuso and the rest leave the other and you take them there—'

'Bergamotti's an old man. Once it gets out he's betrayed these people he'll be begging us to take him into custody. The rest are ours when we want—'

'No!' Her voice was loud, her manner unmistakable. 'Listen to me, Lombardi. You're a jumped-up pen-pusher playing cops and robbers here. We have lives on the line. Men in the middle of these criminals. Screw with these people and they will turn on us. We will be burying colleagues and I promise you this—' she grabbed the mike right out of his hand – 'if there's one drop of needless blood up there in those hills I will pursue you to the bitter end. I'll make damned sure you get hauled in front of the nastiest, most brutal internal inquiry you've ever witnessed. And I will crucify you there.'

The mike went down on the desk. The nearest desk jockey, a man in his fifties with a greying beard and sharp eyes, picked it up and placed it out of Lombardi's reach. 'She knows what she's talking about. So do I. Only a fool or an amateur starts improvising in operations like this. You do that if you have to.' He pointed to the nearest monitor. 'Right now we don't. Look.'

He'd put up the feed from a camera on the autostrada. A line of identical black Mercedes people carriers, was working its way onto a narrow winding road that led to the tracks behind Manodiavolo.

'Jesus,' Teresa whispered, 'they might as well put up a sign.'

She counted them. Six vehicles, all seemingly occupied. 'There could be fifty men there. We've got sixteen. And Peroni.'

'I could – I could call for local backup,' Lombardi stuttered.

She just looked at him and he didn't say another word.

'We watch, we let them go there,' she said. 'We let them walk to the place they're going. When they come out . . .'

Peroni was terrible around guns and violence. Not least because his heavy, imposing presence made him such an obvious target.

'Am I allowed to talk to Casale now?' Lombardi asked with mock politeness.

'I'll do it,' she said and made the call.

It was hard to push from his memory that first visit with Lucia, to stop thinking about her, wondering why she'd vanished so quickly and without a word. Then they followed the narrow winding track into the cavern and dodged beneath the narrow entrance behind the wheezing but determined Gabriele. As they entered the quiet and the dark all thoughts of anything but the task ahead soon vanished.

The chapel was already prepared for the service, by Vanni that morning he guessed. Candles stood in alcoves he'd never noticed, washing the cavern in a warm and smoky light. The faintest breeze was stirring the flickering flames, fanning the persistent fragrance of burning incense over the smell of damp and mould. From the frescoes on the walls the eyes of a

succession of martyred saints seemed to glitter, like an audience waiting for the curtain to rise. An electric lamp had been
set up above the altar, illuminating the precious silver clasp
there and the sarcophagus of Carcagnosso. Around the three
holes in the stone coffin Vanni had set rings of mountain
flowers, yellow and purple and white, garlands for the
ceremony to come.

And the place was full, every chair before the altar occupied, while more men stood in silence at the sides. All in
dark suits, mostly middle-aged, a few older. In the crowded
semi-dark it was hard to guess at numbers. But it could have
been fifty or more. Those seated waited patiently, a few with
hats on their laps, some swatting away flies and the heavy
humid heat of the cave with what looked like coppola caps.
A couple turned and looked at Gabriele Bergamotti as he
entered, muttered a few words in a dialect he still could
barely interpret. Then said nothing more. The summit was
meant for the restaurant in Cariddi, a private occasion where
the politics of organized crime in Calabria, Sicily and beyond
would be on the table for discussion. Not that it would ever
happen.

'Gentlemen,' Gabriele announced in a booming, theatrical
voice, as he strode to the altar, the priest behind him. 'Welcome
to the Chapel of the Holy Clasp. To the resting place of a man
called Carcagnosso who sailed here centuries ago from his
native Spain.' He beckoned at the stone sarcophagus then
clicked his fingers at his brother. 'Him we honour. We have
wine from our vineyards, milk from our cows, honey from
our hives.' Vanni walked forward and placed three small brass
jugs in front of the altar. His brother gestured at the shining
silver clasp. 'But most of all we give thanks for this precious
object. A gift from Heaven to a man called Apollinario back
when the world was different. Father . . .'

The priest stepped forward, nervous in the yellow light.

'They have already chosen,' Gabriele went on. 'One among
them, the most venerable, has been picked for the task. With
your guidance he will touch the clasp then feed our brother
in his tomb. This is a rare occasion, one to be remembered
and shared. I believe most of you in our humble congregation

have never witnessed it before.' He waited and there was no murmur of dissent. 'Good. Now . . .'

He reached out and held onto the priest for support. 'I'm too old to read the passage as I once used to. My brother too dim. My son too young. For that we require . . .' Returned from the altar, Vanni let his hand fall on Falcone's shoulder at that moment. 'A new friend from afar.'

'I'm not a man for reading—' Falcone objected.

'Oh, come, sir.' Gabriele laughed from the front. Vanni urged Falcone forward until he stood beside the tomb. 'You're a cultured soul. I hear it in your voice. The book . . .' The priest passed over a bible, open at the page. 'Just a short passage. That's all.'

Trapped in front of the audience of dark suits there was no way he could escape.

Gabriele tapped the page. 'This is no ordinary service, friend. Not a mass. Not like any you'll find back home. The priest here will perform the ritual. But first an ordinary man, a sinner, must say the words.' He patted Falcone's shoulder. 'You're a sinner, sir. As are we all. The book . . .'

Falcone looked at the sea of faces in front of him. The man was surely there, the one chosen to touch the clasp and make an offering to the tomb. Mancuso. It had to be.

He walked in front of the altar until he found a place where the electric light revealed the passage.

'Genesis,' Gabriele announced, retiring towards the back of the cavern where his brother waited, Rocco too. 'Whence we all came.'

Falcone cleared his throat, cast his eyes over the strange congregation in front of him once more then began.

'Now the serpent was more cunning than any of the wild animals the Lord God had created . . .'

The SWAT team was deep in the fir wood on the slope beneath the chapel, two hundred metres, no more, from the fleet of identical black people carriers parked in a herringbone line against the rocks in the space along the way. In his casual holidaymaker's clothes Peroni felt out of place next to men like these. Combat fatigues, belts full of military gear he

couldn't name let alone understand, an impenetrable lingo all
of their own. And weapons. Automatic rifles, pistols on their
belts, knives in sheaths around their ankles. Casale, the leader,
seemed polite enough but little interested in the opinions of
an ageing street cop from Rome. These men lived in a different,
more rarefied world.

Then Teresa called.

'We counted them from the helicopter,' she said. 'As they
left the vans and walked up the hill. Forty-two all told.'

'Forty-two?'

'That's right.'

'Did they look armed?'

A pause and then she said, 'I don't imagine they'd carry
weapons into a kind of church, would they?'

'So you couldn't see?'

'They didn't look armed, Gianni. To be honest from what
I saw . . . they kind of looked like a bunch of middle-aged
men on a day out. It's not . . . not what I expected.'

'You heard from Leo?'

'Not a word. We daren't call them. We spotted a small group
of people going up the hill from the village. I guess it was
them. Hard to see. They were under cover most of the way.
If they take that path they could come and go and we'd never
notice.'

Casale was glaring at him. With some reason. This was his
party.

'You need to speak to the boss,' Peroni said. 'Tell him what
you told me. He's in charge, not me.'

The SWAT man took the phone and vanished into the bushes
to talk. Peroni looked at the team, looked at himself. He had
on a light blue cotton jacket, creased, that had seen better
days, a thin checked shirt with pockets, dark blue denims,
cheap, no-brand trainers. Could pass for a tourist or a lost
walker if he wanted.

A couple of minutes later Casale came back, handed him
his phone, muttered something about having to wait and see
which he clearly didn't like. Then he went back to his team
and they did the things men like that enjoyed before action:
checked their weapons and didn't talk much at all.

Teresa was still on the line.

'Sixteen against forty-two,' he said. 'Not the best of odds.'

'Thanks for reminding me. Lombardi was talking about bringing in some of the locals to even up the number.'

That was alarming. 'I thought we'd agreed that wasn't a good idea. No guarantee you'd be evening up anything.'

'Not going to happen. Don't worry. I'll see to that. Please take care of yourself. I want to go home. I want you with me. I'm used to sleeping on one side of the bed after all these years.'

'Me too. Also we've got that shower to put in. The new bathroom.'

It was funny how they always reverted to domestic trivia when things got personal.

'Gianni—'

'Don't worry. I'm not going to offer to help with the plumbing. Keep a close eye on the camera from that helicopter. Watch the roads as well. I don't think . . .' He wasn't a complete novice when it came to stakeouts. He'd done robbery work for a time and knew what they were like. Maybe this team had more firepower and surveillance toys than them but the feel of this kind of operation never changed. The tense anticipation. The guesswork. The way you sniffed the wind and wondered what it might tell you. 'I don't think this is quite what it seems. Nothing is in this damned place.'

Something cast a shadow over them in the trees. He looked up and saw a huge bird, a buzzard maybe, wheeling slowly against the searing sun.

'What's your instinct telling you, genius?' she asked.

'Mostly that I'm not a genius. Just a fool chasing wisps of smoke. In the dark mostly. We are still sticking to the plan, right? You've put that idiot back in his box?'

'Yeah. What else can we do? You take those men when they come out. Nic and Leo wherever they are can grab the Bergamotti and get them to the airport. As soon as we see something moving I'll call.'

'Casale. Call Casale. It's his show. Not mine.'

That seemed to puzzle her but at least she didn't question it. Watching that raptor wheel through the air had given him an idea.

They said goodbye in the perfunctory way people who'd lived with one another for years tended to. Then he wandered over to Casale and asked if he'd got a spare pair of binoculars.

'For what?'

'A hobby of mine.'

Peroni took off his cheap jacket and threw it on the ground. Then pulled his shirt out of his jeans, let it hang, rubbed his trainers on the earth until they were muddy. He was good at looking like a lost idiot when he wanted.

One of the team found a pair of small zoom binoculars and handed them over.

'Thanks,' he said. 'Birdwatching. I always like birdwatching. There are kinds here I've never seen before. You guys stay where you are. You're not exactly . . . dressed for it.'

'What are you going to do?' Casale asked. 'I need to know.'

'I'm going to take a look around.' He held up his phone. 'If I find anything, I'll call.'

He slung the binoculars round his neck and ruffled up what was left of his sandy-grey hair. A man out for a walk. A townie who didn't know the way.

Casale didn't argue. Or get the chance.

An hour she'd spent in the back of the white van. It was dark by the time they got to the place they'd chosen. When the Bergamotti wanted a manutengolo to host a guest they usually picked a tame shepherd in the hills. Or, if a woman was involved, Aunt Alessia and her santina's shack hidden away in the woods. Somewhere so remote there was no chance to run, no opportunity to be anything but what they were told: a temporary visitor, welcome provided one obeyed the rules.

The Sicilians didn't seem so hospitable.

The place they'd turned up at was nothing more than a corrugated iron farm store set amidst some fields. As they'd bundled her out she could see lights glittering on the coast a couple of kilometres away. So many it couldn't be a town. Then she'd caught the chemical whiff of petrol on the air and she knew. Beyond Catania, beyond Augusta, before the tourist sights of Siracusa, Avola and Noto, there was a hideous petro-chemical complex built on the site of some precious ancient

Greek settlements. Small farms were dotted through the dry low countryside alongside roads that took huge tankers down to the coast.

It had to be there.

After an hour or two a surly, scruffy man with a beard and a snappy dog had thrown a torch, some bread and cheese and a plastic bottle of water on the rough ground, then slid the door shut and chained it again.

The torch died after an hour. She was surrounded by piled-up crates of lemons. The citrus smell and the stink of petrol stayed with her through the night, along with the dog's barks and the rattle of heavy traffic on a road not far away.

Could have been worse, she thought. They might have left her with Santo Vottari.

When morning came she heard nothing at all. Not even the dog. She'd banged on the metal doors for ages. Tried to find a way out but they must have been padlocked hard from the outside and the storeroom didn't have so much as a window. If it weren't for a few rays of morning sun peeping through the joins between the walls there wouldn't be light at all.

So she finished the water and what was left of the food. Looked through a few of the crates of lemons to see what was there. They smelled sourer than the Calabrian sort and none of them had a hint of the perfume that came from the bergamot orchards back home.

For a while she sat in the corner and waited. Thinking of what had happened, what she'd say, how'd she'd plead for her life.

Because it had to come to that. The Sicilians had been invited to the Chapel of the Holy Clasp by her father. Ever cautious, and with Santo Vottari's help, they'd decided to take a guest as surety for their visit. It wouldn't be long before they knew they'd been betrayed.

A war was coming. They all knew that. The family was supposed to be out of Calabria before that started. But not her.

They'd taken her watch but it must have been about noon. She told herself to stop thinking about her father, the odd, enticing and melancholic man from Rome and what might be happening back on Aspromonte. There were more pressing concerns.

With that in mind she went back to the lemon crates, found a weak point in the wood at the edge of one, worked at it with her fingers, trying to ignore the splinters that kept stabbing at her skin as she prised a long shard of timber from the side. It was about the length of a dagger, the point as sharp though that would survive one strike only. Still she hid it beneath her shirt where the rough timber chafed and rubbed against her skin.

Not long after she heard the chain rattle on the door. It slid open and the blinding Ionian light flooded into the room, silhouetting a figure against a perfect, cloudless sky.

'And the Lord God said, "The man has now become like one of us, knowing good and evil. He must not be allowed to reach out his hand and take also from the tree of life and eat, and live forever." So the Lord God banished him from the Garden of Eden to work the ground from which he had been taken.'

Falcone finished his reading. The priest coughed in a way that told him he hadn't done it well.

'Apologies,' he said and handed back the bible then worked his way through the half-dark, to the edge of the altar where an arm came out and stopped him.

Behind them the priest began reciting some kind of prayer. It had to be in the local Greek dialect. The words were impenetrable, presumably to the Sicilians too since many of the faces in the audience looked puzzled, and a few a little bored.

Then, in Italian, the man in the cope said, 'Now we invite our honoured guest to celebrate the *refrigerium*, the refreshment of the dead.' He held out his white caped arms and gestured at the three bronze jugs in front of the ancient sarcophagus. 'With milk. With wine. With honey. With respect and love. Sir?'

'Mancuso,' Falcone found himself whispering, and hoped no one had heard. It was years since the police had had sight of the Sicilian. The man had proved so elusive they'd no idea what he looked like any more.

There was a murmur among the seated figures then one of them in the second row stood up, bowed and walked to the front. As he bent down over the jugs gleaming in the soft candlelight his face caught in the bright beam of the electric lamp above the altar.

About sixty. That sounded right. Tall, burly, bald as Falcone himself but with a full black beard flecked with grey.

'Recite these words, sir,' the priest ordered, passing him a sheet of paper. 'Even if they mean nothing to you . . . they mean much to us.'

The bearded figure shrugged as if to say, 'If you want.' His voice sounded deep and calm and cultured.

The two men looked at each other. This had been agreed. Costa had his phone out low in his hands, the flash off, the settings of the camera turned up all the way to take pictures in the dark. Five seconds of video and a few stills later he stopped before anyone saw. Then he edged his way along the wall, past the men on the chairs, apologising to the few who were in the way, until he was out near the entrance and there was a signal. Just enough to send the pictures out to Teresa and Peroni wherever they were.

Ten seconds was all it took. He stood in the shade looking at the path leading back to Manodiavolo, listening to the priest's sonorous voice behind him, thinking again of that day she'd brought him there. Then there was movement. The scrape of wooden chairs on stone as men got to their feet. The strange, brief service was over. The visitors would soon walk down the hill. They had, he hoped, an ID for Mancuso. Things seemed to be going so smoothly.

A hand took his arm. It was Falcone. He looked worried.

'What is it?'

The people inside would soon be wanting out of there. He could hear them talking freely now. A few laughing as if it was all a joke.

'Didn't you notice?' Falcone said. 'Bergamotti. The brother. The son.' He glanced back at the line of figures coming up towards them. 'They're gone.'

Teresa Lupo wasn't taking notice of Lombardi any more. Things were happening and they needed her attention. The helicopter was making slow circles over Aspromonte trying to monitor as best they could. She had the photo and video but no time to do a thing with them.

'Where are you, boys? For God's sake call home,' she murmured.

One minute later Falcone phoned. They were outside the chapel, watching the line of men, dark clothes mostly, wander down the hill. A figure in priestly white was at their head. He told her the Bergamotti had vanished.

'Dammit. I saw people leaving,' she cut in. 'Couldn't make out who they were. But they were going back down to the village. I know that. Only two ways out. That was the one they took.'

A pause and she told the nearest surveillance officer to get the camera turned on Manodiavolo.

'Keep holding,' she told Falcone. 'We're trying to work out what's going on.'

She kept her eyes on the screen as the video shifted to the new destination. The desolate square in the abandoned village, the half-toppled campanile, the ruined church and shops. Only one building stood out as intact, the palace with a red and blue-tiled roof.

'Get in closer,' she ordered. The camera zoomed in. People there, by the fountain in the centre. A scarlet car. A khaki three-wheeled farmer's buggy. 'Closer,' she said, heart pumping. 'As much as you can get.'

Three men were standing by the table in the centre. In the back of the open buggy, surrounded by straw, was a figure she recognized. As she watched he shook himself down, climbed out of the back, and stood there looking lost as the buggy puttered off down the lane.

'They're in the piazza,' she said. 'Silvio's with them. He's safe. Go get. Go!'

He was off the line already.

Lombardi had followed the whole thing and never said a word.

'That's our man,' she told him. 'The one they took. Maybe this will work out. Get the cameras back on the hill.' She watched as the view shifted from the helicopter. Saw something she couldn't believe and yelled, 'Stop!'

'What the hell's he doing?' Lombardi asked.

The line of men was coming down the slope. At the bottom

was Peroni, no jacket, a touch dishevelled. Waving what looked like a pair of binoculars.

'I don't know . . .'

'Get Casale in there. Get his men . . .'

She told them to zoom in on Peroni. She knew the man so well. He was smart. Unpredictable too.

'No,' she said. 'Not yet.'

The priest was leading the way, the long sleeves of his white cope flapping against the scrubby bushes as the group made their way down the snaking mountain track. Peroni stood out in the open by their people carriers at the bottom peering at them through his binoculars. The more he saw, the less he felt concerned.

His phone rang. Teresa. 'Busy,' he said. 'Keep Casale out of here until I say.'

'Gianni! I can see you. If I can . . . what the hell do you think you're doing?'

'It's fine. Keep cool. I've got Casale's number. I'll deal with him direct.'

'No! I'm telling you—'

He put the phone back in his pocket and went back to looking at these men through his binoculars. The birds up here were interesting, but not quite so much as this bunch, ambling carefully down the mountainside, some of them leaning on others' arms for support. A few, a good few he saw, dabbing at their cheeks with very white, crisp handkerchiefs. People dressed for religion. Not that he was a churchgoer himself. All the same . . .

He'd taken a good look at the vans they came in beforehand. No sign of weapons. But plenty to indicate they were from Sicily. Spent ferry tickets on the dashboard. In the back some bottles of white Grillo and red Nero d'Avola. And several religious pamphlets with photos of a curious, tent-like church in striking if ugly concrete. The name was there on the cover: the Santuario Madonna delle Lacrime, Siracusa. A funny place he seemed to recall seeing on the TV once.

Then there was the tall, heavy, bearded man he'd seen in

the photos and video from inside the cavern. The images were shaky and indistinct. But there was no mistaking him as he made his way down the hill right behind the priest. He was, surely, their leader. That was obvious in the way they deferred to him, coming to talk, listening, then retiring to the back to let someone else take their place.

It was, he thought, entirely possible that each of these men was carrying some kind of weapon. Sicilians . . . you never knew. But those robbery stakeouts had told him something over the years, along with decades of police experience. Context, atmosphere and the not insignificant issue of surprise mattered too. On occasion more than any hardware you were carrying and a helicopter in the sky.

His phone rang. He glanced at the caller ID. Casale this time.

'Boss?' he said quite casually.

'I'm not your boss,' the SWAT man snapped. 'If I was I'd know what you were doing.'

'I'm going to be a little reception party,' Peroni told him. 'Just say hello. Explain a few things. Let's try and deal with this . . . politely.' The priest had just turned up at the foot of the path. Peroni waved at him and smiled. 'Unless you hear otherwise you and your men wander out in a couple of minutes. Let's see how it goes.'

He cut the call, walked towards the large group of men staggering off the hill, waved again and shouted very cheerily, 'Hello!'

The door squealed open on rusty, ancient fastenings. A gust of petrol stink swept into the warehouse and flooded over the fragrance of fresh lemons. She blinked at the bright light and the blue ocean ahead, then walked to the door to meet whoever was there.

That seemed to surprise him.

A gigantic network of pipes and tanks and industrial buildings ran across this strange horizon, like a massive child's toy stuck together at random. Beyond that giant tankers moved slowly, floating grey whales breaking the view. Aspromonte might have been on the other side of the world.

'Well?' she asked, feeling the long timber splinter riding against her skin beneath the cotton shirt.

There was no dog. No agricultural slave. He'd been surely told to go elsewhere which, in itself, was educational. Instead it was the Sicilian who'd been with Vottari when she was taken. Sciarra. He'd said his name as they'd gagged her in the van.

Just hearing that had made her realize how bad things were. Back home a manutengolo never left a clue about who they were or where they might be found if someone started to look. People became guests for a reason. As surety. As a bargaining tool. Or simply as hostages in a kidnap, to squeeze money out of a family who could usually afford it. You didn't leave any of them some way back to the people and the place that had held them captive. However they left, in a car, on that final trek into the bleak slopes, it was a one-way passage.

'We need to leave,' he said.

'A walk in the hills?'

He was a handsome man and knew it. Nice clothes, nice face and teeth, too much of a tan, though, and his eyes were hidden behind a pair of black-rimmed shades. 'There are no hills, signora.' He gestured to the flat dry fields. The lemon trees were short and withered. Nothing good grew here. 'See for yourself.'

A dark blue van was parked outside, next to a kennel where the dog lay sleeping, tethered to a long chain.

'We must make a short journey—'

'What do you want?'

He laughed. 'What do you have?'

The way he said that she knew full well what he meant. 'And in return?'

Sciarra frowned, a very southern gesture. The sides of his mouth almost seemed to reach down to his chin. He took off the glasses and peered at her. 'Mancuso was invited to your home in good faith. You planned to trap him. Give him to our enemies. Fortunately . . . we knew. And could make arrangements of our own. Signora—' he beckoned to the van – 'there's always a price that must be paid. Without that how would any of us know where we stand?' He patted his jacket pocket and his fingers slid over the unmistakable shape of a weapon. 'Just get in, will you?'

'My father will pay good money—'

'Too late for that. Get in.' He nodded at her hand as she waved it in his face. 'I like that silver bracelet. Nice. I know someone who'll love it.'

'Screw you,' she said and moved back into the shadows, fingers sliding towards the spear of wood, shaking, sweating as they did so. 'Screw Mancuso. Screw all you Sicilian scum and—'

That did it. He was coming for her and as he raced angrily through the door she could see the gun was out.

And in her head a memory. A conversation with the Roman just days before about where she came from and how they spoke.

Agapi for love.

Miso for hate.

Zoi for life.

In the dark he was on her, strong fingers tight around her throat.

Tanato for death.

A single scream and that was it.

'Gentlemen,' Peroni said, grinning as he walked up to meet them waving the binoculars. 'I'm up here birdwatching and seem to be lost. Do you have any idea where we are?'

The one with the beard, Mancuso according to Falcone, shook his head. 'We're strangers here too. Father?'

The men behind gathered in a group around the vans. They looked exceedingly meek.

'Aspromonte,' the priest said, seeming a touch befuddled. 'If you don't know where you are . . . how on earth did you get here?'

'Walking—'

'No one walks this far.'

A few of them were crowding round. Perhaps this wasn't such a great idea at all.

He pulled out his phone, hit the speed dial for Casale and said, 'I think you should join us.'

Which didn't take long. Out of the bushes sixteen SWAT officers emerged, armed to the teeth, rifles raised, all the stock phrases coming out.

Raise your arms.

Drop your weapons.

The priest's bafflement had turned to outrage. 'What in the name of God is this?'

Casale came round while the rest of the team herded the men towards the rock slope behind the vehicles. Peroni pulled out his badge.

'A police operation. Who are these people? Why are they here?' He nodded at the bearded one. 'Let's start with you.'

'Some ID would help,' Casale added, reaching into the man's jacket, hunting for a wallet. He found one, pulled it out, started to go through the cards.

'We are,' the priest declared, 'a group of innocent visitors to a historical site in these hills. We've broken no laws. We've harmed no one. I don't understand . . .'

Close up the average age of this bunch must have been sixty if it was a day. Something in Casale's face told him this wasn't good.

'How long has this trip been arranged?' Peroni asked.

The bearded one stepped forward and had a look about him that said: in charge. 'Since late yesterday. I had a call in my office to say the opportunity was suddenly available after a cancellation.' He paused for effect then added, 'Do you know who I am?'

'I'm sort of guessing you're not called Mancuso,' Peroni told him.

There was a sudden blush behind those bearded cheeks. 'Mancuso? I . . . I don't know any man of this name.'

'Nor me,' the priest added quickly.

The beat of the helicopter was steady overhead. Casale scowled at the craft then thrust an ID in front of Peroni. The one with the beard. A name: Antonio Maltese. Fifty-six. The card issued in Siracusa.

'Who are you?' Peroni demanded. 'Who are these men? Why—'

'We're friends of the museum in Siracusa. And parishioners

of the church of Santuario Madonna delle Lacrime across the road. Making a rare pilgrimage we paid for, paid well last night—'

'At a few hours' notice?' Casale asked.

'At a few hours' notice! As I said! This place is out of bounds to all but those who know about it. When we were offered the chance I couldn't possibly refuse.' He gestured at his wallet. 'Look at my business card in there. Perhaps that will help you see sense. I must say—' his finger wagged at Peroni, much like a school teacher's – 'I don't know what this is about. Or why you're spoiling the peace of this place with that damned machine up there. We've a meal booked in Cariddi. This entire outing has cost us all a small fortune. If we're obstructed in any way this will go further, mark me. I have friends—'

'I'm sure you have,' Peroni said and pulled the card out of the wallet.

He walked away from the priest and the bearded guy who was getting angrier by the minute. Casale joined him and said, 'We've been going through the IDs for the others. It looks like he's telling the truth.'

'No weapons?'

'They're a bunch of rubberneckers. What the hell—'

He waved Casale into silence then called Teresa. She answered straight away and asked, 'You've got him? The one in Nic's photo?'

'We've got him.'

Something in his tone must have told her. 'And?'

'He's not Mancuso. He's not a hood at all. None of these people are. They're a bunch of sightseers from Siracusa who got handed their tickets by the Sicilians last night. We got rumbled. I think—'

'You're sure?'

He looked at the business card. 'Our friend with the beard is the professor of antiquities at Catania university. And a lay officer of that funny looking church in Siracusa.' The conversation back at the vans was getting heated. 'He's also looking forward to lunch down the coast and I think it's best we don't stop him. Or his friends.'

'Oh my God . . .'

'You tell Leo. I'll do my best to calm things down here.'

The phone rang as they reached the piazza. Just two people there: Gabriele in his chair by the table, hat on, picking orange flesh out of sea urchins he was pulling from a bucket. Then passing them to Silvio Di Capua who was stuffing them on bread before wolfing them down.

'He's safe,' Costa told her. 'Silvio's here.'

Teresa Lupo sighed down the line. 'So I saw. Thank God for that anyway. You're not going to like this. The Sicilians. The other 'ndrine. There's not one of them in that party that came down the hill. They're just a bunch of innocents who got roped in last night on the back of a day out.'

Gabriele tipped his hat at the two of them, waved and went back to tearing out the orange innards of an urchin with a knife. A bottle was open in a wine bucket in front of him, the wine sparkling in a champagne glass by its side. Silvio looked as if he'd had a few already.

'What?'

'They must have got wind of what was going on. All those people you saw are just . . . people.'

'That's why they ran.'

'Sorry?' Gabriele tipped his hat and said a very loud 'Buon Giorno'. Silvio began pouring two more glasses and babbling on about how good the urchins were until Falcone's fierce glare quietened him. 'At least we've got the capo.' Gabriele was telling some kind of joke, reeling with laughter. He looked half drunk.

'Just him?' she asked.

'As far as I can see.'

He could hear the distant sound of the helicopter on the other side of the hill. 'Did your cameras pick up anything?'

'Not there. We were watching Gianni. Tell you what . . .' You never had to ask with Teresa Lupo. 'I'll send them round your side. I can route the video to your phone if you like.'

'Do that. We'll get Gabriele to the airport. Now . . .' An argument had started, loud and furious. 'I've got to go.'

'You're *who*?' Falcone bellowed.

'Are you deaf, man? I said. A thespian, for pity's sake,' Gabriele declared with a theatrical wave of his arms. 'I mean, do I look like a criminal? Really?' He threw another slimy orange urchin in his mouth and spluttered, 'Though I've played my share in the past. Any of you see that Montalbano episode *The Urchin's Return*? I played a kind of gangster in that. A very dignified smuggler of seafood. Which made me think of the ricci here. The chap came to a sticky end sadly. I was hoping for another episode . . .'

'He says he's an actor,' Falcone snapped, glaring at him in disbelief. 'An actor!'

The old man held out his hand. Falcone just stared at it.

'Gabriele – that is my real name – Gabriele Amalfitano. Pleased to meet you. Not that I come from Amalfi. Salerno. Though I've trod the boards in many places. Rome. Naples. Palermo . . .'

'Gabriele . . .'

'Maso.'

'I'm Nic. Nic Costa.'

He reached out and pinched Costa's cheeks like a friendly grandfather. 'See. You're good at acting too. A natural. We were all at it. Well . . . me and you and Vanni. That fool son of his was struggling to keep up. The girl, mind . . . she was smart. Though . . .' He looked sober for a moment. 'I think you know that.'

'Well, I have to say—' Silvio was refilling his glass – 'they've been treating me very well indeed.'

'Shut up,' Falcone bellowed. 'Will someone kindly tell me what's going on?'

Costa sat down at the table. 'That would be a good idea, Gabriele.'

It didn't take long and he'd guessed most of it already. Gabriele Amalfitano had been shipped in to pretend to be Lo Spettro, the capo of the Bergamotti 'ndrina, a man so reclusive few would see through the deceit. They'd told him what to do, how to behave, offered a rough idea of what to say.

'To hell with false modesty, improvisation has always been one of my talents,' he went on. 'I worked with Dario Fo when I was starting out, you know. At the feet of the

master. It wasn't hard. We all play our parts. Some better
than others.'

'Vanni,' Costa said. It was as if a curtain had suddenly lifted.
'The capo's Vanni.'

Gabriele nodded. 'A more educated and intelligent fellow
than he made out. A gentleman to me, and to your young
friend here as far as I can see. Though one wouldn't wish to
be on his bad side.' He reached for more wine. 'I suspect we
shouldn't lurk round here long, my friend. Relations among
the locals are likely to be difficult very soon. As for their
compatriots across the strait.' He raised his glass. 'I've never
found comedy to go down well in Sicily. Have you?'

'In the car,' Falcone ordered, snatching the wine out of Di
Capua's hands. 'Both of you. Now.'

They didn't hesitate though Gabriele had to be persuaded
to leave behind the half-full bucket of sea urchins.

Costa got behind the wheel. Falcone turned and glared at
the man in the back. 'I hope they paid you well. I'm throwing
everything in the book at you. I trust you'll feel this charade
was worth it.'

In the driver's mirror Gabriele's face fell very quickly. The
actor was gone. There was a real man there, tired, sad and
scared.

'I had a call from my wife this morning,' he said. 'The first
in weeks. Since this strange production began.' He took out
a handkerchief and dabbed at his cheeks. 'She's well. She's
free finally. They let her go. So yes, sir. I think it was worth
it. In fact I believe it may be the finest performance I'm ever
likely to give.'

Costa was about to start the car when his phone went again.

'We've got them,' Teresa said.

'Where?'

'Four kilometres down the road from you, on the way to
the autostrada.'

'What—?'

'Take out your phone. I'll live stream the video. We're
recording. For what it's worth.'

A picture came up on the screen. Rocco's scarlet Alfa driving
slowly down a serpentine lane. Ahead the terrain seemed to

level and the ordered lines of trees there told him it had to be one more bergamot orchard.

There were cars in the road. Five or six. Blocking the way.

'Silvio. Gabriele. Get out. I'll call for a car.'

Falcone came and looked. 'How long's it going to take us to reach them?'

'I don't know . . .'

'Nic,' Teresa cut in. 'There's a good dozen men down there and unless I'm mistaken they're the ones Casale's supposed to deal with. Not the two of you. Unarmed . . .'

When the old man and Silvio were back on the piazza cobbles, headed for the table, the food and the wine, Falcone climbed in the passenger seat.

'Nic,' she pleaded. 'Nic?'

He didn't say much as Rocco drove slowly down the narrow, winding track. It was hard to find the words. When he was young it had been for mules only. His father had taken him up the hill to Manodiavolo every time one of the periodic local wars broke out. Now, even with the occasional use of vehicles, it was still barely passable.

But after a couple of kilometres the lane became straight and flat, still at altitude, with a view down to the azure sea and the ribbon shore of Cariddi below. All this was his territory by right, by inheritance, bergamot trees mostly with a few orange and lemon bushes dotted around. He knew every field, every stone wall, the feel of the poor, friable soil, the weeds it carried, the pests, the birds, the creatures of the wild.

'This was ours for almost a century,' he said, pretty much to himself, gazing back at the mountain and the fist of Manodiavolo in the distance. 'A long time for one family. We managed well. We did our best.'

Rocco was weeping. He hated to see that.

'Have we heard from your sister yet?'

'No.' The car lurched over a pothole. 'Not a word.'

He looked at his son and found his temper flaring. 'Stop sobbing like a woman. You do us all an injustice.'

They turned another corner and there they were. A line of black cars blocking the way ahead, six or seven men in casual clothes leaning against them, arms folded. A lean, spindly figure at the front, taller than the rest.

'So the Butcher of Palermo did come to see us after all,' Vanni said as they drew up. 'Stay in the car. This is mine to deal with.'

Back on the hill he was pushing the rented Renault. Teresa had told Casale about the gathering on the other side of the mountain. But the SWAT team were even further away, no chance of reaching that part of Aspromonte in much under an hour.

Falcone clung onto the dashboard as they raced round another tight, sharp corner. 'What are we supposed to do?' he asked as the car scraped against the rocky escarpment on their right. 'When we get there?'

'Arrest them all,' he said and took his eyes off the wheel to smile at the man in the seat next to him.

Falcone groaned. Then laughed. 'Right . . .'

'What else?'

He didn't see the gaping hole in the road ahead until they were on it. The nose of the car dipped as it fell, slamming into the hard stone beneath with such force two tyres burst pitching them straight into a crooked pine tree at the side of the road.

The air bags blew and the seat belts bit hard. A branch ripped through the windscreen sending shattered glass all round them. After a long moment they seemed still, listening only to the dying engine. Then came the smell of leaking fuel.

'Out,' Falcone cried, popping his belt, then the driver's.

The two of them scrambled out of the mangled vehicle and stood by the road, well back. It didn't blow. But still they weren't going anywhere. He picked up his phone from the ground. The screen was cracked from top to bottom but it was still working. With shaky fingers he dialled Teresa and said, 'We crashed.'

'Jesus. Are you alright?'

'Yes. We can't get there. Not quickly. What's happening?'

Silence.

'Teresa . . .'

'I'll put the picture back on your phone. If you really want to watch.'

Vanni got out of the car and walked straight up to Mancuso. They'd met three times over the years, the last a decade before to settle a disagreement about percentages on some of the ferry routes. That had ended amicably. It was not always the case.

Two men came and stood in the way and patted him down as he waited, hands up. He kept looking at Mancuso all the time. There were such stories told about this man. About his capacity for cruelty and violence. These habits were not unknown in the Bergamotti 'ndrina, but they were always used for a reason, never mere malice or entertainment. The Sicilians under Il Macellaio were different.

The sons of the Garduña had taken on the characteristics of the lands they came to inhabit over the centuries. Across the water on a rich and exotic island that seemed to be fought over constantly by armies and bands of robbers alike, all seeking to tame its people. In Naples with its restless impoverished millions, glitz and glamour living cheek by jowl with squalid urban sprawl. On Aspromonte and along its savage shoreline where the sons of Carcagnosso could retreat into the mountains, into caves, hide until it was time to come out in the sun again. Unlike the men of Palermo and Naples it was in their nature to be reclusive, to watch the world then hope to shape it. Not the reverse which was the habit of men like this.

'I have no weapon,' he said as the two foot soldiers got down to his ankles. 'Others carry those in my name.'

Mancuso laughed at that and came and embraced him, kissing both his cheeks in that quick and meaningless fashion that was common across the water.

'Bergamotti. You still play that game?'

'It's not a game. It never was. We're different to you. We don't need the world to see our face.'

'No.' He looked so much older. Sick too. There were rumours Mancuso had some kind of cancer and was too frightened to seek proper treatment since then the police would surely pounce. 'But you would show ours to everyone it seems.'

'I'm here, aren't I?'

'True.' The Sicilian nodded. 'Let's take a walk among those trees.'

Vanni didn't move. 'My daughter . . .'

'We can talk of that.'

He glanced back at the car. Rocco was still at the wheel. 'Don't let my son see. He doesn't deserve that. Not after his mother—'

'Your wife was nothing to do with me.'

'As if that matters.' He stood his ground and waited. 'You're a man of your word. Let him go.'

Mancuso hesitated for a moment then nodded. One of his henchmen went over to the Alfa and spoke through the window. Still the car didn't move.

'Rocco!' Vanni yelled. 'Get out of here.' Still nothing. 'Be gone!'

The engine started then and the car moved off. Rocco didn't look back. It was wrong that the last words of his he'd hear were angry ones. He'd tried to be a good father. It wasn't easy.

'I need to go back to Palermo,' Mancuso said. 'That walk of ours . . .'

'Come,' Vanni replied and stepped off the road onto the dry ground, beneath the shadow of the bergamot orchard.

'Why?' the Sicilian asked.

'Because I'm old and tired. Because we've no easy way of renouncing this life. A life I no longer want for my children. They deserve better. Not this . . .' It was hard to find the words. 'Not this constant sense of battle.'

They were walking side by side. For the moment.

'Do you never feel that too?'

Mancuso shook his head. 'Never. I was given this rank by my father. Who earned it killing the man before him. I would disgrace his memory if I walked away. Like a coward.' The man's eyes turned on him then and they were hard and cruel. 'If I handed others over to our mutual enemies . . .'

Vanni laughed. 'Oh please. You would have strung them

out with lawyers. Or escaped more likely. You do yourself so little credit.'

'I would,' he agreed. 'That doesn't lessen the insult.'

The fruit were good this year. There'd be a rich harvest come November. He reached up and picked a fine specimen, running his thumbnail through the rough yellow citrus skin. When he held it up to his nose the smell of home was there, the perfume of bergamot, a fragrance he'd grown up with and, like his father, loved so much they'd use the name to fox all strangers, hiding behind it in their lairs among the peaks.

'They'll fight you if you try to take this territory,' he said. 'It's for us. The Calabrians. We know how it works. We know how to care for it. Don't fool yourself otherwise—'

Mancuso had fallen back until he was half a step behind. He'd take the weapon out soon. There was no reason to see.

'The arrangement,' Vanni added. 'You're an honourable man so I know you'll abide by it. My sister is unharmed. Rocco will leave for good. You'll never see or hear from the Bergamotti again.'

'Agreed.' His voice was faint, his mind it seemed on other things.

'The territories and the land you'll discuss with the other 'ndrine. There were arrangements by which they paid a tithe to me on certain transactions. In return for my looking the other way.' He cut the fruit again and sniffed it. 'That's worth several million euros a year. You will have to bargain with them over that.'

'We will.'

He stopped. It was time. 'And of course . . . my daughter.' Vanni held out his hand. 'A phone call. I was promised. One phone call. To say she's free and well.'

Something in the man's face troubled him.

'Your daughter,' Mancuso said and nothing more.

'I wish to speak to Lucia as we agreed.' He was still holding the bergamot so he dropped it and gestured with his fist. 'As . . . we . . . agreed.'

The Sicilian's gun was out. Small, black, insignificant almost. The type he couldn't guess. Vanni didn't lie when he said he never handled weapons.

'I'm sorry . . .'

The chop of a helicopter's blades were getting louder overhead and they sounded like the ticking of a clock running up to midnight.

'My daughter.' Vanni said more loudly and turned to him.

Mancuso shrugged and waved the gun as if it was an issue of no consequence. 'Things happen. They—'

But he was halfway to the Sicilian now, fist out, fury real and livid. Words no longer mattered.

Two kilometres away, by the wrecked car piled into a tree on the narrow track, they watched the last act of the drama on the cracked screen of Costa's phone.

One shot.

An old man falling.

A group of others quickly scurrying away.

Then, frightened by a sound they couldn't hear, a lone eagle emerging from the bergamot orchard, vast wings opening wide, rising to soar on the hot summer breeze, circling to the jewelled coast below.

# PART SEVEN

# A Momentary Music

## Calabrian Tales

### Chapter XXII: Great Pan is Dead

There are a great many churches across Calabria yet not a single temple to the oldest god many still worship in their hearts, the deity of fertility and the fields, of rustic wilds and savage nature. Of theatre too, tragic and comic, played behind those dramatic masks one still sees in museums.

Pan is his name, half man, half goat. A wild spirit, forever stalking forest glades and mountain passes, pipe in hand, wont to steal nymphs back to his native Arcadia for pleasure. Yet according to the historian Plutarch he's dead. It happened during the reign of Tiberius when a ship's pilot, Thamus, on his way to Italy from Paxos across the Ionian, heard a strange and heavenly voice call out, 'Thamus, are you there? When you reach Palodes, take care to proclaim the great god Pan is dead.'

Now no one knows for sure where Palodes is, but on Aspromonte we believe it to be on our coastline close to the resort of Pellaro. Sure enough when Thamus was off the shore he called out his message and in return heard a terrible, inhuman wailing from the coast and Aspromonte behind: Great Pan is Dead.

The Christians naturally took up Plutarch's story as proof that the pagan world was gone, and the only god still remaining their own. Yet for the poor and the oppressed the more a belief is damned, the more it is likely to flourish, albeit in the shadows. Centuries after Pan's supposed end, travellers in Greece and across Aspromonte reported finding secret shrines and temples to the divinity in rural communities everywhere. Indeed the very chapel in the cavern rumoured to contain the silver

bracelet of the Virgin brought by Carcagnosso was reputed to
be a temple to him before the Christians came.

Perhaps it still is. Perhaps those who worship there say an
unspoken prayer for an older god when they kneel before the
altar. I am not in a position to say, but this I do know. When
I was a child in Manodiavolo, after school, we would sometimes search for him in the bergamot orchards and the fir
forests, along mountain streams and the thrashing torrents rain
and snow would bring in winter. Once – just once – alone,
hunting for rabbits, I caught sight of something through the
trees. It seemed to be a crouching man, two horns on his hairy
head above a pair of twinkling eyes. He gazed at me and
winked as I stood there in fear and amazement. It was winter
and there was ice upon the streams. Yet his chest was naked
and as he moved I saw his hindquarters were furry and bent,
those of a goat not a man, cloven-hooved as he scuttled away
into the woodland whence he came, the fleeting music of his
pipes behind him.

When I met my teacher the next morning I told him what
I'd seen. A wise and educated man, he made me swear never
to mention it outside Manodiavolo, then found a poem he liked
and made me read. I remember the words still. They were by
an American I'd never heard of, Ralph Waldo Emerson.

O what are heroes, prophets, men,
But pipes through which the breath of Pan doth blow
A momentary music.

God of mischief and the savage wilds, god of masks and lies
and drama.

Great Pan is Dead.

Not here.

F ive days on the recriminations had begun. Lombardi was back in Rome where a furious Justice Ministry had opened an internal inquiry. Teresa Lupo, Gianni Peroni and Silvio di Capua had returned too. The word from on high was that the civil servant was likely to carry most of the blame. The team in Cariddi weren't the only ones he'd exasperated. Plenty of his own colleagues were ready to sharpen their knives as well.

The lawyers had just one individual in their sights, an out-of-work actor called Gabriele Amalfitano, and he'd been released on bail after telling them how he was forced into the act after his wife was kidnapped. The prosecutors were reluctant to charge him. Amalfitano had talked freely and frankly of how he'd been seized, given the story he was supposed to recount to the police and the character he had to play. Dragging him into court would only make the embarrassment public and rouse sympathy for a man who'd been forced to go along with the pretence to save his wife.

Costa and Falcone were left to explain to the local force why they'd been kept in the dark throughout. That had gone rather more easily than either expected. There were a few muted protests from on high but the need for secrecy was something the state police and the Carabinieri in Reggio appeared to accept. It seemed to Costa that both were grateful not to have been involved directly. Perhaps they knew how difficult a task it would prove, and how messy the fallout. When he put that to Scuderi, one of the more friendly local officers, the man simply shrugged and said in a resigned fashion, 'The Bergamotti. We only had the faintest idea of who they really were. We knew what they did. But faces, where exactly they lived from day to day, they didn't call the man Lo Spettro for nothing.'

'I believe his real name was Giovanni Ursi,' Costa had said.

'Do you?' Scuderi replied with a smile. 'Well . . . what does it matter now? They're gone. And we get someone else in their place.'

That change occurred without the mob war everyone had predicted. The Corigliano 'ndrina had taken over Bergamotti territory overnight. The arrangement, as far as the police understood, was that the Sicilians would receive the percentage cut once given to the Bergamotti, applied to the whole territory. In return Mancuso and his men had slipped back home, doubtless by private boat from somewhere along the coast, and vanished. Intelligence believed the link man between the two would be Santo Vottari, newly-promoted to crimine within the Corigliano crew.

All of this must have been improvised in the twenty-four hours before Vanni died. There was no sign of the Sicilians by the time Costa, Falcone and Casale's men made it to the bergamot grove. No trace of Vanni either, only blood on the parched September ground beneath the trees. Rocco had been seen vanishing in his scarlet Alfa down towards Cariddi. His car was found later in an autostrada garage. Of him there was no trace. The only news of his sister came from vague reports in Sicily. They suggested she'd been taken hostage as surety for the Sicilians' visit, and murdered when her father's treachery became apparent. Alessia, the aunt he'd first met when she was playing the part of santina as they lured him into the hills, had gone too, all her business interests in Cariddi and elsewhere, the restaurant included, passed over to new masters.

For more than a century this territory had been in the hands of the family that called themselves the Bergamotti. It seemed they'd played the part of rulers, benign mostly, taking their share of public contracts, rigging elections, milking everything from construction works to hospital supply contracts, drug contraband and prostitution. Few ordinary civilians prospered in business or public institutions without their support. Even the church was not immune to their persuasive powers; they had friends and allies everywhere, most of whom now shifted their allegiance to the new regime.

And all the while the capo, Vanni, had lived the quiet

and modest life of a humble farmer in the abandoned mountain hamlet of Manodiavolo, ruling an empire that spanned
businesses around the world while tending his animals and
his orchards. Nothing like this could happen in Rome, in
Sicily, in Naples, anywhere else in Italy. Yet to Costa,
through the time he'd spent as Maso Leoni, it seemed
eminently believable. They were the people painted in that
book he'd been given at the start. Criminals 'full of a strong
goodness'.

It wasn't going to be easy to forget that pool of dark dried
blood beneath the bergamot trees. All that was left of the man.
No corpse. No hard evidence. In Aspromonte even a treacherous, murdered gang lord would never be left for the police
if those who killed him could possibly avoid it.

Five days and everything was petering out. One last lunch
over the water in Cariddi, a meal in which Toni, the waiter,
served them politely but said scarcely a word. Then they picked
up their bags from the house and took the hired car to the
airport.

He drove. Falcone stared out of the window.

'We've nothing to worry about,' he said as they turned into
the airport. 'We did what we were asked. How they found
out . . .?' Falcone shook his head. He looked older, more
gaunt after all this time beneath the harsh Calabrian sun. 'I
doubt we'll ever know.'

'Rocco,' Costa said. This thought had been bugging him
for days. 'They let him live.'

'You think he'd give up his father. His sister?'

It wasn't much of an airport. So few people came here.

'Leo. They let him live. I saw these people on the inside.
If they were going to kill him they'd have done it there and
then. They don't wait on anything. They never have.' He pulled
up outside the car hire cabin. 'Rocco. It has to be.'

One hour to the plane. One hour to Fiumicino and Rome.
They had coffee then Costa's phone rang. A caller who with-
held the number. A caller who didn't speak until he did then
said, 'You're fleeing. Are you happy?'

A croaky, smoke-stained woman's voice he'd first heard in
a shepherd's hut in the hills. 'Alessia. Where are you?'

'The place you just left and never even saw me. Some policeman you are.'

'What—'

'Walk outside. I'm in the cheap little blue car by the gate. I've something for you. Something you need to see as well.'

The line went dead. He walked back to Falcone and said he'd have to fly alone.

'Something,' he added, 'something's come up.'

'What?'

'I don't know. I'll tell you when I do.'

Falcone didn't move.

'Here,' Costa begged. He handed over his case. 'Check that in for me. I'll pick it up as soon as I can. There's a . . . contact. From Manodiavolo. They won't talk with you around. Just . . .' He had to stop. They were calling the flight on the crackly airport speakers. 'I'll phone you when I can.'

He didn't wait for an answer. The car was where she said.

'Get in,' Alessia told him, pushing open the door.

She was wearing black. Black cardigan, long black dress, black boots. Her hair was tied behind her skinny neck in a black bow. Her eyes were clear. The cataracts were contact lenses as he'd suspected. It was hard to picture her as the scruffy santina he'd met with Rosa in the hills. But that was a part she played, an act, like everything else.

Costa settled into the seat and asked, 'Where are we going?'

'What about the man with you? Is he going to follow us?'

'No. He's on the plane to Rome. No one's going to follow us.' All the same she looked round the car park to see.

'Where are we going?'

A quick glance at herself. 'A funeral. Where do you think?'

Half an hour later they were pulling into the piazza of Manodiavolo. There was a hearse parked up by the fountain, a single wreath of lilies and laurel leaves leaning against the front.

The place looked deserted. But then he heard voices, coming from the cemetery behind the church, and they walked there, slowly.

The priest he'd seen in the chapel in the cave stood in the

shadow of the broken campanile, wearing the same white, long-sleeved cope. Four men in black, hired pall-bearers he guessed, waited, hands behind their backs, next to a newly-dug grave, a coffin in simple white pine, a bronze cross on the lid, on the earth by its side.

The priest glanced at them as they turned up. Nervous, Costa thought. He didn't want to be here, any more than the pall-bearers who must have carried the coffin up the shallow hill into the graveyard beneath the cypress trees. Money or the last of the Bergamotti's influence must have brought them here.

'Signora. Do you wish me to say some sort of . . . eulogy?' the priest asked when they arrived. 'I could try and—'

'Just the words,' Alessia told him. 'The usual. Vanni was never one for flattery. Or small talk.'

What followed was in Griko so Costa had to try to match the sonorous tone of the man's voice to what he recalled of the Italian ceremony. The service, such as it was, didn't last long. Then the pall-bearers lifted the shiny black sashes beneath the coffin and manoeuvred it into the grave. The earth looked bone dry and the colour of the bark on the cypresses. When the casket was in place the priest threw some soil on the pale wooden lid, Alessia did the same and nodded at the men to fetch their spades.

'We must speak.' The priest came straight to her. He was pale and his hands were shaking. 'My condolences of course but—'

'But what? Didn't we give you enough money over the years?'

'Of . . . of course,' he stuttered. 'All the same . . . this is not a proper graveyard. No longer hallowed ground. If the authorities were to find out—'

She nodded at Costa. 'They know. Why do you think he's here? They'll do nothing.'

He kept quiet.

'Roman,' she said, tapping on his jacket with a sharp finger. 'My brother's dead. You will never find his murderers. You will not come here and disturb his peace. As to this being hallowed ground . . .' She waved her hand around the little cemetery, the church, the piazza below. 'It was to him. The place he loved. I want him here. Now—' she nodded at the cars – 'get your people to finish their work then go. You'll get your money later.'

The priest didn't argue. The men with the shovels never looked up from their task.

An hour of silence followed, spent sipping water and wine at the trestle table by the old dry fountain. She wouldn't say more with the others around. Then she watched them leave in the hearse, the priest nodding warily as he climbed into the passenger seat.

'I mean it,' she said when the long black vehicle had edged slowly down the hill on the broken cobbles. 'You won't come here and touch him. There'd be no point. You know he's dead. Everyone does. The local police too. They at least have some decency in these matters.'

The weather was colder now, a chill breeze that heralded autumn drifting off the hills. Soon a different family would be harvesting the bergamot crop. Not long after there'd be snow. He wondered what Manodiavolo would look like when that happened and knew he'd never find out.

'Agreed,' he said. 'In return I want two things.'

She stared at him and he saw again that santina in the squalid shack. 'Do you think you're in a position to make demands?'

'Requests. That's all.'

Quickly she snatched his hand and ran her fingers across his skin, found the scar beneath the thumb that Lucia's blade had left little more than a week before.

'She made you one of us. Or tried.'

'Lucia—'

'What I said when I saw you that first time in the hills. I know you think that was all a trick. But I can play the santina. I can see things too. When I want to. Death follows you like a shadow. You like having it around.'

That was too much. 'I didn't betray your family. I was doing my best to try to save them.'

She scowled and looked across at the decaying palazzo. 'They'll let this rot and turn to ruin now. Vottari. The Corigliani.

They want what the Sicilians always do. Money. Luxury. Comfort.'

'Who was it?'

A shrug and then: 'Ask who prospered. Vottari for one.'

'And Rocco.'

'What of him?'

'They let him go. I saw it. We found his car. He's alive somewhere.' Costa didn't take his eyes off her. 'Isn't he?'

Half a laugh and there was something cold and amused in her eyes. 'That is a family matter. For the family to deal with. Not you. Ask the question that's in your head. Or I'll get in that car and leave you here to walk.'

A moment then he said it. 'What happened to Lucia?'

'Don't you know?'

'Not for sure.'

She ran her fingers on the wound then let go of his hand. 'The Sicilians snatched her as security. When they realized what Vanni had in mind they killed her.'

He couldn't speak for a moment. The pain was real. Like a blow to the chest.

'Vanni gave himself up to them. I can't imagine he'd do that without making some kind of bargain. He loved her—'

'We all loved her,' Alessia snapped. 'Don't presume.'

'He wouldn't have offered her—'

'My niece is dead! How many times do I have to say it? I don't know where. I don't know how. We got Vanni back because he wasn't far from here. Lucia . . . they took her across the water. It wouldn't be easy to bring her back. Or safe. So . . .'

Alessia reached inside her bag and retrieved something that took his breath away. It was the silver bracelet, the copy of the Virgin's, that she always wore.

'This is all they sent.' She placed the shining clasp in front of him. 'Take it. The memories I have of my niece are here.' She tapped her head. 'I don't need anything else.'

The silver was cold and more worn than he remembered. Running round a quarter of the circlet was a shiny stain of dried blood.

'I can't . . .'

'Take it! From what I heard she'd have . . . wanted that.
I . . .' Alessia wiped her eyes. 'God. Tears. We're not meant
for them. Take it, damn you. Then I'll drive you to Reggio.
You can go back to Rome. Where you belong. Not here. Never
here again.'

He didn't budge. 'Rocco must have known. It couldn't just
be a foot soldier like Santo Vottari.' Silence. 'Tell me, Alessia.'

'Why? What can you do? What business is it of yours? My
brother and my niece are dead. My nephew's God knows where.
Australia for all I know. He liked it there.' She leaned forward
and took his hand, her eyes full of tears now. 'For your sake,
Roman, learn to let things go. Otherwise those shadows will
return and one day the life they'll claim will be yours.'

She got up, wiped her eyes with the sleeve of her funeral
dress, then walked to the car. 'If you want a ride come now.
You're not the only one who's leaving.'

He didn't get the plane to Rome. Instead he caught the first
flight to Naples, landed there at five, took a cab to the harbour
and the first fast ferry across the bay to Capri. The weather
was warmer even though this was further to the north. But the
boat was quiet, mainly occupied by locals returning from their
daily commute. By the time he reached the island and took
the funicular to the centre even the Piazzetta was barely half
full with tourists gasping at the prices of evening coffees and
cocktails. The way to the ruined imperial villa was called the
Via Tiberio, little more than a footpath, the only traffic the
three-wheel scooters of the rubbish trucks, delivery carts and
transport carriages for elderly locals. Too dark to do much
even if he had an idea what that might be. So he found a room
in a hotel, ate lukewarm flabby pizza in a bar along the road,
took the silver bracelet from his jacket pocket, stared at the
dark stain there, wondering what it might tell him.

He'd fled Calabria so quickly, so impetuously, he didn't
have any luggage and had to beg reception for toothbrush and
a disposable razor. The past few weeks it seemed as if someone
had been hunting him. Now he was the hunter and that felt
good. Rocco was out there somewhere, the reason Vanni and
Lucia were dead. He needed answers.

Back in his room at nine, shirt and socks and underwear drying on the balcony, his phone went.

'Leo,' he said, looking at the number.

'Where in God's name are you? What happened?'

'Vanni's dead. They wanted me to know. To be sure. They don't want anyone looking for the body—'

'Hardly their decision. Where is it?'

Somewhere beyond the window he could hear the sound of animals: goats or sheep perhaps. The little hotel was halfway along the lane that led to the ruined imperial Villa Jovis, an ancient home of Tiberius, away from the tourist glitz and racket of the centre. He could see how it would remind her of Aspromonte.

'I don't know. They wouldn't tell me.'

It hurt to lie but it seemed necessary.

'This lead of yours—'

'May be nothing. Book me out of work. We're owed the time. I'm taking it.'

'Nic—'

'When I've got something to say I'll call. Good night.'

The next morning he checked out of the hotel first thing and walked up the Via Tiberio wondering how he'd find the house. There was something here. Something asking to be found. A piece in the jigsaw that was the Bergamotti, Lucia most of all. He felt that, not that he knew how.

The lane narrowed into a footpath as it wound towards the ruins at the end. Before long he reached the turning marked for the Salto di Tiberio, the precipice where two millennia before a fisherman had died, a lobster rubbed in his face before a soldier threw him off the cliff.

Her words came back.

*It's not just the criminal peasants of Aspromonte who can display a heartless streak at times.*

Opposite, a little way down the hill with a dramatic view over a cliff that fell to stark rock teeth in the bay below, stood a small villa, orange walls, neat garden with fruit trees. Some of them looked like bergamot. There was a for sale notice by the gate alongside a sign that said: Villa Carlotta. It was unlocked so he walked through, down the drive, heart pumping when he heard a distant female voice.

Costa marched straight through the half-open front door. A woman in a long red dress, gold necklace, gold earrings, the very picture of Capri rich, glared back at him. She was with a middle-aged Chinese-looking man in a dark suit who was holding what looked like sheets from an estate agency.

'Who the hell are you?' she demanded.

'I was looking for the family. They live—'

'You said the house was empty,' the man objected.

'It is. They moved out. We're the sole agents.' She led Costa outside and whispered, so the man inside couldn't hear, 'I don't know what you're doing here but I'm closing this sale today. Beat it.'

'The Ursi . . . Father, son, daughter—'

'There's never been anyone here of that name.'

'The woman who lived here—'

'She's gone. Now . . . do I have to call the police?'

There were paintings on the walls. Simple, a little crude. Orchards and a peak he could see was Aspromonte.

Hers. He knew it.

'No you don't.'

It was only a few minutes after nine. Down the lane, on the way back to the Piazzetta and the funicular to the port, there was a sign for a cafe by an arch into a quaint garden. Little more than a few tables set next to someone's vegetable patch. An elderly man with a grey beard was bent over lines of artichokes and squash, not a single customer to serve. Costa went in, sat down and ordered a coffee when he finally arrived. The ferries left all the time. He could get to Naples in an hour then Rome on the fast train in about the same. Call in at the Questura by lunchtime. Get his luggage. Put on his work suit, pick up his ID card. Return to being Nic Costa, a *sovrintendente* in the Centro Storico Questura. He'd escaped those chains for a while when they made him put on the mask of Maso Leoni. That change in identity had opened his eyes in some ways. More than anything, so had she.

'You,' the gardener declared, 'look like a man more in need of a drink. How about I make that a *caffè corretto*?'

Something about him reminded Costa of Vanni, working in his fields. 'Just a *macchiato* thanks.'

A shrug then.

'Well, I'm having one,' the old man announced and after a while came back with two cups and sat down on the other side of the table. 'How's the macchiato?'

'Good.'

'No. It's not. The machine needs fixing. Sorry.' He took a gulp of his own and the rich smell of spirit wafted across the table. Mingling with the scent of orange blossom, it took him straight back to Manodiavolo. 'I saw you looking at the villa up the road.' He laughed and shook his head. 'Six million euros they want for that place. Or so I heard. My uncle Gennaro sold it for a pittance in the Fifties. What he got for it, you couldn't pick up a chicken coop in Capri for that these days. All foreign money. All foreigners.'

'It wasn't owned by foreigners. A woman. A young woman.'

'Ah!' His eyes opened, then he went to the counter, grabbed the grappa bottle, came back and topped up his cup. 'Thirsty work gardening. You're right. They weren't foreigners.'

'They . . .?'

'The family. It wasn't just that young woman.'

'The Ursi?'

The man looked baffled. 'No. They were called Bianchi. Came from the south. Near Reggio, I think. The father was a farmer, I believe. A rich one, I assume. The children . . . I don't know. Wait . . .'

He ambled to the bar again and returned with a photo album and a plate with a piece of cake on it. 'Here. Earlier this summer. It was a birthday. The daughter's, I think. They let me take a picture because my wife cooked dolci. Almond from our trees. Try it.'

The gift he'd brought was sweet and gritty and delicious and he barely noticed as he stared at the picture. It looked like a warm spring day. Vanni was in the centre raising a glass, Lucia happy in a long-sleeved shirt to his left, on the other side Rocco, grinning as he cut into a huge and fancily-decorated cake.

'They were a lovely family,' the gardener said. 'It was always a pleasure to have them.'

'I thought she lived here. Alone.'

He shook his head. 'No. They came and went. No one lives in half these places these days. They rent them out for a small fortune and from time to time they visit. As I said they came from the south. Near Reggio. Though lately . . .' He scratched his rough grey beard, thinking. 'Lately they'd been talking about moving. Not here. Too busy they said. Must be money in farming in Reggio. Me . . . I just own the one home. One's enough.'

Costa finished the coffee. It was lukewarm and weak. 'Moving where?'

The gardener was screwing up his eyes, trying to remember. 'They liked islands. The old man said that. He didn't talk much usually.'

'Venice,' Costa suggested, remembering how Gabriele, the counterfeit capo, had talked of the lagoon, presumably after Vanni's covert briefing. 'Duck hunting.'

'No.' He checked his watch and frowned. 'I must get on.'

'Where . . .?'

'He mentioned the ducks. I remember that. The son was really keen on hunting. Liked guns, I think. Not much of that here.'

'Rocco?'

He nodded. 'Yes. That was his name. Rocco and Lucia. A lovely pair of kids.'

'Burano. They talked about—'

'No, no, no. Not Burano. We went there once. I talked to him about it. All the houses are painted in funny colours. To please the tourists mostly. Rocco didn't want to be near the tourists though I said maybe he could use his guns on them. He wanted to be near the ducks.'

There were little islands all across the lagoon. If someone wanted to hide . . .

The gardener was thinking. 'There was a restaurant the girl talked about. Some American writer went there. The one who wrote about fishing. She was a fan. I remember him.' He grinned and jabbed a triumphant finger in the air. 'Hemingway. Yes.'

'Torcello.'

He could picture it from when he was there with Emily, before they married. A distant island at the very northern tip of the lagoon, a beautiful old basilica from the brief time, more than a millennium before, when it was the most important place in Venice. Hardly anyone lived there. But there was the Locanda Cipriani, a hotel and restaurant Hemingway had used, and all around fields of fruit and vegetables, goats and mules, by the shore the nets of fishermen and the boats of hunters.

The gardener raised his glass. 'Torcello. That's it.' He stopped as Costa got quickly to his feet. 'You don't want another.'

'No,' he said, throwing some coins on the table. 'But thanks.'

He walked, half-ran back to the funicular, checked flights on his phone as the little carriage clunked and bumped the steep way down to the harbour. The high-speed ferry took fifty minutes and it felt twice as long. The cab driver at the other end sped him to Capodichino in thirty. No luggage, just a credit card and personal ID, he got onto the first flight with just twenty minutes to spare.

No time to call Falcone even if he wanted. Besides the battery on the phone was starting to bleat and pieces of glass were falling from the shattered screen.

Marco Polo airport was an hour away, north east across the breadth of Italy. It was just after two when he watched the grey expanse of the lagoon emerge along the Adriatic coast, the familiar shape of Venice coming up beneath the wing, a forest of red tiles and marble buildings, spires, palazzi and squares divided by the winding blue corridor of the Grand Canal. Torcello soon emerged, the tower of the campanile jutting out of the low grey horizon.

A humid haze hovered over the lagoon as he leapt into the gleaming *motoscafo* at the water taxi stand. There was only one person to call.

'Nic?' Teresa Lupo answered straight away. He could hear

the sound of the office behind the rattle of the boat's engine
and the wash of waves against the hull. The Questura never
slept. 'Where are you? Leo's worried. Dammit, I'm worried.'

'Don't be. I'm in Venice. I need something quick.'

'Go on.' She only argued when there was time.

Property records. Just for Torcello. He wanted her to browse
the database and see if there was anywhere with Calabrian
connections. Or a name they recognized. Probably not
Bergamotti. Maybe Ursi. Or Bianchi. Perhaps a connection
with the registered owners of a place on Capri called Villa
Carlotta.

'Don't want much, do you?'

He listened to the clatter of her fingers on the keyboard,
could picture her at work at a desk in the centre of Rome.
'How long's it going to take?'

'I'll get back to you when I have something.'

Thirty minutes in the fast water taxi and he was standing
beneath the outside canopy of the Locanda Cipriani handing
over a hundred and forty euros, almost all the money he had
left. One of the most elegant and expensive hotels in the lagoon
but close up it looked unassuming, just a country inn, much
as it must have done more than half a century before when
Hemingway wrote most of a novel here.

Teresa called back.

'Start talking,' she told him.

'About what?'

'About what you're doing in Venice. That could be a start.'

Diners were coming out of the restaurant, stumbling into
waiting boats, falling on the leather seats in the stern, smiling
at the pale blue sky. A fine late September afternoon away
from the tourist mayhem of San Marco.

'OK,' she said eventually. 'So you won't say. As far as I
can see there's fewer than thirty registered properties on
Torcello. That make sense?'

'Definitely,' he said, looking around.

'The only one that stands out's a place called the Azienda
Agricola San Giovanni. It's owned by a company based in
Monaco. So is the villa on Capri. Different company but that's
as close as I can get.'

'Can you see it on a map?'

'No. There aren't conventional addresses. It's the usual Venice thing. Just numbers. You want me to call the locals and send some backup?'

'No.'

'Wait a minute . . .'

'It may be a dead end. I'll probably be on a plane to Rome tonight. Don't tell Leo. Don't waste anyone's time.'

A pause then. She knew when he was lying. 'Look. If there's something—'

'Sorry. Got to go.'

A smiling waiter was hovering, looking for business. When Costa came off the call the man was over straight away asking what he wanted.

'Advice. I'm looking for some friends. They're from the south. Calabria. Got a little farm somewhere. The Azienda San Giovanni—'

The man nodded. 'You mean the Rossi?'

A pause then: 'Yes.'

'They used to come here from time to time. Don't know why they call that place an azienda. Don't see them selling a thing from the fields.'

'Recently?'

He thought for a moment then said, 'The man. The young one. I saw him in his little boat yesterday, messing around. Looked like he was going shooting.'

'How do I find the place?'

The man pointed down the canal the water taxi took. 'You got to cross the Ponte del Diavolo. The Devil's Bridge.' He laughed. 'Don't hang around if you see a black cat. Means the bad man with the pitchfork's coming for you.'

He had to push through a gaggle of tourists ambling towards the basilica. The afternoon was dead still with a stifling, close humidity to it. He felt exhausted, aware only of the need to go on, not knowing where this led. There hardly seemed a gap between Alessia's grim words and even grimmer gift by the fresh grave in Manodiavolo, Reggio the morning before, Capri, then this remote part of the lagoon.

And the news about Lucia. The subtle, unspoken message

in her aunt's words. She died, along with her father. While
Rocco lived and walked away.

Her silver bracelet still sat in his pocket, the bloodstain in
his head.

There was a cafe halfway along the narrow, rural canal. He
stopped and bought a coffee and a *panino*, asked about the farm
again. The man pointed at a curious low bridge over the canal,
pale brick, no parapets, just open sides.

'Over the bridge. Used to be a monastery until Napoleon
came along and knocked it down,' the barista told him.
'History's all we've got here.'

'Do you know them?'

He thought for a moment and nodded. 'Calabrians.' He
lifted his arm as if to fire a shotgun. 'Bang. That's all the guy
does. Don't know how he gets to eat all those ducks. How the
hell people like him get the money for a place like that.'

He hesitated, just for a moment, then asked, 'Rocco?'

The waiter frowned. 'Yeah. I think that's him.'

Choices.

Decisions.

Forks in the long, long road.

The man went back into the kitchen to find something.

Costa reached over behind the bar and stole the short, sharp
knife that stood beside a half-severed lemon. It jangled in his
pocket against Lucia's silver clasp as he left.

Across the Devil's Bridge the path meandered like an
Aspromonte lane, through tiny vineyards, orchards, past
slender rivulets choked with weed, by the ruins of an ancient
building, a scattering of giant stones across a swampy field.
Then, close to the shore, a house emerged. It wasn't what
he expected, a rundown little farm like one of the Manodiavolo
outbuildings. The place was grand, a mansion, two storeys,
the style Venetian Gothic, ochre walls with wide lancet
windows and green shutters, most of them closed. A small
blue and white motor launch, old and stained by the waters
of the lagoon, was moored by a decaying jetty. Across the
flat, still channel stood the multi-coloured houses of Burano
and the vaporetto stop where one of the mid-sized motonavi

they used for the outlying islands was manoeuvring in to dock.

As he walked round the back a modern swimming pool emerged, an incongruous bright blue, tables and closed umbrellas all round. The place might have made a small hotel but at that moment it seemed quite deserted. Then, as he crept round, close to the wall it came to him: the acrid smell of a cigar. In an instant he was in Reggio, that grimy industrial park on the hot day they'd pretended to murder Falcone and Gianni Peroni.

Ahead there was what looked like the door to the kitchen. Open. A few metres away a ramshackle gardener's hut was leaning at a crazy angle by the path to a vegetable plot full of *cavolo nero*, artichokes and tomatoes, much like the one Vanni had maintained in the south. He could see him here in his head, bending, smiling as he tended the plants, talking to them as he worked.

Creeping round the door his hand crept to his pocket. As his fingers closed on the knife the cigar stink got stronger. There were sudden steps behind, a firm hand on his shoulder, cold metal pressed hard against his neck.

'Jesus,' Rocco whispered close to his ear. 'Your kind never learns.'

He slipped the knife from his fingers to his sleeve, turned round and found himself facing a man he barely recognized. Rocco had cut off all his hair so there was just stubble there and pale scalp beneath. No sunglasses. No designer clothes. He wore a pair of farmers' overalls, blue, dirty. Could have been just another lagoon peasant working on the fields. His face seemed different too. More narrow as if he hadn't eaten much. As if something had been weighing on his mind.

'What the hell are you doing here?'

The gun was at an angle, half-pointed at Costa's chest.

'Looking for explanations.'

A boat's engine sounded on the water. The racket it made sent a couple of pure white egret squawking out of the reeds.

'This was a big mistake, Maso. What am I supposed to do with you now?'

There was that old note of casual cruelty in his voice. Nothing in the world was going to wash him clean of that.

'The name's Nic Costa. I'm a police officer. There was no Maso—'

'We noticed. You never fooled anyone. Why do you think it all went—'

One chance was all he had. His right hand came down and the little knife slipped from his sleeve. Fell straight into his grasping fingers and then the blade flashed quick and sure towards Rocco's gun hand.

A yell of pain. The weapon fell to the ground. Costa threw aside the knife, leapt for the gun, rolled down to the grassy ground, got a grip round the butt, rolled again, stopped.

Rocco was sucking at his hand, his face the picture of fury.

The only sound now was the distant quacking of ducks. Then an explosion somewhere, a shotgun it sounded like.

'It's the hunting season, Rocco,' he said, getting to his feet. The gun felt good. It seemed to lift in his hand of its own accord until the barrel pointed straight at the man in front of him.

'What did your father do with traitors?' he asked.

Rocco frowned. 'The same as me. What do you think? Come on, man. Quit pretending. You said it yourself. You're a cop from Rome. Not Maso Leoni. We invented him. We put an end to his little life the day the Bergamotti died.'

'They didn't just die. Someone killed them.' The gun didn't waver. He glanced around, just for a second to make the point. 'You can tell me. We're out here. No one near. No one to know. No one to see. Everyone gone except you. Why . . .?'

'Why's none of your business.' Rocco stepped closer, held out his hand. 'Use that thing before I take it from you.'

One shot. Good and proper. Bullets cost money. Shouldn't need more.

Footsteps behind. He was still hovering between two worlds. Then a voice close by barked, 'Nic!'

The gun felt heavy. Wrong.

'Give me that,' she said and snatched the weapon from his hands.

\*　　\*　　\*

It took the longest moment to believe it was really her. The hair was shorter too, almost a crew cut, tinted a fashionable steel blue over blonde. Dark-rimmed spectacles that made her eyes seem larger. A gingham shirt. Pale jeans that looked brand new. Two full shopping bags from Conad sitting on the ground.

She might have been an account manager at a trendy advertising agency.

A busy mother returning home.

A teacher.

Or . . . anything.

The Bergamotti, whoever they were, lived like chameleons, forever adapting, changing, shifting shape and nature to stay alive.

'I don't know about anyone else,' Rocco announced, 'but I need a drink.' He sucked his fingers again. 'And a plaster. Don't worry.' He gestured with his hand. 'I probably deserved that. I'll leave you two alone.'

He picked up the shopping and went inside.

Costa said, 'They told me you were dead.'

It was impossible to read her face. Perhaps it always had been.

'Please tell me you weren't going to shoot my brother.'

'Thought of it,' he admitted. 'Thought I had good reason. He pulled the gun on me.'

'You sound like children.' She placed the weapon on the windowsill. 'We don't need a drink. Do we?'

'Just answers. I'm owed.'

Lucia put a finger to her lips, thinking. Then: 'No. You're not. But you'll get them anyway. Sort of.' She came closer and there was a fragrance on her now, a formal, adult scent he'd never noticed before. 'How did you find us?'

'I looked.'

'You're good at looking.'

'It's what I do.'

She smiled and there was sadness in it. 'You're not the only one. Shame.' She glanced at the house, the garden, the quiet lagoon by the dock where two boats were now moored, both old and a touch decrepit. 'Come on. Let me show you our demons.'

\*     \*     \*

The last time he'd been in the Cathedral of Santa Maria Assunta it was with his late wife. He didn't remember much about the place, marooned as it was in this corner of the lagoon, an ancient basilica left behind by time. They'd been too engrossed in one another, too much in love to take notice of anything else. This was different. They had to look. Lucia was insistent. So he sat with her in the quiet, dark nave, back to the altar, as she pointed out the details of the extraordinary scene on the west wall above the door where they'd entered. A panoramic medieval vision of the end of the world, the Last Judgement, rose in front of them, a jewelled masterpiece of golden mosaics glittering in the last of early-evening sun. The chosen rising to heaven; sinners being torn apart by black demons, stabbed by avenging angels, beneath them all the horrors of hell, skulls with serpents snaking out of eye sockets, the physical decay of death.

'Amazing, isn't it?'

'Yes . . .'

'I come here every day.'

There were a couple of tourists around, and an elderly male attendant watching them like a hawk.

'Why?'

'To pray, silly. Why else?' She edged nearer. 'You don't, do you?'

'No.' He gestured at the towering story before them. Sinners being pushed to hell, some of them simply for who they were: Jews and Muslims. Foreigners beyond the reach of the Pope. 'I don't believe in that.'

'Me neither. Not all of it anyway. But I like praying. I like the idea of talking to someone you can't see. Who maybe doesn't exist. But somehow they listen all the same.'

He touched her arm, ran a finger along the olive-brown bare skin. 'The tattoos . . .'

She laughed and looked away. 'Ah. Them. They were only good for two or three weeks. I was worried they'd rub off.'

It seemed obvious now. Part of the disguise, the picture she'd leave behind. 'That's how we'd describe you. When you all ran. A woman with tattoos.' Then he touched the scar. 'That's real anyway.'

'Fell off my bike. When I was twelve.'

'So many stories . . .'

There was a fleeting look of regret then. 'They weren't all lies. I did lose it for a while. I did . . . fall. I think that's when Dad realized we couldn't go on the way we were. When he started to try to come up with some means to get us out, away from all the damage. It was a long time in the planning before we sent word to those people in Rome. Not that it did any good.'

'I'm sorry. He was kind to me. A . . . a good man.'

'Good?' she asked. 'You think that?'

'From what I saw.'

'You saw what we wanted you to see.'

'Alessia took me to Manodiavolo. She showed me—'

'I know what she showed you. I know she told you not to chase us too.'

He shrugged and said he couldn't help it.

'I told her you wouldn't listen. They called him Lo Spettro, remember? It wasn't just Dad. We all grew up learning to be ghosts. That's how we survived. Being anonymous. Being . . . kind of nothing. Which may keep you alive but after a while you wonder . . . who are you really? The Sicilians . . . the other gangs. Apart from Mancuso, they were different. They lived out in the open. They knew one day there might be a visit. From you. More likely from some men with guns. Dad didn't want that for us. In the end he didn't want any of it. Just peace. A place we could be safe. But no one retires from the 'ndrina. Especially not the capo.'

It was starting to come clear.

'So you vanish and leave us Mancuso and the others as an offering? A way to say . . . don't come for us?'

'Half a bargain's better than no bargain at all.'

He had to say it. 'I thought it was Rocco who betrayed you.'

'So I gathered.'

'Rocco and Santo Vottari.'

He could see the old Lucia in her face then. 'Vottari. The bastard got to know somehow. So he and Mancuso's people bundled me into a van and took me over the water. A guest.

No one does that to the Bergamotti. It's like a declaration of
war. The Sicilians called Rocco. Told him they'd worked out
what was going on. Mancuso wouldn't be coming. None of
the other capi. Some people, innocents, in their place. There
had to be a reckoning. I guess Dad didn't think he had a
choice. So he offered his head in return for ours. Not that I
knew. They had me by then. Vottari's got his reward. He's
been shooting his mouth off all over Reggio. If we could do
something.' She shut her eyes all of a sudden. Pain. 'Oh shit.
See. I still think that way. My God . . .'

He tried to hold her but she was too quick, too strong, and
fled outside. He followed slowly. When he found her she was
on the terrace of the Cipriani swirling a cocktail stick in a
glass of spritz, the glasses off her face now, her eyes pink
from tears.

Costa sat down and ordered one for himself. The same
waiter he'd met earlier came out and brought it, a plate of
*cicchetti* too. The drink took him straight back to Venice:
strong, both bitter and sweet, a taste that belonged to the
lagoon.

'What I'd give to go back,' she murmured. 'To see his grave.
Those cypresses. That place. He loved Manodiavolo. I don't
know if he could have lived anywhere else really. It was just
a dream. We fooled ourselves. We were so desperate . . .'

She wiped her eyes and took a long swig of Campari. 'They
snatched me that last night, never told me a thing. So I didn't
know he'd struck a bargain. I thought I was just a surety and
the moment things turned bad they'd kill me. Maybe they were
going to anyway.' Her face turned hard, her gaze stayed on
the cathedral across the way. 'The man who came for me was
called Gaetano Sciarra. You saw him around Manodiavolo. He
was Mancuso's nephew, not that I knew. All I saw was a
Sicilian with a gun and lots of swagger. So . . .' Another gulp
of spritz. 'I didn't wait. I killed him instead. Then ran all the
way here. We're good at running. You probably noticed. Turned
out I could kill a man quite easily too. Though . . . it hurts.'
She turned to him. 'Something always hurts.'

Costa took the bracelet from his jacket and placed it on the
table.

'It has his blood on it, Nic. I can't touch that thing again.'
He pointed to the stain. 'I thought it was yours.'

'I know.'

She wouldn't look at him.

'Alessia wanted me to. So did you—'

'I was trying to be kind! Not cruel!' Her voice was breaking.
Her eyes were wild. 'We just wanted to be free of that damned
prison. To live like other people. Out in the open. Not
wondering if there was some thug around the corner with a
gun. Or a life spent in jail. There's a kind of sanctity in being
ordinary. My father said that all the time. Why do you think
he lived in Manodiavolo? Why do you think we took those
risks?'

She took his hand and closed it on the clasp. 'You keep it.
The woman who wore that doesn't exist anymore. The one
who took her place appreciates her solitude. She craves that.
Talking to a god that probably doesn't exist.'

'Lucia. Please . . .'

'No.' With a rush she was on her feet. 'You need to understand. We have to go. Me and Rocco. If you can find us they
can. Mancuso's nephew. Il Macellaio's offered money for our
heads. He won't stop looking either.'

There was a look of Vanni in her at that moment. His blunt
determination. One that never wavered. All the same he took
her by the shoulders, tried to peer into her eyes, wondered
what and who he saw there.

'You can't spend your entire life running . . .'

'I have,' she threw back at him. 'Didn't you listen?'

'We can change things.'

'How?'

Maso Leoni knew how to lie. How to deceive, fool, pretend.
But he wasn't there. It was just Costa, a Roman, who could
never master that talent.

'How?' she asked again.

'We can try.'

'No,' she said, her composure back. 'We can't. That's the
last thing we must do. Here.' She held out her hands, as if for
cuffs. 'Arrest me. Do it. See how long I live in jail.'

'I can't—'

'Then what?' Her eyes filled with tears again and there was nothing he could say or do to stop them. 'What? I become your secret mistress? A ghost again? Hide away in some dismal apartment wondering if the knock on the door's you or Mancuso's hoods waiting on the other side? Look at me. Look at me. This is who I am, Nic. I run. I hide. I change the way I seem. The way I am. Rocco and me. Brother and sister. Different names. Different people everywhere we fetch up. In Italy . . . in places you'd never think of. This is who we are. *Tra Scilla e Cariddi*. This is the place we live. The only place. If I stop . . . I die.'

'Lucia—'

'I die!'

There was no arguing with the Bergamotti. Never mind what name they used. He held her then. She responded to him, long and slow, a farewell kiss. It had that considered finality to it. Then she whispered, 'Do you think I want this? Do you think that? Really?'

'I will be in Rome,' he said. 'If ever things change—'

'They won't. They can't.' She tore herself away from him. 'We have to pack. He's useless at it. Don't come looking for me. You'll kill us all.' She pointed down the narrow path, past the Devil's Bridge. 'The boat's down there.'

There were barely twenty passengers on the number twelve boat back to Fondamente Nove. If he was lucky he'd make the last fast train to Rome. A place he'd almost forgotten. A life too.

He sat in the outside area at the stern, watching Torcello vanish on the twilit horizon. Their mansion was just visible along the shore. They might flee that very night.

His phone rang and another piece of glass fell from the screen as he answered. 'Leo.'

'Finally. Where are you? What have you been doing?'

The sound of the office was behind him, like a murmur of busy bees.

'Chasing fairy tales.'

'What—'

'I thought I might have a lead for Rocco.' A lone gull

hovered over the churning wake behind him, hoping it might throw up a fish. 'I didn't.'

Home was where your friends were. Family and those you loved. People who didn't feel the need to scurry into the shadows. Fixed points in life. Everyone craved that comfort. Vanni and his family too, but for them it would always be out of reach.

Tra Scilla e Cariddi. A place that seemed to choose them and never let them go.

'I want you in here tomorrow,' Falcone replied and it sounded as if Cariddi and the Bergamotti were behind him already. 'We've got too many damned malingerers in this office and a pile of work to catch up on.'

'I was wondering . . .?'

What did you say? What could you? Give me more time. Let me run. Like her. And maybe one day change her mind.

'Yes?' Falcone always sounded puzzled, a little embarrassed, if he thought the conversation might turn personal.

'Nothing.'

There was no point. He knew it.

The boat was past Mazzorbo. There was nothing to see of the island now except the campanile of Santa Maria Assunta jutting from a low line of darkness at the edge of the lagoon.

A phone that was about to die.

A wallet with fifteen euros and a couple of credit cards.

A choice that had to be made.

'I'll see you soon,' he said and cut the call.

Tired and grubby, he longed to be back in his own bed. One thing only had followed him from Aspromonte: the silver bracelet, a reproduction of an ancient clasp a renegade thief and murderer once spirited from Catalonia to the Mezzogiorno where it lay in a cave next to his tomb for centuries, hidden away in the hills.

He took it out and turned the thing over in his fingers. The blood that had to be Gaetano Sciarra's almost looked like a decoration, a varnish on the soft metal dulled by years of wear.

A gift from a woman whose real name he'd never know.

Diesel fumes swirled all round him from the engine. Someone, somewhere had lit an illicit cigarette. A plane rose from the runway of Marco Polo and roared above the number twelve motonave to Venice, lights flashing, spewing a whiff of avgas over the dank and fusty aroma of the lagoon. The scents of Calabria, the exotic bergamot, the fragrant bitterness of wild thyme, might have been nothing more than memories from a dream.

Costa leaned over the stern of the boat and peered at the turbid, opaque water in its thrashing wake. Then threw Lucia's bracelet over the edge and watched as it vanished beneath the waves.

# Author's Note

This story is a work of the imagination, though one founded on some fact. Four books in particular provided reference points during its creation. Carlo Levi's *Christ Stopped at Eboli*, though not set directly in Calabria and dating from the 1930s, remains an eye-opening revelation of the reality of the Mezzogiorno and the response to it of one, cultured, northern Italian. Letizia Paoli's *Mafia Brotherhoods, Organized Crime, Italian Style* provides a vivid academic insight into the social context of the three principal Italian crime organisations, the Mafia, the Camorra and the 'Ndrangheta. Tommaso Astarita's *Village Justice, Community, Family and Popular Culture in Early Modern Italy* is a fascinating account of a murder trial in Pentedattilo in 1710 which affords a sobering view of the society and culture of this unique region. As in Levi's work, its description of the difficulty of imposing conventional moral and judicial rigours on Calabrian rural communities carries considerable contemporary resonance. *Old Calabria*, written by Norman Douglas, first published in 1915, is strong on the region's Greek roots and offers some laconic observations about the long history of brigandry in the Mezzogiorno.

The complex hierarchy of positions within the modern 'Ndrangheta has been greatly simplified for the sake of brevity and clarity. Those wishing to understand the highly prolix structure behind the organisation will find this described in detail in Paoli's work. The mythical history of the region, from the origins of the crime organisations in the Andalusian Garduña to the persistence of Greek and pagan culture, has been similarly elaborated upon from common folk tales and other sources.

I have reworked the geography of the Strait of Messina for

this tale. Visitors to the tip of Calabria may, however, find echoes of the story in Scilla, on the coast in the Strait of Messina, among certain hamlets in Aspromonte, and in the ghost village of Pentedattilo which lies east of Reggio close to the bergamot-growing region of the Ionian coast.

David Hewson, 2018